Empress of Nymm

David McIlroy

BURTON MAYERS

Content compiled for publication by
Richard *Mayers of Burton Mayers Books.*
First published by Burton Mayers Books 2025.

A CIP catalogue record for this book is available from the British Library
ISBN: 9781917224178

Typeset in **Garamond**

This book is a work of fiction. Names, characters, businesses, organizations, places and events are the product of the author's imagination. Any resemblance to actual persons, living or dead, events or locales is entirely coincidental.

www.BurtonMayersBooks.com

For Betty and Florrie, the true Empresses.

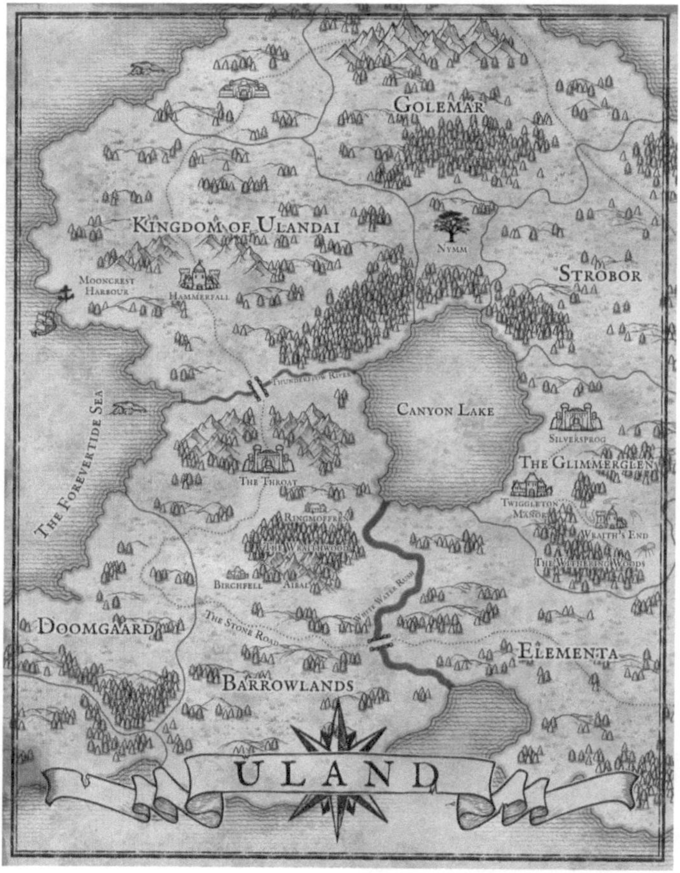
Golemar
Kingdom of Ulandai
Nymm
Strobor
Mooncrest Harbour
Hammerfall
Canyon Lake
The Forevertide Sea
Silversprog
The Glimmerglen
The Throat
Twiggleton Manor
Wraith's End
The Withering Woods
Birchfell
Aibal
Doomgaard
The Stone Road
Elementa
Barrowlands
ULAND

Chapter One:
The Girl With The Golden Eyes

'Are we lost, m'lady?'

Willow flinched.

She hated that phrase. It always tasted false. The way he'd said it somehow made it sound even worse.

Muh-lay-dee.

'No,' she replied, 'we're not lost.'

Far above, a blanket of silvery stars glittered beyond the treetops like the torches of a billion-strong celestial army. Here in the woods, the trees themselves crowded around them, dark sentinels in the night.

Willow saw it all, clear as day.

Next to her, the little man swallowed. She heard the wet gulp noise over the forest's song around them.

'Are you sure?'

'Yes. Sure.'

For a few moments, the only sounds were the rustling of leaves stirred by the breeze and the soft crunch of the little man's boots on the forest floor. But she knew it was coming. He was a talker, and talkers liked to -

'Because,' he went on, 'ordinarily I wouldn't ask, of course, given who you are... given your station, and all that...'

'I don't have a station,' Willow said stiffly.

'... but, you see, it's just that I believe we may have passed this exact same oak tree already, the one there with the big hole in the trunk... more than once, as a matter of fact… and I'm beginning to worry that we might, just might, be - '

Willow sighed irritably. The little man took the hint and stopped, mid-sentence. Out of the corner of her eye, she saw his mouth slowly close.

He'd only start talking again if she didn't explain.

'We're not lost,' she said, fixing her gaze on the trail ahead. 'You don't need to worry.'

He started to open his mouth again and she continued quickly: 'You were right about the oak, though. We have passed the exact same tree. Three times, actually. You did well to notice - most people I escort through the woods don't, in these situations.'

'What… situations?'

She ignored the question. 'You might have also noticed we're going downhill now. Only a little more than before. And the path's becoming straighter. That means we're close.'

'Close?' the little man said. She heard the ring of hope in his voice. 'You mean, we're almost out of this doom-forsaken forest? Thank the Druyads!'

Willow smirked at that. He didn't see it in the gloom.

'I'll take you out of here soon enough,' she said, listening to the trees as she spoke. 'But there's something I have to do first.'

'What… exactly do you mean?' The hope drained away, replaced with concern. 'And what… situation… are we in? I thought you said we weren't lost.'

'We aren't,' Willow said calmly. 'We're being hunted.'

For one glorious moment, the little man didn't speak and Willow allowed herself to believe he'd been stunned into silence. Wouldn't that be something? she thought. And all it took was the truth. Then, his voice flittered back to her through the near-darkness, at least three octaves higher than before, and quivering with fear.

'H-hunted, did you say?'

'Yes.'

'H-hunted… b-b-by what?'

'You really don't want to know.'

'Ohhhhhh!'

She reached out and caught him by the sleeve, just as he was about to tumble into the undergrowth. His arm was plump and spongy between her fingers.

'Don't be afraid,' she said.

He started to moan again and she gave his arm a shake, just enough to make him stop.

Druyads be good, she thought, don't make it any easier for the monster than it has to be.

'Let's keep going,' she continued, cautiously releasing his sleeve. 'We're almost there.'

'O-okay, m-m'lady.'

He fell into step beside her, his little boots once again crunching on dried-out leaves. She could still hear him whimpering softly under his breath.

Willow didn't mind the Gnomish folk. They were intelligent, almost always pleasant, and had treated her with respect long before she obtained her new "station" with the Druyads. Like the Fairies, the Gnomes of Uland were, at the very least, friendly acquaintances of the Woodspeople.

She'd been tasked with escorting this particular Gnome - whose name she hadn't picked up, and hadn't thought to ask for - through an especially dense section of the woods, where the roads petered out into barely-visible, overgrown tracks and the trees grew so close their roots fused together beneath the soil. It was a dark and dangerous place for a creature as small as a Gnome, even in daylight. If the roving wolfpacks didn't make a quick meal of him, the monster surely would.

And it was on their tail now.

'W-where did you say we're going?' the Gnome managed once his whimperings had ceased.

'I didn't,' replied Willow. 'But I suppose I should explain now. You see - '

Something moved through the trees up ahead. She squinted, her eyes momentarily flashing gold in the semi-darkness, but whatever it was had already moved on. The Gnome saw nothing.

'I'm searching for something,' she continued. 'Something very important. It could save someone's life, if I can find it.'

'Whose life?' said the Gnome.

'The life of a very important someone,' said Willow, quietly.

They walked on. The path, barely discernible now, sloped further downwards. The darkness deepened as the trees leered down above them.

'This… thing… you're trying to find,' said the Gnome, just above a whisper. 'It's here? In these woods?'

'Yes.'

'And it's magic?'

'Sort of.' He stumbled and Willow caught him by the arm again. 'It grows from a tree, and the tree lives on deep magic within the ground. Ancient magic. It's a very old tree.'

'Did the Druyads send you to get it?'

'No,' said Willow, 'they didn't.'

'So you're doing this - '

'Without their knowledge, yes.'

The Gnome started to moan again. Willow suddenly grabbed him by the shoulder and he stifled a yelp.

'Can you climb?' she said, fighting to keep her tone measured.

'Climb?'

'Trees. Can you climb a tree? Or do I have to carry you on my back?'

'I-I… I'm not sure - '

Without another word, Willow snatched him up and swung him onto her back. He uttered a little cry, but had the presence of mind to wrap his arms around her neck. Too tight, choking her. But there was no time to waste.

'Hold on,' she said.

She started to climb the nearest tree. Her strong, elegant fingers had no trouble finding branches in the darkness. Her boots - the only thing she wore that wasn't made from woven cloth - didn't slip once as they ascended. She made no sound. And to his credit, the Gnome managed to stay quiet, too.

They were far above the forest floor in moments. Willow steadied herself against the tree's trunk, balancing faultlessly on a branch any non-Woodsperson would've tumbled off in an instant. The Gnome clung to her, his breath coming in frightened tremors near her ear. She would have marvelled at how light he was on her back, under different circumstances.

'W-what's h-happening,' he whispered.

'Don't speak,' Willow replied softly, and he fell silent.

She leaned as far forward as she could, squinting down the length of the tree towards the ground. The silvery starlight dappling the leaves in the treetops wasn't reaching the forest floor. It was pitch black down there, but she could see enough.

And what she saw sent a shiver down her spine.

In the blackness below, the Puca was moving. It melted soundlessly through the dark, following their trail. Creatures without nocturnal vision would never see or hear it coming until it was far too late. Even Willow had barely sensed it at first.

This particular Puca had taken the form of a horse, but it was unlike any horse Willow had ever seen. She stared, wide-eyed and unmoving on the tree branch, as it walked directly beneath them, its unnatural hooves leaving no prints on the soft woodland floor. Its sleek, jet black hair caught a flicker of starlight that'd made it through the tree canopy and she saw it in full, just for a second. Behind her, the Gnome was holding his breath.

Then she heard it, drifting up to them. A voice like silk, whispering yet completely clear, beckoning them from the darkness.

'Climb on my back, sweet friends,' it cooed. 'Come out from your hiding place. Climb on my back and I'll take you somewhere wonderful, just wonderful. Come out, sweet friends…'

Willow heard it first and she tightened her grip on the tree trunk. Then it reached the Gnome, and he began to tremble. Don't let go, Willow thought. Not now.

'Where are you, my sweets?' whispered the Puca, a dark spectre floating between the trees below them. 'Wouldn't you like to take a ride on my back? Come out, come out from your hiiiiiding place…'

Willow squeezed her eyes shut, trying to force the voice from her mind. She knew it wasn't an actual sound. There was no voice. But still, it came anyway -

'I'll find you, sweetlings. I'll find you. Then I'll put you on my back and we'll gallop away, forever and ever and ever…'

Finally, after what seemed like an age, the voice faded.

Willow opened her eyes. Her vision adjusted instantly and she scanned the ground far below them. The Puca was gone.

'Ok,' she whispered. 'We're safe. It's moved on.'

'S-s-safe?' the Gnome spluttered back. 'Did you hear that thing? It s-spoke directly into my h-h-h - '

'Your head, I know,' Willow said. 'They do that. It's how they find their prey.'

'P-p-prey?'

'Let's get out of this tree.'

They made it to the ground in half a minute. Willow set the Gnome down again; his pudgy legs wobbled inside his tweed trousers, but he stayed on his feet.

'I-I can't see,' he whispered. 'It's too dark.'

'Here, take this,' Willow replied, putting the hem of her cloak in his hand. 'And keep up.'

She started forward and he followed. The slight strain on her cloak was all she needed to know he was there. She had no time to stop and look back. They had to hurry.

The trail was gone now, swallowed up in undergrowth. The trees grew so close here they often had to turn sideways to get between them. Willow did this with ease; the Gnome blundered into most of them, letting out a muffled yelp every time.

Maybe this was a bad idea, she thought. I've put him in danger. Maybe I should've just gone myself after all. Some flying thing swished through the trees above them and she quickened her pace. No, this was the only way. They never would've let me do it otherwise.

And suddenly, she heard it. She stopped dead in her tracks and the Gnome walked into her. This time, he cried out: "What is it? Is it that… that thing, again?'

'Sshhh,' Willow replied.

She closed her eyes and listened hard. She'd definitely heard it, hadn't she? It wasn't the Puca again…

Yes! There it was - a new song. An ancient, woodland song.

'This way,' she said.

The song grew louder and more defined as they drew closer. She was hurrying now, forgetting to step carefully through the undergrowth. Behind her, the Gnome was making more noise than ever. Jayne's voice rang in her memory: 'Your overeagerness will get you in trouble someday, Willow. Or you'll get someone else in trouble, and that'd be much worse.'

Almost there, she thought, pressing between the trees, ignoring the low-hanging branches whipping at her green-tinged skin. The song rang clear just up ahead. She knew the Gnome couldn't hear it, but she could. And that song meant -

And just like that, there it was.

They were in what might have once been a clearing in the forest. It was small, not much more than seven or eight feet across, a perfect circle in the midst of the trees. And right in the centre was the one she'd been searching for.

It rose straight up, bizarrely skinny and impossibly tall, with no visible roots at its base. Not a single branch grew from its trunk, all the way to the tree canopy high above them. It looked as though someone had carved a space for it on the forest floor and jammed it straight down from the sky.

And yet, there it was.

'Are we here?' said the Gnome, a little breathless now. 'Did you find it?'

Willow knew the Puca would still be in the area, but there was no time to waste. Not now. If it saw them, she'd hear it coming. She was certain of that.

'Eydrom.'

She snapped her fingers. A ball of emerald light appeared just above their heads, turning the forest clearing bright green. The Gnome cried out, shielding his eyes.

'Oh, sorry,' Willow said.

'Good grief!' the Gnome spluttered, lowering his arms. He squinted around the clearing, and then tilted his head back to gaze at the tree. 'Oh my.'

Willow dropped to one knee, placed a hand on his shoulder, and said, 'I have to leave you now.'

'WHAT?"

'Just for a minute. I can't climb this one with you on my back, and you definitely can't climb it yourself. You'll have to wait here.'

'B-b-but - '

'Just stay quiet. Hopefully the Puca won't return before I'm back down.'

'The... the what?' the Gnome squeaked.

But she was already climbing. The trunk of the tree was so smooth it was almost impossible to get a firm hold, but she managed. Her fingertips dug deep and her boots, made of magic-infused leather, were supple enough to allow her long toes to grip the bark. She climbed fast, never once glancing back down to where the Gnome was whimpering by the base of the tree. The ball of green light followed her up, floating a yard or two away from her shoulder. The Gnome's whimperings turned to squeals once he realised he was about to be left in darkness.

Hurry! Willow thought, climbing faster.

Up she went, hand over hand, the green orb of light hovering nearby as everything below her was swallowed up in shadow. Her breathing remained steady all the way.

Finally, just when she was starting to think the tree might carry on up into the night sky and she'd find herself climbing among the stars, she saw it.

At last! she thought.

The first of the ancient tree's branches had begun to appear just a little further up. Dangling from one of those branches, just below a clump of withered, tangerine-coloured leaves, was exactly what Willow had been searching for.

The healing seed.

'There you are,' she whispered.

She stretched out her free hand, hesitated for a fraction of a second, and plucked the seed nimbly from the branch. It was about the size and shape of an acorn, but instead of a smooth brown shell, there was a jelly-like orb filled with purplish fluid. It fitted neatly in the palm of Willow's hand.

She stared at it for a moment, transfixed by the seed's liquidy contents, watching as the stuff inside the orb pulsed softly against its translucent shell. It wasn't a seed in the truest sense of the word, she knew that. It was something else, something from before her time. And it was alive with deep, ancient magic.

'At last,' she said, aloud this time.

Then, from far below, a shriek.

'Whoops!"

Quick as a flash, she slipped the seed into her pocket and started down the tree. The trunk was so smooth she was practically sliding by the time she reached the bottom.

The green ball of light followed her all the way, throwing crazy shadows around the forest clearing.

She landed soundlessly on the ground and the Gnome almost leapt into her arms.

'There's something here!' he squealed, his over-large eyes bulging in panic. 'I saw it, through those trees. It's that… that poo-kaa thing, isn't it? Oh, ohhh…'

Willow pried him off, her nocturnal gaze following his pudgy pointing finger. 'It's not the Puca, don't worry.'

'How do you know?' the Gnome cried.

'Because if it was the Puca,' Willow replied, adjusting her cloak, 'you'd already be dead. Now come on, let's find the trail again and get out of here.'

The Gnome looked as though he was either going to weep for joy at the idea of leaving the forest or faint on the spot. Willow didn't wait to find out which. She snapped her fingers and the green light winked out, plunging them into darkness again. The Gnome uttered a little cry of surprise and she immediately shepherded him back into the trees. She could hear the healing seed singing softly in her pocket as they went.

She could hear something else, too.

'Hurry up,' she said, weaving between the trees. The Gnome followed close behind, gripping her cloak for dear life.

It was fully dark inside the forest, and the Gnome kept tripping over every protruding root and rock in their path. Willow did her best to ignore his stifled cries each time a low-hanging branch smacked him in the face. She was listening hard.

Soon, however, the trees began to thin out. Before long, there was ample space between them and the first suggestions of trails started appearing. Then, the darkness itself started to draw back as starlight winked through the leafy canopy high above them.

'The path!' the Gnome exclaimed. 'I see it, just up ahead!'

Willow smiled despite herself at the relief in his voice and said, 'Yes, almost there.'

'And… and how long until we're out of the woods entirely?'

'Not long. Travelling will be much easier after this.' She pushed a branch aside, still straining to pick out the sound she'd heard back near the ancient tree. The forest floor was mossy here, almost spongy underfoot. 'We'll have to pick up the pace, though. I want to leave the woods before dawn.'

'I want to know what you found up that tree,' said the Gnome. He was becoming bolder now they were closer to safety. 'I want to know exactly why we had to take that dangerous detour.'

'You'll know soon enough,' Willow replied.

They stepped back onto the path. Above them, the stars were visible once again.

'It was much too dangerous in there,' said the Gnome, folding his arms indignantly. "I have every right to report you, you know. Regardless of your station. I could have been killed.'

Willow sighed. 'Well, you weren't, so there wouldn't be much point in that. Like I said, you'll understand soon.' She turned away, starting up the path. 'It'll all make sense when - '

She heard the snap, far too late.

The rope instantly latched around her ankle and jerked it backwards, whipping her legs out from under her. The Gnome yelped in surprise as she flipped upside down right in front of him, her wavy red hair tumbling from beneath the hood of her cloak. The ground swished past her face, and then she was airborne, suspended several feet above the path.

'Argh! Stupid!' she cried, pushing hair from her face. 'Stupid Willow!'

'W-what happened?' said the Gnome, his boldness now dissolved.

'It's a trap,' Willow replied, fumbling in her pocket. 'I didn't even see it. Stupid!'

She pulled out a short, stubby knife with a pale bone handle, took a deep breath and bent herself double.

Cut yourself down, she thought, grabbing the rope. And run. Get out of the forest.

She put the blade to the rope and drew it across.

The Gnome yelped again as an explosion of white sparks blew the knife out of Willow's hand. It sailed through the air and disappeared into the trees.

'Rats, it's been enchanted!' She winced, shaking her injured hand. Blood was rushing to her head. 'I can't cut it.'

'S-so what should we do?' said the Gnome, staring wide-eyed at her.

'I could try a spell,' Willow said, thinking. 'But I'm not sure - '

Suddenly, her head snapped to the side. She heard it, the same sound from before, clear as day. They were coming, and they weren't disguising their footsteps anymore.

Oh no, she thought,

'Here.' She dug in her pocket and grabbed the healing seed. Somehow, it hadn't fallen out when the rope trap flipped her over. 'Take it.'

She tossed the seed to the Gnome. He just about caught it in both hands.

'What is it?'

'It doesn't matter,' Willow said urgently. 'You just need to… hey, look at me! You need to get it out of here, out of the forest. You have to go now.'

'But what about you? I can't just leave you here, like this.'

'You have to,' Willow insisted. 'There are things coming this way. They set the trap - it was for me. They'll be here in seconds. You have to run!'

The Gnome's eyes bulged. 'Where?' he cried, shoving the seed into his pocket.

'That way,' said Willow, pointing up the path, dizzy now. 'Follow the trail until it forks. Go left, and keep going until you reach the village. Tell them what happened. And don't tell anyone about that.' Her pointing finger jabbed at the Gnome's pocket. 'Hide it if you have to. I'll find you.'

'But.. but - '

'Just go!'

Nearby, something big crashed through the trees. The Gnome turned on his heel and bolted up the path without looking back.

Under the waning light from the stars, Willow's eyes flared gold.

Chapter Two: Brookeworm

Brooke Woods stared at her reflection in dismay.

'I can't do this!' she cried.

The glassy black eyes of the bunny rabbit stared back. If it could reply, she imagined it might say, 'No, but we can. We're in this together now, Brookles.'

Brooke moaned, clapping her hands to her face. The bunny disappeared.

'Sweetheart? Everything ok?'

Her mum's voice drifted through the door.

'Are you crying, dear?'

'No, Mum, I'm not crying!' Brooke shot back, too sharply. She removed her hands from her face, saw the giant white bunny rabbit in the mirror again, and stomped across to her bed.

'I'm coming in,' said her mum, already opening the door.

'Mum…'

Brooke's mother stood in the doorway, hands on hips. Her hair, once blonde like that of her only daughter, was now mostly grey. But her eyes were still bright blue, and right now they were full of concern.

'What's wrong?' she said. 'Does your costume not fit?'

'It fits fine,' Brooke replied. 'That's the problem. I wish it didn't fit.'

'Why?'

'Because I'm a giant rabbit, Mum!' she cried, throwing out her arms. One of her fluffy bunny gloves came loose and dropped to the carpet. 'Everyone else will have cool costumes, and I'll look like this - a giant, dork-tastic bunny rabbit.'

Her mother folded her arms. A small smirk tugged at the corner of her mouth.

'Not everyone will have a cool costume,' she said in a measured sort of way

'Tonya will. Her stuff's always cool.'

'Well, good for Tonya. She's going tonight?'

'Probably.' Brooke tried folding her arms too, then tugged the other bunny glove off and tossed it aside. 'Everyone's going, probably. It's the Halloween party, you'd have to be pretty lame to skip it. Maybe I should just - '

'What about your friends?' said her mother nonchalantly. 'Will they be there, d'you think? Charlie? And Dale?'

Brooke stared fixedly at the bunny glove on the floor, avoiding her mother's casual (yet probing) gaze.

'Yes,' she said. 'They'll be there.'

'Good,' said her mother brightly, reaching for the door handle. 'You can say hello from me, and remind them they're welcome here any time. Now, finish getting ready.'

'But - '

The door closed.

Brooke stood, kicked one of the bunny gloves across the room, and went to her desk. Her history homework, already finished, was neatly laid out on two file pages beneath an upturned textbook titled The Norman Conquest of England. She pushed it aside and stared at the much smaller book it had been covering.

It wasn't much bigger than her hand. Its leather cover was brittle and cracked all over, and the twine used to tie it closed was now badly frayed. But the little book hadn't crumbled into dust like she'd expected. In fact, it seemed to be more solid than ever.

She brushed her fingertips lightly over the wordless cover. The touch alone made the fine hairs on the back of her neck stand on end.

Memories materialised in her mind's eye.

'Here, take this.' Yulerin had whispered as they left the library in Fort Hammerfall, pushing the book into her hands. None of the others had seen it happen. She never told Charlie or Dale about it in the weeks and months afterwards, no matter how much she'd wanted to.

Half a year had passed since they'd returned from Uland.

It still felt like a dream at times. Back in Spring, Brooke had been on a camping trip with her school year group. They'd been hiking up a mountain when a thick, white fog had come down and she'd been attacked by horrible, hairy creatures with glowing red eyes. It hadn't just been her, either - her classmates, Charlie Flint and Dale Reed, had been chased by the creatures as well. They'd managed to catch Charlie, but she and Dale had been rescued by a girl with fiery red hair, green-tinged skin and golden eyes, a girl called Willow - a Woodsgirl - who'd led them through a portal into another world.

The world was Uland, a place filled with magic and monsters and a myriad of other things Brooke could've never imagined in her wildest dreams.

There, they'd embarked on a journey through ancient temples and dark forests and goblin markets to Fort Hammerfall, an enormous city built on the back of a long-dead Giant, in order to find a route back home. Willow had led them all the way (well, Charlie had spent a fair bit of time with a band of friendly trolls, but he'd found them again eventually) and, despite really not understanding them at first, she'd become their very good friend.

While they were in Hammerfall, the city had been attacked by the Doomgaard, a corrupted army led by a traitorous knight called Commander Hysst, who had been pursuing them relentlessly across Uland. Hysst was an agent of Decymero, the most evil being ever to have set foot on the entire magical continent; Decymero wanted to overthrow the allied Factions by wiping out their leaders, who'd gathered at Hammerfall for a war summit. But once he became aware of the "Otherworlders", Decymero wanted them instead.

Another of his agents, Zapharous, had opened a portal with a magical gemstone called the soulburn talisman and tried to capture them, but with the help of Yulerin the Druyad, they managed to escape. They faced off against Hysst in the palace garden, defeated him (it was mostly Willow, really), and saved all of Uland from succumbing to Decymero's chaos. Then they made their way back to the portal and returned home.

It hadn't been a dream, either. She had evidence to prove it.

With a glance towards her door, Brooke carefully opened the book to where she'd last been reading. The pages practically creaked as she turned them; she pressed each one down gently, still fearful of tearing them, though none had so much as crinkled so far.

When she first tried reading it on top of the mountain back in spring, the words had been unintelligible, mere symbols in another language. Most of them were fading, too. But lately, they'd become clearer, more defined. Almost all of the pages were now filled with words.

And she could understand them.

Brooke licked her lips - which she always did without thinking when she was about to read - and began tracing her forefinger across the top sentence on the page.

As always, the jumble of foreign shapes and symbols seemed to shudder as her fingertip passed over them, and there was a tingle of heat against her skin; a second later, when the shuddering had stopped, the symbols had become actual words. Words she could read.

'Awesome,' she breathed.

She saw the sentence in full and read it slowly, mouthing the words in silence. When she came to the end of the line, she said the last part out loud:

'... and the Reckoning will begin.'

Frowning, she closed the book, letting her hand rest on the cover for a moment. The skin of her palm continued to tingle.

'The Reckoning,' she repeated in the quiet of her bedroom. One of the bunny ears on the head of her costume flopped down and she pushed it away absently. 'What does that even mean?'

Then, from downstairs: 'Brooke! Are you ready to go?'

'One second,' she called back.

She pulled open her desk drawer and dropped the book inside. Then, snatching up the bunny gloves, she crossed to the mirror again.

Maybe it's not that bad, she thought, tilting her head. The bunny ears flopped about; the glassy black eyes stared back at her. We'll all be in costume. No-one's going to look cool.

'Tonya will,' she said aloud. 'Somehow.'

A dangle of blonde hair escaped from beneath the head of the bunny costume. She tucked it away. For a split second, she was back in their quarters at Fort Hammerfall, dressed in her banquet gown and forcing a smile while a servant dragged a brush through her hair. Willow was by her side, glowering at her own reflection. Charlie was in his room; Dale was in the House of the Healer.

We were there, she thought sadly. It was all real. I know it was.

She swallowed down the lump hardening in her throat and turned to the door.

Then she stopped.

Without knowing why, or really even knowing she was doing it, Brooke went back to her desk and pulled open the drawer. She took out the little book, unzipped the front of her bunny costume, and slipped it into the pocket of the hoodie underneath. Then she closed the drawer again and headed for the door.

Her mum was downstairs, bright and cheerful as always. She handed Brooke a carrot and giggled at the glare she received back.

'Where's your sense of humour, Brookeworm?' she chuckled, ushering her out the door.

'I'm thirteen, I don't have one,' she muttered in reply.

As the car backed down the driveway, Brooke glanced up at her bedroom window. She thought of the library in Fort Hammerfall again. She thought of Yulerin the Druyad giving her the little old book, and of the words he whispered as they left the room.

'Here, take this.'

And she thought of the words he whispered into her mind, immediately after that:

This is your way back.

Chapter Three: The Halloween Party

Brooke had rarely been in school at night.

The last time was for an open evening at the end of Year 7. Somehow, she'd been roped into showing new students and their families around the art department. She'd spent the whole time saying, 'no, I didn't draw this one - yes it is nice, but I didn't draw it', and, 'please don't put your fingers in the paint pots', mostly to adults.

Now, as a Year 9 pupil, Farmont High was all too familiar. But it was still weird being in the building at night.

Her mum had dropped her off in the car park, helped detangle one of her bunny ears from the seat belt, and drove off with a cheerful wave. Brooke had watched the car disappear around the corner before reluctantly walking up to the school entrance and pushing open the glass door to reception.

Inside, the hallways were dark and eerily silent. Brooke's bunny feet, which may as well have been slippers, made almost no sound on the tiled floor as she meandered through the school.

I'm not the only one here, am I? she wondered, with a tinge of hope.

'Brooke!'

'Ahhh!'

She leapt on the spot as Molly Sharp burst from the girls' bathroom next to her.

'Don't do that!' Brooke cried.

'Sorry!' Molly replied breathlessly. Molly was always a little breathless. 'Did you just get here? I love your costume! Guess who I am.'

Brooke looked her up and down.

'Umm… a witch?'

'No, I'm Wednesday,' Molly moaned. 'You know, from Wednesday? Why does everything think I'm a witch?'

They walked through the school, heading for the gymnasium. Brooke could hear music in the distance, drifting along the empty corridors.

'You're a bunny rabbit, right?' said Molly, tugging at one of her fake, dark pigtails. A curl of mousy brown hair broke free from beneath the wig.

'How'd you guess?' said Brooke.

Molly made a face. 'Wait a second.'

They were in the Year 9 corridor. Molly pulled off her black gloves and started fiddling with the combination dial on her locker.

'What're you doing?' said Brooke, peering up the hallway. The party music was a lot louder now, mingled with laughter.

'Just checking my phone,' said Molly, opening her locker. 'Miss Harrington banned them at the party, which is so lame.'

'Yeah, lame,' Brooke agreed absently. She started twisting the dial of her own locker.

'The party's pretty lame in general,' said Molly, 'but at least… hey, only 300 views? It's been, like, half an hour! I went to the bathroom for nothing.'

Brooke's locker door creaked as it opened. A stack of her textbooks, not needed over the weekend, stared back at her. She glanced at the two remaining photos taped to the inside of the door: one was a big group shot of their class trip to the mountains back in April, taken just before the hike; the second was of her and her mother on the beach last summer, broad grins on their sun-tanned faces.

A couple of tape loops still clung nearby, their photos discarded.

'Are you checking yours?' said Molly, not looking up from her screen.

'Uh, yeah.'

Brooke had left her phone at home. She'd forgotten all about it, somehow. But she had brought…

Casually unzipping the front of her costume, she pulled out the little old book and slipped it into her locker. Safer here, she thought. I'll get it later.

'Vintage!' cried Molly.

'What?' Brooke said quickly, slamming her locker shut.

'The photos, on your door. Actual prints - vintage.'

'Oh, right.'

'I wish I had an old-school camera. All I have is this thing.' Molly sighed, dropped her phone back in the locker and closed the door. 'Come on.'

Molly headed for the gym. After a hesitant glance back at her locker, Brooke followed.

***

Charlie was cornered.

Everything had been going just fine. One minute, Zak and Noah were there, laughing and tossing cheese puffs at Marcus Gale. And then the girls had come over, Zak and Noah had vanished, and Charlie found himself face to face with Tonya Miller.

'So then, I was like, someone else is bound to go as Barbie,' Tonya was saying, 'and I was right, there're three other Barbies here. Three! And I would've just been the black Barbie, which is such a cliche. So I'm glad I didn't do that, you know. I'm glad I came as this.'

She put her hands on her hips, waiting.

Charlie blinked. 'Oh… you're, umm…'

Tonya's eyes narrowed. 'You don't know, do you?'

Charlie shook his head.

'I'm Lucy Gray,' sighed Tonya. 'You know, from Songbirds and Snakes?' When Charlie shrugged, she threw up her hands, exasperated. 'Why did I bother? I should've just been Barbie. Who're you, anyway? You look like an undertaker.'

'I'm the guy from that movie. Oppen-whatever. I don't know his name.'

Tonya grinned, shaking her head in disbelief. Her dark hair fell loose around her face.

'Boys are dummies,' she said. 'You're lucky you're one of the cute ones, Charlie Flint.'

Charlie felt his cheeks redden. Across the gym, he saw Zak and Noah sniggering. The music suddenly seemed too loud.

'Umm…'

'Don't worry, you don't have to say I'm cute too,' said Tonya, inspecting her bright purple nails. 'I know I'm cute. Hey!'

She pointed past Charlie's shoulder. He turned, saw Brooke and Molly approaching, and said, 'I'll be back in a minute.'

Before Tonya had a chance to protest, he walked off. Zak and Noah saw him coming and made heart-shapes with their hands.

'She fancies the pants off you,' Noah said, snickering.

'Everyone does,' Charlie replied smoothly. Noah started to say something else and Charlie punched him on the shoulder. 'What happened to the other girls?'

'Noah scared them off,' grinned Zak.

'Shut up, no I didn't,' grumbled Noah, rubbing his shoulder.

'That's why you guys need me,' said Charlie nonchalantly. 'I'm the babe magnet.'

'You're real humble, too,' added Zak.

Charlie smirked, casually scanning the room. The school gymnasium had been partially transformed since he'd last seen it: paper jack-o-lanterns and skeletons with pinned-together limbs were taped to the wooden climbing bars around the walls; the curtains had been drawn closed and strewn with fake cobwebs (and even faker-looking tarantulas); bat-shaped streamers stretched the width of the ceiling, and someone had even managed to hang an old-fashioned disco ball directly above the centre of the room. It threw a crazy kaleidoscope of light across the floor and walls, almost matching the beat of the cheesy Halloween-themed songs pumping from speakers in the far corner.

It looked like everyone in Year 9 had shown up tonight, in spite of the "lame party" rumours going round earlier in the week. Most of the girls were dancing while most of the boys watched from the sidelines, each acting like they wouldn't join in if their lives depended on it while also casting hopeful, furtive glances towards the dance floor. Charlie saw Zoe Prew, dressed in an elaborate Cleopatra costume, beckoning an embarrassed-looking Henry Pike; Henry shook his head, tried to slip away towards the snack table, and was pushed unceremoniously from the safety of the group by the other boys. Charlie grinned as Henry disappeared into a swarm of giggling girls.

His eyes fell on Mr Green and the grin evaporated.

'Uh oh,' muttered Zak.

The history teacher stalked towards them, his bushy moustache quivering beneath his nose.

'Which one of you three sprayed my car with silly string?' he demanded.

Zak and Noah immediately pointed at each other. Charlie pointed at both of them. Mr Green's moustache quivered harder.

'I know it was one of you,' growled the teacher. 'Or all of you. That's a new car.'

'We're sorry, sir,' said Noah, reddening. 'It was just a - '

'Noah!' Charlie and Zak cried in unison.

Mr Green's smile was triumphant. 'Aha, I knew it! I'll see all three of you in detention after the holiday break. They may as well name that room after you trio, you're in there so often.'

With that, he turned on his heel and marched away. Henry and the dance floor girls parted to let him pass.

'You're such an idiot,' said Zak, punching Noah's other shoulder.

'Me?' replied Noah incredulously. 'It was your idea!'

Charlie didn't listen to the rest of the argument. He didn't care whose fault it was. He didn't even care about getting detention again. His parents would, but that was fine - they should be used to it by now. How much more grounding could he get, anyway?

And was the music getting louder?

There seemed to be more students on the dancefloor than before. Most of the other boys had finally ventured out, now that Henry and Zoe were actively dancing together and Henry didn't look like he minded one bit. It was a chaotic sea of movement and colour, jeering and laughter. And all of it was noise, noise to the eyes as well as the ears.

Getting louder by the second. Thumping, thumping, thumping across the gymnasium in waves, crashing into Charlie.

He blinked. Now he could hear something else.

Instead of music, there was the sound of steel on steel. Blades clashing, metal screeching across metal. Instead of laughter there were screams. Battle roars of fury and pain. Students became soldiers wielding swords and spears, axes and crossbows. Some wore silver-blue armour that flashed as they fought and danced under the light of the disco ball.

The rest wore black.

The black of Doomgaard.

Charlie's hand instinctively went to his side, but there was no sword there. Not anymore. He grasped at thin air with sweat-laced fingers, heart pounding, staring horror-struck at the student-soldiers crowding towards him, fixing on one in particular who was advancing his way with a red-stained broadsword in both hands, ice-blue eyes burning with malice, the ugly scar on his neck contorting as he sneered the words, 'Master Flint...'

'Dude, what're you doing?'

Charlie blinked again. The soldiers became Year 9 students, the battle sounds became music. Zak was there, frowning at him.

'Huh?' said Charlie.

'Your hand,' said Zak. 'Why're you doing that?'

Charlie looked down, saw his right hand poised near his left hip, and quickly pulled it away.

'Nothing,' he muttered.

'You look like you saw a ghost,' said Noah, still rubbing his shoulder. 'Detention's not that bad. Mr Green might even forget by - '

'I said it's nothing!' Charlie snapped. The image of Hysst was still fading. 'The music's… just too loud. They need to turn it down.'

'Don't tell us,' said Zak. 'Tell Dork Reed over there. He's in charge of it.'

Charlie followed Zak's pointing finger to the sound desk in the corner.

'Yeah, maybe,' he said, and walked off.

***

'It's not loud enough,' said Ravi.

'What?'

'I said, it's not loud enough. We need to turn up the volume.'

Dale leaned over to peer at the screen, his lime-coloured wig slipping on his head.

'I think it's loud enough, Ravi.'

'What?' Ravi replied.

Dale settled back in his chair. Most of Year 9 was on the dancefloor now, bathed in shifting, dappled light reflecting off the slowly-rotating disco ball. Henry Pike was directly beneath it, hemmed in on all sides by a gaggle of girls.

'The music isn't loud enough,' Ravi said again, fiddling with the levels on his sound mixer.

Ravi Gupta fancied himself as a bit of a DJ. His hand was the first one up when Miss Harington asked if anyone wanted to take charge of the Halloween party music. Dale volunteered himself too, mostly to avoid what was happening to Henry right now - he'd completely disappeared into the giggling swarm in the middle of the room.

It wasn't just that, either. The gymnasium was Dale's least-favourite place in the whole school, aside from the Art department. Even as he'd helped Ravi set up the sound equipment earlier (which was really nothing more than a laptop, a mixer and two speakers, all owned by Ravi himself), he'd had flashbacks to Mr Gerritsen informing the class that no-one could go for lunch until he'd climbed the rope while Tonya and the other girls sniggered nearby.

If he had to be there at all, it was best to be behind the sound desk with Ravi.

'I'm thirsty,' said Ravi.

'What?'

Ravi leaned over. 'I'm thirsty. I need a drink.'

'Oh.' Dale glanced across at the snack table in the opposite corner. 'Go get one, then. I'll look after the music.'

'No, no,' said Ravi, his hands hovering over the mixer. 'I've got it all just how I like it. I'm worried you'll change something. It's hard to get this just right, you know.'

Dale sighed. 'I'll get us drinks, then.'

He stood and his green wig slipped again. Why'd I think coming as Beetlejuice would be a good idea?

'Get me water,' said Ravi.

Dale looked at him. 'Really. You want water. You know you're at a party, right?'

'I'm thirsty,' Ravi said.

Do they even have water? Dale thought.

He slipped out from behind the desk and started across the room. The white stripes he'd taped to his black suit jacket were already peeling off. He hadn't minded the suit, or even the wig; he had minded getting the white makeup plastered on his face and the dark rings painted around his eyes. His older sister had loved every second of that.

Tonya spotted him and elbowed Cassie Mathers, who started giggling behind her hand. Dale ignored them, heading for the snack table.

Only an hour to go, he reassured himself, then it's over for another year.

Alex Johnson was by the table, shovelling crisps and pretzels onto a paper plate. He glanced sideways at Dale. 'Nice costume, Reed.'

'Cheers.' Dale reached for the plastic cups. 'Who're you supposed to be?'

Alex turned, displaying the 'A' taped to his bulging blue t-shirt.

'I'm Captain America,' he explained. 'Well, I was, anyway. Zak stole my shield as soon as I got here.'

Dale grinned. 'So go get it back, Cap.'

'I will,' said Alex. 'Just have to find it, first.'

He left. Dale filled one cup with fruit punch and started searching for water.

Knew there wouldn't be any, he thought. Ravi can have Sprite, that's close enough to -

'What's up, squirt?'

He jumped. Charlie was at the table, rummaging in the sweet bowl.

'Oh, hey,' said Dale awkwardly, almost knocking the Sprite bottle over.

Charlie popped a Skittle in his mouth. 'Nice wig.'

'Thanks.' Dale poured a cup for Ravi. 'Nice suit.'

'Thanks. I'm the guy from that movie.'

'That... movie? Which - '

'I need to talk to both of you.'

They turned. Brooke was right there, dressed head to toe in a full bunny rabbit costume. Her blue eyes were bright and earnest.

Dale felt his cheeks flush and was immediately grateful for the makeup.

'Oh, hey Brooke,' he said. Charlie nodded and ate another Skittle.

'Can... can we talk?' Brooke said. She threw a look over her shoulder, her bunny ears flopping on her head. 'Here?'

'Umm, I should probably get back to Ravi,' Dale began, and saw Brooke's face also flush.

'Talk about what?' said Charlie.

Brooke swallowed. 'It's about... you know.' She took a step closer; Dale and Charlie leaned in automatically. 'It's about Uland.'

Dale's heart skipped a beat.

'What about it?' said Charlie, lowering the next Skittle.

Brooke's eyes somehow grew wider and, Dale imagined, bluer.

'There's... something I never told you,' Brooke said, barely loud enough for them to hear. 'I didn't think I had to tell you, because there was nothing to tell. Not really. But something's changed. And when I saw you both tonight, I knew I had to. It's time.'

'What the heck are you talking about?' said Charlie, staring hard at her now.

Brooke met Dale's gaze. 'You remember the book? The one Yulerin gave me?'

Dale frowned. 'Sort of. You showed it to me once, ages ago.'

'What book?' said Charlie.

'A little old one,' Brooke said, sizing it up with her bunny-gloved hands. 'It was falling apart, empty inside. I thought it'd just fade away like everything else. But it didn't. And lately… like, in the last couple of weeks… words started appearing in it. And now, somehow, I can read them.'

Dale's heart rate was steadily increasing. All other sounds in the gymnasium had blended into one continuous humming noise.

'What do they say?' Charlie asked.

Suddenly, Dale wanted to leave. He wanted to go back to Ravi and the sound desk. He groped for his plastic cup.

'I don't really understand it,' said Brooke, practically inches away from them now. 'I mean, I can read the words, but I don't know what they're about. It's history, I think. And maybe spells. But that's not the most important thing.'

Dale broke her gaze. He saw Ravi across the room, hunched over his laptop. His eyes dropped a little and accidentally met Tonya's. She was staring at them.

'What's the most important thing?' Charlie said, parroting Brooke's words back to her. All of his usual cool had evaporated.

'I think,' Brooke said, 'it's how we get back there.'

For a moment, none of them spoke. Music and laughter thumped around the gymnasium. Dale could hear his heartbeat in his ears. When Charlie spoke again, his voice was entirely different.

'Get back?' he said slowly.

Brooke nodded. 'I think so. I don't know for sure but… I might soon. I think it's going to tell me, or something.'

The room was beginning to spin. It was all Dale could do to grab his cup from the table.

'So… do you want to see it?' Brooke said, her eyes darting back and forth between them.

'You have it here?' said Charlie.

'Yeah, it's in my locker. I can show it to you.' She looked at Dale hopefully. 'What do you think? You might be able to read it too. And maybe you'll understand what it means.'

He held her gaze for a moment. It was so deep, so blue. Then he blinked and dropped his eyes to the cup in his hand.

'Maybe we shouldn't,' he said.

When he looked up, Brooke's face had frozen.

'What do you mean?'

'Go back,' he said. 'Try to, I mean. Maybe we… shouldn't.'

Brooke stared at him. The red in her cheeks crept up to her eyes. Everything Dale saw behind her was a swimming blur.

'Why… why wouldn't we?' she said, her voice wavering. 'Why wouldn't we go back there?'

Dale opened his mouth, closed it again. His throat had gone dry.

'Maybe,' he managed at last, 'we're not supposed to.'

Now Brooke's eyes were beginning to swim too, just like the rest of the room behind her. But her expression was still frozen, etched into her face like stone.

'Dale,' she said thickly, 'you don't - '

'Ladies and gentlemen!' The music abruptly cut out as Mr Green's voice broke in over the microphone. 'It's time to cast your vote for best costume. No, Tonya, you don't win by default. Everyone, please make your way up here. You too, Zak Marshall.'

There was a hollow bonk and squeal of feedback as Mr Green set the mic down. The Year 9 students began noisily milling towards the front of the gymnasium, where Miss Harington stood with a shoebox, scraps of paper and pens for voting. Ravi waved to get Dale's attention, then pointed at an imaginary cup in his hand.

'I should go,' said Dale. He picked up Ravi's cup, avoiding Brooke's eye. 'I, um, like your costume. I'll vote for you.'

'Dale…'

'Charlie will, too. Wherever he is.'

With that, he walked away from the snack table, leaving Brooke staring at the place Charlie had been standing seconds before.

***

Brooke hadn't seen Charlie leave.

She didn't bother watching Dale go. She was too mad. Her fists were clenched tight inside her bunny gloves.

Miss Harington's voice from somewhere behind her: 'Come on, everyone. The sooner you cast your vote, the sooner DJ Ravi gets the tunes going again. Just one vote each, please.'

Brooke let out a long, slow breath.

She hadn't expected that. She thought they'd be happy. Surprised. Excited, even. It'd felt like the time was right. Tonight had felt right.

And yet…

Why doesn't he want to go back? she thought miserably. *Why wouldn't he want that? I want it. Charlie wants it. Right?*

Where is Charlie?

Everyone was at the other end of the gymnasium crowding around Miss Harington, who was waving pens and paper in the air. Brooke couldn't see Charlie anywhere. Dale was back at the music desk, handing Ravi one of the cups. He glanced her way.

She turned and marched for the doors.

***

The school hallways were unnervingly quiet after the noise in the gymnasium.

Brooke padded along the tiled floor, making no sound herself. She was much too warm inside the rabbit costume.

Suddenly, all she wanted to do was rip it off and go straight home.

'Stupid,' she muttered angrily. 'You're so stupid.'

Stupid, because she'd left her phone at home and couldn't call her mum to pick her up. She could walk back, but she'd get in trouble for it.

Stupid, because she'd assumed Dale and Charlie would feel the same way about the book. She'd expected them to be excited. She'd expected them to at least care.

Stupid, because she'd brought the book here at all.

I should just get rid of it, she thought bitterly. Maybe Dale's right. Maybe we were never supposed to go back.

She turned a corner. Her head was itchy in the costume. She tried pulling back the hood but her clumsy bunny hands wouldn't grip it properly. Exasperated, she tugged the gloves off and tossed them aside.

'And you're stupid because you went to a party as a giant rabbit,' she snapped at herself, throwing back the hooded head of the costume. Her blonde hair was matted to her scalp. Everyone will vote for Tonya, she thought. They always do. At least her parents let her wear a cool costume.

She turned another corner and stopped.

The Year 9 corridor was just as gloomy as before under the low-power evening lighting. And, like before, it was almost empty. Charlie was halfway down the hall, working the dial on one of the lockers.

'Hey,' Brooke said, starting towards him. 'That's my locker!'

Charlie didn't look up. His brow was burrowed, his tongue stuck out to one side. She recognised his concentrated face when she saw it.

'What're you doing?' she said. 'Hey. Charlie.' She reached for his arm.

With a sudden cry of frustration, he let go of the dial and slammed his hand against the locker door. The sound reverberated down the corridor.

'Charlie, what - '

He rounded on her. 'Let me see it.'

'See what?'

'The book! The one that shows us how to get back. Let me see it.'

Brooke stared at him. His dark green eyes overflowed with intensity. She cleared her throat. 'Charlie, you need to chill.'

His mouth twisted. 'Chill?' He punched her locker again and she jumped. 'We could've gone back this whole time, Brooke. We were just going to school and doing homework and living our boring lives, and we could've gone back there at any time.'

'No, we couldn't,' she shot back, bunching her hands into fists again. 'The writing only just started appearing. There was nothing inside it for months. The pages were all blank.'

Now Charlie was the one staring, uncertainty in his eyes. He was at least two inches taller than her, but suddenly that didn't seem to matter.

'Why didn't you tell us about it before now?'

'Because… because there was never a good time.'

'But why - '

'Because we stopped being friends!'

The words left her mouth before her brain could register them. She saw the fire drain from Charlie's eyes. He took a small step back.

'You can't even deny it, either,' she said, vaguely aware her fingernails were digging into the flesh of her hands. 'You were my friend - and Dale's friend - and then you just stopped. As soon as school started again, you dropped us.'

'That's not true,' Charlie said.

'It is true, Charlie Flint. You know it. You were just too cool for us.'

With visible effort, he broke her gaze, looking instead at her locker. Brooke saw a flicker of hurt on his face and felt a sharp stab of regret.

'You… don't know what you're talking about,' Charlie said. He placed a hand on her locker door, as though heat was emanating from inside. 'That's not what… you're wrong, ok?'

A long moment passed. Brooke realised she'd forgotten to take a breath and drew one in slowly, easing back a little.

'Then what?' she said. 'What changed?'

Charlie's hand slid down to the locker dial. He stared at it for another few seconds, then looked at her again. 'Nothing's changed,' he said, 'and that's the problem. Everything here is just the same. That's why I need to go back. We need to go back. Please, Brooke - let me see it.'

'I want to see it too.'

Brooke started. Dale had materialised by her side, gripping his lime-coloured wig in one hand. His chestnut-brown hair was just as matted as hers.

'What're you doing here?' she said, and was instantly surprised by the coldness in her voice.

Clearly Dale was too, but he replied anyway: 'I saw you leave. I felt… bad.'

'Oh, you felt bad?'

'Brooke,' said Charlie, tapping the locker. 'Please.'

She looked from him to Dale, and back again. Two boys in Halloween costumes, each as uncertain and uncomfortable as the other. Waiting on her.

She sighed. 'Fine!'

Charlie stepped back. She moved in front of her locker, twisted the dial back and forth, and pulled the door open.

'There,' she said. 'That's it.'

Dale and Charlie crowded next to her, peering inside at the book.

'That's it?' said Charlie.

'Yes.'

'And how does it help us get back?' said Dale.

'I don't know. I just think it will.'

'What d'you mean, you just think it will,' said Charlie. 'You said it would.'

'I absolutely did not say that.'

'Yeah you did,' said Charlie.

'I heard you say it, too,' said Dale.

'I did not,' said Brooke. 'I said it…'

She trailed off. They all did.

Inside her locker, the book had begun to glow. Silvery light cascaded from between the pages, growing brighter by the second.

'Umm, what's happening?' murmured Dale.

The book was vibrating now. The silver glow grew stronger, rolling in waves, filling the locker with light. Brooke shielded her face with her hands.

'I can't see!' she cried.

'Look, it's opening,' Charlie said.

Brooke could barely see the book anymore. It had indeed fallen open, thrumming on the floor of her locker. All the light seemed to flow from one page in particular - the last one she'd read.

'Agh, it's too bright!' Dale cried, also shielding his face.

'Close it!' Brooke said, clutching blindly for the locker door.

'No wait,' Charlie said. 'That's not what it wants.'

He reached into the locker.

'Charlie!' Brooke yelled, grabbing his arm.

'Brooke!' Dale cried, grabbing hers.

Charlie touched the book. The light flared, brighter than the sun, and the three of them vanished. Dale's wig dropped softly to the floor.

The glow faded.

***

Tonya Miller came around the corner into the Year 9 hallway. She'd heard voices, someone yelling. It sounded like Brooke.

'Hello?' she called. 'Who's here?'

A green wig lay on the floor next to an open locker.

Something inside the locker was glowing. Frowning, Tonya walked towards it.

Chapter Four: The Withering Woods

The music was too loud. Much, much too loud.

'Turn it down, Ravi,' Dale said. 'My ears hurt.'

Ravi didn't turn it down. If anything, the music only got louder. It was rapidly becoming a deafening roar, like foaming white water thundering down Niagara Falls. Or at least, what Dale imagined that might sound like.

It was so loud.

'Ravi!'

But it wasn't music at all, was it? It was something else, a sound he recognised from some other place, from another time.

It was the sound of falling, when you've left one world and another is rushing up to meet you.

The sound of a portal.

Dale's eyes sprang open and he gasped.

At first, his surroundings were nothing more than a blur of green and grey. His arms were outstretched, like he'd been trying to grab hold of something for safety; he was standing, but he couldn't move from the spot he was in.

Then the world began to shift into focus. His senses returned one by one: the green-grey blur became trees; he heard leaves rustling, a bird cawing; the air was somehow thick and cold at the same time. His head was spinning.

'Where...' he croaked.

He tried taking a step and found he couldn't. Looking down, he saw his legs disappearing into something thick and dark, just below the knees. Mud. He was stuck fast.

'Help,' he said, still croaking. He swallowed and repeated it louder. 'Help. Help!'

'Yeah, yeah, I'm coming.'

Charlie emerged from the trees nearby. His black hair was a tangled mess on his head. The sleeve of his suit jacket was torn.

'I'm stuck!' Dale cried, waving his arms.

'I know, I'm not blind.'

Charlie looked left and right. He was on a bank, just above the mud pit Dale had landed in. The bird cawed again somewhere high above them.

'Hurry up!'

'Hang on.'

Charlie momentarily disappeared from view, then reappeared with a long, thin branch in his hands. He extended it towards Dale, who grasped eagerly at it. After a couple of flailing attempts, he managed to get a good grip.

'Ready?' said Charlie.

'Yes, get me outta here.'

With some effort and considerable strain, Dale was just about able to heave his legs from the thick, sucking mud. Charlie pulled hard on the branch, leaning back like he was on the school tug-of-war team. After a few difficult seconds, Dale reached the bank and hauled himself free from the mud pit. He dropped to his knees, panting for breath.

'You ok?' said Charlie, tossing the branch aside.

'Yeah. Thanks.'

'Still got both your shoes.'

Dale rose to his feet on wobbly legs. His shoes were indeed still intact. Both they and the lower half of his trousers were caked in black mud.

'Great,' he muttered.

'Wonder where we are,' said Charlie.

Dale glanced around. They were in a forest populated with pale-barked trees and overgrown, dead-looking grass. It appeared to be daytime but everything was bathed in deep shadow. Enormous dragonflies zipped back and forth through the stale air.

'Wait,' said Dale, 'where's Brooke?'

As if in response, there was a piercing scream from nearby.

'This way!' cried Charlie, bounding off into the trees.

Dale stumbled after him. Charlie was quick and nimble; Dale wasn't, bashing his shoulders painfully off multiple tree trunks in his bid to keep up.

'Slow down!' he cried.

Then Brooke screamed again, closer now, and he ran faster.

They found her on the third scream, not far from the mud pit. Dale had bundled into Charlie, who'd stopped dead between two withered old trees. When he saw why Charlie had stopped - and what Brooke was screaming about - he recoiled in fright.

'No way,' said Charlie.

'Get me out of this!' Brooke yelled.

She was trapped in a massive cobweb, the biggest Dale had ever seen (or dared to imagine in his worst nightmares). It looked more like candy floss than webbing, really. And every inch of Brooke's bunny rabbit costume was covered in it.

'Don't just stand there,' she cried, struggling. 'Help me!'

'Umm… Dale?' said Charlie.

'You first,' Dale replied.

The web stretched between several thick tree trunks and disappeared into the leafy branches above their heads. All manner of small creatures were caught in it, but it was impossible to tell what they were - they'd been thoroughly wrapped. Like presents, Dale thought morbidly.

'Guys!' Brooke yelled.

'Ok, ok!' Charlie said.

After a moment's hesitation, he stepped down into the dried-up gully the web had been spun across and grabbed Brooke's entangled arm.

'Yuck! This stuff's gross.'

'Tell me about it,' Brooke snapped. She looked up. 'Dale, you can't be serious.'

'You know I don't like spiders.'

'Do you see any spiders?'

'Do you see the giant web you're stuck in?'

'Dale!'

'Fine!'

He dropped into the gully and started working on her left foot. The webbing immediately clung to his hands and sleeve. It was smooth as silk and incredibly difficult to break. Touching it sent gooseflesh racing up and down his back.

'Argh, come on,' Charlie muttered. 'If only we had a knife.'

'Or a flamethrower,' said Dale.

'Guys.'

The change in Brooke's tone made them both stop right away. She was looking straight up at the tree branches above them, her blue eyes bulging. Dale didn't have to look to know what she'd seen, but he couldn't stop himself.

When he saw it too, his breath caught in his throat.

'That's a big spider,' said Charlie in a flat voice.

Dale watched, mesmerised with paralysing fear, as eight hairy black legs slid gracefully from the tree canopy, followed by a bulbous black body splashed with fierce scarlet marking. The spider's head was as big as a basketball. Its dripping fangs slowly opened and closed as it regarded them with eight shining black eyes. When it stepped onto the web, Dale felt the whole thing tremble.

'Guys…'

'It's the size of my bed,' said Charlie.

'GET ME OUT!' Brooke shrieked.

Dale and Charlie snapped back into action, furiously tugging at Brooke's arm and foot. The spider started down from the branches, carefully placing its clawed feet on the web, eyeing each of them simultaneously. Its fat, hairy torso quivered; Dale thought he heard it hiss.

'There!' Charlie cried.

Brooke's right arm broke free from the webbing. She instantly unzipped the front of her rabbit costume and began wriggling the arm out of her sleeve. Above them, the spider drew steadily closer.

'Help me!' Brooke yelled, pulling her left arm out of its sleeve. The rabbit costume remained stuck in the web.

Charlie grabbed one hand and Dale grabbed the other. Together, they yanked the top half of Brooke's body out of the costume. The bunny head came loose, its floppy ears fully tangled in sticky webbing.

'Hurry!' Brooke cried. 'Pull me out!'

They pulled, and pulled. The spider was halfway down the cobweb now, its horrible hairy legs spread across it, its fangs snapping open and closed, dripping venom. Dale strained with all his might, half worried he was going to pop Brooke's arm from its socket, mostly worried the spider was about to reach her, and then them.

'Pull, Reed!' Charlie shouted

'What do you think I'm doing?'

'Both of you, pull!' Brooke cried.

And then, suddenly, the costume released her legs and all three of them tumbled backwards, landing in a heap in the gully. The bunny remained stuck in the web. The spider was right above it.

'Go!' said Charlie.

They scrambled out of the gully, just as the spider reached the costume. Its fangs sank into the fake fur, immediately staining it green with liquid poison. Then it spat it out and eight shining dark eyes turned on them.

'Run!' Dale yelled.

They bolted away from the cobweb and ran without looking back once.

***

Brooke wasn't sure how long they kept running.

At first, she was sure the spider was right behind them, all eight of its feet thudding hard on the forest floor, its fangs snapping at their heels like hedge clippers.

But after what seemed like an age of stumbling headlong through wilted grass between gnarled old trees, they could run no longer. All three of them collapsed where they were, gasping for breath.

Slumped against a tree, Dale managed: 'Is… is it gone?'

Charlie wiped a hand across his brow. 'Yeah. I think so.'

Brooke was on her knees in the dead grass, trying to slow her breathing. She saw a beetle scuttling towards her and wobbled back to her feet, grasping the nearest tree for support.

'That was… that was,' she said, '... really scary.'

'Yeah,' Dale agreed. 'I'd take a ghoul over that thing any day.'

Brooke looked up. 'Ghouls? So… we're back?'

Dale shrugged. 'I mean, aren't we? It looks like Uland.'

'It's different,' said Charlie, turning on the spot. 'I don't think we've been in this forest before. It's a lot… older.'

'Ancient,' Brooke agreed, running her fingers over the pale bark of the tree. It flaked off and crumbled into powder.

'So we're in a different part of Uland, then,' said Dale. He closed his eyes, wincing like he was in pain. Brooke recognised it as his "thinking hard" face. 'I can't remember every forest on the map. There were loads.'

'I don't remember the map at all,' Charlie said, still turning slowly, peering into the woodland shadows. 'Were there other forests?'

'Of course there were… are… other forests,' said Dale. 'It's an entire continent.'

'Easy, squirt. I saved your life back there, remember?'

'From the mud? Sure you did.'

'You'd still be there if - '

'Boys!' Brooke snapped. They looked at her, taken aback.

Then Charlie smirked. 'Boys?'

'What are you, a teacher?' said Dale, also grinning.

'We're sorry, Miss Woods - '

'Shut up!' Brooke said. She put her hands on her hips and quickly took them away again. 'First of all, thanks for saving me. Sort of.'

'Sort of?' Charlie replied incredulously.

'Second of all,' Brooke continued, 'we have to get out of these woods. There're probably worse things here than giant spiders.'

Dale shivered. Charlie's smirk had evaporated.

'Now,' Brooke said, 'I was in Scouts, so I know a little navigational stuff. We need to look for trees with moss on one side… I think it points north… and then - '

'Why don't you just use that?' said Charlie.

'Use what?'

He pointed. She looked down. The book was sticking halfway out of her hoodie pocket. She pulled it out slowly.

'How… did it get in there?'

'Beats me,' said Charlie. 'I thought we were inside it.'

'You thought we were inside the book?' said Dale. 'How would that work?'

'I dunno, dorkus, how does any of this work?'

'Bo… guys,' Brooke cut in. 'Enough. I'll check if there's a map in here.'

She flicked through the crinkled old pages. The indiscernible writing was still there, ending just where it'd done before. But there was no map.

'Nothing?' said Dale.

'Nothing,' said Brooke, closing the book.

'Let's just go this way,' said Charlie, already walking away.

'Hey, wait!' Brooke said, stuffing the book back in her pocket. 'We can't just... Dale!'

Dale had started after Charlie. He shrugged. 'We can't just stay here. That spider could be following us, couldn't it?'

Brooke hesitated, glanced back the way they'd come, and hurried after them.

***

The woods seemed to grow darker the further they walked. The pale trees appeared ghostly in the gloom, and here and there, the wilted grass gave way to swampy mud pits buzzing with flies. If there was a sky above them, they couldn't see it. But Charlie had somehow spotted a vague trail in the grass and hadn't paused long enough to think about where it was leading them.

Brooke followed just a few steps after Charlie, with Dale just behind her. Bizarrely, she'd already begun to miss the bunny costume. She felt vulnerable without it, and the bottom hem of her jeans was starting to get soaked in the grass. Her trainers were sodden.

Mum'll kill me for losing the costume, she thought. Well, if a giant spider doesn't kill me first.

'Where do you think this trail's going?' said Dale.

'Dunno,' said Charlie. 'Somewhere.'

'As long as it gets us out of these woods, it's fine by me,' said Brooke.

They trudged on in silence for a minute. The forest was oddly still around them; above, the leaves of the pale-barked trees barely rustled.

'So... what do we do?' Dale said, finally breaking the quiet. 'Where do we go?'

'We'll get help,' Charlie replied confidently. 'Someone will help us. Just like before.'

Brooke was surprised by the surety in his voice. 'What if there's no-one around here to help us, though?' she said. 'It might not be like before. I mean, I don't think we came through one of those Druyad portals this time. We could be anywhere.'

'We could be in Doomgaard,' suggested Dale.

Charlie slowed, his head swivelling left and right. Then he resumed his unrelenting pace. Brooke felt a stitch beginning in her side.

'We need to find Willow,' she said. 'She'll help us.'

'How do we find her, though?' Charlie replied over his shoulder. 'She found you guys last time, remember? We can't just, like, phone her.'

'You didn't bring yours?'

'No, left it at home. Before the party.

'Weird. I did too.'

She thought about the party. How much time had passed since they got sucked into her locker? Would anyone have noticed they were gone?

'If it is like last time,' she said, 'then we only have three days to get back. That's the rule, right? Three days before we turn to stone.'

'Geez,' said Charlie.

'Or maybe that only works if someone turns the big hourglass thingy. Or maybe we have to come through a proper portal. I don't know. We need Willow. Or Yulerin. Or Jayne, even. Hey Dale, how do we…'

She looked back as she spoke, then stopped.

'Charlie?'

'Yeah.'

'Where's Dale?'

Charlie stopped and turned.

Dale was gone.

***

'Dale!' Brooke yelled, cupping her hands around her mouth. 'Where are you?'

'Oi, squirt!' Charlie shouted. 'Come back!'

Their calls echoed back to them through the woods. In the distance, some creature with wings took flight, crashing noisily into the tree canopy. Aside from that, the forest was still.

There was no sign of Dale.

Brooke's heart thumped hard in her chest. 'Charlie, where is he?'

'I don't know.' Charlie drew in a breath and bellowed, 'Dale Reed! Where are you?'

'Dale!' Brooke joined in.

They stood where they were, calling his name until their throats ached. There was no reply. Around them, the woods only grew darker and more silent, if that was possible.

'What if something got him?' Brooke said, and found her voice was trembling. 'What if the spider came back?'

'Or the ghouls,' said Charlie.

'Don't say that!' Brooke cried.

'Ok, ok,' Charlie said, holding up his hands. 'Look, let's keep going. The trees end just up ahead, see?' He pointed in the gloom. Brooke saw he was right - the trees seemed to thin out in the near distance. Maybe they were at the edge of the forest. 'We can get help and come back for him. He'll probably find his own way there, anyway.'

'You think so?'

Charlie shrugged. 'What else can we do? We can't just stay here and wait for that spider to find us again. Or a pack of wolves, or whatever.'

Brooke looked up at the tree canopy, wondered if they could climb to safety, and thought better of it.

'Ok,' she said. 'Let's go find help and come back.'

They carried on up the trail, continuing to call Dale's name. There was no response. Around them, the trees grew more and more sparse. Patches of navy sky began poking through the forest canopy in places. Brooke spotted stars at one point.

And suddenly, the rough trail in the grass became a stoney path beneath their feet.

'Look!' said Charlie.

Something had appeared up ahead. Brooke squinted. It was a metal archway on stone pillars, extending over the path. As they drew closer, she saw words worked into the metal, mouldy and rusted with age and strewn with cobwebs. She imagined it had once been an impressive, ornate entryway into whatever lay ahead. Looking at it now sent shivers creeping up her spine.

'What does it say?' Charlie murmured next to her. The woods were totally still around them.

'I don't know,' she replied softly.

But she did know, didn't she? The words on the archway were in a foreign language, just like those in the book. Yet, as they passed beneath it, the words seemed to twist and morph before her eyes. And then she could read them.

'What is it?' said Charlie, staring at her.

'I can read it,' Brooke replied tonelessly.

'And what does it say?'

She swallowed. 'It says, "Welcome to Wraith's End".'

Chapter Five: The House in Wraith's End

Charlie hadn't been entirely sure he wasn't dreaming until that moment. Even when he'd dropped out of the portal onto the wilted grass and banged his knee on that rock standing up, or pulled Dale out of the mud, or helped rescue Brooke from the cobweb. None of it had seemed completely real. He'd dreamt about Uland plenty of times over the last six months.

But then Brooke had read the words on the archway, and thick, dark dread had begun swirling around in his stomach, and he knew for sure it was all really happening.

It was the same thing he'd felt when Commander Hysst first looked him in the eye.

'Charlie.'

Brooke was a few paces beyond the archway, looking back.

'What?'

'It's a village,' she said. 'But I don't think anyone's here.'

He forced his feet to start moving again. Once he reached Brooke, he saw she was right - there was a village just up ahead. The stoney path sloped downhill from the archway to a small square surrounded by buildings made from dark, weathered stone; some were houses, others were shops and places of trade. One building had a spire on top that made it look like a church. The whole village was hemmed in on every side by the forest.

As they descended the hill and approached the first buildings, something else became obvious right away: Wraith's End had clearly been abandoned for some time.

'This is super creepy,' Brooke said in a low voice.

Her words carried easily to Charlie's ears because the village was so very quiet. No birds were singing, no dogs were barking. A breeze whispered softly between the buildings, stirring tree branches overhanging the village boundaries and sending crinkled old leaves skittering across the cobbles in the square; a faded sign creaked on rusted hinges by the door of what must have been a tavern. Brooke saw him trying to read the words and said, 'The Hanging Bat. That's what it says.'

'Charming,' Charlie replied.

They were in the square now, standing by a well built from the same dark stone as the path into the village. It had been boarded up long ago; overgrown vines snaked all over it, slithering down to the cobbles by their feet. Every building facing into the square appeared to be falling apart: rotted wooden doors clung desperately to thresholds; window panes were cracked and covered in green mould; several roofs had caved in, exposing more of the creeping vines within. One building in particular - Charlie thought it might have been a blacksmith - was completely covered in the same sticky white cobwebs they'd seen in the forest.

When Brooke spoke again, her voice was little more than a whisper: 'I don't like this place.'

'Me neither,' said Charlie.

There was a clear, evening sky above them, but the air was so still. He could smell the village decaying around them. Clearly, no-one had lived here for a long, long time. And yet, he sensed something deeply unsettling about the place, something that made his skin crawl. Someone, or something, was watching them…

'Dale!'

He jumped. Brooke was running across the square, the soles of her shoes slapping on the cobbles.

There was Dale, standing beneath a street lamp, gazing up at the broken panes of its long-disused lantern.

Where'd he come from? Charlie thought.

'Where were you?' Brooke cried. She reached him, stopped just short of a hug, and instead thwacked him on the shoulder with her palm. Dale dropped his gaze from the street lamp and stared at her blankly.

'Dale,' Brooke repeated.

'We thought you were spider food,' said Charlie, joining them. Dale looked at him expressionlessly. The black makeup around his eyes made his face look like a skull in the low light. 'Why'd you disappear back there?'

Dale blinked.

'Say something,' Brooke demanded. 'You can't just walk off and not tell us why.'

Dale looked at her again. Then his eyes trailed back to the square, as though it was slightly more interesting than them. Charlie saw Brooke's hands become fists.

'Fine!' she snapped. 'Don't talk. If you want to huff, that's your decision.'

She wheeled away and stomped across the square.

'Dude, why're you being weird?' said Charlie. 'Haven't you annoyed her enough already?'

Dale didn't respond. He was staring beyond the square now, his eyes fixed on something in the darkness. Charlie followed his gaze, squinting.

'Hey,' he said, 'over there.'

Brooke turned, arms folded, and looked where he was pointing.

'What is it?' she said.

'I think it's a house,' Charlie replied. 'A big one.'

The house was just beyond the square, a little way down another street. It was at least three stories tall, towering above the other crumbling buildings around it. Two chimneys on either end of the roof jutted up towards the sky like horns.

And then Dale was heading towards it.

'Where're you going?' said Brooke.

Dale ignored her, walking swiftly across the square in the direction of the house. Brooke stamped her foot. 'What's wrong with him?'

'I don't know,' said Charlie, 'but we better keep up before he disappears again.'

He started after Dale.

'I really don't like it here,' Brooke muttered, following them.

***

The house seemed to grow even larger and more ominous as they approached. The front of it was just as dilapidated as the rest of Wraith's End: grimy windows, rotting door frames, flaking paint. Fallen roof tiles protruded from a jungle of weeds in the overgrown garden. Brooke noted, with a shudder, that there were a number of gravestones there as well.

She glared at the back of Dale's head. Why was he leading them up here? This seemed like the last place they should be going right now. They needed to get out of the woods.

And why wasn't he speaking to them?

The huge house loomed over them, dark and silent. Curtains had been drawn over the windows so they couldn't see inside, but Brooke wasn't sure she wanted to, anyway. She did her best to avoid looking through the filthy glass for fear of seeing something peeking back at them.

A low, rickety fence formed a square in front of the house. Dale stopped at the gate and looked down at it, as though he'd never seen one before.

'What're you doing?' said Charlie. 'Just open it.'

Dale turned his blank stare on him, blinked once, then reached down and pushed open the gate. It creaked loudly on its hinges, the sound knifing through the still evening air. Then, with a snap, the gate simply fell off and disappeared into the weeds.

'Solid work, right there,' Charlie said.

Dale went into the garden and they followed. Their feet crunched on the gravel path leading up to the door. A long-forgotten wheelbarrow full of weed-infested soil sat next to the doorway, with an old spade still leaning against it.

'Hope they fired the gardener,' Charlie said.

'It's more like a graveyard,' said Brooke. 'Dale, what're we doing here?'

Dale didn't respond. He stood at the foot of the steps, facing the door. It was enormous and in just as much disrepair as the rest of the house. The only unblemished part of it was its large brass knocker, moulded into the shape of a bat.

'Can we not go in there, please?' Brooke said.

'We probably shouldn't,' said Charlie, 'but I'm guessing Dale… yep, there he goes.'

Dale started up the steps. Brooke and Charlie waited at the bottom.

'I really don't think we should go in there,' Brooke said.

Dale arrived at the top step. He looked up at the knocker, glinting in the weak light from the evening's first stars.

'Seriously Dale,' Brooke said earnestly. 'I have a bad feeling about this place. Dale!'

He reached for the knocker.

'Dale…' Charlie began.

'Brooke! Charlie!'

They spun around. Brooke gasped.

Dale was running up the path to the house. His chestnut hair was askew, his green eyes wide with fright.

'What the what?' Charlie exclaimed.

'Dale!' Brooke cried. 'How?'

She looked at Charlie. He looked at her. Slowly, they both turned to the door.

The Dale they'd followed to the house was suddenly halfway down the steps and facing them. His arms were by his sides and his expression was just as blank as before. But as they watched, a grin slowly crept into the corners of his mouth, a grin that was so wide and so unnatural it sent Brooke's heart racing with alarm.

'Get away from it!' the other Dale yelled as he ran up the path towards them.

The Dale by the door smiled, bearing his teeth. Brooke had just enough time to see that those teeth were pure white and pointed at the tips before Charlie pushed her aside. The old gardening spade was in his hands.

'Back off!' he said.

Pointy-toothed Dale took a step towards him. Charlie swung the spade at his head; Dale caught it with one hand and thunked Charlie hard in the chest with the other, sending him sprawling backwards. He landed among the weeds, wheezing.

'Charlie!' shouted the approaching Dale, running at the open gate.

Pointy-toothed, smiling Dale turned to look at Brooke, who'd managed to stay on her feet after Charlie's push. She stared into his eyes. They were no longer green, and there was something moving behind them. He came towards her.

'Get down!'

Brooke dropped.

There was a flash of blue light and a whoosh of static-filled air. Brooke rocked onto her back. Pointy-toothed Dale was blasted sideways with an inhuman shriek of surprise. He hit the ground and exploded in a shower of sizzling blue sparks.

Brooke struggled back to her feet. Dale - the real version - was standing in the garden, panting hard. His hands still glowed blue, but it was already fading.

'Are you ok?' he gasped. 'Did I hit you?'

'No, I'm good,' she said shakily.

Next to her, Charlie also rose to his feet. He rubbed his chest, wincing.

'Alright,' he said, 'what the heck is going on?'

'Yeah, what was that?' Brooke said, jabbing a finger at the charred spot where the other Dale had been seconds before. 'It looked exactly like you.'

'I'm not sure,' said Dale. He took a deep breath and let it out slowly, then continued: 'I got lost in the woods. I thought I heard someone behind me on the trail and I looked back, and when I turned round again, you were both gone. And then it seemed like the actual path was gone, too, and I was just wandering around among the trees.'

'We were calling for you,' Brooke said.

Dale shook his head. 'I couldn't hear you. I was just stumbling around out there. It was getting dark, and I kept thinking about the spider…'

He trailed off, dropping his eyes. Brooke felt a sharp stab of regret for being angry with him moments ago. That wasn't even him. He hadn't been the one ignoring them. He hadn't led them to this house.

'How'd you find us?' Charlie said, breaking up her thought pattern.

Dale sniffed. 'I found the village eventually. It just appeared out of nowhere. I was walking through the streets and it was mega creepy - '

'Right?' said Brooke, nodding. 'So creepy.'

'So creepy,' Dale repeated. 'And then I saw you two going up the hill with… someone else… and I thought maybe you'd found help. So I started running after you. And then I saw that it wasn't someone else at all. It was me. And it knocked Charlie over like a rag doll - '

'Well…' Charlie started.

'And then it was coming for you, Brooke,' Dale said, 'and I just panicked. And that's when my powers came back.'

He looked down at his hands again, flexing his fingers.

'So we can, like, do stuff again?' said Charlie. 'Did anyone see a sword?'

'Maybe that's why I'm able to read the writing,' Brooke wondered aloud. Dale frowned, and she explained: 'I could read the words on the archway coming into the village. It's called Wraith's End.'

'Oh,' said Dale. 'That's… appropriate.'

'Guys,' said Charlie.

'But we still don't know what happened here,' Brooke continued. 'It's like the whole place was just abandoned overnight a long time ago, and no-one's been here since.'

'Guys!'

She and Dale turned. Charlie pointed towards the village.

Someone else was walking up the hill in the direction of the house.

'Is that…' Dale said.

'Yup,' said Charlie.

'It's… me,' Brooke said.

Another version of Brooke was indeed walking their way. It was dressed exactly the same as her in blue jeans, green hoodie and white trainers. Its blonde hair was ghostly under the strengthening starlight.

'Uh oh,' said Charlie. 'Look.'

They looked. Dale gasped.

'It's me again!'

Another Dale was approaching the house from the trees off to the left. It looked exactly like the first one, and even from a distance, they could see it was also grinning.

'There's a Charlie,' said Brooke.

The Charlie version was clambering over a wall behind a house directly opposite them. It dropped awkwardly to the ground, picked itself up, and started towards them.

'My days,' Charlie breathed. 'They're everywhere.'

Within seconds, there were at least a dozen Brookes, Dales and Charlies making their way towards the house from all different directions. Some appeared from between other buildings in the village; others stepped out of the buildings themselves, pushing open rotting doors and gates, walking slowly up the hill. Brooke saw another version of herself covered from head to toe in thick cobwebs and realised it must have come from the blacksmiths in the square.

'What do we do?' said Charlie urgently.

'Dale,' said Brooke, 'can you use your magic?'

'Umm, maybe.' Dale held up his hands; the glow appeared briefly, then faded. 'Nope. Can't control it. Don't know how.'

'Let's get out of here,' said Charlie, backing away. The nearest Brooke was at the garden gate, grinning at them.

'Where?' cried Brooke, watching another Charlie and Dale climb over the fence at the end of the garden. 'Where?'

'Inside,' said Dale. 'Quick!'

They hurried up the steps to the house entrance. Dale's hands scrabbled around the middle of the door.

'There's… there's no handle!' he exclaimed.

Brooke looked back. There were multiple doppelgangers in the garden now, shuffling towards them, cutting off their escape. One of the Brookes smiled with sharp, pointed teeth.

'Do something!' she cried.

'How?' Dale said. 'How do we open it if there's no - '

Charlie reached past him, grabbed the big brass knocker, and thwacked it three times. Knock, knock, knock.

There was a hollow clunk. The door swung open.

'Inside!' Dale yelled.

The doppelgangers rushed at them.

Charlie tumbled through the door. Dale and Brooke followed. She heard one of the creatures behind her hiss. Her heart missed a beat.

'Close it!' Charlie shouted.

Dale was the last one inside. He threw himself at the door, slamming it shut. A split second later, dozens of hands were thumping furiously on the other side. They were all hissing now.

'That was too close,' said Charlie.

'Agreed,' Brooke said, watching Dale back away from the door. It was now trembling within its frame as more and more doppelgangers pounded on it. 'Way too close.'

'At least we're not out there anymore,' Dale said.

She looked around. There wasn't much to see - it was dark inside the house and her eyes hadn't adjusted yet. She thought there might be a staircase just behind them and a hallway leading off to the right. The air was damp and musty.

'So what now?' said Dale.

'You tell us,' Charlie replied. 'It was your idea to come in here.'

'You opened the door.'

'Only because you couldn't.'

'There was no handle - '

'Guys,' Brooke said over the pounding on the door, 'I don't think it's going to hold.'

'It'll hold,' Charlie said. 'Did you see how thick it was?'

Down the hall, a window smashed.

'Oh no,' Brooke said.

Another smash. And another.

'They're coming through the windows!' Dale said.

'You think?' Charlie said.

'What do we do?'Brooke cried. 'There's nowhere else to go!'

'There must be a way out,' Charlie said. 'A back door, or something. What about the stairs?'

'We'll get trapped up there,' said Dale.

Footsteps echoed down the hall, dozens of them. They were coming.

They're going to kill us, Brooke realised in horror. And her next thought arrived before she could stop it. Or eat us.

'Upstairs!' Charlie shouted.

'No, we can't!' Dale shouted back.

The door rattled on its hinges. Brooke heard a sharp crack as the wood split. Footsteps thundered in the hall.

We're going to get eaten alive, she thought, by a bunch of us.

Suddenly, a bright orange light flared in the darkness behind them. They spun around,

'Hurry! This way!'

Brooke saw a very short man - or something that looked like a man - holding up a lantern, frantically beckoning them towards another hallway by the staircase. His eyes, huge and urgent, flashed in the orange glow.

'Follow me!'

He turned away, taking the lantern light with him. In the same instant, a Dale-sized fist smashed through the front door, showering them in splintered wood.

'Come on!' yelled Charlie.

They rushed after the little man and his lantern, bundling into each other in the semi-darkness. Up ahead, the orange light disappeared around a corner. They followed and saw a door swing open, just as dozens of footsteps pounded into the entrance hall. Furious, hungry hisses reverberated through the house.

'Quick!' the little man cried. 'Down there!'

In the swinging lantern light, Brooke caught a glimpse of an open trap door. There wasn't time to take in anything else about their surroundings.

The little man closed and locked the door, jabbed a pudgy finger at the open hole in the floor and repeated, 'Down there! Hurry up!'

'Who - ' Dale started.

'No time,' said Charlie, and pushed him into the hole. Dale uttered a cry of surprise as he vanished into blackness. Charlie immediately dropped down after him.

The little man was by Brooke's side. His bulging, indigo-coloured eyes met hers.

'Please, m'lady,' he said, 'it's the only way.'

Footsteps in the hallway. They'd be here in seconds.

'Thank you,' said Brooke simply.

She dropped through the trap door into the darkness.

Chapter Six: Underground Escape

At first, there was nothing but black.

Dale hadn't been ready for the fall and immediately buckled to the ground, breath squeezing from his lungs like an accordion. He rolled onto his side, wheezing. A second later, he heard rather than saw Charlie land next to him, and then Brooke. She gasped as her feet hit the loose gravel, and promptly fell over.

Then the little man with the lantern joined them, pulling the trap door closed as he dropped down into the hole. An unseen latch automatically snapped shut somewhere above them.

'Get in,' he said.

In the lantern light, Dale saw they were now in a passageway with a low ceiling supported by thick wooden beams. They'd landed beside a railway track of sorts; the darkness ate it up in both directions beyond the reach of the orangey glow. The air was damp and chill, like they were inside a fridge. An empty wooden minecart rested on the tracks.

Dale got to his feet. Charlie had already scrambled into the cart and Brooke was following close behind.

'After you, young sir,' said the little man, gesturing. 'And please, do hurry.'

Still wincing from the fall, Dale clambered up into the minecart between Charlie and Brooke. With some effort, the little man followed. They heard the muffled sound of the door to the room above being thrown open.

'Other young sir,' said the little man, addressing Charlie, 'do you see a lever on the side of the cart?'

Charlie leaned over. 'Yeah?'

'Would you give it a good pull, please?'

Reaching down, Charlie grasped the lever and pulled it with a grunt. There was a loud clank from below.

'Hold tight, please,' said the little man.

The cart began to slowly trundle along the tracks, its rusted wheels squeaking in the gloom. Dale resisted the urge to brush his fingers against the tunnel's earthen walls, which were well within touching distance. Above, the army of Brookes, Dales and Charlies hammered on the trap door.

'Umm, does it go any faster?' Brooke asked nervously.

'Oh yes,' replied the little man, clutching the lantern. 'It just needs a second to warm up, and then we'll be on our-'

They were all thrown back as the cart suddenly lurched forward. In the blink of an eye, the trap door was far behind them, the pounding of the doppelgangers replaced with a long shrieking roar of metal on metal.

'Whoa!' Brooke cried, her blonde hair blown back from her face. Charlie's legs bicycled in the air next to her as he struggled to sit up again.

The cart rocketed along the tracks faster than Dale would have thought possible, his stomach turning over and over inside him. The wooden beams flashed past just above their heads in a blur. If it hadn't been for the little man's lantern, it would all have been happening in complete darkness.

'This is better than a rollercoaster!' Brooke laughed, rocking into Dale and Charlie on either side of her. Charlie had managed to get himself into a sitting position again and was clinging to the cart with white-knuckled hands.

It's like we're back in the fairy passages, Dale thought, trying desperately to ignore the nausea sensation building inside him.

They seemed to be gaining speed. The cart rattled faster and faster through the tunnel, rounding bends so quickly Dale was sure they'd tip off the tracks. At times they were going uphill, and he'd have to grip the edges of the cart to stop himself tumbling back into the little man and his swinging lantern. More than once, the track plunged into a dip, and that was somehow much, much worse.

'Nearly there, I think,' the little man called over the noise.

Brooke actually said 'Aww'; Dale and Charlie, both a deep shade of green by now, stared at her in disbelief.

Finally, the cart began to gradually slow down. The beams and walls became visible again; Dale noticed with uneasy disgust that they were laced with sticky white cobwebs, just like those in the forest. Up ahead, they could see the starry night sky beyond the end of the tunnel.

'Hold on,' said the little man. 'I think we're almost at the - '

The cart hit the metal buffer at the end of the track with a tremendous clang that ricocheted back down the tunnel. The rear of the cart lifted right off the ground and Dale suddenly found himself pitched airborne, sailing into open space. He barely had time to get his arms up in front of his face before hitting the ground with a thump. The breath was instantly squeezed from his lungs. He rolled once, twice, three times, then finally came to a stop. His head spun; at least a minute passed before the stars high above him settled into focus.

Groaning, he sat up. They were now at the top of a grassy hill on the outskirts of the forest. The tunnel had ended in a square hole cut into the hillside, framed by the same wooden beams that supported its ceiling. The grass around the tunnel opening was heavily trodden. Off to one side, a rusted pickaxe still leaned against a weather-beaten crate filled with broken stone pieces. The gnarled, pale trees seemed to peter out roughly where the tunnel began.

It's a mine shaft, Dale thought, getting shakily to his feet. I'll bet it runs under the entire forest, too.

'Oww,' he heard Brooke moan. She was sitting a few feet away, rubbing the back of her head. 'That wasn't fun.'

'You were having a great time,' Dale said.

She threw him a glare. 'I didn't expect it to end like that.'

There was a retching sound from nearby. Charlie emerged sheepishly from behind the crate of stones, wiping his mouth with his sleeve. He waved away their concerned looks as he approached.

'Ah, back out in the open at last.'

The little man appeared from the tunnel entrance, briskly brushing himself down. Under the brightening starlight, Dale saw him properly for the first time: he wore a charcoal-coloured jacket over a white shirt and waistcoat trimmed with gold, along with matching trousers that came down to where his knees must be; white stockings covered the rest of his stumpy legs, which disappeared into overlarge leather boots. He couldn't be more than three feet tall.

'Where are we?' said Brooke, standing.

'Somewhere safe, for now,' replied the little man, coming over to them. 'Safer than back there, anyway. Though I'd really like to get further away from these trees, if you don't mind my saying so.' He had curly grey hair, thick sideburns and a trimmed moustache, which made him look a lot older than his height suggested. But his eyes were large and bright, with irises the colour of eggplants, and those eyes were studying them curiously now.

'You're from a distant land, I imagine,' said the little man, looking at Brooke's hoodie in particular. 'Somewhere cold, perhaps?'

'You could say so,' Dale replied.

'What are you, anyway?' said Charlie.

The little man was taken aback. 'I beg your pardon? Whatever do you mean?'

'That was rude, Charlie,' said Brooke reproachfully. She addressed the little man: 'He means, umm… where do you come from?'

He straightened up. 'I am, of course, a Gnome of the Glimmerglen. Quite a nobleborn Gnome, if you must know. You'll have heard of Twiggleton Estate, no doubt?'

Brooke, Dale and Charlie shook their heads. The Gnome was aghast.

'Goodness, you really aren't from around here, are you? Everyone knows of Twiggleton.' He drew himself up to his full height, adding proudly, 'My father is the venerable Lord Twiggleton himself.'

Charlie snickered. Brooke dug him in the ribs with her elbow.

The Gnome glowered at Charlie. 'It seems gratitude for my help has worn off already. Farewell, then.' He turned to leave.

'No wait!' Dale said. 'He didn't mean anything by that.'

'He was just being an idiot,' Brooke said, 'as usual.' Charlie nodded, rubbing his mouth to hide the grin.

The Gnome stopped, turning to face them again.

'I accept your apology,' he said, folding his arms. 'I await his.'

Charlie looked at Brooke and Dale. He sighed. 'Sorry.'

The Gnome's face brightened immediately. 'Water under the bridge, so to speak.' He extended one of his very small hands. 'My name is Quillorin, son of Lord Brambleby Twiggleton, of Twiggleton Estate. Pleased to make your acquaintance.'

Brooke shook his hand. 'I'm Brooke Woods.'

Dale and Charlie introduced themselves in turn. Quillorin the Gnome shook their hands, nodding politely. Dale saw the flash of puzzlement on his face at each of their surnames.

'Well,' said Quillorin, picking up his lantern. 'I suppose you'll have to come with me, then. It would be most unwise to stay here, so close to the Withering Woods.'

'The what?' said Charlie, looking back over his shoulder.

'I confess, I don't know them very well myself, either,' said Quillorin, fiddling with the lantern. Its little flame bloomed, bathing them in orange light. 'I've spent my whole life within sight of them, and this was perhaps the third time I've ever set foot beyond the forest edge. It's a dark, dangerous place.'

'You're telling us,' said Charlie.

Quillorin blinked. 'Yes… that's correct.'

'Where is your estate?' said Brooke. 'Is it close?'

'Oh yes,' said Quillorin cheerfully. 'It's not far. You can see it from here.' He pointed to a distant woodland grove, about a mile from the foot of the hill; a roof was just visible above the treetops. 'If we head straight across these fields, we should be there in no time. I'm sure the cook wouldn't mind making us some supper, even at this late hour.'

Dale's stomach growled at the word supper.

Quillorin looked back at the Withering Woods, startled. 'We seem to have attracted some wildlife. Let's make haste, shall we?'

He started away from the mine shaft entrance, holding the lantern aloft. Dale, Brooke and Charlie followed.

Chapter Seven:
Quillorin

Night had fully descended by the time they neared Twiggleton Estate. The sky was a blanket of glittering stars stretched above them in every direction, and the moon - or whatever it was called here in Uland - was a glowing orb of white. They barely needed Quillorin's lantern under so much celestial illumination.

Brooke decided she liked the Gnome the moment he introduced himself. She'd come across enough creatures in this world (and, maybe, in her own world) to know not all of them are pleasant. Most creatures, in fact, would sooner eat you than offer you something to eat. They were lucky to have stumbled across a Gnome this time, especially a Gnome as nice as Quillorin.

At first, he walked a little ahead of them, his head swivelling left and right in the orange glow of the lantern. Brooke knew why - they were crossing open fields, at night, in a place populated by giant spiders and copycat monsters. And despite Dale appearing to have regained his powers, they were still just three kids and a very small man with no weapons.

I wish I knew where we were, Brooke thought.

As if reading those thoughts, Charlie said, 'Where exactly are we?'

'The Glimmerglen, of course,' Quillorin replied. He slowed until they were walking by his side. 'The prosperous and peaceful land of the Gnomes.'

'Is it near… the Barrowlands?' Dale asked.

'The Barrows? Goodness, no. That region is quite some distance from here, even by Peryton. What's left of it, anyway.'

'What d'you mean, "what's left of it"?' said Brooke.

Quillorin glanced at her. 'Well, it's been rather torn by war, hasn't it?' When they didn't respond, he continued patiently: 'The Barrowlands is in Suthdren, right between Elementa and Doomgaard, just to the south of Ulandai. After the war began, the Doomgaardians and Ulanders met in battle in the Northern Barrows. Many, many skirmishes took place there. There was much bloodshed. And even now, when we appear to be at peace - '

'Wait,' said Dale. 'This war… what started it?'

Quillorin rubbed his chin. 'Well, I believe it began shortly after the Battle of Fort Hammerfall. I'm sure you know of that one, even if you're from a foreign land. It's rather famous.'

Brooke, Dale and Charlie glanced at each other over Quillorin's head.

'After that particular battle, the leaders of Uland agreed to abide by the Pact, the ancient accord binding each region to the other, for the preservation of all. Goodness, don't I sound like a history scholar? Anyway, all of the Factions - with the exception of Doomgaard, naturally - united in solidarity for the good of the realm. An army marched south from Ulandai, led by King Sol himself. They say it was quite the spectacle, all those soldiers in their shining armour, all those flags waving in the wind. People in the villages lined the streets to throw flowers and whatnot. Of course, we Gnomes saw none of it here in the Eisdren region of Uland. We only heard the stories, after the fact.'

'What happened?' said Brooke, watching the field grass swish past her feet.

Quillorin's tone darkened. 'War often seems like a glorious thing before it truly begins. And then it's not so glorious anymore. The Doomgaard army was much larger and more powerful than the other Factions had anticipated. Even with their combined strength, the enemy were not easily defeated. They were not defeated at all, in fact. So many lives lost, so much destroyed.'

The Gnome shook his head. They waited for him to continue as the trees surrounding Twiggleton Estate grew closer.

'After some time, it became clear that Doomgaard could not be crushed, or even fully pushed back behind their own borders. The Factionheads became restless. The Pyres of Strobor were the first to withdraw, though many say they were of little help anyway. Then the Elementals retreated back to their own land. And finally, even the Giants. In the end, the war came down to Doomgaard and the Kingdom of Ulandai. And neither really won. It was years before the first signs of peace - '

'Hang on,' Charlie cut in.

'Years?' Dale said.

Quillorin nodded. 'Oh yes. Many seasons have passed since the war began. And even with this tentative "peace" we have now, I imagine it won't truly end anytime soon.'

'Years?' Dale said again. 'How many years?'

'Oh,' Quillorin said, thinking. 'I'd say there've been at least a dozen shiftings of the season since Hammerfall. So… about six years.'

'Six?' Brooke and Dale exclaimed in unison.

'But it was only six months ago,' said Charlie. 'Six months since we were last here. Right?'

'What are you talking about?' Quillorin said.

'Time moves differently,' Brooke said, her mind drifting back to their last return from Uland, when they'd arrived before they left. 'It must have happened again. Six months for us…'

'... was six years here,' finished Dale.

Quillorin stopped dead.

'Hold on,' he said, lifting the lantern higher. 'What did you say your names were?'

'Brooke,' said Brooke. She pointed at the boys in turn. 'Charlie. Dale.'

Quillorin's puzzled expression melted into wide-eyed surprise, and then awe.

'You're… you're… it's you!' he exclaimed.

'That's right, it's us,' said Charlie, shrugging.

'You're them!' Quillorin said excitedly. 'You were there, in the battle. You defeated Commander Hysst. You saved Fort Hammerfall!'

'Well, sort of,' said Dale. 'It wasn't so much us as - '

The Gnome's eyes bulged. 'You're the ones they spoke of! You were with her!'

Brooke frowned. 'Who's her?' Yet even as the words left her mouth, she knew. And as the realisation dawned, she couldn't believe it wasn't the first thing they'd thought of: 'Willow!'

'Yes!' Quillorin cried. 'Ohhhh, this is wonderful! Such a fortuitous turn of events!'

'You know Willow?' said Charlie.

'Indeed I do,' said Quillorin proudly. 'Lady Willow was escorting me through - '

'Lady Willow?' said Brooke incredulously.

'Bet she loves that,' Dale said, grinning.

'Yes,' said Quillorin, nodding eagerly. 'Lady Willow, of Nymm. The Lady Willow of Nymm. It was hard to believe, really, when she volunteered to guide me. It was an honour to even meet her, never mind journey under her protection.'

'Where is she now?' said Brooke. She pointed towards the estate. 'Is she there?'

Quillorin's smile faded. 'I wouldn't imagine so, though I haven't yet made it home myself. I've been lost for days, you see. Those woods, and the things in those woods…'

'We know,' said Charlie. 'They took our faces.'

'Cursed creatures, yes. That village was lost to them some time ago. It's the last place I wanted to come across in there.'

'Where's Willow?' Brooke asked again.

The Gnome met her gaze. She saw his hand move towards his pocket.

'Perhaps we should get inside,' he said. 'It seems we have much to discuss, and I'd rather do so by the fire with a warm drink in my hands. This way.'

He started across the field again and they hurried after him.

Chapter Eight:
Twiggleton Manor

Twiggleton Manor was an enormous house in the centre of an equally enormous estate, surrounded on all sides by dark green fir trees and a tall red-bricked wall. The idea that it was home to a creature as small as a Gnome seemed completely bizarre to Charlie. But then again, he reasoned, they were back in Uland, and everything was bizarre all the time.

They left the fields and joined a dusty road shortly before arriving at the entrance to the estate. Huge iron gates fashioned to look like wings blocked their path; lamps glowed softly on top of the pillars on either side. Quillorin waved his lantern and called, 'It's me, I've returned.'

At first, nothing happened. The gates remained closed. Quillorin chuckled nervously.

'I'm sure everyone's asleep,' he said, 'they may not have heard me.'

He cleared his throat and started to call out again, louder this time. Before he could finish, the gates parted of their own accord and slowly creaked open. The lamps on the pillars burned a little brighter.

'Ah, there we go,' said Quillorin, relieved. 'Shall we?'

They passed through the entrance and headed up the gravel drive towards the enormous house. The gates closed again as soon as they were inside, and more lamps on pillars set at intervals by the drive flickered to life as they went by. Between their light and that cast from the stars and moon above, they got a good view of the gardens: sprawling, trimmed lawns were bordered with brightly-coloured flowers and many more kinds of trees, extending all the way to the red-bricked perimeter wall; hedges and shrubs shaped like animals were dotted across the grounds; the water of a large pond off to the right glittered under the stars, and Charlie was sure he saw something that looked like a turtle sleeping by the edge of it.

'I do hope I haven't disturbed everyone,' said Quillorin. 'I'm sure they weren't expecting me back at this late hour.'

'When were you supposed to get here?' Brooke said, gazing around the garden.

'Oh, at least a day ago. Maybe two days. I confess I may have lost track of time in those awful, forsaken woods back there. If I hadn't remembered about the mine shaft, I'd likely still be trapped in that haunted house.'

'Haunted?' yelped Dale.

'Indeed,' said Quillorin gravely. 'And not by the good kind of ghosts, either. Oh look, here comes the welcoming committee!'

Something was coming down the drive at speed. Charlie squinted, trying to make out what it was. It definitely wasn't a Gnome, anyway - the thing was bounding towards them in the darkness, crunching on the gravel, panting noisily.

'Halt!' a voice cried, 'who goes there?'

'It's me,' Quillorin called back, holding the lantern aloft. 'I'm back. And I've brought company.'

The noisy panting thing finally bounded into the lantern light and skidded to a stop. It was a massive brown dog with black paws and a black-tipped tail. Charlie thought it looked like a cross between a Great Dane and a Bloodhound, if there was such a thing. He looked around, expecting to see the owner of the voice appear in the dog's tracks.

'Aww, look at him!' Brooke gushed. 'He's so handsome.'

The dog cocked its head to one side, studying each of them suspiciously. Then it turned to Quillorin.

'What are these?' it said.

Charlie felt his jaw drop. He looked at Brooke and Dale and saw matching expressions.

'Now now, Magnus,' said Quillorin. 'That's no way to greet guests, is it?'

The dog - Magnus - snorted.

'Guests?' he replied through slobbery jowls. 'Trespassers! We must alert the house!'

Magnus threw back his head and bayed loudly. Lights began appearing in the windows of the house behind him.

'Magnus, please!' Quillorin said. 'There's no need for that. These are not trespassers.'

The dog stopped baying and looked at them again. Then his tail began to wag.

'Not trespassers,' he repeated in his gruff canine voice. 'Friends?'

'Yes,' said Quillorin. Charlie got the impression he'd had this exchange with Magnus many times before. 'They're friends, from a far-off land. It's good to see you by the way. Did you even notice I was late returning?'

The dog's face lit up. His tongue lolled from the side of his mouth.

'Master Quillorin!' he said, as though he'd just seen the Gnome for the first time. 'You're back! You're back at last!'

Seconds later, Quillorin was down on his knees, trying and failing to fend off the dog's snuffling nose and slobbering tongue. Charlie watched bemusedly, thinking how at the start of the year everything he was seeing right now might have been completely strange, and now it was just… normal.

'Can I pet him?' asked Brooke, edging closer.

'Certainly,' said Quillorin.

'Certainly!' echoed Magnus, turning to her eagerly.

Brooke patted his head and rubbed behind his ears, giggling. The dog's tail thumped rhythmically on the gravel. 'Oh that's good, oh that's good,' he said happily.

'Magnus, tell the house we're on our way,' said Quillorin, getting to his feet. 'Have them light a fire and prepare us something warm to drink.'

'Yes, Master Quillorin,' said Magnus. 'I will do that right now.'

The dog wheeled away, kicking up gravel in his wake, and bounded back up the drive towards the house.

'Sorry about that,' said Quillorin, dusting himself down. 'He's… enthusiastic.'

'How did you teach him to talk?' said Dale.

'Teach him?' Quillorin said, puzzled. 'He's always been able to talk. It's getting him to stop that's the problem. Come to think of it, I've yet to meet a dog that doesn't talk. Now that would be something indeed.'

He picked up the lantern and they made for the house.

***

The doors flew open as they mounted the steps. A female Gnome stood there, hands on hips. She wore a pink dressing gown, matching nightcap and large round spectacles.

'Quillorin Twiggleton, where on Uland have you been?'

'Apologies, Brigwynn,' said Quillorin sheepishly. 'It's a long story.'

Quillorin told it - the part about how he'd met Charlie, Brooke and Dale, anyway - as they were led through the house. Brigwynn, who Charlie assumed must be the head maid, shuffled grumpily ahead of them in fluffy pink slippers. Elsewhere, they could hear Magnus thundering around upstairs, throwing open doors and yelling, 'Guests are here! Come and see the guests!'

Brigwynn guided them along a maze of hallways with thick sheepskin rugs and huge paintings hung on wood-panelled walls to a dining room with a gigantic mahogany table. A warm fire already blazed in the hearth. She ushered them into chairs, fussing and scolding, before waddling from the room. As the doors swung closed by themselves, Charlie heard her bellow, 'Someone get that dog!'

Quillorin breathed a sigh of relief, sinking back in his chair. 'Home at last,' he said.

'It's beautiful here,' said Brooke, gazing around the room.

'Oh yes, it is. This estate has been in my family for generations. My great, great, great, great Grandgnome built it shortly after the fall of the Giants, back in the Sixth Age. What a time that must have been.'

'Is there food?' said Charlie.

'Charlie!' Brooke snapped.

'Is there?' Dale said. Brooke sighed. Charlie heard her mutter, 'Boys...'

'Certainly,' Quillorin said. 'Brigwynn is no doubt rustling something up as we speak. I'm sure you're all famished after your long journey. I… assume you've had a long journey?'

They looked at one another.

'Well,' said Dale, 'we've come from somewhere far away, if that's what you mean.'

'You said you've heard of us?' Brooke said.

'Oh yes, you three are quite famous,' said Quillorin, beaming. 'Although you're a tad shorter than I imagined. In the tales, one of you is a mighty warrior - '

'That's me,' said Charlie, sitting up straighter in his chair.

'Of course,' Quillorin said, nodding. 'The one who duelled Commander Hysst. I've heard the stories. That must have been something.'

'Yeah,' Charlie said. 'Something.'

Dale cleared his throat. 'You said you were with Willow?'

'Indeed,' said Quillorin, drumming his pudgy fingers on the table. 'She was my guide. I was stuck in a town some distance away on the far side of the forest. She offered to escort me back to a nearby village called Fizzleforge - I could have made my way home from there. But she was… captured.'

'By who?' said Brooke, leaning forward. 'Ghouls?'

'Heavens, no!' said Quillorin, aghast. 'The ghouls were eradicated in the first year of the war, though I'm sure there are still some in Doomgaard. She was taken by a bounty hunter, I think. I can't say for certain, she ordered me to flee…'

He stared sadly at his hands. Brooke, who was seated closest, reached towards him. 'I'm sure she's fine. Willow is… tough.'

'That's putting it mildly,' said Dale.

'Who sent the bounty hunter?' Charlie asked.

Quillorin seemed to sink further into his chair. 'Well, again, I can't be certain. There are… rumours… across the continent. Rumours and stories, really, of one who… may or may not be…'

'Decymero,' said Brooke.

Quillorin stiffened. Charlie saw the blood drain from his face.

'We don't… like to use that word,' he managed.

'We know,' said Dale. 'It's like a swear, isn't it?'

The Gnome nodded slowly. 'Yes. Like a swear. But worse.'

'Do you know where Willow is now?' Brooke said.

Just then, the doors swung open again. Magnus came lopping in, tail wagging furiously. Brigwynn followed close behind, pushing a little trolley laden with food.

'Ah!' said Quillorin, sitting up again. 'Just in time.'

'Supper! Supper!' Magnus barked, prancing around the room.

Brigwynn muttered to herself as she began moving warm plates and covered platters from the trolley to the table. Brooke immediately got up to help her; Charlie and Dale followed suit. The table was the right height for humans, Charlie noticed, and the Gnomes had to really stretch to reach anything on it. Quillorin, who hadn't got up to help and still looked a little pale, needed a large cushion on his chair to sit comfortably for his meal.

Once the food was distributed, Brigwynn pushed the trolley over to the wall, offered a small bow and left the room. Magnus curled up by the fire but kept one eye trained on the table.

Charlie didn't realise quite how hungry he was until the platter covers were lifted and the food aroma hit them. His stomach rumbled louder than Dale's at the sight of fresh-baked bread with butter and raspberry jam, thick sausage rolls wrapped in flaky pastry, an enormous wedge of cheddar cheese, and what appeared to be a three-tiered chocolate fudge cake topped with sliced strawberries. A huge china tea pot beside a jug of cold milk spouted a steady trickle of steam into the air. Brooke passed cups to everyone; Dale was already cutting himself a slice of cake.

'You're all hungry, then,' Quillorin observed with a smile.

'Starving,' Charlie replied through a mouthful of bread.

'Have as much as you like,' said Quillorin, with a wave of his hand. 'There's more than enough here. And whatever you don't manage, Magnus will polish off afterwards.

Magnus's tail thumped happily on the floor at the mention of his name. No-one spoke for the next few minutes. They all ate hungrily, clearing the platters in no time. Quillorin, who must have been famished himself, only nibbled on some cheese and sipped his tea.

Finally, each of them flopped back in their chairs, pleasantly full. Magnus padded over to the table and sat next to Dale, staring intently at his plate.

Charlie wiped his mouth with a napkin. 'That hit the spot.'

'Yup,' Brooke agreed. She stifled a burp and instantly looked horrified with herself. Charlie smirked, reaching for the tea pot.

'So, about Willow,' Dale said, glancing nervously at Magnus, who was inching closer all the time. 'D'you know where she is now?'

Quillorin sighed. 'Not for sure, but I can make certain. I'll send Magnus and the other dogs to find out.'

Magnus cocked an ear but kept his eyes fixed firmly on Dale's plate.

'How was she captured?' Brooke asked.

They listened, a little sleepily now with supper in their bellies, as Quillorin relayed what had happened in the forest several days ago: just barely escaping the prowling Puca; Willow leaving him in the dark while she scaled the old smooth tree; the bounty hunter's trap snagging her on the path to Fizzleforge; how he'd just about managed to survive on his own while lost in the Withering Woods. Charlie could feel sleep tugging at his eyelids but took in everything the Gnome said, right up until the moment he set the glowing purple thing on the table.

'What's that?' said Brooke.

'She gave it to me,' Quillorin replied, gazing at it. 'She said I had to take it and keep it safe, and not…' - his eyes flicked up to them - '... tell anyone about it. I don't know what it is, but it's bursting with magic. I've been somewhat more courageous while it's been on my person.'

Charlie felt a brief pang of unease. For a split second, he was back in the Druyad Tower at Hammerfall, frozen in place while the Soulburn Talisman burned red on the floor.

'She said she'd come find me,' Quillorin added, 'but I doubt that's going to happen now.'

'Then we need to find her,' said Brooke, with some finality. 'We need to find out where she is and... and rescue her. She'd do the same for us.'

'She did the same for us,' Dale clarified, shrinking away from Magnus's drooling mouth.

'Just give him something,' Brooke said irritably.

As Dale nervously offered a piece of sausage roll to the dog, Charlie said, 'Even if we find out where she is, how do we rescue her? I mean, look at us. We're still in Halloween costumes and we don't have any weapons.' Then, with a sudden flash of remembrance: 'Are the trolls near here?'

Quillorin's eyes grew wide. 'Trolls? Here? Good heavens, I hope not.'

'Why?' said Charlie evenly. 'What's wrong with trolls?'

'Well, for one thing,' said Quillorin, sipping his tea, 'they're rather fond of eating Gnomes.'

'Oh.'

'We know some good trolls,' explained Brooke. 'They helped us, last time we were here.'

'If it wasn't for them, we'd have lost the battle at Fort Hammerfall,' said Charlie.

Quillorin's eyes widened further, somehow. 'Really? I've never heard that before. How very fascinating. Trolls, saving people...'

Charlie opened his mouth to say something else and Brooke quickly put in, 'They might be quite far away, if we're in the east of Uland. I think we were in the west last time. Wosdren, if that's what it's called.'

Quillorin nodded. 'That's correct, m'lady.'

Brooke flushed at that. Next to her, Dale wiped his slobber-covered hand on his suit jacket while Magnus scoffed down the last of his sausage roll.

'I think,' said Quillorin, 'we should all get some rest. It's rather late. I, for one, haven't slept properly in days. Magnus here will escort you to the guest rooms, and then I'll send him out to find Lady Willow.'

Magnus looked reluctantly from Quillorin to the remaining food on the table. 'What about that?' he said. 'Is it for me?'

'Once you get back, yes.'

With a woof of delight, Magnus bounded to the door, his big paws thumping clumsily on the floorboards. 'Come on, come on!' he said, tail swishing excitedly. 'Time for bed. Come on!'

They pushed back from the table, thanked Quillorin for supper, and followed Magnus from the dining room. Charlie glanced back as they left - the Gnome was over by the fireplace, staring into the flames.

Magnus clattered up the stairs ahead of them and raced down the hall, almost knocking another Gnomeservant flying along the way. He showed each of them to their individual rooms and promptly ran back downstairs with an enthusiastic bay of delight, waking anyone who might have still been asleep in the enormous house.

Charlie's room contained a four-poster bed, a huge wardrobe, a chest of drawers as tall as him and a wash basin in one corner. Flames crackled in a fireplace next to the bed, throwing a warm flicker across a thick sheepskin rug on the floor. For a moment, he simply stood by the closed door and took it all in, picturing his own room back home at the same time: worn clothes strewn everywhere, TV and games console on his desk, an acoustic guitar he'd tried to learn to play now gathering dust in the corner. This room couldn't have been more different.

I'm still not sure this isn't a dream, he thought.

He kicked off his shoes and went over to the basin, recoiling at the sight of himself in the mirror above it. His black hair was a tangled mess, his skin grimy with dirt and sweat. How had he been at a school Halloween party just a few hours ago? Now that was beginning to seem like a dream.

But this was real, wasn't it? It'd happened again. They were back in Uland, in this bizarre, upside-down place where he wasn't just Charlie Flint, a gangly almost-fourteen-year-old from England who'd just been given yet another detention. No, here he was Charlie Flint, the one who'd fought alongside trolls, who'd duelled an insane, scar-faced knight in a burning mountainside city. Here, he was Charlie Flint, the warrior.

He grinned at himself in the mirror and started to wash up.

Chapter Nine:
The Nighttime Passer-By

Brooke hadn't really had time to take in her surroundings.

Magnus the talking dog had nosed open the door to her bedroom, did a couple of noisy tail-chasing spins on the rug, and bounded out again, almost knocking her flying along the way. She heard him ushering Dale down the hall, saying, 'Hurry, hurry! I'm on a quest! HURRY!', and closed her door.

Just like Charlie in the next room, she went to the basin in the corner to wash her face and was just as startled at her own appearance. The basin water was warm, though, and the bar of soap next to it smelled like fresh summer roses. She washed her face, did her best to clean her hair (she was disgusted to find a sticky strand of cobweb behind her ear), and used the plush towel next to the basin to dry herself off. The rest of her could wait until morning.

She peeked through the heavy velvet curtains but saw only darkness outside, and went straight to bed. The mattress was unbelievably soft; within seconds, her eyelids were drooping.

We're here, she thought, watching the light from her fireplace dance across the ceiling. We're back. I knew it wasn't just a dream.

One final thought came before sleep took her, and it almost jolted her awake again:

Did someone turn the Time Keeper?

The flickering lights faded into black.

***

'Brooke. Brooke, wake up.'

'Huh?' she groaned, rolling away.

There was a hand on her shoulder. 'Brooke. Hey.'

She sat up suddenly and cried, 'The city's under attack!'

'What? No.'

Dale was standing by her bed holding an oil lamp. Its yellow flame cast shadows across his face, making him look older than he was.

'What're you doing in here?' Brooke said groggily. Then she looked at him properly. 'And what the heck are you wearing?'

Dale was no longer in his Halloween costume. Instead of his striped suit, he wore a deep blue tunic over a white shirt, dark grey breeches, a brown leather belt with a hip pouch, and matching leather boots. Even in the weak lamp light, Brooke could see his face reddening.

'When I woke up my clothes were gone,' he said, 'and they'd left this instead.'

Brooke snorted laughter. 'You look like a real sorcerer now.'

'Wait 'til you see Charlie,' Dale said. He motioned with the lamp. 'Think they've left something for you, too.'

Brooke looked at the clothes folded neatly at the foot of her bed, briefly wondered how they'd gotten there, and said, 'I'm not wearing that.'

Dale shrugged. 'That's your call. But they want us downstairs as soon as possible.'

'Why?'

'No idea. A Gnome knocked on my door to tell me.'

A Gnome knocked on my door, Brooke echoed, marvelling at the weirdness of it all.

'So,' said Dale, 'are you coming?'

'I will,' said Brooke, 'when you leave, so I can get changed. I'm only half dressed.'

'Oh,' he said, the red in his cheeks deepening. 'Right.'

He turned and crossed to the door.

'Dale?'

'Yeah?'

'Leave the lamp. It's still night time.'

'Right.'

He set the lamp on her chest of drawers and left the room.

Brooke swung out of bed. She could hear voices downstairs now, lots of them. Someone hurried past her door.

What's going on? she thought.

Picking up the neat bundle of clothes at the foot of her bed, she moved closer to the lamp and dropped them on the floor. She stood looking down at them for a moment, then sighed.

'Oh well,' she murmured aloud. 'Suppose I'll have to look stupid too. It's only fair.'

She started to change.

***

The noise in the downstairs hall was deafening.

Magnus had returned, and he wasn't alone. At least a dozen other dogs had joined him, all bouncing excitedly around the room, their paws hammering on the floorboards. A dishevelled Brigwynn was right in the middle of them, scolding and shushing in vain.

As Brooke descended the stairs, Quillorin appeared from another hallway, brow furrowed as he fastened the buttons of his coat. It was navy with gold trim and looked more expensive than anything she owned back home.

He saw her coming and bowed.

'Lady Woods,' he called over the din. 'I see you found the clothes we left for you. I trust they're to your liking?'

'Yes, thank you,' said Brooke.

She'd stared at herself in the mirror for a full minute before venturing from her room. The Gnomes had given her a knee-length, emerald-green tunic with intricate gold embroidery and a brown leather belt; they'd also given her a flowing, ankle-length undertunic and woollen tights, but she'd decided to stick with her jeans instead, even if they were a little muddy. The grey leather boots they'd left by her door had, somehow, also fitted her perfectly.

Quillorin beamed. 'Good! I believe your companions will be here momentarily. Master Flint requested something from the armoury.'

Brooke reached the foot of the stairs. A shaggy Wolfhound padded up to her and gently nudged his head into her hand. The other dogs continued to crash around the hall, some barking, others yelling in voices she could understand.

'A quest! A quest!'

'We found her!'

'Look at us! We're so clever!'

Magnus strutted proudly up to Quillorin and sat down by his side. Even then, he was almost as tall as the Gnome.

'What's going on?' Brooke said, raising her voice.

'I sent Magnus and his pack out a few hours ago to scour the countryside for Lady Willow,' Quillorin explained. 'One of them got word from a passing eagle that she was spotted at the gates of Silversprog Bay, a citadel some distance north of here. As expected, she was in the custody of a bounty hunter. A whole posse of them, in fact. Ah!'

Dale and Charlie entered the room, flanked by two more dogs. One of the dogs, a Labrador, was happily leading Dale by the sleeve. Dale had a fixed grin on his face.

Charlie had also changed his clothes. He now wore a deep red leather doublet over a black tunic, a thick brown belt with scabbard, dark grey breeches and black boots. Unlike Dale, he seemed pleased with his new outfit. He seemed especially pleased with the shortsword in his right hand, which he now held up to the light. It flashed in the glow of the entrance hallway lamps.

'Ah yes,' said Quillorin, nodding in approval. 'That one belonged to my cousin, the great Nimblefoot Twiggleton. He was one of the few true Gnomish warriors of my generation. That blade has seen a fair bit of action.'

'I like it,' said Charlie, sheathing the sword. Then he saw Brooke. 'Hey, when did Princess Woods get here?'

'Shut up,' Brooke said, flushing. Dale caught her eye and quickly looked away.

'Oh my, you're royalty?' gasped Quillorin. 'I had no idea, m'lady! I should have offered you my father's suite instead of a lowly guest room.'

'No, no,' said Brooke, 'he was - '

'Those were lowly guest rooms?' said Charlie.

'I'm not a real princess,' Brooke finished, feeling stupider by the second. 'He was just making a joke. A dumb one.'

Charlie smirked. Quillorin scratched his chin in puzzlement. Next to Dale, the Labrador's tail thumped steadily on the floor.

'Sir,' said Brigwynn, extracting herself from the melee of dogs, 'the carriage is outside.'

'Oh yes, of course,' said Quillorin, receiving a wide-brimmed hat from a tubby Basset Hound. 'That's why we're up at this late hour, after all.'

'What carriage?' said Dale.

Quillorin tapped his round nose. 'Ah, you'll see momentarily. Follow me.'

***

Outside Twiggleton Manor, the night air was still and cool. The lamps along the driveway had been lit again, and the sky was speckled with winking stars. Their boots crunched noisily on the gravel as they headed for the gates; Quillorin had ordered the dogs to stay in the house, but Magnus had been allowed to accompany them. The Great Dane trotted proudly by the Gnome's side.

'So what's the plan?' asked Charlie, one hand resting on his scabbard. 'Bust into this place, grab Willow and get out?'

'Yeah, that would go well,' said Dale.

Quillorin chuckled. 'No, nothing like that, I assume. I've had quite enough excitement for one day, let me tell you. When I was a young Gnome in my fifties, maybe. But not now.'

'So what, then?' said Charlie. 'How do we rescue her?'

'Well,' said Quillorin, adjusting his hat, 'we're in luck there. It just so happens my uncle lives in Silversprog. He serves in the Queen's court, as a matter of fact. Quite the distinction for any Gnome.'

'The Queen?' Brooke said, watching shadows dance in the garden as they neared the gates. 'Of all Uland?'

'Oh no, nothing like that. There is no Queen of Uland, hasn't been for a long time. She's the Queen of the Glimmerglen, the Gnomish land. Some call her the Glimmerqueen. Her real name is Merriwind.'

'So there's no Queen of Uland…' Charlie said.

'No.'

'... but there's still an Empress? In Nymm?'

In the low light, Brooke rolled her eyes. She remembered Charlie's face when the leader of the Woodspeople had planted a kiss on his cheek after the Battle of Fort Hammerfall.

'Orchidema,' said Quillorin. The gates swung open ahead of them and Magnus bounded through. 'Yes, indeed. But no-one's seen her in quite some time.'

Charlie didn't ask any more questions after that.

They passed through the gates. Just up ahead, a carriage drawn by two large white horses waited on the road. As they approached, Brooke noticed how tarnished and rickety it was. It looked like it might fall apart if they hit a pothole. Even the curtains covering the inside of the windows seemed like they'd seen better days.

Magnus had been waiting dutifully by the foot of the carriage steps. Quillorin scratched behind his ear and said, 'You're in charge until I get back, ok?'

'Yes, master,' said Magnus. 'I am in charge.'

'You're coming with us?' said Brooke.

'Certainly, I believe I'll be of service. My uncle should help get us passage into the Queen's court, and then we can find out where Lady Willow's being held. Besides, it's the least I can do for her. And I have to return this strange object, too.' He patted his pocket, where the purple orb must be.

'Whose carriage is this anyway?' said Dale.

'Just a passer-by in the night,' Quillorin said. As he spoke, the carriage door unlocked and creaked open a couple of inches. 'They showed up at a most opportune time - my own carriage wouldn't have been ready to go until morning, and there's really no time to waste.'

'But who - '

'Inside now,' said Quillorin briskly. 'We must get going.'

He ushered them up the steps. Charlie was the first one in, followed by Dale. Brooke glanced back at the house, and then at Magnus. The dog smiled back in the way only dogs can, his pink tongue drooping lazily from his mouth.

'After you, m'lady,' said Quillorin warmly.

Brooke mounted the steps and pushed through the curtains.

***

'What? How?'

Brooke heard the amazement in Charlie's voice, and part of her knew what she'd see before her eyes finished adjusting to the light.

'How is this possible?' Charlie said.

Brooke saw the dining table with the crystal bowl full of fruit and the sheepskin rugs on the floor and the big squishy armchairs by the fireplace, where logs crackled merrily in the flames. She heard the kettle whistling on the stove, and caught the scent of fresh-baked cookies in the air. She saw the enormous bookcase and the reading chair and the spiral staircase in the corner. Her face broke out in a grin.

Behind her, Quillorin bustled inside, closing the door behind him. He uttered a little gasp of surprise. 'Oh my! I didn't expect this at all.'

'Where are we?' asked Charlie.

'Jayne's house,' replied Dale, matching Brooke's grin. 'This is Jayne's house.'

'The Seer?' said Charlie.

'Oh my,' Quillorin repeated, awestruck.

Just then, a familiar voice called from above: 'Up here!'

Dale immediately made for the spiral staircase. Brooke followed, almost tripping over one of the floor rugs. 'The Seer,' they heard Quillorin breathe behind them.

Brooke clattered up the steps behind Dale. They emerged onto a second floor. Here, there was a short hallway, decorated in much the same way as the ground floor below. Paintings hung on the walls that Brooke somehow knew Jayne had created herself. There was a closed door on the left and right wall, and an open one at the far end: through it, they could see the end of a huge bed draped with silk sheets. The smell of summer flowers hung in the air.

'One more,' Jayne called.

The spiral staircase continued further up. Dale and Brooke took the steps two at a time, with Charlie and Quillorin trailing in their wake. They came out onto a third floor, which was really just one big room with the same wooden floorboards and panelled walls. Most of these walls were covered with bookcases, each packed to bursting with leather-bound tomes. An open fireplace on the right threw a warm amber glow across the floor; on the ceiling, a massive skylight window offered a stunning view of the night sky above them. At the far end of the room, an enormous mahogany desk and high-backed leather chair drew their attention, as did the smiling woman perched on the end of it.

'Jayne!' Brooke and Dale cried in unison.

Her grin widened. 'Hello again,' she said. 'I had a feeling I'd be seeing you two tonight.'

Perhaps it was the warmth and comfort of the room, or perhaps it was simply seeing someone she recognised in this strange place, but Brooke suddenly found herself bursting with happiness and crossing towards Jayne with her arms outstretched. The Seer slipped off the end of the desk and spread her own arms.

Dale got there first, throwing himself into Jayne's embrace. Brooke did the same. She hugged them both fiercely for a moment, then released them. Dale staggered back, red-faced and flustered. Brooke looked up at Jayne, beaming, 'It's so good to see you again,' she said.

'Likewise,' said Jayne, studying her with deep hazel eyes. Those eyes flicked past Brooke to the spiral staircase as Charlie and Quillorin emerged into the room. 'Welcome, new friends.'

Brooke turned. Charlie and the Gnome were gazing in wonder around what must be Jayne's study. She suddenly remembered Charlie hadn't actually met Jayne the last time they were in Uland, and said, 'This is Jayne Butterfield. She's the Seer.'

'Pleasure to meet you both,' said Jayne, extending her hand. Each of her slender fingers was adorned with a gemstone-encrusted ring. Charlie and Quillorin crossed the room and each shook her hand in turn. Quillorin also offered a low bow, which Jayne immediately waved away.

'I apologise, m'lady,' said the Gnome. 'I had no idea you were the passer-by. Those dogs of mine can talk, but many of them don't think. Had I known, I'd have invited you in for - '

'No need, Master Twiggleton,' said Jayne kindly. 'I was, as you say, merely passing by. It was simply good fortune to run into these old friends in the process.'

'Yeah right,' Brooke said, grinning. 'Like you didn't know we'd be here.'

Jayne winked and whirled away towards the fireplace. This time, she wore a sky blue dress under her brown leather bodice, with a matching blue sash around her waist. Her curly brown locks flowed to the middle of her back.

Brooke, noticing Dale noticing Jayne, quickly added, 'Are we inside the carriage?'

'I suppose so,' Jayne replied nonchalantly. She lifted a poker from the rack and jabbed at the logs in the fire. 'Though it does seem rather improbable, doesn't it?'

'You're telling me,' Charlie said from across the room.

Jayne straightened up and turned. 'Charlie Flint,' she said, 'come here.'

Brooke watched as Charlie hesitantly crossed towards the fireplace. Behind him, Quillorin's purple eyes were wide.

'What's that by your side?' asked Jayne.

'This?' Charlie looked down. 'It's a sword. Why - '

Brooke gasped as Jayne swung the hot poker straight down towards Charlie's head. It connected with Charlie's blade with a reverberating clang of metal on metal; Brooke hadn't even seen him unsheath and raise the sword, such was the speed with which he'd done it. Quillorin's jaw was practically on the floor.

Jayne held the poker there for a moment, then slowly lowered it. Charlie, teeth gritted, matched her movement.

'At last,' Jayne said. 'The true warrior. It never hurts to be sure.'

She replaced the poker on the rack. Charlie stepped back and sheathed his sword again.

'What if I hadn't been?' he said, a little gruffly.

Jayne shrugged. 'Then I suppose our first meeting would've been very brief indeed.' Charlie didn't say anything else, but Brooke saw the flicker of pride cross his face.

'Don't worry,' said Jayne, looking at Dale. 'I'm not going to test your sorcery skills just now. That'll be for another time. Now…' She produced her gold-rimmed spectacles from nowhere and slipped them on. '... tell me everything.'

Chapter Ten: The Road to Silversprog

They spent the next twenty minutes telling Jayne everything that had happened since the book pulled them into Brooke's locker at the Halloween party. Jayne listened patiently, nodding along in places. Quillorin did the same, though he seemed to grow more and more puzzled as the story went on. Finally, Brooke, Dale and Charlie finished and turned to the Gnome, who hastily relayed his side of things, beginning with Willow offering to escort him through the forest and finishing with their escape from the monsters in Wraith's End.

Jayne's smile was grave this time. 'Ah yes, *those* things. They're called Shadowmorphs, though some refer to them as Fetches. Dangerous, despicable creatures. They tend to lay claim to places once the inhabitants have been… disposed of. You were lucky to get out alive.'

Brooke shivered.

'You said Willow gave you something?'

'Oh, yes,' Quillorin replied, fishing in his pocket. He produced the purplish orb and handed it to Jayne, who held it up to the light.

'This,' said Jayne, 'is a healing seed. They only grow on a handful of trees across the entire continent. Young Willow did very well to find one. Though I can't really say I'm surprised.'

She tossed it back to Quillorin, who just about caught it.

'Careful with that,' said Jayne. She turned her attention to Brooke. 'Any dreams yet?'

Brooke blinked, thinking. 'Umm, no. I haven't really slept yet. Properly, anyway.'

'Hmm. Give it time, they'll come.'

'Quillorin says it's been six years since we were last here,' Dale said, abruptly changing the

subject. 'Is that right?'

'Twelve seasons, yes,' Jayne replied. 'That'd be about six years for you, if my calculations are correct. And they are. Either way, a long time has passed here. I imagine you'll find things to be rather different since your last visit to Uland. Your journey won't be quite as easy this time.'

'*Easy?*' all three of them exclaimed as one.

Jayne grinned. 'Why yes - did you think it would become *less* difficult? The entire world is at war now, in case you hadn't heard.'

Quillorin interjected with, 'M'lady, I believe there's been a peace accord between - '

'Nothing but a distraction, Master Gnome,' said Jayne, the golden firelight dancing around her head. 'Just a delaying tactic by the Doomgaard. While the other Factions rest, Decymero's forces rally in secret.'

Quillorin shrank back at the word Decymero.

Jayne's tone softened. 'Never fear, my friend. Help has arrived once again.' She looked at Brooke, Dale and Charlie, who looked at each other.

'Us?' said Dale.

'You,' Jayne said. 'You, and Willow. It's rather a perfect combination, don't you think? You bring out the best in one another.'

She walked to her desk. They all turned to watch her.

'Destiny has conspired to bring you here once again,' said Jayne, easing into her chair. 'And there'll be a reason for that, trust me. When evil stands, good rises to meet it. Evil's been standing for a while now…' She opened a heavy-looking book and started flipping through its pages.

'... so it was only a matter of time before the deep, ancient magic of Uland brought you back. Your presence turned the tide once before. Or have you forgotten?'

'No,' said Brooke. 'We haven't forgotten.'

'It felt like a dream sometimes,' said Charlie.

'Quite the opposite,' said Jayne. 'Here, you're wide awake.'

As if in response, and before she could stifle it, a yawn escaped Brooke's mouth. Charlie and Dale saw it, and then they were yawning too. Jayne grinned without looking up.

'Perhaps you three should rest awhile,' she said. 'Why don't you have a seat?'

'What seat?' said Dale, turning. 'Oh.'

A plush green sofa had appeared by the fireplace. Brooke was certain it hadn't been there a moment ago. Certain, but not surprised.

The boys immediately flopped down, jostling for the most comfortable spot. Brooke watched them tussle for a moment, then said, 'I think I'll go downstairs, if that's ok?'

'Of course,' said Jayne, motioning towards the staircase.

Leaving Dale and Charlie ('Budge over!', 'Gerroff!') to contest the sofa, she crossed the room to the stairs. Quillorin, who'd drifted over to one of the bookcases, tipped his hat as she passed. She descended to the middle floor, hesitated at the sight of the open bedroom door, and carried on down to the ground floor.

Here, flames continued to crackle in the fireplace and the smell of fresh baking still hung in the air. It was gloriously peaceful. Brooke's eyelids suddenly quadrupled in weight. She shook sleep away and went to the kitchen, trailing a hand over the table as she passed. She'd eaten the best breakfast of her life at that table, not so long ago. Or *was* it long ago, in actual fact? Over half a decade had passed here, according to Quillorin and confirmed by Jayne. Yet she, Dale and Charlie were only six months older.

I wonder how old Willow is, Brooke thought, not for the first time.

A plate of chocolate chip cookies rested on the kitchen counter. She picked one up, found it was still warm, and started nibbling. She couldn't hear the boys squabbling over the sofa from down here. Amazingly, she *could* feel the almost imperceptible sway of the carriage beneath her as it trundled along the road to Silversprog Bay. They were inside it, somehow.

'Magic,' she murmured, taking another bite of the cookie.

She crossed to the fireplace and sank into one of the armchairs. The flames bathed her in pleasant warmth, tickling her skin softly with their heat. Her eyelids grew heavier, but the cookie was giving her a timely sugar boost and she managed to fend sleep off, at least for the time being. She stared into the fire, watching it dance and twirl over the logs, listening to the steady crackle of burning wood. The flames began to blur.

'You've come a long way again, Brooke.'

Jayne was next to her in the other armchair. Brooke kept her eyes on the fire, transfixed.

'It didn't feel so far this time,' she replied dreamily.

'Maybe not. It's certainly different now, isn't it? No Druyad temple. No ghouls snapping at your heels.'

A shudder ran down Brooke's spine. She shifted a little in the chair. The chocolate chips were melting between her fingers.

'No Commander Hysst, no Wee People,' Jayne continued casually. 'You're not even *in* my forest this time. And yet, here I am. All the way across the continent, beyond the great Canyon Lake, in the land of the Gnomish folk. Do you know how long it's been since I was last here?'

'Thirty-seven years,' Brooke said in a far-off voice.

'Yes! That's quite a stretch, isn't it? I'd barely even left the Forest of Lost Souls in all that time, for the most part. And now it's gone…'

'... burned…'

'... right to the ground. All of it.' Next to her, Jayne sniffed. 'Those Doomgaard beasts. Black armour to match their black hearts. They set my forest alight just to stop the Ulandai advance from the north. And for all the good it did.'

Brooke blinked. The flames swam back into focus for a moment, then began to blur again.

'I knew it would happen, of course,' Jayne said sadly. 'I'm cursed to know all things. Cursed, and blessed, I suppose. I knew you'd be back, for instance. Knew it from the moment I waved you off on the road to Ringmoffren. Knew it when the first stories about Hammerfall reached the Barrowlands. Those stories about the four of you spread fast, you know?'

'Yeah?' Brooke whispered.

'*The Four Heroes of Hammerfall*,' Jayne said with a flourish. '*The Duel in the Garden. Willow and the Other-worlders.* That's my favourite version. In that one, Master Reed transforms into a phoenix and burns half the Doomgaard army to cinders. In another, you subdue Commander Hysst with a sweet song from your own land. Few of the stories come close to the truth, which may be for the best.'

Brooke took a sluggish bite of the cookie; crumbs tumbled down the front of her tunic.

'They tried to give Willow a title after that, you know. She refused, but they started calling her *Lady* Willow anyway, which she hates. The Lady Willow of Nymm.' Brooke didn't have to look over to know Jayne was smiling. 'She pledged herself afresh to the Druyads, to Yulerin, in place of her former master. She spends all her time in their service now, running errands that take her from one end of Uland to the other. For the longest time, I thought she was just… distracting herself. Trying to regain some sort of purpose. Maybe that's how it started. But now I know what she was *really* doing. She'd been searching for it all along.'

'The seed.'

'And she finally found it, and suddenly you three are here again. Right on cue.'

'How?' said Brooke. The flames were beginning to hurt her eyes but she found she couldn't look away. 'Who brought us back? The Time Keeper…'

'It's gone,' said Jayne. 'Destroyed. The Druyads got themselves in quite the tangle trying to understand how you managed to get here through one of their portals. Yulerin encouraged them to revisit their thinking. They spent years doing so. Eventually, they concluded that the Time Keepers were actually *hindering* their magic, that travelling through time itself was more dangerous than they'd ever imagined. So they had them all destroyed.'

'We won't… turn to stone?'

Jayne chuckled. 'I have no idea. That's not the thread I'm being shown right now.'

'Thread?'

'You'll know soon enough. It'll start to unravel for you, too. I'll teach you how to pull on your own thread, to draw it out, but I don't have much longer. It'll have to be in your dreams, and you might not remember them. Dreams are funny that way, I suppose.'

Brooke blinked again.

'Can you see… our futures?'

'In part,' said Jayne. 'The parts that matter, anyway. But there's also something there I don't want to see. I've learned not to strain too hard into the days to come. The days that're here now are more than enough to deal with. For tonight, let's not look beyond the good Lady Willow in Silversprog Bay. We'll deal with the rest later.'

'How do we save her?' Brooke murmured.

'Who're you talking to?'

She jumped. The remains of the cookie fell from her hand.

Charlie was standing by the fire, frowning down at her. Brooke looked to her right. The other armchair was empty.

'Umm... no-one,' said Brooke, lifting the cookie from her lap. 'Just myself.'

'Ok then.' Charlie rubbed his eye sleepily. 'Jayne told me to come get you.'

'Jayne?'

'Yeah. Seer lady, you know? The one Dale's following around up there like a puppy?'

Brooke felt a brief, unwelcome flutter of resentment in her stomach. She struggled up from the armchair.

'Where'd you get that cookie?' Charlie said.

'You finish it.'

She thrust it into his hand and headed for the stairs.

***

When they arrived back on the third floor, Quillorin was perched on the sofa, thumbing through a book. Jayne was still behind her desk. Dale was by her side, peering down at the page she was reading. He glanced up as they approached, flushed, and stepped back.

'Jayne was just showing me some stuff about sorcery,' he said, doing his best to ignore Charlie's knowing grin.

'Yes, he's picking it up with ease,' said the Seer cheerfully. 'I trust you got some rest?'

'Umm, a little,' Brooke replied slowly.

Jayne held her eye for a split second, then winked. 'Good, you'll need it for what's ahead. You all will. But first, let's make a plan.'

She swept around the desk with a flourish and stood with her hands on her hips, studying each of them in turn. For a moment, no-one spoke. Quillorin carefully closed the book he'd been reading, watching Jayne uncertainly.

Brooke could feel Dale's eyes on her and kept hers fixed on Jayne.

'Master Gnome,' said Jayne, finally breaking the oddly thickening tension. 'Join us, please.'

Quillorin came around the sofa and stood next to Charlie. Without meaning to, they'd formed a rough circle in the middle of the study.

'What can you tell us about where we're heading?' Jayne asked.

Quillorin cleared his throat. 'Silversprog Bay is the capital… town… of the Glimmerglen. For want of a better word, anyway. It's too small to be a city, you see, but it's much larger than any other settlement in our modest region. We Gnomes are not zealous for land. We're content with our place in the world.'

Jayne nodded. 'Most admirable.'

Quillorin stood an inch taller at that. 'It was once a simple fishing port,' he continued, 'but over time, it became more of a market town. All of our trading passes through Silversprog: ships sail from all corners of Canyon Lake to barter with the Gnomish people. Many underestimate us due to our size, but we're formidable in ways most of the Tallfolk can't comprehend.'

'And you have an uncle there?'

'Oh yes, Eldric Twiggleton. He's *Lord* Eldric now, I believe. The Queen elevated him to her court some time ago. I haven't seen him in months. But he'll help us, I'm sure of it.'

'Good.'

Brooke had been watching Jayne closely as Quillorin spoke. She was nodding along thoughtfully, her gold-rimmed spectacles glinting in the light, a curl of chestnut hair dangling by her temple. She understood now that Jayne had never been downstairs with her at all. She'd been speaking with her using - what was it called again - *telepathy*, while simultaneously holding conversation with the others.

For all Brooke knew, she could have been doing the exact same thing with Charlie. But somehow, she doubted it.

Or, rather, she *knew* it.

Is that what it's like to be the Seer? she wondered. *Telepathy? Knowing the future? Being able to squeeze your entire house into a carriage?*

For the first time, Brooke began to understand something about Jayne Butterfield that she hadn't really grasped before, even after everything she'd heard her say and seen her do: there was real power inside her, deep magic, flowing through her veins. Power that was very, very old, and somehow, a little frightening.

And, according to Jayne and Yulerin, Brooke had the same power herself.

Or at least, I'm supposed to.

She glanced at Dale, accidentally caught his eye, and returned her gaze firmly to Jayne again.

'... shouldn't be a problem,' Quillorin was saying. 'If I can speak to my uncle in private, I can explain that this has all been a big misunderstanding. The Lady Willow was never meant for capture. He may even see the funny side of it, you know.'

Quillorin chuckled. When none of the others joined in, his laugh petered out.

'If only it were so simple,' said Jayne, rubbing her chin. 'Willow's been taken by a bounty hunter in the employ of Decymero himself.' Quillorin uttered a little whimper and she continued: 'It's not just a matter of strolling inside, asking the Queen to give us her prisoner, and leaving again. She's offered this hunter sanctuary until the Doomgaard contingent comes to retrieve Willow - if they arrive to find her gone, who knows what those beasts might do? No, the Glimmerqueen won't release Willow without something in return. That, or you'll have to sneak her out.'

'How?' said Dale. 'They'll be guarding her, right?'

'Oh yes, most heavily,' nodded Quillorin.

'We can fight our way out,' said Charlie confidently, one hand resting on the Gnomish sword strapped to his side.

Quillorin shook his head vigorously. 'No, we can't shed blood. I won't have that.'

Charlie sighed. 'Fine.'

'If some of us distract the Queen,' said Dale, staring up at the skylight, 'someone else can find Willow in the, umm…'

'Dungeons,' said Quillorin and Jayne in unison.

'Yeah, there. And then we can sneak her out another way. We'll be miles from there before they realise she's gone.'

Brooke took a deep breath and said, 'I'll get her.'

'You?' Dale said, miserably failing to mask the dubiousness in his voice.

Looking back on it later, Brooke wasn't quite sure why she reacted like she did next. Maybe she was weary from running through that forest, or was still suffering the lingering terror of Wraith's End; maybe it had something to do with her "conversation" with Jayne, and the dawning realisation of what being the Seer might actually mean. All she knew, on reflection, was that she couldn't have stopped it if she'd tried.

She could tell Dale also knew he'd made a big mistake, but it was too late. The word had barely left his mouth when a hot surge of anger rushed through Brooke like molten lava in an erupting volcano and she rounded on him, teeth gritted, fists bunched.

'What d'you mean, *me?*' she snapped. 'Why can't *I* do it?'

'I didn't mean - '

'What *did* you mean? Did you mean because I'm a *girl* I can't rescue Willow? Or because I'm not a *sorcerer* or *warrior* and I can't use a sword or shoot fire from my hands, so I could never do it? What did you mean by "you", Dale Reed? Huh?'

Dale had shrunk back against Jayne's desk. Next to him, Charlie's eyes were like saucers.

Brooke opened her mouth again, but no more words came. She ducked her head, letting her hair fall over her beetroot-red face. She suddenly felt small and stupid. Tears were coming, and she didn't want them to see. She didn't want *him* to see.

'Actually,' said Jayne, as though nothing had happened, 'I believe Lady Woods here will be perfect for this rescue mission of ours. She is, after all, holding the map.'

What?

Brooke looked up, frowning. Whatever tears of embarrassment had been ready to burst a second ago seemed to retreat. Dale was staring hard at the floor.

'What map?' Brooke said.

'If I were you,' said Jayne, 'I'd have a read through that little book of yours. The one in your pocket. I get the feeling it's ready to serve you again.'

Brooke's hand dropped to her hip. The book was there. She didn't remember bringing it from her room earlier.

Jayne clapped her hands together and they all jumped.

'So it's settled, then,' she said. 'Brooke will rescue Willow while the rest of us hold the attention of the Queen's court. Once they've gotten to safety, we'll bid our Gnomish hosts farewell and be on our merry way. I'll be sure to leave Queen Merriwind with a very convincing story to tell the Doomgaard when they arrive. Or perhaps a strong sleep potion. One step at a time, I suppose.'

'Wait,' Brooke said. 'I can't rescue Willow on my own!'

'You won't be on your own,' said Jayne. 'You have your book.'

'But - '

'We'll iron out the finer details in a moment. First, I need a drink. I believe a mug of hot chocolate would hit the spot right now.'

'Yes!' cried Charlie, like he'd been holding the word in all night.

'Downstairs, then,' said Jayne. 'After you, Lady Woods.'

Chapter Eleven: The Bay of Gnomes

Silversprog Bay was, for all intents and purposes, little more than a round, stone castle surrounded by a collection of smaller wooden buildings on the shore of the lake. Yes, it had a high exterior wall built atop earthen ramparts, and large entrance gates with a drawbridge and portcullis; yes, there were guard towers and cobbled streets and *some* grey-stoned buildings dotted among the wooden ones; and yes, there was a good-sized harbour just below the castle, with ships coming and going on the still, early morning waters. But Dale certainly wouldn't have called it a city.

They came within sight of Silversprog just after sunrise. Charlie had spotted streaks of violet in the sky above Jayne's study and they'd gone outside. Stepping out of the carriage and seeing how small it really was had a weird, jarring effect on all of them. Except Jayne, of course. She spoke in whispers to the two large horses that had apparently been pulling the carriage all night, though neither of them looked remotely tired. They snorted happily when she scratched their pink noses.

They'd stopped on the crest of a hill overlooking the bay. Quillorin pointed down at it, following the gentle curve of the road with his finger.

'We're on the Queen's land now,' he said. 'Everything from here onwards, all the way down to the city itself. Seems like everyone's still asleep. But look! You can see the first merchant ships of the day arriving, down there at the docks. See the one with the blue and silver flag? That'll have come all the way from Ulandai.'

Dale allowed his gaze to drift out over the lake, tracing the rippling pathways the trading ships had cut in the water. It looked more like an ocean to him, stretching into the far distance, deep and blue and coated with early morning mist. He couldn't see a speck of land anywhere on the horizon. Above, Uland's vast array of nighttime stars were fading fast in the steadily-lightening sky.

'What's the Queen like?' said Charlie.

'Oh, she's most fair indeed,' Quillorin replied. 'She's been on the throne since the infamous Goblin Revolt, many years ago. That didn't happen here, of course, since Goblins and Gnomes take little to do with each other unless there's trade to be had, but Merriwind… I mean, the Queen… has always been a just ruler. And much respected across Eisdren. The Glimmerglen has enjoyed a long spell of peace under her.'

'Do you think she'll listen to your uncle?' said Brooke. 'Maybe he'll convince her to let Willow go?'

'Perhaps,' said Quillorin thoughtfully. 'We can only try our best.'

'Enough dilly-dallying,' Jayne called. 'I believe we have a Woodsperson to rescue.'

They turned to go back to the carriage. Dale gave Brooke a wide berth, trailing behind the others. It was too early in the morning for another telling-off.

He knew he'd said something stupid last night the moment he saw the look on her face. His stomach had instantly curled into a knot and his cheeks blazed red. He'd never seen Brooke that angry in his life, even when he'd accidentally tipped juice over the pages of her book in Primary School. It was… scary.

I should apologise, he thought, pushing through the carriage curtains into Jayne's house. Except, I'm not entirely sure what I'd be saying sorry for.

Once they were back inside, the carriage trundled on down the hill towards Silversprog. While Jayne and Quillorin spoke quietly by the dying embers of the fireplace and Charlie rooted around the kitchen for yet more food, Dale turned the plan over in his head again. It was simple enough: Jayne would get them into the castle (no-one would refuse the Seer), where they'd be invited into the Queen's court; there, Quillorin would take his uncle aside and try to persuade him to release Willow; if he said no, or it wasn't in his power to do so, Brooke would sneak down to the dungeons, find Willow and help her escape.

Jayne had been right about the book, too - a hand-drawn map of Silversprog Castle had materialised on the next empty page, showing a clear route from the courtroom to the dungeons. There was even a secret door leading out of the castle. Brooke said the path she needed to take glowed faintly when she touched the page, but no-one else could see it.

No sooner were they back inside the carriage than Jayne announced they'd arrived. She gave each of them a cloak that perfectly matched the colour of their clothes, just like the last time they'd been in Uland.

'Keep your faces hidden until we're in the castle,' Jayne instructed, wrapping a royal blue cloak around herself. 'I don't want anyone recognising you and causing a commotion.'

'How could they recognise us?' said Charlie, fastening the silver pin on his cloak. 'We were only here for, like, three days. And it was six years ago.'

'You have a memorable face, Master Flint,' said Jayne. 'Also, your statue is an incredible likeness.'

'*Statue?*' Charlie exclaimed.

'Yes, they built a big one of the three of you - and Willow - at Hammerfall. Right where you fought Hysst. People came from far and wide to see it. Gnomes, too. Anyway, out you go.'

They stepped from the carriage into bright morning sunshine. Dale winced, shielding his face from the abrupt glare. After a moment, his eyes adjusted and he saw they were just outside the gates of the town. A nervous Gnomish stablehand was tying the horses up by the road, or trying to, at least - they towered above him, snorting and pawing at the ground, and it was all he could do to gather the reins in safely.

'They'll want a drink and some hay,' said Jayne, 'if you don't mind. We won't be long.'

Without another word, she swept across the drawbridge and they hurried after her. The Gnomish guards, battle-clad in boiled leather armour and armed with spears twice their height, glanced at them sleepily as they passed beneath the portcullis and into the town.

Even at this early hour, Silversprog was already beginning to wake. As they made their way through the cobbled streets, shopkeepers were opening doors and setting out stalls; Dale caught the rich aromas of baking bread and frying bacon (or something that smelled like bacon, anyway), and got a good whiff of strawberries and oranges as they passed a fruit shop on the corner. The town rang with early morning noise, too: smithies hammering on anvils; dogs barking at the heels of their Gnomish owners; residents shouting across the streets to one another, laughing and arguing and exchanging the morning news.

'Did y'hear about Ravencrest? Burned to the ground last night, it was.'

'My cousin's friend's sister told her the Giants is movin' south, so they are.'

'More Doomgaard in the Barrows now, I heard.'

'Some commotion up in them woods the other night. Wonder what that was all about.'

This place is like Crookedstone, Dale thought, stepping aside as a plump Gnomish mother and her two knee-high children brushed by. *Except it's a lot less… hectic.*

Indeed, compared to the chaos of Crookedstone and The Throat, the Gnomish capital town was a pretty pleasant place to be so early in the day. The Gnomes themselves were mostly polite and cheerful, if a little jumpy maybe, tipping their hats and offering smiles as they passed. Even their arguments seemed full of jest. The Goblins had been sneaking, sneering creatures, tracking their every move with menacing yellow eyes in the markets; the Gnomes seemed to be the polar opposite, and Dale was glad of it. Still, he wasn't tempted to remove the hood of his cloak. Jayne had seemed pretty strict on that one.

'Do Gnomes live all over Uland?' Brooke asked as they walked.

'Oh yes,' replied Quillorin. 'You'll find us most anywhere on the continent. But we like it here in the Glimmerglen. We have the lake to our front and the woods at our backs. It's safer this way, usually.'

'Gnomes are survivalists,' Jayne added, her boots clocking on the cobbles. 'They've been around for thousands of years, almost as long as the Giants. They have a knack for endurance. And they're really rather clever.'

Quillorin's chin went up. 'Well, we're always eager to learn.'

They were going downhill now. As they drew closer to the castle, the little wooden houses and shops gave way to larger stone buildings. Dale caught a glimpse through an open door of a library, complete with a bespectacled Gnomish librarian wobbling precariously at the top of a bookcase ladder.

There were more guards here, too, patrolling the streets with their spears and shields. Every one of them offered a cheerful, 'Good morning' as they passed. Dale wondered how good they'd be in a fight. He saw Charlie eyeing them and suspected he wondered the same.

'There it is,' said Quillorin, with a little thrill of excitement in his voice. 'Castle Silversprog.'

The road ahead widened and sloped more sharply downhill to the harbour, where ships of all shapes and sizes were already coming and going in the morning sunlight. Gnomes swarmed all over the docks, jumping up and down gangplanks, fastening thick ropes to cleats along the weathered wooden quays, talking animatedly with sailors from other regions of Uland. Dale saw a group of burly Ulanders with tattooed arms clumped around a single Gnome, who seemed to be either welcoming them or demanding they leave at once. On another quay, a skinny Pyre merchant scrutinised crates as they were loaded onto his ship. Dale shivered at the sight of him, remembering Ravocus, the creepy, vampire-like Factionhead from Strobor he'd briefly seen at Fort Hammerfall.

Castle Silversprog itself loomed over the harbour, a round stone structure with a domed top ringed with battlements. A green flag in the centre of the dome fluttered in the breeze. Gnomish soldiers armed with crossbows peered out across the water from between crenellations on the battlement wall, their helmets glinting in the morning light.

'Ah, it's good to see it again,' said Quillorin as they neared the castle.

'A fine citadel indeed,' said Jayne. 'And, I believe, never been breached?'

'Never,' Quillorin said proudly. Then: 'Of course, it's also never been attacked.'

'Not once?' said Charlie.

'No. I doubt the rest of Uland sees us as a worthwhile target. Which is fine, naturally - it's one of the reasons we Gnomes are so adept at survival. But if the Factions ever found out about the vast stores of gold beneath our…' He trailed off. 'Actually, never mind. We're here.'

They'd arrived at the castle entrance, a pair of thick oaken doors at the top of a flight of stone steps. Two more spear-wielding guards stationed here watched them approach. As they mounted the steps, they moved to block their path.

'No visitors,' the one on the left said gruffly.

'Certainly not,' said Jayne, flashing a smile. 'We're *delegates*, you see, summoned to the Queen's Court for an audience with her Royal Highness. I'm afraid we're rather late, so if you wouldn't mind?'

The guards stayed where they were, eyeing them suspiciously.

'Didn't hear about no delly-gates,' said the one on the right. 'Would've been told.'

'Brethren,' said Quillorin, stepping forward. 'My uncle is a member of the Queen's Court. Lord Eldric Twiggleton, if you know him? He's most eager to see us, and we've travelled rather a long way - '

'No visitors,' repeated the first guard staunchly.

'We don't have time for this,' Charlie muttered. Dale saw his hand inch towards where the sword was hidden beneath his cloak and his heart skipped a beat.

'I agree,' said Jayne pleasantly. 'Gentlegnomes, have you seen one of these before?'

She held out her hand. A blue-winged moth rested on her palm. The guards frowned.

'What's this?' the second one said.

The moth began to beat its wings, rising from Jayne's palm. The guards instantly became transfixed, staring dumbly at it with glazed eyes. The moth fluttered away and the guards followed, letting go of their spears. Brooke and Charlie caught them before they clattered to the ground.

'A little friend of mine,' said Jayne. 'Awfully interesting when he wants to be.'

Dale watched the guards bumble down the steps and down the road after the moth. Some passers-by stopped to stare at them.

'Oh my,' said Quillorin. 'I think we'll need to hurry. Look.'

Three galleons were approaching the bay, each of them driven by black sails. A Gnome was waving them towards one of the quays.

'Doomgaard,' said Charlie bitterly.

'Here to retrieve Willow, yes,' said Jayne. 'We'll need to make this quick. Master Reed, does that key fit the lock?'

'What key?' Dale said. He looked down and saw a large brass key in his right hand. 'Oh, ok.'

Brooke and Charlie set the spears down as Dale slipped the key into the lock. He turned it once and the doors opened with a *clunk*.

'Good work,' said Jayne, patting him on the shoulder. 'And Lady Woods, I believe you know the way?'

Brooke fumbled the book from her pocket, opening it to the castle map.

'Follow me,' she said.

They entered the castle, locking the doors behind them.

Chapter Twelve: The Queen's Court

Their footsteps echoed along the stone corridors of the castle as they made their way to the throne room. If there were any more guards in their path, which there surely would be, they'd hear them coming a mile off.

Charlie didn't care, though. He finally had a sword strapped to his side again. It felt good, it felt *right*. He hadn't felt either of those things since they left Uland. Not properly, anyway.

He was the Warrior. He'd take on anyone who got in their way.

'Umm, I think it's this way,' Brooke murmured, turning to go left at the end of the corridor. 'No wait... this way.'

They went right. This corridor was just as cold and empty as the last one. Torches flickered along the walls between hanging tapestries, battered old shields and ancient-looking swords. Every so often, they'd pass over a faded ornamental rug and the clapping of their footsteps would momentarily cut out. They met no-one along the way.

'Where *is* everyone?' Dale said.

'Shhh,' Brooke hissed, 'not so loud.'

'I wasn't being loud.'

'Yes you *were*.'

'Both of you shut up,' said Charlie. He saw Jayne and Quillorin exchange a glance.

They turned another corner and Brooke abruptly stopped. Charlie bumped into the Gnome, almost knocking him flying. 'Whoops, sorry,' he said.

'Quite alright,' said Quillorin, readjusting his hat.

'I think it's up there,' said Brooke, motioning with the little leather book.

They were at the foot of a wide set of stone stairs, curving up and around a massive supporting pillar. The torches continued on up the wall, throwing shadows every which way. And for the first time, they heard sounds. Muffled voices. Music.

'Sounds like a party,' said Charlie.

'It certainly does,' Jayne agreed. 'Any cause for celebrations, Master Gnome?'

'Not that I know of,' replied Quillorin uneasily. 'It's most irregular for the Queen's court to stage a… party… this early in the day.'

'I like irregular things,' Jayne said. 'Let's take a look, shall we?'

They made their way up the stairs. As they ascended, the voices and music grew steadily louder. Charlie could hear flutes and fiddles, and some sort of drum. A woman - or female Gnome, he assumed - shrieked laughter.

'What the heck is going on?' said Dale.

The stairs ended at another set of oaken double doors. Spears were propped against the wall on either side of them. *The guards left their posts*, thought Charlie.

They stood there for a moment, listening. Finally, Brooke said, 'Should we knock?'

'We could,' said Jayne, 'but I doubt we'd be heard. Master Quillorin, would you like to lead the way? Four cloaked non-Gnomes may look a little odd without a native escort.'

'Oh. Yes, yes of course.'

Quillorin twisted the iron ring handle on the right-side door and pushed it open. The once-muffled noises from inside immediately flooded out, ringing loud and clear in the stairwell. They followed the Gnome through the doors.

And they stared.

'Oh my,' said Quillorin.

The throne room of Castle Silversprog was a huge, cathedral-ceilinged space ringed with thick stone pillars. On one side, three enormous windows looked out over the water; warm morning sunlight spilled through, illuminating the entire room and making the smouldering wall torches redundant. On the opposite wall, three colourful stained-glass windows faced towards the town itself; each window seemed to depict different stages of Silversprog's development, from a single earthen mound with a green flag planted on top to the many houses and streets and royal buildings of the current era. A stone throne sat on a raised area at the far end of the room and high above them, a silver chandelier burned with hundreds of dripping wax candles.

Under different circumstances, Charlie imagined it would have been a grand, regal space, certainly fit for royalty. Right now, however, it was in chaos.

They appeared to have stumbled into the dying embers of a full-blown party. The room was filled with revellers, most of whom were Gnomes in fancy robes, though several non-Gnomish people seemed to have joined the fray. They were all laughing and shouting and singing, apparently unaware of how early it was. A band of weary-looking musicians played in the corner, belting out a lively jig; a number of party-goers were merrily dancing along to the music at the foot of the throne steps. At some point, a banqueting table laden with food had been dragged into the room - most of which was now gone or scattered on the floor around it. Charlie spotted one of the door guards slouched in a chair with a half-eaten meat drumstick in his hand.

'This is the Queen's court?' said Brooke in disbelief.

'I... I...,' Quillorin stammered, gawking around the room. 'I mean... I...'

'This looks miles better than our Halloween party,' said Dale.

'I take it this is, in fact, rather irregular?' Jayne said, half concealing a smile.

'Yes! *Most* irregular!' Quillorin cried. 'My good lady, I beg you, don't let this tarnish your image of the Gnomish people. We're normally not this... rambunctious. I've never seen anything like this in all my life. You there!'

Quillorin grabbed the arm of a passing servant. The other Gnome had sticky pink jam and chocolate smeared on his shirt. There were dark bags under his eyes.

'Sir?'

'What's going on here?' Quillorin demanded. 'Where're the members of the Queen's court?'

The servant blinked dazedly. 'You're looking at them. Well, most of them, anyway. I think the rest are up on the roof.'

'Doing what?'

'Last I heard, throwing food at seagulls.'

He staggered off into the crowd. Quillorin was aghast.

'Never,' he said. 'Never, in all my days...'

'It shouldn't be hard getting Willow out of this place,' Dale observed. 'No-one'll even notice she's gone.'

'I believe that could be true,' said Jayne. 'Though we should be quick about it. Those Doomgaard ships weren't far away.' She turned to Brooke. 'Is there a way to the dungeons from here?'

Brooke consulted the book, squinting at the map. She pointed across the room. 'There're stairs through that door. They should take us all the way down.'

'Excellent,' said Jayne. 'Let's make haste.'

They started across the throne room. The Gnomes of the Queen's court - if that's who they really were - didn't pay them much attention. One particularly merry female Gnome with thickly-painted eyelids and pouting lips tried to get a hold of Charlie's arm as he passed, and he hurriedly jerked it away. Dale slipped on a discarded meat pie, just about managing to stay on his feet. They were right in the middle of a crazy cacophony of noise and colour and sickly-sweet perfume - Charlie guessed there must have been at least a hundred people there, and none of them seemed to be entirely in their right minds.

'This way,' Brooke shouted over the din, pushing towards the door in the corner.

'I'm so sorry, so very sorry,' Quillorin apologised as they went. 'This is most unbefitting of Gnomes. I've never seen such a thing, not once in all my days. How very embarrassing...'

'Are we all going to the dungeons?' Charlie called. 'Or should one of us - '

The corner door flew open with a *bang* and someone squealed in surprise. Those nearest turned to look. Quillorin bundled into Brooke from behind and the book dropped from her grasp.

'Make way! Make way!'

Gnomish guards in green cloaks poured through the door. Unlike their counterparts elsewhere in town, these soldiers wore a combination of leather and metal armour, and had green feather plumes on top of their helmets. They also carried shortswords instead of spears. Brooke just about managed to grab the book from the floor before she was stepped on.

'Make way for the Queen!'

The shouting and laughter and singing immediately died out, and a ripple of hushed anticipation swept across the room. The band ended their jig and switched to a more regal tune. As one, the crowd turned to face the throne, murmuring with excitement, craning to see.

'Oh my,' Quillorin blurted.

The last of the guards emerged through the doorway with the Glimmerqueen between them. Charlie was surprised to see she was actually taller than the other

Gnomes - not far off Dale's height, in fact - and walked with a little swagger. She wore a full-length green robe fastened with an elaborate silver chain, and a glittering silver crown studded with emeralds balanced on her head. Like the other Gnomes, her eyes were big and purple-irised.

Queen Merriwind waved to the crowd as she mounted the steps to her throne. 'Hello, everyone,' she said, grinning toothily. 'Who's having a good time, huh?'

The onlookers erupted with cheers and raucous laughter. As the guards took up their positions around the throne and Merriwind climbed onto her seat, a chorus of 'Long live the Queen! Long live the Queen!' spread across the room. Charlie noticed that the corner door was now closed and guarded by two soldiers.

Merriwind motioned for silence and the enthusiastic chanting gradually died down to a bubbling murmur. The band had switched to a slower tune on the harp and violin. All eyes were on the Queen.

She continued smiling down at the crowd, her small Gnomish hands clasped in her lap. Several moments passed, and still no-one spoke. Charlie frowned. *What's she doing?* he thought.

Finally, a much older Gnome with a bald head and drooping grey moustache stepped up and whispered in her ear. She nodded.

'Oh, I'm supposed to welcome you.' She spread her hands awkwardly. 'Umm… welcome!'

The crowd responded with a brief, hesitant cheer. The older Gnome whispered to her again.

'So, the Queen's court is now in session,' Merriwind added. 'Does anyone have anything, like, important to say?'

The crowd exchanged glances. Charlie caught Brooke's eye and saw she was frowning too.

Why does she sound so familiar? he thought.

'My Queen,' said a Gnome in a blue tunic, stepping forward. He still held a half-eaten, half-melted slice of cake in one hand. 'We saw Doomgaard ships in the bay. Why are they here?'

More murmurings in the crowd. More whispers from the moustachioed Gnome.

'They're here for the, um, prisoner,' said the Glimmerqueen. 'Once they have her, they'll be on their way. Nothing to worry about, apparently.'

'*Apparently?*' Dale whispered.

'Most irregular,' said Quillorin.

Another Gnome stepped from the crowd and said, 'Shouldn't she stand trial? All prisoners are meant to stand trial. It's the law.'

The murmurings became rumbles of agreement. Someone called, 'No Doomgaard here' and others began echoing it. Soon, it was filtering through the whole crowd.

'She should stand trial!' someone shouted.

'They can't just take her!'

'Where's the Queen's justice?'

Merriwind grimaced, wringing her hands in her lap. Her Gnomish advisor whispered to her a third time and she said, 'Would it help if I brought her out?'

An affirming cheer went around the room. The Queen beamed again, pleased. Some of the guards headed for the corner door.

'Oh, that was easy,' said Jayne. 'They're bringing Willow to us.'

'But how do we get her out,' Brooke said anxiously. 'There're so many people here. We can't just grab her and run, can we?'

Jayne seemed to consider it for a moment, then shook her head. 'No,' she said, 'I believe this may require some diplomacy.'

Half a dozen guards had exited through the door. The crowd were jabbering excitedly again, edging towards the corner. Charlie tried to stand his ground as they pressed into him from behind. *They can't see past us*, he realised. *We're taller than most people in the room.*

'Master Quillorin,' said Jayne, raising her voice to be heard. 'That gentleman by the Queen is your uncle, isn't he?'

'He is,' replied Quillorin. 'I didn't know he'd become her advisor, though.'

'It could work to our advantage,' Jayne said.

'Look!' said Brooke.

The guards were returning. They seemed to move as one, shuffling back into the throne room, grumbling for others to move aside. And right in their midst, draped in a tattered brown cloak with wrists bound in heavy manacles and her face shrouded in fiery red hair, was Willow.

'It's her,' said Dale.

'Willow,' Brooke said.

There were gasps in the crowd as the guards escorted Willow towards the throne. The Gnomes in their path moved quickly aside, keeping a safe distance.

'That's a Woodsperson,' one said.

'Haven't seen a Nymmite in years,' said another.

'What's she doing all the way down here?'

'Wait, is she…?'

While all eyes were on Willow, someone else had entered the room behind her and the gaggle of guards. Charlie had barely noticed him at first. But as soon as he saw him, he instantly knew who he must be.

The bounty hunter.

He was humanoid in appearance, probably well over six feet tall, with skin the colour of the moon, tinged purple; his nose, jaw and cheekbones were sharp and striking, and his ring-studded ears extended up through his long, sleek purple hair like two fleshy daggers. His dark eyebrows also stretched far beyond the limits of his face, curling a little at the tips. He surveyed the room with cat-like, neon green eyes that glowed each time he passed through shadow.

'Who's that?' said Dale, catching sight of him.

The bounty hunter glanced their way, unsmiling. He wore a dark cloak that covered everything from the neck down. Charlie suspected there were a number of weapons concealed underneath it. He gripped the pommel of his sword, watching the hunter trail after the guards.

Jayne spotted him and said, 'Well, well. So that's how Decymero finally captured our dearest Willow. He enlisted the Whispering Blades of Sable Fen.'

'The what of the what?' said Charlie.

'Bounty hunters,' explained Quillorin. 'Frightfully good ones, too. They're as ruthless and deadly as they come. And, I believe, they're not easily bought. Ohhhh dear.'

The Whispering Blade melted into the shadows near the wall as the guards assembled around Willow. If it hadn't been for his glowing green eyes, Charlie would've lost track of him right away.

'Here she is,' announced the Glimmerqueen, spreading her arms. 'Just like I said.'

Willow stood at the foot of the throne steps, facing towards the crowd, who'd withdrawn a few paces. Her head was down, her shoulders slumped. The guards had formed a rough semi-circle between her and the Queen.

'Now,' said Merriwind, 'you've seen her, so I'll just send her back to - '

'Justice!' someone yelled.

'Justice for the Nymmite!' added another.

The Queen's face fell. 'Gosh, you people are never happy, are you? All the food, all the parties. That elephant-looking thing I let you ride around the courtyard. You're *never* happy. What do you *want?*'

'Justice!'

'Don't let the Doomgaard take her!'

Merriwind threw back her head and sighed, exasperated. Charlie suddenly realised he was staring at her, frowning so hard his face felt like it might crumple. Something about her movements, her voice. It was… so…

'Justice for - '

'Shut up!' cried the Glimmerqueen. 'Just shut up, all of you!'

A gasp went through the crowd. The guards glanced uncertainly at each other. Quillorin's uncle moved to speak to the Queen again, but she brushed him aside.

'No, enough,' she snapped. 'I'm *so* done with this. She's going with the *doom-guard*, right now, and that's final. I've spoken. I'm the Queen, and what I say - '

'Your Majesty, may I interject?'

Charlie started as Jayne spoke up, her voice carrying easily over the crowd. A couple of the soldiers spun to face their way. The Glimmerqueen squinted down at her.

'Who the heck are you?' she called back.

'Just a passer-by,' Jayne replied, sweeping forward. The Gnomes scattered, staring up at her in surprise. Quillorin, Brooke, Dale and Charlie automatically followed her. In the shadows by the wall, a pair of neon green eyes locked onto them.

'So what?' said Merriwind, hands on her hips. 'Can't you see I'm running a court here?'

'Most admirably, too,' said Jayne pleasantly. 'But could I make a suggestion?'

'What suggestion?'

Jayne was near the front of the crowd now. Willow's head lifted slightly, then suddenly jerked up. Her eyes flashed golden beneath the tangle of her hair.

'I'm not sure you're aware,' Jayne continued eloquently, 'but the prisoner you're holding there really isn't yours to hold. She's a rather important person, in fact.'

More murmurings in the crowd. Everyone was staring at Jayne now, including the guards.

'Uh, my good lady,' said Quillorin's uncle Eldric, raising an objecting finger. 'I'm sure you mean well, but this prisoner was brought to us by an outside party, who sought sanctuary within our walls. We Gnomes are duty-bound to offer help to strangers, especially in these uncertain days of… conflict. She is not our responsibility.'

'Then you won't mind setting her free?'

'My lady, I really don't think - '

Jayne pulled back her hood. Several members of the court gasped and pointed.

'That's the Seer!' cried one.

'The Wise One of the Forest,' declared another.

'Lady Butterfield!' gushed a third.

Willow's eyes burned bright now. Her face was set, but the corners of her mouth were trembling. Charlie saw a spark of emerald light between her fingers.

'Who?' said Merriwind, shrugging at Eldric, who looked flabbergasted.

'Trust me, Your Highness,' said Jayne. 'It's not in your best interest, or the interest of your people, to hand this Woodsperson over to the forces of Doomgaard. They won't stop there. But have no fear! I'd be happy to take her off your hands if - '

In the blink of an eye, the Whispering Blade appeared between Willow and Jayne. Charlie hadn't seen him move. The bounty hunter's hand slowly withdrew from his cloak, revealing a silver dagger. When he spoke, Charlie felt ice fingers running down his back:

'She is mine.'

Jayne measured him with her gaze, her smile unwavering. 'Perhaps we can come to an arrangement?' she said.

The Whispering Blade shook his head, the rings in his ears tinkling softly.

'No arrangement.'

'A price, then?'

'No price.' The hunter pulled the blade out further; those nearest backed away. The room was thick with tension.

'Ah, but everyone has their price,' said Jayne, almost cheerily. 'Tell me yours and my Gnomish friend by the Queen there will meet it.'

Eldric's jaw dropped open. 'I most certainly shall not!'

'Uncle,' said Quillorin evenly, moving to Jayne's side. 'Please listen to Lady Butterfield.'

'Nephew?' cried Eldric. 'What on Uland are you doing here? This is no place for you.'

'My lord,' Quillorin said, dipping his head. 'Give this gentleman whatever he wants. It's imperative that you do. I know you have the means.'

'Well of *course* I have the *means* - '

'What the heck is going on here?' cried Merriwind.

Suddenly, Brooke stepped forward. 'Please, your... umm... majesty,' she said. 'Don't let the Doomgaard take her. Let her go. It's the right thing to do.'

The Glimmerqueen sighed. 'And who are you?'

'I'm a friend of Jayne's,' Brooke replied, pulling back her hood. 'I'm from somewhere far away. My name is - '

'BROOKE!'

Every single person in the throne room jumped at Merriwind's cry. The Queen's eyes bulged from her head. There was a look of pure astonishment on her face.

Willow shared that astonishment, staring disbelievingly at Brooke with her mouth hung open. Eldric, the guards and the other officials nearest the throne looked confusedly from the Queen to Brooke to Willow, unsure of what to do.

And then several things happened at once.

The double doors at the back of the throne room suddenly burst open, causing nearby members of the court to cry out in surprise. Charlie turned and saw five soldiers in black armour in the doorway. Four wore helmets, their faces concealed behind visors; the fifth, now striding into the room, had his helmet under one arm.

In the same moment, the Whispering Blade materialised right behind Willow. Before anyone could react, he had his dagger pressed against her throat and her head bent back with his other hand. Someone in the crowd noticed and screamed.

At the sound of the scream, guards swarmed around Merriwind, shielding her from harm. The Glimmerqueen disappeared behind a moving mass of leather armour and green cloaks. Charlie heard her yell Brooke's name as they bundled her towards the corner door.

Then the Doomgaard soldiers drew their swords and the room descended back into chaos.

The crowd scattered in every direction, shouting and screaming as the black-armoured soldiers pushed their way through. Someone ran into Dale and knocked him flying. Charlie saw Jayne grab Brooke's cloak and pull her aside, just as a candelabra toppled from one of the tables and crashed to the floor. Quillorin had vanished into the sea of Gnomes.

At the front of the room, the Whispering Blade still had his dagger at Willow's throat. He'd begun edging her off to the side, towards the big windows overlooking the water.

'Stop right there!' barked the unhelmeted Doomgaard soldier, pointing at the bounty hunter as he advanced through the dispersing Gnomes. 'She belongs to us.'

'Jayne!' Brooke cried. 'We have to help her!'

Then, even louder from the corner: 'Brooke! It's me!' The guards were ushering Merriwind through the door. 'Upstairs! BROOKE!'

She was gone.

And then, just as abruptly as it began, the chaos stopped.

Charlie found himself standing in a circle of empty space. He'd drawn his sword at some point and now gripped it in both hands, poised ready to fight. Jayne and Brooke were nearby. Dale had disappeared into the crowd of Gnomes, who were bunched at one end of the room below the stained-glass windows.

At the other end, the Doomgaard soldiers stood between them and the Whispering Blade, who had edged Willow all the way over to the lakeside windows. His neon green eyes flashed malevolently as he pressed the dagger harder to her throat. Willow grimaced in pain.

The leading Doomgaard soldier dropped his helmet to the floor with a clatter, pointed his sword at the bounty hunter and said, 'Release her.'

For a split second, no-one spoke. The room was almost completely silent. The only sounds were the Queen's muffled shouting beyond the door in the corner and the terrified whimpering of some in the crowd.

'I want double,' said the Whispering Blade.

The Doomgaardian sneered. 'You'll get what was promised and not a coin more.'

'Double,' repeated the bounty hunter, 'or I spill her blood right here.'

More whimperings from the crowd. Charlie tightened his grip on his sword. *It's too far*, he thought. *I'd never be able to reach her in time.*

The Doomgaard soldiers fanned out, their boots clunking on the stone floor. They didn't seem to notice anyone else in the room - they were completely fixated on Willow. The hunter shuffled her closer to the windows.

'Not one more step,' he said icily. 'I want the money - all of it - or she dies.'

'She's going to die anyway,' replied the Doomgaardian. 'You'll just save Decymero the bother of having to do it himself.'

Several Gnomes gasped at the mention of "Decymero". Charlie heard someone wilt to the floor behind him in a dead faint. He kept his eyes fixed on the Doomgaard soldiers, listening to the steady thump of his heart beneath the doublet and wishing there'd been actual armour in Quillorin's house.

I can take them, he thought. His sword arm felt strong and ready. *I can do it.*

No you can't, came the reply. He started at the sound of Jayne's voice inside his own head and glanced towards her. She was facing the soldiers, not looking at him. But her voice came again, clear as day: *Don't fight. You won't win, not here. Wait.*

'We have your money,' the leading Doomgaard soldier was saying. He motioned and one of the others held up a heavy-looking coin purse. 'Release her, take your reward, and go. You'll have Decymero's thanks.'

The Whispering Blade seemed to think it over, then said, 'I don't want anyone's thanks. I want *double*. Give me that and I'll let her go.'

'You're not in a position to - '

'Gentlemen!'

The Doomgaard soldiers whipped their swords in Jayne's direction, their heavy armour rattling as they spun to face her. Their leader turned slowly, eyeing the Seer as she approached. Over by the windows, the Whispering Blade watched the situation unfold warily.

'Who are you?' said the Doomgaard leader.

'No-one special,' Jayne replied breezily. 'Just someone who enjoys a good party. And what a party this was!'

She spread her hands as she said it, indicating the mess all around her. As she did so, Charlie caught sight of a blue-winged moth fluttering through an opening in one of the windows.

'This is none of your business, m'lady,' the Doomgaard leader said coolly. 'Step back if you value your life.'

'My, my,' Jayne chuckled. 'How very menacing.'

Charlie was half-watching the moth floating towards Willow behind the Doomgaardian's backs when he suddenly realised Brooke had vanished. She'd been standing next to Jayne, and now she was gone.

Dale, Quillorin, and now her. I'm the only one left.

'Stop,' said the Doomgaard leader, levelling his sword at Jayne. 'If you take another step, I'll take your head.'

'Sir,' said one of the others hesitantly. 'Isn't that - '

'I know who she is. And I know what she can do. If she comes any closer, cut her down.'

Jayne held up her hands defensively. 'Boys, please. You're mistaking me for someone else. There's no need for all this animosity.'

The moth had reached Willow. The bounty hunter was focused entirely on Jayne and the soldiers, and didn't see it fluttering towards her. Charlie watched as it floated down her front and landed gently on the manacles binding her wrists.

'That's it, I've had enough,' the Doomgaard leader snarled. 'Kill her.'

Two of the soldiers started towards Jayne. Someone in the crowd cried out in alarm.

Clunk.

They stopped. Slowly, the soldiers all turned back towards the windows.

Charlie saw the blue-winged moth fluttering up to the ceiling. The metal manacles lay at Willow's feet. The bounty hunter craned over her shoulder, peering down at them.

'How - ,' he began.

Willow's eyes bloomed golden and the dagger at her throat became a leaf. The Whispering Blade had just enough time to drag it harmlessly across her skin before she jerked her head back and butted him in his sharp, pointed nose. He yelped in pain and staggering backwards, dark blood spurting from his nostrils.

'GRAB HER!' the Doomgaard leader yelled.

The soldiers flew at Willow, but it was too late. Her hands were already up, green sparks fizzing between her fingers. She smiled, said something Charlie didn't hear, and clapped her palms together.

There was an ear-splitting *bang* and a blinding flash of green lit the room. The Gnomes screamed, cowering together in a mass huddle below the stained glass windows.

Charlie winced, rubbing his eyes. After a few seconds, his vision readjusted and he looked towards the Doomgaard soldiers.

Or rather, where they *used* to be.

The five hulking men in black armour had been replaced by five fat, lime-green toads. They hopped clumsily around the floor, croaking in confused panic. One by one, the Gnomes began to realise what had happened - there were gasps, cries of disgust, and more than a few cheers.

'Was that really necessary?' Jayne said.

'No,' Willow replied. 'I just wanted to do it.'

'WILLOW!'

Her head whipped in Charlie's direction at the sound of his yell. The frown on her face melted into delighted recognition, and then immediate understanding - she dropped to the floor, just as the bounty hunter's dagger cut through the air an inch above her scalp. The blade sliced cleanly through a strand of her swinging hair, sending it sailing into a nearby bowl of punch.

Now they were fighting - or rather, Willow was expertly dodging his crazed attacks - and Charlie found he was running across the throne room towards them, sword at the ready. He half-expected Jayne to block his path, but she simply stood where she was, watching whatever was about to happen.

The Whispering Blade backed Willow away from the windows, stabbing again and again in her direction, shrieking with rage each time his dagger failed to find her. She dipped and ducked and danced away from the weapon with ease, her long red hair flowing every which way like it had a mind of its own. They were almost in the far corner by the time Charlie reached them.

With a grunt of effort, he swung the shortsword at the Whispering Blade and would have taken his head clean off if he hadn't dropped at the last second. The sword *whummed* harmlessly just above the tip of his left ear.

And then the bounty hunter was coming at Charlie, green eyes blazing, pointed teeth bared in fury. He parried the first blow, then the second. His boots scraped noisily on the stone floor as he readjusted his position again and again, his sword spinning this way and that, blocking the oncoming slices and stabs from the hunter's dagger. He was backing off, but the Whispering Blade couldn't land a blow on *him* either.

How am I doing this? Charlie somehow managed to think between moves. *I haven't used a real sword in six months.*

Jayne's voice: *A warrior never forgets.*

He could see Willow in his peripheral vision, edging around them as they fought, waiting for an opening to use a spell. But none came. And now Charlie could feel himself beginning to tire. The Whispering Blade was strong and very fast, attacking relentlessly in a blur of dark armour and glinting steel. Each blow from the dagger sent shockwaves jarring through his muscles and into his bones.

I'm going to make a mistake, he thought desperately, *and Willow won't be able to stop him in time. He's going to kill me!*

And no sooner had the thought entered his head than his heel caught on some discarded thing on the floor and he went down hard. The breath left his lungs in an instant. His sword arm went limp.

The Whispering Blade didn't hesitate long enough for Willow to react. He lunged at him, dagger raised, screaming in triumph.

Whoosh!

Freezing blue light burst just above Charlie's face. The bounty hunter's battle cry cut short as his body was tossed to the side. Charlie caught a brief glimpse of him encased in solid ice, neon eyes frozen wide in shock, before he hit the floor and shattered into hundreds of pieces.

'What on earth…?' he wheezed.

He looked up and behind, and there was Dale. His hands were still up, still glowing faintly blue. He appeared almost as shocked as the bounty hunter had been.

'Didn't know I could do that,' he gasped.

Charlie scrambled to his feet, panting. 'You… can freeze stuff now?'

Before Dale had a chance to reply, they were both nearly knocked to the floor as Willow pounced on them. Charlie found his face buried in her hair as the remaining breath was squeezed from his lungs. She smelled like trees.

'You're back, you're back!' she cried, hugging them tighter. 'You actually came back!'

Charlie returned the hug, still gagging for air. Dale was laughing now.

'It's great to see you too,' he said.

'Yeah… yeah it is,' Charlie managed, between coughs.

'I thought I'd never see you again!' Willow released them from the hug but kept her grip on their cloaks. 'It's been *such* a long time, you know. Seasons and seasons.'

'Twelve, we're told,' Dale said. 'It was different for us.'

'Wait,' said Charlie, seeing Willow properly for the first time. 'You look the same. Like, *exactly* the same. Shouldn't you look at least… a *little* older?'

She grinned, letting them go. Her skin, clearly green under the light from the chandelier, was just as unblemished as it had been the last time they'd seen her. Her irises were fading to hazel again, flecked with gold.

'You know we age differently,' she said. She looked him up and down. 'You're taller.' And then, to Dale: 'You're not.'

Charlie snorted. Dale's brow furrowed.

'This is a splendid reunion,' Jayne said, suddenly appearing by their side, 'but I think it's time to go.' The Gnomes of the Queen's Court were staring at them in silence.

'Brooke Woods was here,' Willow said questioningly. 'Where is she now?'

'I believe,' Jayne said, 'she's somewhere above us.'

Chapter Thirteen: Brooke Meets The Glimmerqueen

Brooke had been staring in horror as the Whispering Blade pressed his dagger to Willow's throat when Jayne's voice echoed through her skull, crystal clear. It may as well have been a thought of her own: *Go to the Queen.*

She'd looked at Jayne, saw she wasn't looking back, and knew there was no time to ask questions. It'd been an order.

While all eyes were on the Doomgaard soldiers squaring up to the bounty hunter, Brooke quietly retreated to the door in the corner of the throne room. Some of the Gnomes saw her go but said nothing, even moving aside to let her pass. To her surprise, the door wasn't locked, either - she twisted its iron ring handle, pushed through into the gloom beyond, and eased the door shut behind her.

She found herself in a cold, shadowy stairwell, dimly lit with flickering torches. Stone steps curved down to what she assumed must be the dungeons, far below the throne room and everything else in the castle; the steps also carried on up another floor above.

Upstairs! Brooke!

Go to the Queen.

'Ok then,' Brooke whispered to herself. 'Here I come.'

She started up the steps. It was hard to see clearly and there was no rail, so she had to run her hand over the cool stone to keep her bearings. Here, the only light came from small, smokey torches fixed to the wall at intervals and the occasional arrow slit looking out over the town below. She didn't pause to peer through any of them - Jayne's words still rang in her head.

Soon, the door to the throne room was far behind. If something was happening below, she couldn't hear it. The only sounds in the stairwell were the soft crackles and pops of the torches and the clicks of her boot heels on the stone steps.

'What're you going to do when you get there?' she asked herself aloud, and jumped at the sound of her own voice. *Go to the Queen.* 'And how did she know my name?'

The stairs continued curving upwards, higher and higher. Climbing them reminded Brooke of their time in the Druyad Tower in Fort Hammerfall and she quickly pushed the memory aside. Her heart was pounding now; her palms were slick with sweat.

Why did Jayne send me? she thought. *Why not Charlie, or Dale? I hope Willow's ok.*

And then, as if from no-where, the stairs simply ended at another oaken door with an iron ring handle. A final torch flickered on the wall next to it.

What do I do?

Brooke hesitated, then did the only thing she could think of - she reached out and gave the door three firm raps with her knuckle. *Knock, knock, knock.*

She waited, listening. Nothing happened.

Did I go the wrong way? she wondered, her heart thumping harder. The little leather book was still in her pocket. *Maybe I should check the map?*

Instead, she knocked on the door again, harder this time.

Almost immediately, there was a loud *clank* from the other side and the handle turned. The door opened a crack. Brooke saw no-one at first, then dropped her gaze - a Gnomish guard was staring up at her.

'Whadya want?' he muttered.

Brooke cleared her throat. 'I, um… need to see the Queen.'

The guard's purple eyes narrowed. 'Why?'

'It's, uh… private?'

The Gnome snorted and replied, 'Queen's not here.' He started to close the door.

'Please!' Brooke cried, jamming her boot in the crack without thinking. 'I need to see her now. She… she *told* me to come here.'

'Go away,' snapped the Gnome, leaning against the other side of the door. 'The Queen doesn't want to see - '

'Merriwind!' Brooke yelled. 'Your Majesty! I'm here!'

'Hey!' barked the guard. 'Be quiet!'

'MERRIWIND!'

'Brooke?'

The guard stopped pushing against the door; Brooke gratefully felt the pressure on her foot release and drew it back.

'Let her in.'

The door creaked open. Brooke stepped inside and it was instantly slammed shut behind her.

She was now in a large, circular room with four tall, evenly-spaced windows, all covered with scarlet drapes. Morning light filtered through them, bathing the space in a soft, red glow. At the far end of the room, a second set of spiral steps - wooden this time - curled up into the ceiling.

The only furniture Brooke could see was a plush red couch, a bookcase, a desk and chair, and a single candelabra on a brass stand. An enormous ornamental rug covered the floor. Standing on it, facing her with their swords drawn, were the Gnomish guards. There must have been at least a dozen of them.

And as Brooke watched, the Glimmerqueen emerged from behind them. She stared at her in open amazement, wringing her little hands. The guards parted to let her through.

'Brooke,' said Merriwind. 'I… I can't believe you're here.'

Brooke studied the Gnome, trying to read her. 'You… know who I am?'

Merriwind nodded.

'How?'

The Queen glanced awkwardly at the small army of guards gathered around her.

'Maybe we should go up to the roof.'

'Your Majesty,' the nearest guard interjected, 'that may not be wise. The Doomgaard vessels are still in the bay, and - '

'We'll be fine,' Merriwind said. 'You guys stay here and, like, guard us. We'll be right up there. Don't let anyone else through that door.'

'Yes, my Queen.'

Merriwind crossed to the spiral stairs and started up them. After a moment's hesitation, Brooke followed.

They came out on top of a turret. It was about the same size as the room below, lined with weathered crenellations. Two enormous cannons faced out towards the bay, where the Doomgaard ships were anchored. All boat traffic in and out of Silversprog harbour had ceased.

For a moment, Brooke and the Gnome Queen just stared at one another. A breeze tugged at their cloaks; seagulls screeched in the distance.

Finally, Brooke spoke: 'How do you know me?'

To her surprise, Merriwind's big purple eyes grew watery and her lip began to tremble.

'Oh, Brookles,' she said in her high Gnomish voice. 'I thought I'd never see any of you again.'

Brookles?

She frowned, steadily holding the Gnome's gaze, straining to see beyond it. There was something on the other side of those eyes, wasn't there? Something else, something she somehow recognised.

Brookles, she thought. *No-one ever calls me that. No-one, except for…*

Then her own eyes widened. Her mouth dropped open.

It can't be…

'Ton?'

The Glimmerqueen nodded vigorously and her face broke out in a wide grin. Tears rolled freely down her cheeks.

'It's me,' she said.

'Tonya?' Brooke repeated disbelievingly. 'I… I don't understand…'

Merriwind rushed across the turret roof and threw her arms around her. Brooke hugged her back. She could feel the Gnome's body trembling against her.

They broke apart. Merriwind sniffed, wiping her eyes with the sleeve of her dress.

'Tonya,' Brooke said, forming the words slowly, 'are you telling me you've… *turned into a Gnome?*'

Merriwind - or Tonya - shook her head, blurting a chuckle.

'Sort of,' she replied. 'Not really. I just… *look* like one. I have since I got here.'

'What d'you mean? *How* did you get here?'

'I have no idea.' She sniffed again, but the tears were no longer coming. 'I was at the Halloween party, and I saw you leave the gym. And then Dale went after you so I followed because, you know, you'd seemed upset or whatever. Then you were both gone, but there was this light coming from your locker. And I went over to look, and I must have touched it or something, and then there was this flash and I woke up here.'

She spread her arms. 'And that was a *month* ago.'

'Wait, what?' Brooke said, flabbergasted. 'You've been in Uland for a *month?* How's that possible? We just got here.'

'I told you, I have no idea,' Merriwind/Tonya replied. 'All I know is, I've been in this place for weeks. When I woke up, I was in a little park or something on the edge of town, and the Queen was there - the *real* Queen - and she was alone, crying. I went over to ask where I was and she was, like, really shocked to see me. But I could see she was all upset and stuff, so I took her hand to comfort her, and then I just *changed* into her. It was like we were both looking in a mirror. And then she got really excited and said it was just the chance she'd been praying for, and she said I could be Queen in her place, and then she just *left*.'

'She left?' Brooke said, straining to take it all in.

'Yeah. The guards must have been giving her space in the park and she was able to slip out. I think she hated it here. So anyway, they came back and assumed I was her, and they brought me to this castle, and I've been here ever since, pretending to be the Queen of the flipping Gnomes!'

Brooke still couldn't quite believe what she was hearing. But hearing Merriwind talk, and knowing it was really Tonya's voice coming from her mouth, somehow made the situation completely absurd. Hilarious, even. And before she could stop herself, she'd begun to laugh.

Merriwind scowled. 'Don't you laugh at me, Brooke Woods. You have no idea what this is like. I've been stuck here for weeks with these boring Gnomes, listening to all their problems and trying to rule them. It's *sucked*.'

Brooke tried and failed to fully suppress her laughter. Merriwind stamped one of her tiny feet and only made it worse.

'I tried throwing all these parties just to make things more interesting,' she said, 'but they must have never partied before, and now I think I've broken most of them. You should've seen what they were like when the pointy-eared dude brought the prisoner here. Brooke!'

'I'm sorry, I'm sorry,' Brooke gasped, wiping tears from her own eyes now. 'It's all just so random. I'm glad you're ok, at least you were safe here. It wasn't like that for us the last time we were here.'

'Last time?' Merriwind said. 'What last time? And who's here now?'

Brooke told her about how she, Dale and Charlie had been sucked into the locker and landed in the Withering Woods, and about the spider, and the shapeshifting monsters, and Quillorin. She explained how Jayne had brought them here, and why they wanted to free Willow, and what was happening in the throne room below them.

'I'll tell you the rest later,' she said. 'It's a long story. But for now, we all need to get out of here. With Willow.'

Merriwind nodded. 'Yes, please. I'm *so* ready to go. In fact…'

She squeezed her eyes shut, straining. Brooke watched in amazement as the appearance of the Glimmerqueen simply fell away - crown and all - and Tonya Miller stood there instead, dressed once again in her Halloween costume. She opened her eyes, just as the last remnants of purple faded from her brown irises.

'Oh man, that feels so much better,' she said in her normal voice. 'I could only change back at night when I was alone.'

'Couldn't you have just changed and walked out any time?' Brooke said, looking her oldest friend up and down. 'They wouldn't have known it was you.'

Tonya shook her head. 'They were watching me like a hawk. It was easy to see why the real Queen was so unhappy here. She was like a prisoner.'

Brooke frowned. 'This might be tricky.'

'I don't care,' said Tonya. 'I'll parachute off this tower with a pillow case if I have to. Let's just find a way out of here, and fast.'

***

Brooke really wasn't sure how they were going to escape from the tower. There were at least a dozen Gnomish guards with swords in the room below them, and in spite of Tonya's suggestions, leaving directly from the roof itself wasn't an option. They had no choice but to go down.

To their surprise, however, the room below was almost entirely empty when they descended the spiral staircase. All of the guards had left. Only two Gnomes remained, speaking together in hushed tones by one of the windows. As Tonya closed the trap door at the top of the staircase, they turned to face them.

'Quillorin!' Brooke exclaimed. 'I thought you'd run away or something.'

'Quite the opposite, Lady Woods,' replied the Gnome, offering a small bow. 'I sought help instead. This is my uncle, Eldric Twiggleton.'

The older Gnome also bowed, displaying his shiny bald head in the process.

'Uncle,' Quillorin continued, 'this is, of course, the famous Lady Woods. You'll know of her from the stories. And this…'

He trailed off as Tonya joined Brooke at the foot of the staircase.

'This is… umm…'

'Hi, I'm Tonya Miller.'

'This is Lady… Miller, who I assume is a friend of Lady Woods?'

Brooke nodded.

'Where is the Queen?' said Eldric, frowning.

Brooke and Tonya glanced at one another. Brooke opened her mouth, but Tonya got there first: 'She's gone.'

'Gone?'

'Gone.'

'Gone where?'

'Away. On… holiday. She just left.'

'Holly-day?' Eldric repeated, absently stroking his moustache. 'That is most… irregular.'

Tonya nodded in agreement. 'Totally.'

'But how - '

Just then, the door to the room flew open and several people bundled inside. The first was Jayne, who beamed as she swept towards them.

'Ah, well done!' she said, with a clap of her hands. 'I was beginning to worry you'd gotten into trouble up here.'

Next was Charlie, and then Dale. They both stopped dead at the sight of Tonya.

'What the…?' Dale said.

'Tonya?' said Charlie.

'Nice to see you too,' Tonya said with a smirk. 'What, by the way, are you wearing?'

'Ton's here,' said Brooke, unnecessarily. 'And you won't believe what - '

She was cut short by Willow, who had crossed the room in a single bound and threw her arms around her with a cry of 'Brooke Woods! You came back too!'

Brooke returned the hug, laughing. As they broke apart, Willow's eyes turned to Tonya and narrowed.

'Who is this?'

Brooke briefly explained who Tonya was (to Willow, Jayne and the Gnomes) and how she'd come to be in Uland (to Dale and Charlie). She left out the fact she'd been masquerading as the Glimmerqueen the whole time she'd been there. Tonya wisely kept her mouth closed and merely nodded along.

'A month?' Dale exclaimed. 'I can't believe you survived all that time.'

'Why, because I'm a girl?'

'No… what? That's not what I - '

Tonya smirked again and punched Dale on the shoulder. 'Relax, Reed. I'm joking.'

'Oh. Yeah, sure. I knew that.'

Willow watched this exchange curiously. Brooke noticed her watching, smiled, and turned to Jayne. 'What do we do now?'

'We leave,' said Jayne. 'But first, I believe Master Quillorin here has something that belongs to Willow.'

'Heavens, of course!' Quillorin cried. 'I do hope it hasn't been damaged.'

He fished inside his cloak and pulled out the white orb, offering it to Willow. It glowed purple in the room's diminished light. Willow's eyes grew large.

'The seed!' she cried, snatching it from Quillorin's palm. 'You still have it!'

'I kept it safe, just as you asked,' Quillorin replied proudly. 'Though I can tell you now, it was no easy task, especially when - '

'We need to go, right now,' Willow interrupted. 'I'm sorry… thank you, Master Gnome… but this can't wait. There's no time.'

'Is that intended for who I think it's intended for?' said Jayne.

'Yes.'

'Then young Willow is right. We need to make haste.' She looked at Eldric. 'My Lord, what's the fastest and safest way out of this castle?'

Eldric tugged on his moustache, flustered. 'The front entrance, I expect. But no! We can't go that way, not anymore. The Doomgaard have Silversprog surrounded.'

'They do?' said Quillorin.

'Regrettably, yes. We spied a battalion of their soldiers making land further up the coast and suspect they're hiding at the edge of the forest, waiting for anyone trying to escape. I believe they expected the bounty hunter to try double-crossing them during the exchange of the, umm…'

He motioned to Willow, who folded her arms and said, 'Prisoner?'

Eldric nodded, his Gnomish face reddening. 'Yes. My apologies, Lady Willow. I wasn't sure it was you at first, and then the Doomgaard were on their way and it was far too late. But perhaps I can make up for it by helping you now.'

He turned back to Jayne. 'There is a way out, through the dungeons. But the only route of escape from there will be via the docks. You'll have to take a ship.'

'Splendid,' said Jayne breezily. 'Do you have one at the ready?'

'I do, but we'll need to hurry. This way.'

Eldric shuffled towards the door and they followed. As Charlie passed Tonya, he said, 'I can't believe you survived that long, either.'

'I get by on my looks, remember?' she replied.

Charlie grinned and they left the room. Willow followed just behind, frowning.

Chapter Fourteen: Fleeing Silversprog

'He's rather spry for an older chap, isn't he?' said Jayne.

They'd descended the stone spiral stairs in a hurry, bypassing the throne room along the way. As they went, Quillorin explained how he'd taken his uncle aside during the chaotic encounter between the Doomgaard and the Whispering Blade, filling him in on their plan. Fortunately, Eldric had understood the situation at once. Then, after spotting Brooke leave through the corner door, they'd followed her up to the Royal Reading Room and sent the guards down to help restore order among the members of the Queen's Court below.

'I've also sent orders to seal the castle and stop any Doomgaard troops from moving into town,' Eldric called over his shoulder between breaths. 'We can delay them, at the very least. Once you're on the water, you'll have a good chance of escaping alive.'

'Just a chance?' said Dale.

'Better than nothing,' said Charlie, skidding on one of the steps.

'Where should we go?' asked Brooke. 'Ulandai?'

'Goodness no, you'd never make it all the way there,' said Quillorin from somewhere in their descending column. It was hard to see in the gloomy half light of the stairwell. 'The Kingdom of Ulandi is on the far side of Canyon Lake, a great many miles away. And the Doomgaard ships are fast. No, you'll need to head north and make land as soon as possible. From there, you can continue your journey.'

'Where're we going, anyway?' said Dale.

'We're going to Nymm,' replied Willow.

'What's that?' said Tonya. 'Is that a place?'

Brooke heard Willow mutter something from further back in the line. Jayne replied for her.

'Nymm is where Willow is from,' she said. 'They're her people, her tribe. It's a place, yes. But it's a *hidden* place.'

'Oh,' said Tonya. 'I've only been in this town, and I don't even know anything about it. Someone needs to show me a map, or something.'

'We will,' said Brooke. 'We've got *loads* to tell you.'

'I still can't believe you're here,' said Charlie. 'And you're not freaking out.'

'I've been freaking out plenty, trust me.'

Eventually, they came to a smaller wooden door with a final torch flickering weakly next to it. The stairs continued on down to the dungeons, according to Eldric, but this was their exit.

'Beyond this door is an alleyway,' explained the older Gnome. 'At the end of the alleyway, turn right, and you'll be at the harbour. Go to the fourth dock. Find a ship called *The Copperdawn Voyager*. Tell them Eldric sent you, and give this to the captain.' As he spoke, he removed a silver chain from around his neck and held it up to the light - there was a pendant on the end with a Gnomish symbol carved into it.

'The family crest!' exclaimed Quillorin. 'You can't!'

'It's the only way, nephew. They'll never believe them otherwise, and we can't go with them. This will grant them safe passage from Silversprog.' He handed the chain and pendant to Brooke, who took it reluctantly.

'Wait, you're not coming?' said Dale.

'Won't you be in danger if you stay?' said Brooke, slipping the pendant into her pocket.

'Maybe,' said Eldric. 'But it's imperative we remain here and help bring order to this chaos. If we flee now, the Doomgaard will simply sweep into town and take it for themselves. The last thing we need is for them to gain another foothold in Eisdren, especially with the Glimmerqueen off on holly-day, whatever that means. No, the rest of you must go.'

Quillorin nodded in the dim light. 'It's been a pleasure to meet you all. Truly.'

'We still have your clothes and stuff,' Brooke pointed out, swallowing down an unexpected lump in her throat.

'And I have your sword,' Charlie added.

'Gifts,' said Quillorin, smiling. 'It's the very least I can do in exchange for an excellent adventure. And after all, Lady Willow did technically save my life. Now, get going before that ship leaves the harbour.'

At that, he and Eldric turned and started back up the stairs. Brooke heard Eldric say, 'What *is* a holly-day, anyway?' and caught Tonya's eye in the wavering light.

'You heard them,' said Jayne briskly. 'Let's get going, shall we?'

Charlie turned the iron ring handle and pulled open the door with a grunt. They all flinched back as warm morning sunlight spilled inside.

'Geez, that's bright,' said Dale, rubbing his eyes.

'Hmm, more time may have passed than we realised,' said Jayne. 'We won't have long to reach the dock. Willow, can you lead the way?'

Without a word, Willow brushed past them, pulled up her hood and walked out the door. They hurried after her.

Just as Eldric had said, the door led to a narrow alleyway at the base of the castle. Brooke's nose wrinkled at the sharp stench of rotting fish, and something else she didn't want to consider. Willow didn't pause, continuing quickly towards the far end of the alley, her earthen brown cloak flapping behind her.

'How long will it take us to reach Nymm?' asked Brooke as they followed.

'Not long, I think,' replied Jayne, 'It depends where the gateway is now. The Woodspeople like to move it around, you see. It's how they've endured for so long.'

'Like the Gnomes,' Dale said. 'Survivors.'

Jayne nodded. 'They're not unalike. Both are ancient races, some of the oldest in all of Uland. But the Nymmites are among the *most* ancient.'

Willow paused at the end of the alleyway, peering up and down the street beyond. When they caught up to her, she said, 'It looks clear enough. Come on.'

Brooke thought about asking her to slow down a little, but she knew there'd be no point. The more time they spent here, the more she remembered about their last visit. Willow wouldn't stop, or slow, until they reached their destination.

She slipped out of the alleyway and they followed. They were now in a steeply-declining street with a sharp bend up ahead. The cobblestones here were damp and slippery. Dale lost his footing twice and Charlie caught him both times. Jayne glided along as though she was walking on a perfectly-flat carpet.

They rounded the bend at the bottom of the street and abruptly found themselves at Silversprog harbour.

Brooke was instantly reminded of the Goblin Markets at Crookedstone. There were people everywhere: Gnomes, Ulanders, various other races she didn't know the names of, all bustling around between the boats moored in the harbour. She spotted a giant at the end of one of the wooden docks, heaving huge crates into a merchant ship, and a group of Elementals in brightly-coloured cloaks. And unfortunately, she noticed more than a few goblins. Their lime-green skin, leering grins and penetrating yellow eyes took her right back to their encounter at The Throat. Suddenly, she just wanted to get out of Silversprog as soon as possible.

'Over there,' said Willow, pointing across the harbour. '*The Copperdawn Voyager*. That's it.'

'How can you see that from here?' said Tonya, shielding her eyes with her hand. 'Are you sure that's the right one? It's not very big.'

'The name's written on the side of it,' Willow said shortly. 'That's it.'

'She has super good eyesight,' Brooke clarified. 'If she says she can see it, she can see it.'

They started along the docks, weaving between merchants and sailors and those there to barter for goods from other regions of Uland. There was a lot of shouting and laughter and crashing as heavy items were moved on and off the boats. No-one (apart from the few goblins scattered across the harbour) paid them much attention. They were all far too busy, and the sight of the Doomgaard galleons just outside the bay seemed to have everyone on edge. It was palpable in the air.

'Oh,' said Tonya as they neared the boat. 'She was right. There's the name on the side.'

The Copperdawn Voyager was a fairly small merchant vessel, at least compared to some of the other boats moored in the harbour, though it seemed more than big enough to Brooke. Its sturdy wooden hull, chipped and weathered by countless journeys across the waters of Canyon Lake, loomed above them as they drew near. The name of the ship had been painted (and repainted) on the starboard bow in an oddly-flourished hand. Sailors laden with crates and barrels thudded around the deck, yelling orders back and forth, tying down goods ahead of the next trip. They were already beginning to unfurl the mainsail.

A Gnome wearing comically-large leather boots and a wide-brimmed hat was perched on a mooring bollard next to the *Copperdawn*'s gangway. He was peeling an apple with a knife and didn't look up as they approached.

'Yeah?' he said.

'Good morning, sir,' said Jayne. 'We're here to request passage on your fine vessel.'

The Gnome - who must have been the captain - continued peeling the apple. 'That right?'

'Indeed.'

For a moment, nothing happened. The Gnome kept peeling while the deckhands beyond him kept shouting. A ragged-looking seagull landed on the ship's mast and eyed them curiously.

Jayne cleared her throat. 'Sir, are you - '

'We're all full,' said the captain. He carved off a slice of apple and popped it in his mouth, finally looking up at them. 'Too many of you, anyway. And we're just about to leave.'

Just then, a bell started tolling in the castle. They looked back and saw some commotion near the entrance. Brooke caught glimpses of black and green, flashes of glinting metal. Shouts carried across the harbour; merchants and sailors stopped what they were doing to peer towards the source.

The Gnome captain also paused his apple-eating long enough to listen. Then he looked at them properly, studying each of them in turn.

'Who'd you say you were?'

'Just some travellers, seeking passage,' said Jayne. For the first time, Brooke picked up a hint of urgency in her normally-calm voice. Then she remembered the pendant and fished it from her pocket.

'Eldric… Lord Twiggleton told me to give you this,' she said, letting it dangle on its chain.

The captain squinted at it, then held out a pudgy hand. Brooke stepped forward and dropped the pendant into his palm. He held it up, turned it, then stuffed it in his pocket.

'This'll pay for one of you,' he said. 'Maybe two. But I ain't taking you all. Some of you'll have to stay.'

Brooke looked up at Jayne uncertainly. Out of the corner of her eye, she saw Tonya side-step behind Charlie and Dale.

'My dear captain,' Jayne said, spreading her hands. 'Are you sure you can't squeeze them in? They're really quite small. And I'm sure they'll be of use.'

'You have to take us,' Willow said, taking a step forward. 'There's no time.'

Jayne put a hand on her shoulder. The captain's expression darkened.

'Do I, now?' he said. Behind him, the mainsail rolled down and immediately grew fat with the breeze. The *Copperdawn* strained on her moorings, eager to leave. 'You'll need to pay more, m'lady. That's all there is to it.'

The gold in Willow's eyes began to come together beneath her hood. Brooke saw Charlie's hand slide towards his sword.

'Excuse me.'

The captain looked past Brooke and promptly dropped his apple; it bounced twice on the dock boards and fell into the water below with a *plop.* He jumped to his feet and bowed.

They turned. Queen Merriwind was standing between Charlie and Dale, her green cloak flapping gently in the breeze. She put her hands on her hips.

'Are you denying my friends and I passage, captain?'

'My Queen!' cried the captain, bowing low. 'Of course not. I didn't mean… I didn't know…'

'What didn't you know?'

Everyone bar Brooke and Jayne were staring at the Glimmerqueen in confusion. Willow cast her gaze around, searching for Tonya. The shouts and cries near the castle were growing louder.

'I didn't know *you* needed passage too, Your Majesty,' the captain stammered. 'My ship is yours, naturally, if you'll do me the great honour.'

Merriwind studied the nails of her left hand. 'I guess so. Can I have my own room?'

'Maybe we should just get on board,' said Brooke quickly. 'Your… Majesty.'

'Oh yeah, good idea.'

The Gnomish captain beamed and ushered them to the ship. The sailors on board gawked as Merriwind started up the gangplank. Willow, Charlie and Dale followed, still visibly confused.

Brooke was about to go too when Jayne grabbed her arm.

'This is where I leave you,' she said in a low tone.

'What?' Brooke cried. 'No, you can't!'

The others, now on deck, looked back. The few Gnomish guards stationed on the docks had begun running towards the castle, drawing their swords. The bells continued ringing out across Silversprog.

'Don't worry about me,' Jayne smiled. 'I'll be right as rain. I believe everyone's quite preoccupied.' She placed the tip of her finger on Brooke's forehead. 'You *know* I'll see you again very soon, yes?'

Brooke held her gaze. She *did* know, didn't she? Somehow, she knew.

'Yes,' she said. 'But I still wish you could come.'

'You'll be just fine. You're together now, and that makes all the difference. Get on that boat.'

She gave Brooke a gentle push towards the gangplank. Gnomish sailors were hurriedly untying the *Copperdawn*'s mooring lines from the dock; those on deck were doing their best to clear a tidy path for Merriwind.

Brooke mounted the gangway as quickly as she could. No sooner were her feet on deck than the last two sailors jumped aboard and the plank was pulled up behind her.

'Why isn't she coming?' Dale said anxiously, joining Brooke by the bulwark.

'I don't like this,' Charlie added on her other side. 'And where the heck did Tonya go? Is she here?'

'I'll explain that in a second,' Brooke replied.

Jayne stood on the dock, smiling and waving. They saw the little blue-winged moth from the castle entrance flutter past her shoulder. At the far end of the harbour, a line of Gnomish guards had gathered with swords and spears. Sailors and merchants were rushing to their ships.

'Weigh anchor!' bellowed the captain, who was now standing behind the wheel at the stern of the *Copperdawn*. 'Cast off!'

Within seconds, the ship had begun to pull away from the harbour. Jayne threw them a final exuberant wave, turned on her heel and strode back up the dock. They immediately lost sight of her in the chaos of the harbour.

'So what now?' said Charlie.

Brooke looked at him, and then Dale. Just beyond him, Willow hung from the riggings, peering back at the docks.

'I think we all need to have a conversation,' she said.

Chapter Fifteen: The Copperdawn Voyager

Charlie scratched his head again and said, 'I don't understand.'

They were in the captain's quarters of *The Copperdawn Voyager*. The captain himself - a grumpy seafarer by the name of Cogwhistle - had insisted Queen Merriwind take it. He seemed to think they were her entourage, which suited them just fine.

Dale, who'd never been on a proper boat in his life and so far didn't intend to do so again, summed it up: 'She's a shapeshifter. That's her power here. She can change her appearance.'

'Just like me being the Seer, and you being the Warrior,' Brooke added from her seat by the porthole. 'I think Tonya is the Changer of the Uland Seven.'

'The what?' said Tonya.

Once the captain had ushered them into the room and they were certain the door was secure, Tonya had transformed back into herself. Dale and Charlie had stared bug-eyed as Merriwind disappeared and the Tonya Miller they knew from school materialised in her place. Brooke hadn't flinched; Willow, perched on a stool in the corner, had studied the floorboards.

Naturally, Tonya had many questions, and they'd done their best to answer what they could. They explained they'd first entered Uland during the school trip six months ago, and about the Wee People, and Jayne; they told her about the trolls, and the Doomgaard, and Commander Hysst; between the four of them, they managed to relate most of the story pretty well, with Willow clarifying certain points along the way. As it turned out, Charlie was the best storyteller among them, especially when describing battles and swordfights. Even the part about the Uland Seven came back to him easily. Finally, they told her how they'd returned home, and then all eyes shifted to Willow.

She held their gaze in silence for a moment, twisting the hem of her cloak between her long green fingers. Then she said, 'You were gone a long time. Many things have changed. Uland is different.'

Brooke nodded, brushing a blonde dangle from her face. 'It *feels* different.'

Willow nodded: 'We're at war now, though most people will say we're not. They're pretending, you see. Like it's not really happening anymore. Like the whole of the Barrowlands hasn't been burned to the ground.' Her last few words dripped with bitterness.

Dale, gripping the edge of the captain's table where he was seated, said, 'Quillorin mentioned something about that, I think. He said the war ended up being between Ulandai and Doomgaard.'

'Mostly,' said Willow. 'It was hard to keep the other Factions involved when they were so far from it. People start to forget a war's happening when they can't see it. When it isn't happening to *them*. But it hasn't really stopped. It's just changed, and it's changing the entire continent. We haven't had peace in many seasons.'

'That sucks,' announced Tonya. Willow glanced at her but didn't reply.

'What about you?' said Charlie. He was seated in the captain's chair with his sword across his lap, cleaning it with a rag. Dale hadn't seen a speck of dirt on it but decided not to point it out. 'What were you doing in those woods, with that Gnome?'

'Quillorin,' Tonya corrected. 'They have *names*, you know.'

'Sorry, I forgot you're one of them now.'

'Yes, how'd you end up in the Glimmerglen,' Brooke said quickly as Tonya started to rise from her chair.

'I was on a mission,' said Willow, her eyes darting between Charlie and Tonya. 'The Gnome - Quillorin - needed safe passage through the woods, and I volunteered. That's it.'

Brooke drew her gaze and held it, waiting.

'And?'

'And what?'

'Why were you *really* there? Don't lie to me. I'm the Seer.'

She'd never called herself that before, Dale thought.

Willow wrinkled her nose. 'I'm not lying, Brooke Woods. I really *was* there to help Quillorin. It just… coincided… with something more important.'

'The healing seed?' said Dale.

Willow looked at him, nodded. 'It only grows in a few places in Uland. I found out it was there, but I couldn't just go all the way to the Withering Woods without a reason. I'm in the service of the Druyads, remember? They have to send me, or agree to it at least.'

'What are drew-adds?' said Tonya.

'Magic old men with beards,' said Charlie. 'Like wizards.'

'That's *not* what they are,' Brooke corrected crossly. 'Stop being thick, Charlie. It's unbecoming.'

Charlie smirked and said, 'La-dee-da', but lowered his head to avoid Brooke's glare.

'The Druyads,' Willow said, 'are the most ancient beings in Uland. They're the keepers of old knowledge and magic. They defeated the Giants at the end of the Fourth Age. In fact, the lake we're sailing across now was formed from the explosion that killed the seven Great Giants. The Druyads did that. The entire continent would've still been enslaved by the Giants if it wasn't for those "magic old men" and their ancient power.'

Charlie focused more intently on cleaning his sword. Dale said, 'Where's Yulerin now?'

'I haven't seen him since the crescent moon,' said Willow. 'That was a while ago, when he agreed to let me travel to the Glimmerglen. He's probably back in the High Druyad temple, though.'

'Who's the healing seed for?' said Brooke, though the answer had already floated into her mind even as she asked the question.

Willow hesitated, glancing warily at Tonya, who had her boots up on the captain's table. Tonya saw her look and sighed. 'Who am I going to tell, huh? Those Gnomes out there? I don't even know who you're talking about.'

'Clearly she can keep a secret,' Brooke added.

Willow, seeming satisfied enough, said, 'It's for someone who's sick. Very sick. The seed is the only cure. I've been searching for it for a whole season.'

'Who's sick?' said Dale.

'Orchidema,' replied Willow gravely. 'The Empress.'

Charlie didn't look up, but Dale saw the movement of the rag slow on his blade.

'She fell ill overnight, almost two seasons ago. What you might call a year. None of the physicians in Nymm could cure her. The other Factions wanted to send help but, with the war going on, our leaders didn't think that would be wise. She's been confined to her bed ever since, and she grows worse by the day.'

'A whole year,' Brooke said. 'That's so long.'

'Illness works on Woodspeople more slowly than most other races,' Willow said. 'But even so, the Empress doesn't have long. I'm not the only one searching for a cure, but I think I'm the only one who's found it. That's why it's so important I get back to Nymm as soon as possible.'

'How did she… Orchidema… get sick?' asked Tonya.

'She was poisoned,' said Brooke.

They all looked at her.

'How'd you know that?' said Dale.

Brooke shrugged. Daylight from the porthole cast a golden hue around her, giving her a strange shimmery appearance. Just for a moment, Dale thought she looked like someone else entirely and his heart did an odd little somersault in his chest.

'She's the Seer,' said Willow, 'and she's right. The Empress *was* poisoned. By Decymero.'

Tonya slid her boots off the table. 'I've heard that word,' she said. 'The Gnomes don't like it. I mean, they *really* don't like it.'

'It's like a swear,' Dale explained. 'You'd get detention for saying it here.'

'It's an evil word,' Willow agreed. 'Decymero had Orchidema poisoned somehow. But I'm not sure he actually means to kill her. Yulerin thinks he did it to draw me out. He knew I'd want to find the cure, that I wouldn't be able to stop myself from looking. And he was right. And I don't care, because I'm not afraid of him.'

'Neither are we,' said Brooke.

No-one spoke for a moment, but something passed between them all. Some silent resolve, an understanding. Even Tonya seemed to feel it, Dale thought, judging by the look on her face.

'The Druyads wanted to keep me hidden, after what happened at Hammerfall,' said Willow slowly, still fiddling with her cloak. 'They kept me near the temples, only let me do basic, easy missions. I barely left Wosdren for… years. And then, Orchidema.'

'Why does Decymero want you?' Dale said. 'Because of Hammerfall?'

'Maybe. There might be something more, I don't know. But it doesn't matter.' She took the healing seed from her pocket and held it up to the light. It glowed purple between her fingers. 'We just need to get this to Nymm.

Once Orchidema is healed, I can go back into hiding again. And you four can go home, I suppose.'

Dale, Brooke, Charlie and Tonya all looked at each other.

None of them had thought about going home all day.

***

The waters of Canyon Lake stretched into the infinite distance, glittering blue beneath the clear morning sky. There was nothing on the horizon to the south or west. *The Copperdawn Voyager* ran parallel to a low, green strip of land to the east, and Dale thought it was shrinking further away from them with each passing minute. If he squinted, he imagined he could see suggestions of mountains to the north, barely visible at this range. They seemed to be as far from anywhere as they could get.

He'd done his best to ignore the nausea building in the pit of his stomach, but after a couple of hours in the captain's cramped quarters, he couldn't stand it anymore. Seasickness was brand new to him and he hated it already; he'd wobbled across the deck with a face as green as Willow's and hurled what little was in his belly into the lake. The Gnomish sailors nearby laughed raucously and continued on with their business.

He began to feel better after that. The cool, fresh air whipping across the deck of the ship helped, as did the warm sunshine on his face. After a while, he even started to enjoy it.

How do we get back?

Truthfully, he hadn't thought about it much until Willow mentioned it. They'd spent their entire time in Uland so far running for their lives or rescuing other people, and then running for their lives *with* them. None of them had a chance to think, to compute what was happening. Uland had begun to feel like a faded dream until last night - now, it was very real again. All of it. And it wasn't just his powers that had returned.

He touched his chest. Beneath the clothes Quillorin had given him, the scar had also come back. He hadn't noticed until he was changing in his room in the manor house. The ghoulish claw mark was clear as day on his skin, like it'd only just happened. He ran his finger along it and shivered.

'What's up?'

He turned from where he was leaning on the starboard bulwark and saw Tonya striding across the deck. The sailors glanced at her curiously.

'Should you be out here?' Dale said, adjusting the front of his tunic.

'Course,' said Tonya brazenly. 'I'm the Queen, remember?'

'Shhh!' Dale hissed, pulling her to the rail alongside him. 'They'll hear you.'

'Oh come on, as if they care.' Tonya looked back over her shoulder and for one horrible moment, Dale thought she was going to announce to the whole crew that she'd been Merriwind all along. It would've been typical Tonya. Instead, she turned back and leaned over the bulwark, peering down at the white waters rushing past the ship's hull below them. 'This is a funny old place, isn't it?'

'Yeah. It's funny.' Dale watched her staring at the water. 'Have you been on a boat before?'

'Loads of times,' she said. 'Even went on a cruise once. It was kinda lame, though - you're just stuck in one place with your family and there's no escape. Sort've like being the Queen of the Gnomes, I guess.'

'I can't believe you were there a whole month.'

'Me neither. I was *really* glad to see you guys.'

'Even me?'

'Even you, you dork.' She stretched her arms into the breeze, leaning further over the side. Dale inched nervously closer, preparing to grab her if she fell.

'I think this is the longest we've talked to each other. Like, ever.'

'Maybe,' Tonya said, 'but it's only weird if you point it out. Besides…' She straightened up again and Dale breathed a silent sigh of relief, '... we all need to stick together, right? We're the only humans here. Even that girl - Willow - isn't human, is she?'

'No. But she's close.'

'I don't think she likes me.'

'She didn't like us at first, either. Give her time.'

Tonya studied her nails, ignoring the wind whipping at her dark curly hair. 'It's kinda cool having powers, though, isn't it? I'm not into superhero stuff n' all, but I can see why people like it.'

'You think we're superheroes?' Dale said, amused.

'Well *these* guys don't have powers, do they?' she replied, gesturing towards the Gnomish deckhands. 'They're just super short. And most of them don't know how to party.'

'Why doesn't it surprise me that you slipped so easily into being a queen?'

Tonya threw him a look. 'Reed, please.'

Dale grinned and squinted past the bow of the ship. The distant mountains seemed a little clearer now.

'I hope Nymm isn't as far away as it looks,' he said.

'Yeah. So what's going on with you and Brooke?'

He spun round, almost tripping over his own foot in the process. 'What? Nothing. What're you talking about?'

Tonya's smile was sly. 'You heard me. What's up with you and Brookles?'

'Nothing!'

'Then why's your face red?'

'It's not!'

The nearest sailor paused mid-mop to listen. Dale saw him and turned back to the bulwark.

'Stop just saying things, Tonya,' he muttered. 'You don't… know.'

'I know enough,' Tonya replied casually. 'I know you and Brooke and Charlie hardly spoke in school before that dumb hiking trip, and then after it you were best friends. It makes sense now, even though it was *super* weird at the time. Brooke never told me what happened but I knew something was up - she hung out with you guys all summer, I hardly saw her. And then, after school started, all three of you just… stopped.'

'Stopped what?'

'Being friends, I guess. Proper friends, anyway. I wouldn't know though, Brooke still barely talks to me. To anyone, really. Same goes for you.'

Dale stared at the water. His head felt light - maybe the seasickness was coming back again.

'It's not… there's more to it…'

'Here's what I think happened,' Tonya said, her smile widening. 'You and Brooke started being friends, and then *best* friends, and then you started fancying her.'

'No…'

'And why wouldn't you? She's pretty, even though she pretends she isn't. Or doesn't know she is, or something. I don't know.' Tonya leaned closer. 'And I think you *told* her you like her, and she didn't… reciprocate - is that the right word?'

'Yes. I mean, no - '

'And then it got all awkward and stuff, and here we are.'

Tonya leaned back, folding her arms. The smile was still there, triumphant now. Dale could tell she'd been waiting to say all that for a while; the embarrassment brewing inside him started bubbling over into anger.

The Gnomish deckhand had lost interest and gone back to mopping. Dale straightened up, drawing in a slow breath.

'That's not what happened,' he said. 'You don't know everything. Some of what you said's right - Brooke and me and Charlie aren't friends like we were before - but we're back here now and we don't have a choice. We *became* friends last time to survive, and we'll do it again. I might even have to be friends with you, too. But I guess we'll see.'

He pushed away from the bulwark and stomped away towards the captain's quarters. Behind him, Tonya muttered something, but it was lost in the wind.

***

'I don't know how it works,' Brooke was saying, 'or when it started exactly. But I can definitely read it.'

Charlie watched as she ran her index finger over the strange foreign lettering in the little leatherbound book. He didn't see anything change and the words remained as incomprehensible as ever, but Brooke's face broke into a grin.

'This part's about us,' she said, reading the words. 'The Warrior, the Sorcerer, the Time-Bender, the Healer, the Seer, the Trickster, the Changer.'

'The Uland Seven,' said Willow.

'The Changer,' Charlie said, still running the rag along the blade of his sword. 'That's gotta be Tonya, right?'

'Maybe,' said Brooke, looking at Willow for clarification. Tonya herself had just left the room for some air, like Dale.

The Woodsgirl stroked her green-tinged chin, gazing down at the pages pinned open by Brooke's hand. 'It's likely. Very few creatures can shapeshift, and none of them look like Ulanders. If Tonya Miller is the Changer, then she has a very great power indeed. One she seems to have mastered already.'

'And how can I read these words?' Brooke asked, brushing across the page again. 'They look like total gobbledygook until I touch them.'

'Gobbledy-what?'

'Never mind. It must be a Seer thing.'

'Most likely. Even I can't read it.'

'Question,' said Charlie, tossing the rag onto the captain's table. 'How'd the book get us back here? Is it a portal?'

'I don't know,' Willow replied, pulling out a chair next to Brooke. 'I've never heard of such things. Maybe it's a gobbledygook?'

Charlie and Brooke exchanged a glance and grinned. Willow saw it.

'What? Did I not use that word right?'

'I have no idea,' said Brooke. She closed the book. 'But whether the book's a portal or not, it got us back here. And the map helped us find you, which is the main thing. It faded away as soon as we left Silversprog, so it must've been there for that reason alone. Maybe Yulerin will know. I hope he's at the High Druyad temple, assuming that's where we end up. I have questions. Like, what's the Reckoning?'

Willow, who'd been lowering herself into the chair, seemed to freeze.

'Where did you hear about that?' she said slowly.

'It was in the book. Something about pieces coming together to start the Reckoning of Uland. What's that about?'

Willow's golden-brown eyes flicked from her to Charlie to the book. She picked up a used tankard from the table, held it aloft for a moment, and set it down again with a *thunk*.

'It's a prophecy,' she said. 'An ancient one, from the beginning of everything. The Reckoning is a period of time that's supposed to be the bridge between the Sixth and Seventh Ages of Uland. When it ends, the final Age begins - they say it will either be one of unending peace and contentment, or of horror and destruction. It all depends on the outcome of the Reckoning.'

'So no big deal, then?' said Charlie.

Willow went on, 'The prophecy says the Reckoning will be ushered in when three fragments of an ancient artefact are brought together and activated by the Druyads, who hold the key to unlocking their power. It'll be a time of conflict between good and evil itself. No-one will escape it.'

She paused. Charlie and Brooke waited. The ship continued rocking slowly back and forth beneath their feet.

'Yulerin thinks Decymero's been searching for the artefacts,' she said. 'It's partly why the Druyads destroyed the Time Keepers, in case any of them turned out to be one of the three pieces. If he managed to find the artefacts and bring them together, he'd start the Reckoning. And then he could swing the entire fate of Uland towards a final Age of unending destruction.'

'But why?' said Brooke earnestly. 'Why would he even want that?'

Willow held her gaze. 'Because he's evil. And that's all evil really wants. The end of all good things.'

They jumped as the door swung open. Dale stood there, red-faced and tousle-haired from the breeze. He glanced at each of them, lingered on Brooke for a second, then slammed the door behind him.

'The heck's wrong with you?' said Charlie.

'Nothing,' Dale said, going over to the fireplace in the corner. 'Just felt seasick, that's all.'

'Where's Tonya?' said Brooke.

'Out there, getting some air.' Dale crouched by the fireplace and started prodding the cold embers with a poker.

Charlie sheathed his sword. 'Well, I hope I get a chance to take Decymero on someday. If he's anything like Hysst, he won't be so bad. I think I could take him in a straight fight.'

'He's nothing like Hysst,' said Willow sullenly, 'and you wouldn't have a hope of beating him alone. Not if he's as powerful as the Druyads fear.'

'Maybe *you* could beat him, though,' said Brooke. 'You were pretty awesome at Hammerfall. I'd like to see you do that to Decymero.'

Willow shook her head, red hair tumbling over her face. 'I don't want to ever meet him. Ever. And that'd be the last thing Yulerin or the other Druyads would want. No-one really knows what Decymero can do, or how he'd do it, or even what he *wants* for sure. It's all… guesswork. And I think that's how he likes it. The less we know about him, the more he's able to get away with.'

'Are we definitely sure he exists?'

They all looked at Dale. He was standing by the fireplace now, kicking at the dead embers on the hearth. Outside, one of the deckhands shouted something they couldn't quite hear.

'What do you mean?' said Willow.

'Yeah, Dale,' said Brooke, with more than a little coldness. 'What d'you mean?'

Charlie remembered something Brooke had told him about the Throat, when she, Dale and Willow had almost been captured by Hysst. She said Dale had been asking worrying questions about Decymero, that he'd fallen out with Willow for a bit because of it. And he saw the way she was looking at him now.

'I mean,' Dale said, 'is it possible he's not even real? Maybe he's, like, the boogeyman, or something? Maybe people have made him up to scare each other, to get what they want. It'd be easy to trick people into making bad decisions if they thought - '

'Are you thick?' said Charlie. They all looked at him in surprise. 'Do you even remember what happened last time, up in that tower? It was *you* who destroyed the Soulburn Talisman, that thing that opened the gate to Decymero. He was *right there* with his hand out. That all felt pretty damn real to me.'

Dale blinked. Then his face hardened.

'I'm not the thick one here, Flint,' he said. 'I'm just the one… asking questions. Maybe we should all be asking more questions. About all of this.'

'Are you calling me thick, squirt?'

'If you weren't, you'd know I am.'

Charlie started to stand up; Dale turned to face him.

'Stop this,' said Willow.

'He started it,' said Dale, pointing.

'Yeah, and I'll finish - '

'Both of you *shut up*!' snapped Brooke. 'Listen.'

They all stopped. On the other side of the door, more sailors were shouting. They could hear footsteps pounding across the deck.

'Something's happening,' Willow said, rising.

'Dale,' said Brooke, 'where did you say Tonya is?'

Dale looked at her.

They all made for the door.

***

There were hysterics on deck.

Gnomish sailors darted every which way, yelling in panic. Some were hurriedly trying to fasten down crates and barrels with ropes, others were scurrying up and down the masts and rigging. A handful were fleeing below deck; one blundered past Brooke and said, 'I'm not paid enough for this, no sir,' before disappearing through the cargo hatch.

'What the heck's going on?' she cried.

'Ships,' replied a passing Gnome. 'Coming up fast on our stern. Appeared from nowhere, they did.'

'What ships?' said Charlie, dodging out of another sailor's path.

'Those bearing black sails.'

Captain Cogwhistle stomped across the deck in his overlarge leather boots. He pointed a pudgy accusing finger at them. 'Tell me, why are three Doomgaard galleons in our wake? They're after *you*, aren't they?'

This time, he pointed directly at Willow. She didn't flinch.

'I should've known there'd be trouble when we took a Woodsgirl on board. You're that prisoner everyone was talkin' about, right? The one the Queen had locked up in the - ' He stopped, casting around. 'Wait, where *is* the Queen? Isn't she with you?'

'She's sleeping,' Charlie lied. 'In your quarters. Told us not to disturb her, no matter what.'

'How the blazes can she sleep through this racket?' the captain barked. 'Those Doomgaard ships will be on us in no time.'

'How close are they?' said Dale.

'See for yourself.'

They all went to the bulwark and looked towards the rear of the ship for the first time. Its stern rose above deck level; a Gnome was up there behind the wheel, glancing anxiously over his shoulder. Beyond him, a green flag flapped noisily in the wind. And beyond it - much, much closer than Brooke would've liked - were three Doomgaard galleons with full black sails, tearing through the white wake of *The Copperdawn Voyager.*

'Uh oh,' said Dale.

'Big understatement,' added Brooke.

'How long before they reach us?' Willow asked. She was standing *on* the bulwark rail, hanging from the riggings like before.

'Just long enough for a pint of rum,' laughed Cogwhistle sardonically. 'May be the last one I ever have. If the Glimmerqueen fancies a drink, tell her I'm below deck with the rest of my crew.' He started towards the cargo hatch.

'You're not going to fight?' Charlie said indignantly.

'With what, young sir?' Cogwhistle replied over his shoulder. 'This is a merchant vessel. We don't have any weapons worth talkin' about. I suggest you all make ready to surrender or abandon ship - you might be able to swim some way before the crocs get you.'

He headed for the hatch. Most of the remaining crew on deck followed.

'So they're just going to hide?' said Charlie. 'Like cowards?'

'They're Gnomes,' said Willow, dropping back down to the deck. 'They know how to survive. It's their way.'

'So what do we do?' Dale said. 'Abandon ship? Is there, like, a lifeboat?'

'They'd mow us down,' said Willow. The noonday sun flared briefly between scudding clouds above them, catching the golden glow in her eyes. 'And like the captain said, if they didn't get us, the water beasts would. Leaving isn't an option.'

'So we fight,' said Charlie. It wasn't a question.

'We hold them off,' Willow replied. 'At least until… hey! Stay there!' She jabbed a finger at the sailor behind the ship's wheel, who looked as though he was about to make a break for the cargo hold. 'Keep us on course. We'll protect you.'

'We will?' said Dale.

'Tonya!' Brooke cried suddenly. 'Where is she?'

'Up here.'

The voice came from high above them. They all looked up and saw Tonya waving down from the crow's nest. Her hair whipped crazily around her head in the wind.

'What're you doing up there?' Brooke shouted. 'Come down!'

'Those boats are pretty close,' Tonya replied, pointing towards the Doomgaard ships. 'And I think they have cannons.'

That was enough for the few remaining sailors on deck. They all dropped what they were doing and bolted for the cargo hatch; the one behind the wheel hesitated longest before rushing after them.

'Well that's great,' muttered Dale.

'Brooke Woods,' said Willow, 'do you know how to steer a boat?'

'Me? What, no - '

'Just keep us on course,' Willow said, pushing her towards the steps. 'We'll do the rest.'

'On course?' Brooke said, staggering across deck. 'How will I know - '

'You're the Seer. If anyone knows, it'll be you.'

As Brooke mounted the steps to the wheel, Willow shouted up to the crow's nest. 'Tonya Miller, how long until those boats reach us?'

'How should I know?' came the reply.

Willow sighed in frustration. 'Make a guess!'

There was a pause. Then: 'Maybe five minutes?'

Boom.

Something whistled through the air, just a few feet wide of starboard.

'What was that?' cried Dale.

'Oh, but we might be in range of those cannons,' Tonya called.

Another *boom.* Another dark object shot past their portside this time.

'Yep, definitely in range.'

Brooke was behind the wheel now, cheeks ruddy in the breeze, blonde hair blown back from her face. 'They're shooting at us!' she cried.

'We know!' Charlie replied.

'Those galleons will rip this boat apart,' said Willow. 'We have to stop them getting alongside us. Charlie Flint, are you strong?'

'Well, I - '

'Dump everything overboard that's not tied down. We'll go faster with less weight.'

'Got it.'

Charlie ran for the nearest barrel. Willow grabbed Dale by both shoulders and looked him in the eyes.

'Now's the time to use your powers, Dale Reed,' she said.

'I'm still not sure how,' he said. Willow's fingers dug into his flesh. 'Ow!'

'Just try,' she said. 'It's all you can do. I'll try, too, though my magic isn't best suited to being on the water. You take port, I'll take starboard, ok?'

'One down!' Charlie wheezed, heaving a barrel over the bulwark.

Boom. Boom.

'Watch out!' Tonya cried from above.

Another cannonball blurred past, right next to the mast. The fourth clipped the bulwark a few feet to Brooke's left, showering her in splintered wood. She screamed, covering her head.

'Portside!' yelled Willow, pointing.

'I'll try,' Dale replied, crossing the deck. He looked down at his hands, flexing his fingers; beneath his shirt, the Ghoulish scar burned on his chest. 'I'll try.'

***

With a grunt of effort, Charlie shoved another casket over the bulwark railing. Its contents smashed as it tumbled down into the churning waters below.

Boom. Another cannonball hurtled past, just a few feet from the edge of the hull.

Getting closer, he thought. *They'll stop missing soon.*

'Dale, are you ready?' he heard Willow shout. She was on the right-hand side of the boat - starboard, he remembered it was called - near the foot of the stairs. Her hood was down and the wind was playing havoc with her hair.

'Ready,' Dale called back from the opposite side of the deck. He didn't look ready at all.

'They're really close now,' Tonya shouted anxiously from above. 'Is someone, like, going to do something?'

Charlie saw she was right. Two of the three Doomgaard ships had caught right up to them and would soon be level with *The Copperdawn Voyager*. They were both larger and clearly faster than the Gnomish merchant vessel. Their cannons were primed and ready to fire, just as soon as their target was in sight - when that happened, they wouldn't stand a chance.

Doomgaard sailors in black armour moved around the decks of both ships. Charlie could hear them barking orders to one another, pointing their way. He saw swords and spears and crossbows, and he licked his lips.

If only I could reach them, he thought. *They're in for a big surprise if they try boarding us.*

'Willow?' Dale yelled uncertainly over the roar of the wind and water. 'I don't know if I can do this.'

'You can,' Willow shouted back. 'Just pretend they're all Whispering Blades.'

Boom. Boom.

Brooke squealed as another cannonball grazed their stern, rocking the boat. The impact knocked her to one side and she let go of the wheel.

Immediately, the ship began veering right, straight into the path of one of the Doomgaard galleons. Charlie saw enemy sailors rushing to the bulwarks, grabbing ropes.

They are *going to board us!*

'Brooke!' Tonya cried from above. 'The wheel!'

Charlie sprinted across the deck and mounted the stairs, two at a time. He reached the spinning wheel just as the first of the Doomgaard grappling hooks clattered over their bulwark and just about managed to grab two handles. It almost pulled him off his feet before he got his boots firmly planted. Then, gritting his teeth and straining every muscle in his arms, he started to turn the wheel back the other way.

The Copperdawn Voyager's bow began angling away from the approaching Doomgaard galleon, but there were already three grappling hooks latched to their bulwark. On the enemy deck, dozens of black-armoured sailors heaved on the ropes, trying to pull the two ships together.

'Willow!' Charlie yelled.

She'd already seen them. Gripping the rail with one hand, she stretched her free one towards the ropes. Green sparks flurried around her fingers. There was a sharp burst of light and the clawed metal hook heads became papery green leaves, immediately releasing from the bulwarks. The ropes themselves turned into thick, snake-like vines in the Doomgaard sailors' hands. Several of them yelled in surprise as they tumbled backwards.

'Yes!' Charlie cried, still turning the wheel.

Brooke clambered to her feet, grabbing his arm for support. Her hair was stuck to her forehead and her blue eyes were dazed.

'I don't like boats,' she said.

'Me neither,' said Charlie. 'Here, take this.'

Brooke grabbed the wheel and instinctively started turning it a few degrees to the right, angling them back on course. Charlie didn't have time to wonder about it. He had to get help.

He glanced back. The third galleon - significantly larger than the other two - was still some way behind them, but its two monstrous forward cannons were trained on their stern. One accurate hit and they'd be done for. If the waters of the lake weren't so choppy, Charlie thought, their hull would be full of holes already.

You might be able to swim some way before the crocs get you.

Charlie rushed back down the stairs. There was a flash of blue light to his left, followed by screams from Doomgaard sailors on the other ship. He saw Dale stagger back from the rail, his hands still glowing blue.

'Geez, that was a good one!' the other boy cried. 'I froze a bunch of them solid!'

'Freeze the cannons!' Willow shouted, hurling a bolt of green light at the galleon on her side.

This is nuts! Charlie thought.

He reached the cargo hatch and threw it open, dropping to his knees. Bright sunlight spilled down into the hold below; the Gnomes shrunk away from it, shielding their eyes.

'Close that door!' the captain shouted. 'Let us have our drinks in peace.'

'They're going to sink your ship!' Charlie yelled back furiously. 'Do you not care at all? You'll all die if you stay down there.'

'Maybe,' replied the captain. 'But at least we'll have bellies full of rum. That's a fine way to go, if you ask me.' He hiccupped.

Boom. A cannonball sliced through the mainsail just below the crow's nest. Tonya squealed.

'You're all cowards!' Charlie yelled down at them. 'This is *your* ship and we're defending it. We're just kids! Get up here and help us!'

The Gnomish sailors exchanged looks. Someone said, 'He's right, lads.'

'He's not right,' hiccupped Cogwhistle. 'He's just an Ulander. He doesn't know nothin' about survival. Break open another barrel, boys - it'll be your last!'

With a snarl of anger, Charlie punched the deck and got back to his feet. Over by the bulwark, Dale hurled another bolt of blue light at the Doomgaard galleon. A second later, he cried out and ducked as an arrow whizzed past his head.

'They have crossbows!' Tonya shouted.

'We know!' Willow replied, dodging arrows from her side.

Charlie spotted a barrel lid a few feet away and made for it. He dropped, just as an arrow fizzed past his ear, and grabbed the lid by the handle. Raising it like a shield, he staggered towards Willow.

'How do we get out of this?' he cried. 'We can't win.'

'We have to try,' Willow replied, desperately spellcasting in the direction of the enemy galleon. Most of the Doomgaard arrows transformed into dandelions and floated harmlessly to the deck, but some made it through. One *thunked* into Charlie's makeshift shield, almost knocking him over. 'If we can hold them off for long enough, we might be able to - '

Boom.

Brooke and Tonya screamed in union as the stern of *The Copperdawn Voyager* exploded. Chunks of splintered wood rained down on the deck; the whole ship rocked forward and Willow tumbled into Charlie, knocking them both to the floor. The Doomgaard sailors cheered.

'We're hit,' Charlie gasped, winded.

'I know,' said Willow, scrambling back to her feet.

Charlie looked towards the ship's wheel. Somehow, Brooke was still hanging on, her hair a tangled mass of splinters. Tonya was still screaming up in the crow's nest; the Doomgaard bowmen had started firing at her too. The enemy galleons were almost level on either side of their mortally-wounded ship, barely a dozen yards away. Dale was still furiously hurling bolts of ice at their cannons while dodging their arrows.

We can't win this, Charlie thought exhaustedly, dragging himself to his feet. *We're going to sink and get eaten by crocodiles, if they don't shoot us with arrows or cannonballs first.* And then, crazily: *At least I'll get out of that detention with Mr Green.*

He watched in a sort of daze as the first of the Doomgaard soldiers swung towards their ship, sword drawn, black armour glinting in the sunlight. Willow hit him with a blast of green light and he dropped with a scream into the foaming water between the boats. But the next two were already coming, swinging on ropes from the galleon mast. Both of them landed with heavy thuds on their deck. One instantly advanced on Willow; she dodged nimbly away from his sword, her golden eyes blazing, green sparks crackling around her fingers.

The other one came for Charlie.

He drew his sword with a *shiiiing*, adjusting his feet on the wet wooden boards. The soldier, covered from head to toe in the same black armour Commander Hysst's men had worn, stomped towards him. He could see the man's eyes behind his visor, wide and white with bloodlust. Charlie squeezed the hilt of his sword and gritted his teeth.

Come on, then, he thought. *Do your worst.*

'Back, you beast!'

Something *clanged* off the soldier's helmet and he staggered to a halt; an iron kettle landed on the deck at his feet. He looked down at it, looked up again, and was immediately smacked in the face by a brass dish. The Doomgaardian stumbled backwards, dropping his sword with a clatter.

'Keep at it, lads!' bellowed the Gnomish sailor by the open crate. 'Don't let up!'

Suddenly, there were Gnomes everywhere, heaving cargo items from the remaining crates and barrels at the oncoming Doomgaard soldiers. As more landed on *The Cooperdawn Voyager's* deck, they were pelted straight away with pots and pans and dishes and crockery. One soldier took a heavy wooden chopping board to the chest and was sent tumbling over the bulwark; others did their best to advance, trying to use their swords and spears to block the barrage of flying kitchenware.

'That's it, lads!' cried the lead Gnome. Charlie recognised his voice as the one who'd disagreed with Cogwhistle, who was nowhere in sight. 'Keep the beasts back.'

Charlie wasn't sure how long the fight raged on like that. He joined the Gnomes in hurling cargo while Willow and Dale continued blasting them with ice or transforming their weapons into plants. Tonya, who they were no longer firing at, yelled instructions from above; Brooke kept the ship on course.

But all the while, the galleons drew closer, the unfrozen cannons trained on *The Copperdawn Voyager's* hull. The biggest ship, still some way behind them, had stopped firing while the Doomgaard soldiers were on deck, but Charlie knew its job may already be done. The stern of their ship was slowly, but surely, dipping into the lake. And the Gnomes were already running low on throwable cargo.

We're just delaying the inevitable, he thought, hurling another pot.

Sure enough, Doomgaard soldiers stopped swinging onto their deck. Those that were already on board stood their ground at the starboard bulwark, weapons at the ready. Charlie and the Gnomes had all but run out of cargo to throw.

A black-armoured soldier on the starboard-side galleon clambered up on their bulwark and, cupping a hand around his mouth, yelled, 'It's over! Lay down your arms and surrender now.'

'It's cooking stuff, idiot!' Charlie shouted back. 'You drop *your* weapons.'

The soldier, who must have been the ship captain, removed his helm. He was as bald as Eldric and about four times the Gnome's size. He sneered, baring mustard-coloured teeth.

'You're in no position to bargain, boy,' he said, one arm hooked around the rigging to steady himself. 'We'll board you or sink you. Your choice.'

'You can't sink us,' Tonya shouted from the crow's nest. She pointed down at Willow. 'You need *her*, right?'

One of the bowmen loosed an arrow at her and she ducked out of sight. The Doomgaard captain's yellowy grin widened.

'We don't mind fishing her out of the water,' he said. 'The monsters down there'll finish off the rest of you. Now, what's it going to be? Surrender and live, or fight and die?'

Charlie's teeth remained clenched, but his grip on the teapot he was holding loosened. He looked across at Willow, who was still poised in a spellcasting stance, her green-tinged skin glistening with sweat. The Gnomes bunched on the portside of the deck around Dale glanced nervously at one another.

'Smells like surrender to me,' laughed the Doomgaard captain. 'Drop those weapons of yours and get on your knees.'

It can't end like this, Charlie thought wearily. *It just can't.*

He looked at the teapot in his hand, started to set it down. The Gnomes did the same.

Then: 'Sir!'

All eyes whipped towards the Doomgaard sailor, who was pointing in fright towards their stern. Charlie followed his trembling finger and felt his own eyes grow wide.

The big galleon, the one that had punctured the hull of *The Copperdawn Voyager*, was on fire.

'What in the blazes?' cried the Doomgaard captain.

They all watched in amazement as orange flames raced up the hull of the huge ship, licking into the wood like it was bone-dry kindling instead of soaking timber. Sailors plunged screaming into the water. In seconds, the enormous black sail of the ship also caught fire and dropped away from the mast in clumps of ash.

'How?' one of the Gnomes said.

'Dale, was that you?' said Charlie.

'No way, it's too far!'

'Look!' cried Brooke.

Two more ships had appeared on either side of the burning Doomgaard galleon. They were smaller and sleeker, with clean white sails. Even from this distance, Charlie saw the flag atop each of their masts - it featured a diamond divided into four sections: green, red, blue and purple. Balls of fire were shooting from each ship, eating into the hull of the already-sinking Doomgaard galleon.

'The Elementals!' exclaimed Willow.

'We're saved!' cried one of the Gnomes. The rest immediately joined in, whooping and cheering for joy.

'Take them!' roared the Doomgaard captain.

The black-armoured soldiers on *The Copperdawn Voyager's* deck advanced. Charlie dropped his teapot and flew at the nearest soldier, swinging his sword in a wide arc. The soldier jerked back in surprise, got his sword up in time, and started duelling.

As their steel rang, the Gnomes hurled the remaining cargo at the other soldiers; Willow turned the ship's rigging into vines and snagged a couple of them, pulling them to the floor. On the portside, Dale heaved a blast of bright light at the reloading bowmen, obliterating several of them into blue sparks.

All the while, no-one seemed to notice the fingers of ice creeping up the hull of each Doomgaard vessel. As swords clashed and pots flew on deck, and the bigger galleon was consumed in fire further behind them, the wooden bodies of both flanking enemy boats began to crack. Finally, one of the Doomgaard soldiers spotted the magicked ice slithering up the bulwark and sounded the alarm, but it was already too late.

With a loud whine of splitting timber, the deck of the starboard side galleon broke apart. The sailors, soldiers and bowmen who'd been waiting to board the Gnomish ship disappeared down into the galleon's belly with shrieks. The ship's mast tilted sideways and the sail collapsed, flopping down over the remaining sailors like an enormous black bedsheet. The captain was knocked from the rigging and vanished into the lake.

The soldier duelling Charlie was momentarily distracted by the commotion on the other ship - Charlie saw the opening and delivered a powerful blow to his arm, knocking the sword from his black-gloved hand. The Doomgaardian yelled in pain, staggered backwards and clattered over the bulwark into the frothing lakewater below.

'They're sinking, they're sinking!' Tonya cried triumphantly from above.

She was right. The enemy vessel had collapsed in on itself and was rapidly taking on water. The sailors who hadn't fallen through the gap made by the ice were throwing themselves into the lake. The galleon itself would be underwater in minutes.

It was only then they saw the third Elemental vessel on the other side of the Doomgaard boat. It was smaller than the others, driven by oars instead of sails. In all the confusion of battle, no-one had noticed it approaching the enemy ship. Elemental warlocks lined its deck, still hurling bolts of ice at the hull of the half-sunk Doomgaard galleon.

The Gnomes were cheering now, tossing the last of the cargo in the air. Charlie couldn't help but join them, waving his sword over his head.

'We're not done yet!' Willow shouted.

The other Doomgaard ship was still intact, despite most of its lower hull having turned into an iceberg. A fourth Elemental vessel had snuck up on its portside but had withdrawn after the Doomgaard soldiers turned their bows on them instead - the warlocks were freezing their arrows mid-flight.

'Their sail!' Brooke shouted from the wheel. 'Destroy it!'

'How?' Charlie yelled back. 'We need fi- '

Whump.

A swirling ball of orange-red fire shot from between Dale's hands and hit the Doomgaard galleon's sail, punching a hole straight through it. The flames spread instantly, licking into the canvas. The Doomgaard sailors tried in vain to pull the sail down but the damage was already done.

'It's working!' Brooke cried.

Sure enough, with no way to propel itself, the enemy galleon began to fall back. In no time at all, their cannons were no longer level with *The Copperdawn Voyager*. They watched as the Doomgaardians ran about the deck in panic, trying in vain to put out the burning sail.

'Nice one, Reed,' Charlie called. Dale grinned back, shooting him a thumbs up.

'Look out!' someone cried.

Charlie spun round, just as the mast of the other barely-afloat Doomgaard galleon finally snapped. With a low groan, it toppled sideways, straight towards their deck.

'Brace yourself!' a Gnome bellowed.

The bigger, heavier Doomgaard mast slammed into theirs, rocking the whole ship to one side. Charlie lost his footing and landed painfully on his arm. As he went down, he saw Brooke also hit the floor on the raised deck. Willow was bowled over by several Gnomes. Dale, who'd already been leaning against the bulwark, managed to stay on his feet.

High above them, Tonya screamed.

'Oh no!' Brooke cried.

Charlie looked up. Tonya was clinging to the edge of the crow's nest, her legs kicking desperately in mid-air. She must have been over fifty feet above the deck.

'Help her!' Charlie managed to shout. 'Quick!'

Willow struggled to her feet. Several Gnomes staggered across the tilted deck towards the mast. Charlie tried to haul himself up, wincing at the pain in his arm.

But they were all too late.

With a loud *crack*, the mast of *The Copperdawn Voyager* snapped. The whole thing toppled to the side under the weight of the Doomgaard mast. Tonya hung on to the crow's nest, screaming all the way down.

'No!' Charlie cried.

Then the mast snagged on the rigging and abruptly jerked to a halt. The sudden stop was enough to break Tonya's grip on the nest; she sailed through the air like a rag doll, still screaming, and splashed into the foaming water where the second Doomgaard galleon had been just moments before.

'Someone get her!' Brooke cried.

Charlie crawled across the sodden deck towards the bulwark, but he could barely put weight on his right arm. He knew he wouldn't be able to swim, even if he somehow managed to jump into the lake. Still, he had to try.

'WHY ISN'T ANYONE GETTING HER?' Brooke yelled.

'Gnomes can't swim,' replied one of the sailors ashamedly.

Willow met Charlie's gaze with wide, stricken eyes. 'Neither can I.'

'My days,' Charlie gasped, pulling himself up on an empty crate. 'My arm's shot, I can't do it. I would if I could, but… Dale?'

The other boy had thrown off his cloak and was swinging his leg over the bulwark. He looked back fearfully.

'Wish me luck,' he said, and jumped.

Splash.

'Dale!' Brooke cried. She'd gotten to her feet and was stumbling down the stairs from the raised deck. Behind them, Charlie could hear the remaining Doomgaard sailors yelling and flailing in panic as the galleon sank beneath the surface, now detached from the mast entirely.

He staggered across the tilted deck and grabbed the bulwark rail for balance with his good hand. Brooke and Willow met him there. They stared down at the churning water.

'Where are they?' Brooke cried in a high, terrified voice. 'I can't see them!'

'Me neither,' said Charlie.

The Doomgaard galleon with the smouldering sail had fallen further back out of range. *The Copperdawn Voyager* was slowly turning on the spot, its wheel spinning out of control where Brooke had left it. A couple of Gnomish sailors ran to stop it.

'Can she swim?' said Willow shakily. 'Can… can Dale?'

'I've no idea,' said Charlie. 'I remember dunking him in the pool once, but I can't remember if he - '

'There!' cried Brooke, pointing.

They looked. Dale had reappeared a few yards from the ship's hull, sucking in lungfuls of air. His brown hair was now slicked black against his scalp.

Tonya was in his arms; her head was slumped motionless against his shoulder.

'He's got her!' Brooke exclaimed.

'She's not moving,' Willow said.

Dale waved at them and ducked under for a second. He came up again, coughed hard.

'Rope!' Charlie shouted. 'We need rope.'

The Gnomes had already gathered it and were racing to the bulwark. They hurled it down to Dale; it unfurled in the air and slapped into the water next to him. He grabbed hold of it, straining to keep Tonya above the surface.

'Pull!' Charlie shouted.

The Gnomes heaved on the rope. Brooke and Willow joined in. Charlie tried but his uninjured arm was too weak to make much difference, so he called out instructions instead.

'Pull! Keep going, they're almost out. Dale, tie it around you. That's it. Now, hold on!'

A few minutes later, they had them back on deck. Dale sat on all fours, coughing lakewater onto the boards as Willow thumped his back.

'You did so well,' she said gently, hitting him again and again. 'So brave. Most valiant.'

Brooke crouched next to Tonya, crying softly. The other girl lay on her back, head to one side, still unmoving. The Gnomes stood around them, wringing their hands anxiously.

'Does anyone k-know CPR?' Brooke blubbed.

'What's that?' said one of the Gnomes.

Charlie dropped to his knees next to Tonya's soaked body. His heart was pounding blood into his ears so loudly he barely heard himself say, 'I'll do the breathing if you press?'

Brooke looked at him, disbelieving.

'I…I don't know how.'

'I don't know either,' said Charlie, taking Tonya's chin in one trembling hand. He stared at her closed eyes, her open lips. 'But we have to try.'

'Ok,' said Brooke, shuffling closer.

'Ready?'

'Ready.'

Charlie leaned down and drew in a deep breath.

'Stand back, you dozy landlubbers.'

Brooke was shoved aside as Cogwhistle dropped to his haunches next to Tonya. He glowered at Charlie from beneath his hat.

'Let her go,' he muttered. 'I'll handle this.'

Charlie obeyed. The Gnomish captain looked Tonya up and down for a moment, mumbling to himself. Charlie could smell beer on his breath.

'Hurry,' Brooke whispered anxiously.

'Hold your horses, I know what I'm doing.'

The Gnome placed one pudgy hand on Tonya's abdomen and closed his eyes. Charlie saw a faint golden glow around his fingers, just for a second. Then, with a grunt, he thumped his other fist down on his hand. And again. And a third time.

On the fourth thump, Tonya's eyes sprang open and she sat straight up with a wheezing gasp.

'Ton!' Brooke cried.

Tonya looked round at them all in shock, her hair in her face, her jaw slack. Then she leaned over and vomited lakewater onto the deck at Willow's feet. The Woodsgirl took a quick step back.

Cogwhistle hauled himself back up, leaning on one of the sailors for support. He looked down at Charlie, sniffed noisily, and spat a wet gob of something onto the boards.

'Some Gnomes can do a little magic,' he said, 'even if we are cowards.'

He turned and headed for the wheel.

Chapter Sixteen: The Elementals

'I really thought you were dead,' Brooke said.

'Me too,' Tonya croaked. 'I swallowed about a gallon of water back there. My throat's *killing* me now.'

They were in the cabin of the Elemental ship, seated near the fireplace wrapped in thick woollen cloaks. The cabin was larger than the captain's quarters of *The Copperdawn Voyager*, and much more ornate - Brooke thought the elegant wood-panelled walls, red velvet curtains and luxurious, tasselled cushions wouldn't have been out of place inside Twiggleton Manor. They could've been in some fancy drawing room if the floor hadn't been swaying gently beneath their feet.

'It looked like you barfed up half the lake,' Charlie observed, clutching his injured arm. Willow had given him one of her purple healing beans and it was already taking effect - he hadn't been able to move his fingers until a few minutes ago, and now his whole hand felt fine again.

'Seemed that way,' Tonya said, tugging her cloak tighter around herself. 'Good thing *one* of you could swim, huh?'

'Hey, my arm!' said Charlie.

'Woodspeople can't swim,' said Willow. She was in the far corner of the cabin, hugging her knees. 'You'd have ended up having to save me too.'

'I *can* swim,' Brooke clarified. 'I'm just not very good at it.'

'Neither am I,' Dale put in from the other corner. He was bundled up in two cloaks - his face poked out from between them like a turtle in its shell. 'You were lucky the Gnomes pulled us back in when they did.'

'Lucky you weren't a wimp, you mean,' said Tonya.

Dale said, 'You're… welcome?' and Tonya smiled. He returned it, ducking his head.

'So what now?' said Charlie.

The Elementals had taken them aboard their ship as soon as the battle was over. Cogwhistle and the Gnomes had chosen to stay on *The Copperdawn Voyager* while one of the other Elemental vessels towed it to safety. It was in bad shape but, according to the gruff Gnomish captain, would make it shore at least. Somewhere along the way he seemed to have forgotten about the Glimmerqueen - Brooke hoped they'd be far away before he remembered.

'The Elementals have offered to take us onward,' Willow explained. 'Once we reach the northern shore of the lake, we can go the rest of the way ourselves. It'll be about a day or two's journey on foot. Less if we move quickly.'

'Sounds exhausting,' sighed Tonya.

Brooke saw Willow's eyes glow faintly golden and said, 'That's actually not too far. The last time, we had to fly part of the way just to make it in time.'

'Fly? They have, like, planes?'

Charlie snorted laughter; Dale buried his face in his cloak.

'What's a plane?' said Willow.

They did their best to explain air travel to Willow - who grew more confused by the minute - while also describing for Tonya what it was like to fly by peryton. She seemed too weary to question the idea of a huge flying stag with feathered wings, so they left it at that.

After a while, an Elemental deckhand arrived with food and drinks. It was the first time Brooke had gotten a proper look at one of them since they were pulled aboard: she was a young girl with sunkissed skin and aqua-coloured eyes wearing a knee-length blue dress and blue leather ankle boots; her hair, which she wore in a long, over-the-shoulder plait, had been dyed royal blue. Her eyebrows - also dyed blue - arched when she saw Willow in the corner of the cabin.

'I… I was told to bring you refreshments,' she said nervously. 'I hope you like carrot cake and walnuts. And there's hot chocolate if you're still feeling - '

'Yes please!' Charlie cut in, snatching a steaming mug from the tray.

Brooke took a mug and a slice of cake, pointedly saying 'Thank you' with a sharp glance at Charlie, who was stuffing walnuts in his mouth. She noticed the Elemental girl's fingernails had also been painted bright blue.

'Thanks,' said Dale, waddling back to the corner in his cloak shell.

The girl gazed around the room, unable to suppress a beaming smile. 'You're *them*, aren't you? The heroes of Hammerfall? I've… I've heard the stories. We all have.'

'Stories,' said Willow. 'That's all they are.'

The girl's face fell a little. Charlie must have noticed, because he quickly added, '*True* stories, though. We were really there, we really won. It was… quite the battle.'

Now it was Brooke's turn to snort.

The Elemental girl's smile returned. 'I *knew* it was you. Charlie Flint, the great warrior. Brooke Woods, the wise Seer.' She squinted towards the corner. 'Dale Reed, the mighty sorcerer. And Willow of Nymm, who defeated Commander Hysst.'

Charlie sat up straighter. 'Well, I - '

'You've got it exactly right,' said Brooke with a smirk. 'Willow saved the day.'

The girl's awestruck gaze came to rest on Tonya. 'I'm afraid I don't know you, my lady. I do apologise for my ignorance.'

'I'm Tonya Miller,' Tonya said casually, 'Queen of the Gnomes.'

'Queen of the - '

'She's joking,' Brooke said quickly, nudging Tonya with her toe. 'Thank you for the food and hot chocolate, it's delicious.'

The girl seemed disappointed but took the hint with a smile. She offered a polite bow and left the room.

'No more Glimmerqueen talk, ok?' Brooke said. 'From now on, you're just Tonya.'

'I'm never *just* Tonya,' the other girl replied, popping a walnut in her mouth.

'So are we famous, like, everywhere?' said Dale.

'Most places,' replied Willow, inspecting a piece of carrot she'd extracted from the cake. 'But like I said, most of what people know of you are from stories. Words get... embellished. Many people believe Charlie to be seven feet tall with enormous muscles and unrivalled sword-fighting skills, for instance.'

Charlie grinned toothily. 'Well...'

'And I've heard drinkers in taverns discussing how Brooke flies around on a white horse with a silver mane, and Dale conjures ferocious ice beasts with the snap of a finger.'

'Can I really do that?' Dale said.

'The Elementals are no different,' Willow went on. 'Some of their forces took part in the battle at Hammerfall - though to hear them tell it, you'd think they did most of the fighting - and stories were carried across the continent to Elementa. So yes, your *myth* is everywhere. And it won't be long before word spreads that you're back.'

'But the Elementals are good, right?' said Brooke. 'I mean, they saved us back there. And they're helping us now.'

'Yes,' said Willow slowly, curling a strand of red hair around her finger. 'They *did* rescue us. But they also let one of the Doomgaard ships go when it was already damaged. And I'm not sure why they were so far north on the lake when - '

'I'm tired,' announced Tonya, standing. 'Dale, budge over.'

She crossed to the cushioned window seats; Dale drew himself further into his cloak shell to make space. At the word "tired", Brooke felt a wave of sleepiness wash over her. 'Maybe we should get some rest,' she said. 'It's been a long day already.'

'You're telling me,' said Charlie, gulping down the last of his hot chocolate.

'Sleep if you need to,' Willow said, getting to her feet. 'I'm going to get some fresh air. It's stuffy in here.'

'Ok,' Brooke replied, her eyelids already growing heavy. 'Wake us when you're back.'

Willow looked at each of them in turn, muttered 'humans', and left the cabin.

Brooke closed her eyes, welcoming the chance to sleep. It'd been a long day already and showed no sign of ending anytime soon - how she wished she was back in her own bedroom, with her geeky movie posters tacked to the wall, and her neatly-arranged desk, and her books…

Her eyelids fluttered open again. Frowning, she reached into her pocket and pulled out Yulerin's little leather book.

Why am I looking at this now? she wondered wearily.

She unbound the twine seal on the book and flipped it open, casting a glance around the cabin as she did so. The others were already asleep or on the verge of it.

'What're you doing?' Charlie mumbled, his eyes only half-open.

'Nothing,' she replied. 'Go to sleep.'

Charlie obliged, his head drooping forward. Brooke carefully turned the book's pages, marvelling afresh at how they didn't crack or tear between her fingers in spite of how ancient they must be. She came to the page where the map had been and stopped.

The drawing of Silversprog Castle was completely gone; a new image had taken its place.

It was barely visible. Brooke brought the book close to her face, squinting at the hand-drawn lines of ink on the page, trying to discern what it was.

Is it... a tree? she thought, puzzled. *And what's this round thing below it? A rock?*

She stared at it for another minute before deciding she had no idea what it was. But that was ok - she knew, somehow, that it'd become clear soon enough, if they needed it to. Just like the map.

With a weary sigh, she closed the book, tied the twine, and slipped it back in her pocket.

And almost immediately, she was fast asleep.

***

The sun was high in the blue afternoon sky. Gulls circled the Elemental ship, squawking noisily, watching for opportunities to steal unguarded food. Waves slapped rhythmically against the hull of the boat as it cut through the water.

Willow stood outside the cabin door for a moment, her face upturned to the sky, enjoying the soft prickle of warm sunlight on her green-tinged skin. Unlike the Other-worlders, she'd managed to remain mostly dry during their fight with the Doomgaard forces that morning, which was a good thing considering how much Woodspeople disliked getting wet. Rain was fine, of course - it came from the sky, where water *should* be. But lakes and rivers and oceans were something else entirely. She couldn't wait to get her feet back on solid ground again.

The Elemental deckhands cast curious glances her way as she walked along the bulwark, trailing a hand on the wooden rail. She shielded her eyes and squinted across the water, but there were still no signs of beaches or trees or mountains just yet. Soon, she hoped.

'My lady.'

She turned. One of the male deckhands approached, bowing his head politely. He was dressed all in green, with matching green hair and a green beard. *One of the Land Elementals*, she thought, noticing with amusement that even his eyelashes were dyed green.

'Do you require assistance?' he asked.

'No,' she replied. He nodded and started to turn away. 'No wait, yes. How long before we reach land again?'

'I'm… not quite sure. Perhaps by tomorrow's sunrise?'

Tomorrow? She sighed.

'We'll do our utmost to accommodate you all in the meantime,' said the deckhand politely. 'There'll be a substantial meal later, and we'll keep the fire lit throughout - '

'It's fine,' Willow said. 'Just get us there as fast as you can.'

'Of course.'

The young man bowed again and walked away. Willow watched him go for a moment, wondering afresh at the strangeness of the Elementals: the half-Ulander, half-magical people of the south, with their bizarre internal divisions and nonsense rituals. She'd never truly understand them. But they were allies, and that was all that mattered right now.

She crossed to the other side of the deck and leaned over the bulwark, watching the foaming white water churn against the hull. They were making good time, for sure. But not making it fast enough for her liking.

The lake is huge, she reminded herself, *as wide as it is deep*. No ship could traverse it in less than a day, not even the fastest clipper vessels favoured by the merchants of The Gilded Compass. And it was filled with all manner of aquatic monsters, some of which could swallow a ship whole. The wisest captains knew how to navigate the waters safely without straying into the hunting grounds of those hidden, hungry beasts, which meant they could rarely travel in a perfectly straight line. Just like on land, really.

Air is best, Willow thought. *Maybe we can build one of those air-plane things and just fly everywhere. That'd be nice.*

She turned away from the railing, folded her arms, and muttered, 'Why does everything always have to be so *difficult?*'

Another passing deckhand glanced her way. Like most of the adult Elementals on the ship, he was at least a head taller than her. In their eyes, and in the eyes of most non or half-magical beings in Uland, she knew she appeared as young as her friends in the cabin. That appearance sometimes served her well.

'Can I help you, m'lady?'

Ugh, that word. Why do they all keep using it?

'You cannot.'

'Very well, m'lady. Perhaps you'd like to go back inside? Sometimes, when you're out on the deck for too long, the sun can be…'

She allowed a little gold to shimmer through her irises. He saw it and stiffened visibly.

'... but you're more than welcome to stay out here, of course.'

'Thank you.' Willow smiled pleasantly until he walked away. That smile became a smirk - Elementals, like all semi-Ulander beings, were just a little bit scared of the fully magical races.

Part of her still didn't completely trust them, either. There was just something about them, something she couldn't quite put her finger on. Since the war began, the Elementals were often the slowest Faction to act when Doomgaard moved; some said their sluggishness contributed to the destruction of the Barrowlands, and there was even talk of their Council dissuading the Pyres from sending supplies to the Ulandai battalions camped along the Thunderflow river because it would *cost* too much. They were notoriously obsessed with wealth.

And yet, they'd come to their aid today. Quickly, decisively. It was unlike them.

And how did they know exactly where we were?

How did they know we *were on the Gnomish ship?*

Willow let the questions float in her mind, as the Druyads had taught her to do. The answers would come when they were ready, and not a moment before. For now, there was no need to force it.

She tilted her face back to the sun and closed her eyes.

***

Dale wondered if he'd ever be truly warm again.

The waters of Canyon Lake had been heart-stoppingly cold. As soon as he'd plunged beneath the surface, the very breath in his lungs had seemed to freeze. For a horrifying few seconds, he thought he was going to sink like a stone into the murky, swirling darkness and never be seen again.

Then, somehow, he'd rallied himself. He wasn't a strong swimmer - he could *barely* swim, in fact - but when he glimpsed Tonya's limp form floating a few feet away, her hair cascading around her head like the ghostly body of a jellyfish, his limbs started working. He got one arm round her and dragged them both to the surface, kicking furiously, determined to keep them both alive.

He knew it was his fault she'd been up in the crow's nest in the first place. She'd climbed that mast because of what he'd said, and there was no way he was going to let her die as a result of his stupidity. He'd have jumped in the water even if everyone else had done it first.

The Gnomes hadn't pulled them aboard a moment too soon, either. As he'd kicked his way towards *The Copperdawn Voyager*, one arm hooked around Tonya and the other around the rope, something big had brushed against his foot in the waters below. He'd always look back on that as the moment he'd been seconds away from becoming crocodile food.

And now, despite being dressed in dry Elemental robes and bundled up in thick woollen cloaks in a toasty warm cabin with the curtains drawn, he still couldn't get the lakewater chill to leave his veins. A shiver overtook his whole body for a second, and next to him, Tonya's head lifted.

She blinked at him with sleepy brown eyes and said, 'Still cold?'

He nodded, pulling the cloaks tighter. 'You?'

'Yup.'

Across the room, Brooke was slumped to one side, her mouth ajar. Charlie snored softly in the chair nearest the fireplace. They hadn't seen Willow leave.

'I can still taste it,' Tonya murmured. 'The lake. It was… bitter, or something.'

'Yeah, it was. Bitter and freezing.'

'Maybe I should've stayed in Silversprog,' Tonya said, fidgeting in her purple Elemental robes. 'You guys have been *nothing* but trouble since you got here.'

Dale grinned. 'I know. You were a queen and everything.'

'I *am* a queen, and everything.'

She looked at him again, and he felt his face flush. It occurred to him how alien this situation would've been just a couple of days ago. Here he was, Dorky Dale Reed, bunched up next to Tonya Miller, one of the most popular girls in school. And not just Tonya from Farmont High, but Tonya who now knew about Uland, who'd *lived* in Uland for weeks. It was totally bizarre.

He wondered if she could see that familiar, annoying redness creep back into his cheeks in the flickering firelight. If she could, she didn't show it.

'Thanks for… you know… saving me, and stuff,' she said.

'No worries. Someone had to.' She grinned, and he swallowed. 'And I'm sorry for what I said before. Back on the other boat. That was dumb.'

'*So* dumb,' she agreed, still grinning. 'But I get it. I shouldn't have said what *I* said, about… you know…'

She nodded in Brooke's direction. Dale felt a sudden rush of panic, half expecting Brooke to sit up and say, '*What* was that about me?', but she continued sleeping, blonde hair strewn across one side of her face.

'Just… don't say anything, ok?' he whispered. 'Not that there's anything *to* say. Because there isn't. But still…'

Tonya leaned close and whispered conspiratorially, 'Your secret's safe with me, Casanova.'

'Casanova? What - '

The door to the cabin swung open, banging off the wall. Across the room, Charlie sat up with a start and blurted, 'Orchidema, wait!'; Brooke's eyes fluttered open, settled on Tonya and Dale huddled together on the bench, and widened.

Willow shut the door behind her. Her eyes burned golden in the dimmer light as she swept the room. Dale was conscious he was seeing her without her usual earthen-coloured cloak on for the first time: beneath it, she was dressed in a moss green tunic and dark olive leggings under segments of boiled leather armour; a simple rope belt was looped around her slender waist, and instead of boots, she wore thin-soled shoes that were scuffed and muddied from travel. She pushed fiery red hair from her face.

'Are you all awake now?'

Dale and Tonya sat up. They didn't see Brooke's gaze lingering on them.

'What happened to you?' Charlie said, rubbing his eyes. Then he jerked his hand back. 'Hey, my arm! It's working again.'

'It was the bean,' said Willow. 'Why do you never remember what the bean does?'

'Beans aren't that special where we're from,' Charlie replied.

Just then, the door opened behind Willow. She whipped around, her cloak billowing.

The same Elemental girl from before stood there, one hand on the doorknob. She looked at Willow, startled.

'Oh, I'm so sorry, my lady,' she said, embarrassed. 'I didn't mean to disturb you.'

When Willow didn't immediately reply, Brooke said, 'You didn't disturb us. Is something wrong?'

The girl shook her head. 'No, nothing's wrong. I've just been sent to summon you all out to the deck. The captain wants you out here. We have a guest.'

***

They followed Willow from the cabin to the open deck of the Elemental ship. Outside, the air was still and warm, and the waters of Canyon Lake sparkled under the bright, sunlit sky. Dale was glad of the heat, and judging from Tonya's expression, she was too.

Most of the Elemental sailors seemed to have cleared the deck. Only four remained, each robed in one of the customary colours of their Faction: red, green, purple and blue. They all carried staffs with colour-matching gemstones embedded in the heads. The girl who'd summoned them was nowhere to be seen.

'What's going on?' said Charlie, addressing both Willow and the Elementals on deck.

'Not sure,' Willow replied warily, eyeing the warlocks. Dale noticed her fingers twitching restlessly by her hip.

Brooke moved forward. 'What's happening here?' she said to the Elementals. 'Why were we called outside?'

'Step back, please,' replied one of the warlocks flatly.

'Why?'

'Just step back. It's for your own good.'

'I don't like this,' muttered Charlie, hand drifting towards his sword.

'Me neither,' said Willow. A single green spark popped between her fingers.

'What is *that*?' Tonya cried.

Whoosh.

A shadow raced across the deck and they all looked up, shielding their eyes. Something big had just passed through the air above the ship.

Whoosh. Whump, whump, whump.

At first, Dale couldn't make out what the thing silhouetted against the sunlight was. It hovered directly above the ship, cutting in and out of view in the glare. As it held there, it *whumped* rhythmic blasts of warm air down on them, over and over. The Elemental warlocks didn't move or even look up.

'Is that a helicopter?' Tonya called over the noise.

The *whumping* sound slowed, and Dale finally understood what it was: wings. Enormous feathered wings, beating in midair directly above their heads. And as the beating slowed, the thing descended closer and closer to the ship, its shadow pooling on the deck boards, until finally it was below the tip of the ship's mast and they could see it clearly for the first time.

'It's a peryton!' Brooke exclaimed delightedly.

Dale saw she was right. An enormous peryton, half deer and half bird, floated down to the deck. The blast from its wings almost knocked them off balance as first its long, peacock-like tail and then its hooves touched down on the boards. The deck creaked beneath its weight - it was much larger than Percius, who's taken them from Ringmoffren to Crookedstone all those months (or years?) ago.

'So *that's* what a peryton looks like,' said Charlie in an awestruck voice.

Of course, Dale thought, *he's never seen one up close before.*

The creature's antlered head swivelled in their direction and its onyx eyes settled on Charlie, who shrunk back a step. Dale grinned at that. Then he saw who was seated on the back of the peryton, and his grin became an 'O' of surprise.

'Wait,' said Brooke. 'Is that - '

'Lady Luno of Elementa!' bellowed one of the warlocks.

All four of the Elementals ducked their heads as Luno slipped from the stag-like creature's back and dropped gracefully to the deck. As soon as she was down, the peryton folded its wings tight to its body and snorted.

'There you are!' Luno exclaimed.

She strode towards them, spreading her arms. Just like before, when she'd represented her Faction at Fort Hammerfall, she wore a floor-length scarlet dress with a slit up one side, exposing an alabaster leg and high-heeled red boots as she walked; a gold sash was tied around her waist just below a red leather bodice, and a red silk cape draped over her shoulders, fastened just below her throat with a gold pin. Her bright red hair was tied up in a bun. As she approached, the sunlight caught her eyes and they flashed like rubies.

'Lady Luno,' said Willow, bowing her head.

The others did the same. Tonya's eyes ping-ponged between Luno and the peryton, which was now staring fixedly at one of the warlocks.

'Please, my friends, none of that,' Luno said dismissively, with a wave of a red-gloved hand.

Then, to Dale's surprise, she swept Willow up in a luxurious hug, pulling her tight. Willow awkwardly hugged her back.

'Oh it's just *so good* to see you again, Lady Willow!' Luno exclaimed, baring pearl-white teeth between perfectly-painted red lips. 'I couldn't *believe* it when the news reached me about your capture in the Glimmerglen.' She released her and, as Willow staggered backwards, turned her open arms towards Brooke. 'And Lady Woods of the Other World, you're *back!*'

As Brooke was gathered up into the red dress, Dale exchanged a glance with Charlie. Willow stood rigidly just behind them, arms by her sides.

Luno hugged Charlie and Dale in turn, gushing about how *wonderful* it was to see them, and how *delighted* she was to have them back in Uland, and then she came to Tonya. 'And who might you be?' she asked, cocking a red-dyed eyebrow.

For the first time in his life, Dale saw Tonya Miller squirm.

'I'm, uh, Tonya,' she said. 'I'm... friends... with this lot.'

'Then you're a friend of mine,' said Luno, taking Tonya's hand in both of hers. 'Welcome to Uland, my lady. I look forward to learning *all* there is to know about you.'

Tonya nodded, and Luno dropped her hand. She beamed at them; behind her, the peryton pawed restlessly at the deck boards.

'I simply had to come,' said the Elemental Factionhead, her unnaturally-bright red eyes drifting over them. 'I was in Eisdren on diplomatic business when word reached me about the Doomgaard assault on Silversprog.'

'Assault?' Tonya said quickly.

'Oh yes, I'm afraid it's been *quite* devastated,' said Luno, like she was passing on a snippet of juicy gossip. 'There was a full Doomgaard battalion waiting in the woods. Many Gnomes were killed, I believe, and half the town was burned to cinders. But fear not - once I got wind of what was happening, I sent my forces there to restore order right away while I myself came after you. It was easy enough to spot the Doomgaard vessels on a clear day like this, and they were so concerned with that Gnomish ship of yours that they didn't even see us coming. Most of them are at the bottom of the lake now, and good riddance.'

Tonya's face had fallen during Luno's recount, but the Elemental didn't seem to notice.

'And when I heard you were on your way to Nymm, I was simply *compelled* to offer my assistance. After all, you're the famous Hammerfall trio - if it wasn't for you, and Lady Willow, I myself may not even be here. And now there are *four* of you! I imagine the Council will be intrigued to hear how you managed to return after all these seasons.'

Dale could see Willow out of the corner of his eye as Luno spoke. She was still standing completely still, her eyes locked on the Factionhead.

'I'm here to escort you onwards,' Luno said. 'This ship is fast, but the lake is open and dangerous. More Doomgaard galleons will be on their way by now. And I believe time is of the essence.'

'How do you know that?' Willow asked abruptly.

Luno measured her with eyes so bright they almost glowed. 'Why, isn't time for your friends limited here? Something about turning to stone after three days?'

Tonya opened her mouth; Dale nudged her with his foot.

'Yes,' Willow said after a slight pause. 'Time is… of the essence.'

'Exactly.' Luno clapped her palms together. 'We'll travel by air. I'm afraid this particular beast is loyal only to me, she'll gore anyone else who tries mounting her. But we have a more amenable pair ready and waiting for you.'

She gestured to the sky. Dale looked up, and for the first time, noticed two more perytons circling high above the ship.

'They'll get us there in no time at all,' said Luno, smiling. 'Now, gather your things, my friends. Let's get you all to Nymm.'

Chapter Seventeen: Northward

Brooke tightened her grip on the peryton's mane and leaned into the wind, laughing breathlessly. The hood of her cloak had blown back long ago, leaving her hair free to whip about in the breeze; behind her, Tonya recoiled as another long blonde strand tried to enter her mouth.

'Brooke!' she cried over the rushing wind, 'quit moving around, your hair's in my face!'

'Sorry!' Brooke called back. 'I can't help it.'

'Just sit still!'

Behind Tonya, Willow peered down past the peryton's huge feathered wings as the waters of Canyon Lake blurred beneath them. Above, the sun was beginning its slow descent towards evening. The Elemental ships had already disappeared on the horizon.

'How much longer before we get there?' Tonya called over her shoulder.

'Get where?'

'To Nymm.'

Willow squinted past Tonya's head. The mountains were beginning to grow distinct in the distance. 'A few hours, maybe.'

'Hours? Geez,' moaned Tonya. 'My butt hurts already. These things should have saddles.'

Their peryton snorted and thrashed its head; its antlers gleamed dangerously in the sunlight.

'Careful,' said Willow. 'He can hear you.'

'He… knows what I'm saying?'

'Every word. If you keep insulting him he might decide to buck you into the lake.'

Tonya didn't say another word after that.

As soon as Luno was airborne, the other perytons had scooped them up from the Elemental ship and immediately set off for Nardren, the northern region of Uland. The girls were on one (Brooke had nabbed the front spot right away) and the boys on another, seated behind an Elemental warlock. Even from some distance away, it was clear neither of them were enjoying the experience as much as the girls - Dale was green, and Charlie was clinging to him for dear life.

Two more perytons had joined them mid-flight, each carrying three Elementals as part of Luno's entourage. She flew just ahead of everyone else on the largest peryton, which she'd greeted as Cinderwing during her remount on the deck of the ship.

Brooke knew something was up with Willow. She didn't have to be a body language expert to tell the Woodsgirl was on edge, but there hadn't been time to ask her about it before they'd taken flight. And now they were surrounded by Elementals, all of whom were in earshot.

She was a little suspicious of Luno herself. Seeing her again had taken her right back to the banquet at Fort Hammerfall, just before the battle. She remembered standing there awkwardly in that stupid Ulandai dress while the Factionheads scrutinised them and hundreds of banqueters pretended not to watch. She remembered King Sol, who refused to take their warnings about Decymero seriously, and Ravocus the Pyre, who looked as though he'd just crawled out of a coffin and might try to drag them back in with him. She remembered Murblok the Giant, and Empress Orchidema, and Yulerin the Druyad, who'd sent them back home.

Where is *Yulerin, anyway?* she wondered, watching Cinderwing glide ahead of them. *Willow said she hasn't seen him since the crescent moon, however long ago that was. Weeks? Months?*

Either way, Brooke hoped they'd see him again soon. It was the old man who'd given her the little leather book, and the book was what brought them back to Uland. Surely he *had* to be involved in all this somehow.

'Look!' said Tonya, pointing past her.

Brooke ducked her head to the right, squinting between the peryton's antlers. The mountains weren't quite as clear to her as they were to Willow's keen eye, but she could see them well enough - they had that dull blue quality mountains often have when they're far away, and they seemed to stretch all the way across the horizon, rising ever higher as the perytons skimmed above the lake.

'Nardren,' Willow called from behind them. 'The north. The giants live there now.'

'Are all of those mountains… you know… *dead* giants?' Brooke said. 'Like, the really old ones that used to rule Uland?'

'Wait, what?' said Tonya.

'Only the biggest ones,' Willow replied. 'The smaller mountains are usually just actual mountains. The largest ones are the Ancient Giants. You'll know them when you see them.'

'What are you two talking about?'

'We'll give you a history lesson later,' said Brooke, leaning forward again.

As they continued north, the blue of the sky deepened. Purple streaks started to appear over the mountains in the distance, and Brooke began to discern snow on some of their peaks. She could also feel the air growing colder and buried her fingers deeper in the peryton's thick mane, trying to keep her eyes on the static horizon rather than the constantly-moving waters below.

Finally, Willow said, 'There it is.'

'Nymm?' Tonya blurted in Brooke's ear. She'd been leaning against her back and Brooke wondered if the other girl had fallen asleep.

'No, not yet,' Willow said. 'But we're coming to the end of the lake. See?'

They looked and saw she was right. Just up ahead, Canyon Lake abruptly ended at a stony shore dotted with tiny houses, which in turn quickly gave way to low woodland; the woods merged into a dense, sweeping forest of dark green pine trees that seemed to stretch all the way to the feet of the mountains on the horizon.

'We'll have to put down soon,' said Willow.

'Aw, what?' moaned Tonya. 'Why can't we just fly straight to Nymm?'

'We just can't,' Willow replied, a little irritably. 'Trust me, I know where I'm going.'

'I didn't say otherwise,' Brooke heard Tonya mutter.

At Willow's urging, Brooke politely asked the peryton to speed up. It obeyed, and soon they were flying almost level with Cinderwing. The other three perytons also flew faster to keep up, their massive wings *whumping* in the still early-evening air.

'Lady Luno!' Willow shouted.

The Elemental Factionhead looked their way, her red cloak billowing impressively behind her like a superhero cape.

'We need to land,' Willow called, jabbing her finger downward. 'We can't fly here.'

Luno frowned, then nodded. She leaned forward and spoke to Cinderwing, and the creature immediately began to descend.

Within minutes, the lake was gone and they were racing above the stony shore. Brooke saw not-quite-human people near the tiny houses pointing and waving up at them, and she waved back. Then the shore was gone and they were sweeping over an endless legion of trees, the hooves of the perytons almost brushing their topmost branches.

'Where do we land?' Brooke said, looking left and right. 'I don't see any space.'

'Just wait,' said Willow.

Sure enough, bare hilltops soon began popping up here and there among the trees. They passed several before Willow said, 'There!' and pointed at one in particular with a wider, flatter summit than the others. The perytons circled down towards it before settling one after another onto the smooth terrain of the hilltop, their hooves clicking on the speckled grey stone. Brooke's peryton snorted fussily as they dismounted; the boys slid awkwardly from the back of theirs and Dale immediately made for the bushes on the hilltop perimeter, clutching his mouth.

The Elementals gathered together and bowed their heads as Luno slipped gracefully from Cinderwing's back. A green-cloaked warlock with dreadlocked hair handed her a staff made from pure white wood, set with a glittering ruby in the head. Luno tucked a long strand of scarlet hair behind her ear and turned to Willow.

'Why did we land?'

'It's not safe here for these particular perytons,' Willow said, watching a pale-faced Dale return from the bushes. 'There are creatures in these woods that'll prey on them.'

'Prey on *these?*' exclaimed Tonya, gesturing towards their mount. It was scenting the air with huge hairy nostrils, its massive antlers tipped back against its mane.

'Yes,' Willow replied. 'These are Suthdren perytons. They're big and powerful, but there are beasts in the north that've learned how to kill them. They'll pull them right out of the air. We'd need Narsdren perytons to keep flying, and we don't have any. We'll go on foot from here.'

Tonya sighed and muttered, 'Great.'

'Speaking of which,' Willow continued, addressing Luno, 'we can make the rest of the journey by ourselves, my lady. You don't need to come with us. We appreciate your help but I'm sure you have… better things to do, as a Factionhead.' She offered a small bow.

Luno smiled. 'Lady Willow, you flatter me. But your cause is absolutely crucial right now, and we won't rest until we've seen you safely to your destination. Elementa is at your disposal.'

Brooke thought Willow's reciprocated smile was somewhat forced.

'Which way?' said Charlie.

Willow turned in a full circle, scanning the forest with keen golden-brown eyes. A cool breeze swirled across the hilltop, snatching at everyone's cloaks and hair. Brooke shivered, pulling her own cloak a little tighter.

It's so much colder here, she thought. *And the mountains still look really far.*

Willow bent, picked a tuft of grass growing from a cleft in the rock, and let it float away on the breeze. She watched it for a moment, then pointed in what Brooke assumed must be a north-western direction.

'That way,' she said.

'By your lead,' said Luno, inclining her head.

'You'll need to send the perytons back,' said Willow. 'They won't be safe here, especially after dark.'

Luno snapped her fingers. The Elementals grabbed their staffs from the perytons and spoke quietly to each of them. One by one, the great beasts took flight again, almost knocking their former passengers over with the blast of wind from their wings. They watched them circle back into the sky and fly off towards Canyon Lake in a 'V' formation, with Cinderwing at the head.

'Alright,' said Willow. 'We'll try to cover as much ground as possible before darkness falls, but we'll have to hurry. This way.'

She started across the hilltop and the others followed. Brooke glanced back once at the silhouetted perytons gliding towards the lake and found herself wondering, quite unexpectedly, what had happened to Jayne.

***

The woods closed in around them almost instantly.

As soon as they were off the flat, bare hilltop, the ground began sloping steeply down into a dense green forest, its floor carpeted with jutting rocks and pine needles. The trees grew thick and tall around them, but unlike the dark, spider-infested Withering Woods of the Glimmerglen, this forest was airy and bright, illuminated with shafts of golden sunlight knifing through the leaf canopy above them. Birds twittered and whistled among their branches, flitting from tree to tree.

It reminded Charlie of the woods in the Barrowlands, where he'd first met the trolls after they rescued him and the other Birchfell villagers from the Doomgaard prisoner wagon. That seemed like a lifetime ago now. He wondered - not for the first time since arriving back in Uland - what had happened to them. Were they all still alive? Had they gotten caught up in the war? Would he see them again?

'It's so steep,' complained Tonya. 'Why's it so *steep?*'

'It's a hill,' said Brooke.

Dale tripped. Charlie caught him by the arm, right before he went down.

'Thanks,' said the other boy. His face still hadn't entirely returned to its usual colour since the peryton flight. Charlie, who'd been quietly terrified the whole time, understood.

'No worries,' he replied. 'Try not to break your face before we get to Nymm.'

'I'll try. I wish she'd slow down.'

Willow ranged ahead of them, darting nimbly between the trees while they did their best to keep up. The Elementals didn't help, either - the warlocks insisted on moving in a tight procession behind Luno, who didn't seem to be in a big hurry herself.

'Argh!' Tonya cried, swiping at the air. 'Those bugs are huge! I *hate* the woods.'

'How did you ever survive on that camping trip?' said Brooke.

Charlie saw Willow stop and look back, which she'd already had to do several times since leaving the hilltop. He quickened his pace, catching up to her just as she started off again.

'You always go this fast?' he said.

'Always,' she replied. 'I'm going at a *normal* pace. You're all just slow.'

They carried on without speaking for a minute. A little way behind them, Tonya continued complaining about everything in sight. Luno and the Elementals said nothing.

'How far to Nymm?' Charlie asked between breaths.

'Not far,' Willow said. He noticed she made no sound as she walked. 'There's a path up ahead. It'll be easier then. We'll go faster.'

'Wanna bet?'

She looked at him, gold flecks catching the light. 'Bet? Why?'

'Never mind.' He almost tripped too, just about keeping his balance. 'When we get there, will there be food?'

Willow snorted. 'Of course there'll be food. Is that all you ever think about, Charlie Flint?'

'No. I think about other stuff.'

'You'll have food,' said Willow. 'And trees to sleep in.'

'Trees?'

Willow nodded. 'Very comfortable ones, too.'

Charlie shook his head, grinning at the thought of Dale trying to sleep in a tree. Then: 'This… healing seed, you found - it'll work?'

'Yes,' said Willow. 'It should. I think.'

'You *think?*'

'It's… sort of our last hope,' she said. 'We've tried almost everything else, for months. Nothing's worked. The Empress fights hard, but her illness is… determined.'

'You said it was poison?'

'Yes. Very powerful. It would've killed anyone else already, but she's strong.'

'Yeah. Strong.'

Willow looked at him again, lingering this time. Charlie deliberately avoided her gaze until she looked away.

'How long does she have?' he asked. 'Yunno, until she…'

'Dies?' Willow said. He nodded. 'Days. Months. Hours. No-one really knows. We thought her time had arrived more than once. But as I said before, I don't believe Decymero actually meant to kill her. He did it to draw me out.'

'Why?' said Charlie. 'Why you? Because of Hammerfall?'

Willow didn't reply for a moment. Beneath their feet, the ground was starting to level out.

'Something more than that,' she said, finally. 'I'll tell you about it later. It's not… safe to do so right now.'

'Ok,' said Charlie, though he didn't really understand.

Behind them, Tonya whined, 'Are we there yet? How much *further?*'

'Your friend is annoying,' Willow said matter-of-factly.

'Wait til she finds out she has to sleep in a tree.'

***

A short time later, they came to the foot of the hill and the forest floor flattened out under their boots. Willow led them on a meandering path between the trees, abruptly changing direction every so often, but always heading in a general north-westerly direction. Charlie kept pace with her; the others trailed a little behind them. The air was still and pleasant here; luminescent insects flitted through the shafts of light from the forest canopy above them, buzzing by their ears, zipping away before they could be swatted. Brooke had the impression the bugs were following them.

'Ugh, I hate these things,' Tonya muttered, swiping at one that looked like a plump, blue dragonfly. It retreated to a safe distance and continued drifting after them.

'Be thankful they're not dangerous,' Luno said behind them. It was the first time she'd spoken since they left the hilltop. 'The Fyreflicks in Elementa would've left burning bites all over your arm by now. And then we'd have had to freeze it off, just to save the rest of you.'

'Freeze it off?' said Brooke, looking back. 'Like, her whole arm?'

'Why, yes,' Luno replied, her red irises glinting in the shadows cast by the trees. 'It's the only way to stop the Fyreflick spread. Freeze the limb, smash it, and seal what's left. It isn't pretty.'

Brooke and Tonya both shivered; neither of them swiped at the bugs after that. They walked on a bit before Luno spoke again. 'How exactly did you come to be here again, Lady Woods?'

Up ahead, Brooke thought she saw Willow turn an ear their way, as though she'd heard the question. She paused for a second before answering.

'We're not really sure. It just sort of… happened.'

'We fell into a book,' said Tonya breezily.

Ton…

'A book?' said Luno. Casually, Brooke thought, but her interest had been piqued.

'Yes,' Brooke said, before Tonya could divulge any more. 'It was just random. Like I said, we don't really know how it happened.'

'And, if I might ask, where did this book come from?'

'The old man gave it to you, right?' said Tonya. 'That's what you said on the boat.'

Tonya, shut up!

'Yes.'

'The old man?' said Luno. 'Do you mean Yulerin, of the Druyads?'

Again, Brooke hesitated before replying. Something told her to word her answers carefully, for whatever reason. 'Yes. Yulerin.'

'How intriguing. And did Master Yulerin tell you *how* the book could bring you back here?'

'No. We don't know how it happened. It just did.'

'I see.' There was a momentary stiffness in Luno's tone, but it quickly melted away. 'Well, it's marvellous to have you back again. All of you. Do you expect to stay longer this time?'

'Maybe,' she said. 'It... might not be up to us, I suppose.'

'Well, the Elementals are here to assist in any way we can.' Luno drew in a breath and let it out slowly. 'I must say, these woods are extremely pleasant indeed. I am *so* looking forward to visiting Nymm for the first time. And it'll be simply wonderful to see the Empress again. Such a *shame* what's happened to her, don't you think?'

'Yes, a real shame. Excuse me, Lady Luno - I just want to check if Dale's feeling alright after the flight. He didn't look well.'

'He full-on barfed his guts out,' Tonya said.

'Yeah. We better make sure he's ok.'

'As you wish,' said Luno.

Brooke took Tonya by the arm and quickened her pace, putting a little distance between them and the Elementals. Dale, who was still some way behind Willow and Charlie, jumped when they reached him.

'Hey, sicky,' said Tonya. 'Feeling better?'

'Mostly,' Dale replied, staring at the ground. His colour had returned but Brooke thought he still looked worse for wear. 'I don't think I like perytons.'

'Just warn us if you're gonna hurl again,' Tonya said.

'Let's not say anything else until we get to Nymm, ok?' said Brooke, looking pointedly at Tonya. She could feel

Luno's eyes on her back. 'We can discuss everything properly when we're there. It'll make more sense then.'

Tonya frowned, then shrugged. 'Fine by me. I just hope we get there soon. Do you think they'll have baths? The Gnomes drew one for me every night and I've kinda gotten used to them.'

'Maybe,' Brooke said.

Tonya sighed. 'I miss being the Queen.'

Dale glanced sideways at both of them and said nothing.

A few minutes later, they arrived at a path. It was paved with ancient, crumbling stones, and was just wide enough for three people to walk side by side. Brooke remembered the magical Stone Road that ran in a complete loop all the way around Uland, and wondered how far they were from it right now.

They walked on for some time, following the path as it wound through the forest. Mysterious birds sang in the trees and squirrel-like creatures scurried off into the undergrowth as they passed. The shafts of light cutting through the tree canopy grew gradually weaker the further they went. Brooke could also feel the air getting colder and hugged her cloak tighter to her body. Even Tonya eventually became too tired to complain, and they all fell silent.

Finally, after what felt like at least two hours of constant walking, the Elementals abruptly stopped and Luno announced, 'We rest here.'

Willow turned, her golden eyes flashing in the shadows. 'We should keep going… my lady.'

'In good time, Lady Willow,' said Luno, handing her staff to one of the warlocks. 'But we all need rest and sustenance if we're to continue on at this pace. This looks as good a place as any for a break, don't you think?'

Willow cast around. 'It's not safe,' she replied, 'but it'll do.'

They all took a seat on the nearest rock or log, apart from Willow, who stood impatiently on the path. To Brooke's surprise, the Elementals immediately handed them little parcels of food, each of which contained a selection of nuts, berries and sweet cake. They guzzled it hungrily. Afterwards, the warlocks made a big show of conjuring water in jars and distributed some to each of them. It tasted a little sour to Brooke but she was too thirsty to turn it down.

'We should keep going,' Willow said as soon as they'd finished eating and drinking. 'There's still some way to go.'

Luno got back to her feet. 'Of course. I'm sure you're anxious to get to Nymm. As am I.'

Willow nodded, just once, and said, 'Let's go, then.'

The further north they travelled, the more the forest seemed to change around them. At first, there were only trees on either side of the ancient stone path; they grew tall and straight, and the waning early evening light lanced easily between them. It reminded Brooke of how the Forest of Lost Souls had looked after their night in Jayne's house - in daylight, it'd been peaceful and pretty, and she hadn't minded the walk at all. This northern forest felt the same.

But after a while, the stones paving the path started to show cracks, and the trail itself became less distinct. The trees drew in closer around them, becoming greener and more gnarled with each passing minute, until there wasn't a patch of brown bark in sight - every tree was completely covered in a thick layer of fuzzy green moss from their roots to their topmost branches, and they leered over them as they walked. The carpet of pine needles had also been replaced with spongy green moss, punctuated here and there with strange, orchid-like plants that seemed to unfurl their white petals as they passed. The air grew thick and heavy, like they were in a giant green sauna, yet Brooke felt herself getting chillier with each passing step.

One by one, the shafts of golden sunlight from above faded away until there was nothing but green around them in every direction: green ground, green trees, a bright green leaf canopy overhead. The path itself was soon overtaken by moss and the stones disappeared, leaving them to walk on what felt like a soft, flexible carpet. The scent from the white orchids was almost overpowering.

'I feel… kinda weird,' said Tonya.

'Me too,' Dale replied. 'Like I'm… asleep. Are we? Asleep?'

'Just keep going,' said Willow from just ahead of them. 'We're almost there.'

'I feel funny too,' said Brooke. And then she giggled, surprising herself. She tried to stifle it with her hand and only giggled more.

'What's so funny?' said Charlie, looking at her. Then he started too, chuckling quietly at first before erupting into full-blown laughter. Dale was laughing too.

Brooke heard tittering from behind them and looked back. The Elementals all had their heads down, trembling with barely-suppressed laughter. Even Luno had a hand over her mouth and was staring hard at the ground.

'What's… h-happening?' Brooke managed, tears of laughter rolling down her cheeks. 'I-I… I can't stop!'

'Neither c-can I,' Tonya said breathlessly. Next to her, Dale doubled over.

'It's the forest,' Willow said. She was grinning but seemed to have her laughter in check. 'It's trying to force us away, so we're very close. In fact…'

She abruptly left the path, disappearing between the moss-covered trees. The others stood where they were, bent double with laughter. Brooke could barely breathe; stitches dug deep into her sides. Charlie had fallen to the ground and was curling himself into a ball. The Elementals were leaning on their staffs to keep from dropping, too.

The air was heavy with magic. Brooke knew she was breathing it in and couldn't stop.

Willow reappeared and said, 'This way. Hurry!'

They managed to haul themselves after her through gales of laughter, holding on to one another for support. Brooke staggered into Dale and clutched at his arm. He held her too, crying laughter into her shoulder.

Willow led them between the trees, clambering over exposed mossy roots and decaying logs peppered with colourful mushrooms. Brooke's mind was a jumbled blur and her midriff was in agony from the constant laughter. She continued holding onto Dale, who seemed like he was about to fall to the ground at any moment. Her head was spinning.

And then, suddenly, the trees ended.

They came out into a wide, empty space. Up above, the red evening sky was clearly visible through a circular gap in the forest canopy. Marigold sunlight knifed between the trees in places, catching them in the eyes.

Just as abruptly as it had started, their laughter died out. It was as though they'd been starved of oxygen and someone had twisted a valve somewhere, flooding this new space with fresh air. The pungent scent of the white orchids faded. Brooke looked at Dale, saw his nose was just inches away from hers, and quickly let go of him. She stumbled back, flustered and dizzy.

'What… the heck was that?' said Tonya, holding her temples.

'Where are we?' said Charlie.

Brooke looked around, taking in the space properly for the first time. It was a clearing, wide and circular, matching the gap in the leaf canopy above them. Instead of spongy moss beneath their feet, there was ankle-high grass. Birds flitted between the trees along the edges of the circle, chirruping excitedly.

'What's that?' Dale said.

She half expected to see a little gnarled white tree in the middle of the clearing, but it wasn't there this time. There were no flutes or fiddles, either. Instead, the perimeter of the circle was ringed with dark grey stones, each as tall as her and flat on the inward-facing side. Runes had been crudely carved into them around head-height.

'A passage circle,' Luno said, gazing around the clearig.

Willow walked to the centre of the circle and beckoned them. They joined her, still wiping laughter tears from their eyes. The Elementals cast wary glances at the stones.

'What happens now?' said Tonya.

'Just wait,' said Willow.

They waited, watching. The copper sunshafts coming from one side of the clearing grew lower and stronger. Brooke had to shield her face with her arm to avoid getting blinded by the setting sunlight. The entire circle glowed like it was on fire.

'Ok,' said Willow slowly. 'Everyone turn around. Look for a passage.'

'What d'you mean, "a passage"?' said Dale.

'You'll know it when you see it.'

They did as she said, turning on the spot, squinting towards the stones. Brooke saw nothing but trees beyond them. She expected the runes to turn blue like those in the Great Cavern, but they didn't. There was nothing to see except sunlight and trees and shadows and -

'There!' Charlie cried.

They followed his pointing finger.

'There what?' said Tonya.

'I don't see anything,' said Dale.

'I see it!' cried Brooke.

'As do I,' said Luno.

Something had happened to the trees between two of the stones on one side of the circle. They seemed to have lined up, forming a new, narrow trail extending straight into the forest. It was as though they'd been planted that way a very, very long time ago, but Brooke hadn't seen any suggestion of it until Charlie pointed it out.

'That's it - well done,' said Willow. 'The passage only makes itself known for a few minutes at sunset, and it's never in the same place.'

'Bonkers,' Dale said.

'Indeed,' said Luno softly.

'This is the way to Nymm,' Willow said. The final embers of evening sunlight faded and her eyes bloomed gold. 'Follow me.'

Chapter Eighteen: Nymm

They left the stone circle and entered the passage.

The scent from the white orchids was gone and they were no longer laughing, but Dale's sides still ached; he couldn't catch his breath at one point and wasn't entirely sure how he'd managed to stay on his feet. It'd started to feel like drowning in the open air. He wondered how many other people had reached that part of the forest, and what had happened to them.

'Hey,' said Tonya. 'Where's the path gone?'

They looked back. The stone circle had disappeared - there were only thick green trees behind them now, blocking off the end of the passage. No way back.

'Why doesn't that surprise me?' said Brooke.

'Come on,' said Willow.

They carried on along the narrow trail along a carpet of soft green grass between the passage trees, which grew up and over their heads in a sort of tunnel shape. The bright green moss was completely gone now - the trees here were slender and white, with leaves the colour of fire: orange, yellow, red, and some gold. They all gleamed lustrously, though Dale was no longer sure where the light was coming from.

He also wasn't entirely sure how long they'd been walking for (had it been just a few minutes or several hours?) when the end of the passage came into sight up ahead.

'Finally!' said Tonya. 'My feet are killing me.'

As they drew closer, the passage end gradually became brighter, and brighter, until none of them could look directly at it. The trees lining the passage seemed to simply end, framing a shimmering, luminescent wall that threw back a distorted reflection of their faces. Dale thought it was like looking into liquid glass. The brightness seemed to emanate from somewhere beyond it.

'This is the gateway,' said Willow, standing close to the liquid glass wall. It dappled her green-tinged skin with golden light. 'Well, *one* of the gateways, anyway. Nymm's on the other side. When you walk through, lean as far forward as you can. And hold your breath.'

'Why?' said Brooke.

'You'll see. Lady Luno, why don't you go first?'

Luno looked slightly taken aback, but came forward anyway. She peered closely at the shimmering wall, glanced sideways at Willow, and stepped through. The wall rippled, but not quite like water, Dale thought. Luno's red cloak blurred for a moment on the other side, and she was gone.

One of the warlocks hurried up to the wall. 'We must go next,' he said.

'Fine by me,' said Willow.

Six of the seven Elementals went through the liquid glass wall and disappeared. The seventh remained behind, leaning on his staff.

'After you,' he said, smiling amicably.

Willow seemed to hesitate, then motioned towards the wall. 'Brooke, you go.'

She did, pushing through with her arms outstretched. Dale heard her take in a gulp of air right before she disappeared. The green of her tunic blurred for a moment on the other side before she vanished.

Charlie went next, then Tonya, who let out a low moan before disappearing. Finally, Dale stepped up to the wall. He was a little surprised to feel a chill coming off it, and hesitated.

'Breathe in,' said Willow. 'And lean forward.'

'Okey dokey.'

He took a breath, stepped forward and pushed through the wall.

And then he was underwater.

Or at least, that's how it felt. The ground was suddenly gone and he found himself kicking in open space, his arms waving uselessly in front of him. The sounds of the forest - the rustling of leaves, whisperings of wind, twittering of birds - was also gone, replaced with a muffled nothingness, like some invisible substance was pressing in against his ears. It pressed at his eyes too and he tried squeezing them shut but discovered he couldn't. The distant light was still there, drawing closer. But he wasn't moving.

Suddenly, he realised he couldn't breathe. He began to panic, kicking his feet furiously in the liquid nothingness, his arms pinwheeling in slow motion. His mouth fell open and whatever was occupying the space around him tried to roll down his throat, choking him.

Lean forward! he screamed inside. *Lean forward!*

But he couldn't.

He was stuck, floating in something that felt like water, flailing in panic. He couldn't breathe, couldn't really see anything beyond the distant, blurred light. The others were gone. He'd messed it up somehow. And now here he was, drowning at the entrance to Nymm when he'd managed to survive the crocodile-infested waters of Canyon Lake.

Lean… forward…

Darkness closed on the edges of his vision. He knew it'd be over soon. His eyelids started to close. He stopped kicking.

Then there was a hand on his back. And another, right on the back of his head. Pushing, tilting him forward. The light grew brighter, colours rushed towards his face. He reached out with one weak hand…

Someone grabbed it, yanked him forward, and he burst out into open air.

'There he is!'

Charlie had him by the arm, pulling him. Dale sat up, gasping in lungfuls of air. His head was spinning, his eyes struggling to come into focus.

'Are you alright?' he heard Brooke say.

'He's fine,' said Willow, emerging behind him, one hand still on his back. 'He just got a bit disoriented on the way through.'

'What… what was that?' Dale spluttered.

'Stand up, squirt,' said Charlie.

Dale looked around. He was sitting up to his chest in the same shimmering liquid. Charlie was also in it up to his knees, smirking down at him. He offered his hand again.

'Really screwed that one up, didn't you?'

Dale took in a final deep breath and grabbed Charlie's hand. The other boy hauled him to his feet. They both looked down.

'How are we standing in this?' Dale said. He looked Charlie up and down. 'And how are we bone dry?'

'Not a clue,' said Charlie.

Willow brushed past them, stepping out of the shimmer. She was also completely dry. The others were gathered by the edge along a low stone wall, watching them. Dale caught Brooke's concerned gaze; she blinked and turned away.

They stepped out. Dale looked back and saw they'd emerged from what appeared to be a pool of luminescent water, ringed by stone. Except it wasn't water, because his entire body was dry. And he'd sat up in it, as though there was a firm surface beneath. Which meant…

'It's at a right angle to the passage entrance,' he said absently, picturing it in his head. 'When we came through the wall, it was as if we were lying flat in there.' He looked at Willow. 'So basically, I almost drowned in a foot of water.'

'It's not water,' said Willow. 'I told you, Woodspeople can't swim. And you didn't *almost drown*, you just needed to sit up.'

'Don't worry, I did it too,' said Tonya. 'Just not as dramatically as you.'

'Certainly a clever way to enter,' said Luno, studying the pool. 'Most ingenious.'

The pool itself was in the centre of a woodland clearing, hemmed in on all sides by more of the thin, white-barked trees. The grass beyond the rim of the pool was just as soft and thick as that in the passage from the stone circle, except here it was peppered with dry, crunchy leaves. An old, ornate lantern hung from a crooked pole just above the pool, casting a warm, silver-white glow around the clearing - it was the source of light they'd been able to see through the shimmer wall.

'It's so quiet here,' said Brooke, gazing up at the star-filled sky above them.

Willow nodded. 'It is,' she agreed, before adding, 'Lady Luno, your people will need to put their staffs down for a moment.'

Luno frowned. 'Why?'

'Who are you?'

They all jumped, apart from Willow. The voice had come from right behind them. They turned as one to look.

A male Woodsperson stood a few yards away, watching them with glowing golden eyes. Like Willow, he wore a plain brown cloak, pinned just below the throat and parted in the middle to reveal green leather armour underneath. His skin was also tinged green, perhaps more vibrantly than hers. He was taller than her, too, and the hair beneath the hood of his cloak was light brown rather than fiery red. His green hands were clasped loosely as he leaned against one of the trees.

'Lay down your weapons,' Willow said slowly.

The Elementals looked to Luno, who nodded. One by one, they laid their staffs down on the grass. Luno handed hers to the nearest warlock, who placed it at her feet. Charlie unsheathed his sword and set it down.

Willow took a step forward, briefly ducked her head, and said, 'Rowan-thir.'

The Woodsman returned the nod. 'Willow-mir.'

Dale frowned. 'Wait... Willow-*meer*?'

'It's my proper name,' she said. Beneath the lantern light, her cheeks reddened. 'It's only used here, in Nymm.'

'Oh.'

The Woodsman ignored Dale, continuing to scrutinise Willow; the gold in his eyes had faded a little, revealing rich blue irises beneath.

'Who are these strangers?' he asked evenly.

'These are my friends,' Willow said, gesturing, 'from the Other-world. They were here many seasons ago. And this is Lady Luno of Elementa.'

Rowan-thir's eyes flicked briefly to Luno, then returned to Willow.

'Why?' he said curtly.

'Rude,' Dale heard Tonya mutter.

'I have something for the Empress,' Willow said. 'A cure for her ailment.'

Rowan-thir's eyes flared. 'A cure?'

'Yes. A healing seed from the Glimmerglen. I need to take it to her at once.'

The Woodsman straightened up. 'At once.' Then, addressing the rest: 'We'll return your weapons later, once the Council has been informed of your arrival.'

Dale heard the Elementals gasp in surprise. He looked down and saw their staffs (and Charlie's sword) were gone - they were now in the hands of several more Woodspeople, who'd appeared from between the trees around the clearing. No-one had seen them take the weapons.

Luno's eyes flashed red in the lantern light. 'I don't believe we gave our permission for that, good sir.'

Rowan-thir smiled. 'You're in Nymm now, Lady Luno of Elementa. We do not need anyone's permission here. Now, if you'll all follow me.'

With that, he turned and disappeared between the trees, where a narrow path was now visible. The other Woodspeople waited, watching them in silence.

'Ok, let's go,' said Willow.

'After you, Willow-mir,' said Charlie, bowing.

She threw him a look and started down the path.

***

The trail wound between the white-barked trees at shoulder-width, forcing them to walk in single file. It was dark here and the trees appeared ghostly in the gloom. Willow and Rowan-thir led the way, with the other Woodspeople following just a few yards behind the Elemental procession at the rear. No-one spoke, though Dale was sure he heard a couple of the warlocks muttering under their breath.

Soon, the path began to ascend, and stone steps appeared beneath their feet. The trail continued to wind through the woods, never widening, growing steeper by the minute. Dale felt a stitch digging into his side and began to wish they were back in Twiggleton Manor or seated by the fireplace in Jayne's impossible house.

Every non-Woodsperson was getting a little out of breath by the time the path abruptly levelled out and the trees thinned around them. They emerged onto a grassy plateau with another ornate lantern to one side. Above, the night sky was blanketed with a billion glittering stars and a fat, white moon.

And below, Nymm stretched out before them.

'Wow,' Brooke breathed.

'Majorly,' added Tonya.

Dale's mind struggled to immediately comprehend what he was looking at.

At first, it appeared to be a vast forest filled with enormous trees and dotted with pools of multi-coloured light: pinks, blues, greens, yellows and purples, all wavering between the shadows. Then, as his eyes adjusted, he saw that many of the trees were in fact buildings of some sort, blending seamlessly into the woodland landscape around them, and the pools of light were open spaces, like public squares, paved with smooth stone and ringed with lanterns. The lanterns burned in an array of different colours, and the squares were connected to one another by paved stone roads, also lined with lanterns. Figures moved along the paths and through the squares, going to and fro between the tree-buildings.

'Look at *that*,' said Charlie.

His head was tilted back. Dale tracked the line of his gaze and felt his own eyes widen.

The trees of Nymm grew hundreds - if not thousands - of feet above them, their branches extending out in all directions, interconnecting with each other to form a vast, leafy bough web that blocked out portions of the night sky entirely in places; many of the boughs were as thick as the steel beams Dale had seen in unfinished skyscrapers, and suspended from them were hundreds and hundreds of smaller tree-buildings, each lit warmly from within by lantern light. The whole city, if that's what it could be called, looked like it was upside-down.

And as his eyes grew sharper, Dale realised he could see many more Woodspeople up in the trees than were down on the ground, strolling leisurely along the branches, leaning out of windows in their hanging houses, ascending or descending from the complex, glittering canopy on rope ladders or staircases that snaked around the trunks themselves. Fireflies danced among the leaves of the trees, keeping just out of reach of the strange, bat-like creatures swooping just below them, creating a kind of sonorous music with the beat of their tiny wings. The air here was cool and refreshing, and bristling with magic.

'Welcome to Nymm,' said Rowan-thir, hands still clasped casually by his abdomen. 'Please, this way.'

He started down another path from the plateau and they followed. Brooke, who was gazing in wonder up at the tree canopy, stumbled into Charlie, who in turn bumped Tonya.

'Careful,' said Willow. 'It's steep here.'

She was right. The trail from the plateau was even narrower than the path from the pool, zig-zagging down a grassy incline to the forest floor. There were no rails here - if any of them slipped, they'd tumble all the way to the bottom. Dale kept his eyes fixed on the back of Tonya's head, refusing to look down until he felt the path growing flatter under his boots. It reminded him vaguely of the staircase in the Great Cavern inside Mount Aibal, where they'd first arrived in Uland. That'd been six months ago for them, six years for Willow.

But it seems like a lifetime ago now, he thought, as the path levelled out again.

Then they were on the forest floor, and the real size of Nymm started to become apparent. From there, the trees seemed truly enormous, towering above them all the way up to the forest canopy; among them were the tree-like buildings, which perhaps had once been trees themselves and were now hollowed-out versions dotted with glowing windows and wooden balconies, topped with flat roofs overhanging the trunks themselves. Every tree-building was a unique height, shape and design - Dale thought they all looked somehow thrown-together and, simultaneously, intricately constructed with great care. The buildings spread right to the distant perimeter of the city, where the open forest floor ended abruptly at the wall of white-barked trees.

They followed Rowan-thir along one of the paved stone pathways, passing beneath the lanterns and through the little squares where multiple roads converged. Beyond the pathways, the entire forest floor was covered in a thick layer of lustrous green grass, broken up by patches of colourful wildflowers; bumblebees the size of tennis balls buzzed lazily back and forth between each patch, bumping into one another in mid air. Dale spotted a creature that looked like a fox with the wings of an eagle sprouting from its back, curled up in a hollow between the roots of a tree. It observed them with keen yellow eyes, flexing ferocious talons where its forepaws should be.

Willow saw him staring. 'It's an Enfield,' she said. 'They're guardians of the forest. Don't worry, it won't hurt us.'

'You sure?' said Dale, trying and failing to break eye contact with the creature.

'I'm sure. Just don't touch one if it comes close.'

More Woodspeople were passing them on the road now. They were all dressed in a similar way to Willow and Rowan-thir, and all of them had the same flecks of gold in their eyes as they gazed at their group. Some looked younger than Willow, others appeared much older than Rowan-thir; some were tall, others short; some had dark hair while some were brunette, or even almost blonde. Occasionally they passed one with red hair but none were quite as fiery as Willow - even here, she stood out from the others.

And, Dale noticed, passing Nymmites were staring at her just as much as them.

'This place is beautiful,' said Brooke in an awe-struck tone, her head tilted as far back as it would go. 'And it's *huge*. How many people live here?'

Rowan-thir regarded her with a flicker of curiosity as he glided along the road. 'There are many of us, but not as many as there *once* were. The people of Nymm have been… condensed… into this place by other Factions across Uland.' He glanced at Luno as he said this, but she appeared not to notice. 'There was a time when we were everywhere. I'm surprised you haven't learned this already from the histories.'

'They don't know the histories,' Willow pointed out. 'They have their own.'

Rowan-thir nodded. 'In any case, what you see here is what's left of our people, for the most part. We were once an Empire, and now we're not.'

'I need to see Orchidema,' Willow reiterated.

'You will. I've sent word to the palace. I believe they're expecting us presently.'

'What palace?' said Dale.

No sooner had the words left his mouth, however, than it appeared up ahead. It couldn't have been anything other than the palace, either: it was a tree in itself, growing right in the centre of the forest floor, its massive boughs spreading out over the smaller tree-buildings gathered around it; Dale guessed it must be half the height of the biggest trees and three times their width. Thousands of brightly-coloured lights winked in and out among its uppermost leaves, which were all red and orange and brown and gold, and more lights burned steadily in the hundreds of windows carved into its trunk. Eerie music drifted from somewhere inside it, hanging in the air around them as they approached.

'That's a big tree,' Charlie said, gazing up at it.

'Palace,' Willow corrected.

'Fascinating,' said Luno. The warlocks murmured their agreement.

As they drew closer, a younger Woodsboy hurried up to Rowan-thir, whispered something in his ear and darted off again.

'The Empress is expecting us,' he said. 'Apparently she's eager to see the Other-worlders in particular.'

'I'm content to wait,' Luno said courteously, though Dale picked up a tinge of something else in her voice. 'Perhaps you could provide us with refreshments? We've had a long journey.'

Not as long as ours, Dale thought.

'Of course,' said Rowan-thir, motioning towards another path leading to one of the tree-buildings nearby.

'If you follow my men, they'll take you to the banqueting hall.'

Luno nodded and walked briskly after a pair of Woodspeople, with her entourage of warlocks in tow. The remaining Woodspeople of Rowan-thir's party followed; he waited for them all to move out of earshot before addressing Willow: 'You brought Elementals here? Are you mad?'

The others looked at him in surprise. Willow blinked and replied, 'I had no choice. They rescued us from the Doomgaard. It would've been incredibly suspicious if we'd turned down their offer of help.'

'Even so,' said Rowan-thir, the gold flecks in his eyes flaring. 'The Council will not welcome their presence here.'

'The Council can blame me,' Willow said, 'as usual.'

Rowan-thir made a *hmmm* sound and started towards the great tree in the centre of the city.

***

Dozens of golden eyes turned on them as they made their way through the palace.

Inside, the colossal tree was warm and bright, illuminated with lanterns and stone fireplaces set into the trunk. Brooke had no idea how those fires weren't burning the tree to the ground, but she'd learned long ago not to question what went on in Uland.

'It's a city full of Willows,' Charlie murmured next to her.

The Woodspeople within the palace would stop what they were doing to stare openly at them as they passed. Here, the Nymmites were dressed in more regal-looking cloaks and often had their hair tied up in elaborate plaits, but for the most part, they all looked exactly like Willow and Rowan-thir, at least as far as Brooke could tell.

We probably all look the same to them, she thought.

'Do they… know who we are?' Dale asked.

'Maybe,' Willow replied. Brooke noticed she was keeping her head down as they walked along the curved hallways of the palace. 'You look like Ulanders, remember? They won't have seen many of those here.'

The hallway ended at a wide staircase, which continued curving up the inside of the tree. Rowan-thir paused briefly to speak to a pair of guards at the base. The guards stepped aside and they continued on.

The stairs seemed to go on forever. Every so often, they'd pass a window carved through the tree trunk, followed by a lantern, followed by another window, and another lantern. On and on they went, climbing higher and higher, passing more Woodspeople along the way. The closer they got to the top of the tree, the more regally-dressed the Nymmites became. And the more they stared at them.

Tonya was beginning to mutter about the number of stairs and Dale was clutching at his side by the time Willow announced they were near the top. Brooke couldn't have been more glad to hear it - her calves were burning and sweat was trickling down her back, and her breath was becoming more laboured with each passing step.

I should've kept going to field hockey practice, she thought.

And suddenly, they reached the end of the staircase.

There was no door here - they simply emerged from the stairs into a new space. And once Brooke saw where they were, her mouth fell open.

They were at the base of a colossal branch, easily as wide as one of the single-laned roads back home. It curved up from the end of the staircase and disappeared into the dense leaf canopy above. Woodspeople were ascending and descending the branch with ease, despite the fact there were no steps or railings to hold on to. Other branches - some smaller, some just as large - sprouted off in different directions from the top of the tree, vanishing into the leaves or hanging aloft over the forest floor far below.

'Look at *that*,' breathed Tonya, her complaints about the stairs now forgotten.

Brooke saw what she was staring at, and stared too. The tips of some of the branches seemed to have been purposefully cultivated into tree-buildings like those throughout the rest of the city, curving back on themselves into dome shapes, like fists at the end of arms. Some of them were huge, too, easily the size of houses, and all lit up inside. There must have been at least a dozen below the line of the leaf canopy - they hadn't been able to see them from the forest floor.

Up here, the air seemed thicker to Brooke, like she was inside a closed room rather than a treetop. It was beautifully scented too, like fresh roses after heavy summer rain. And, if it was possible, it was also *musical* - she could hear a soft melody in the air as though there were invisible wind chimes all around them, tinkling in the breeze.

'This way,' said Rowan-thir, starting up the branch.

They followed. Willow and the Woodsman strolled easily up the curve of the branch while the others stuck rigidly to the centre, almost on all fours. The bark of the branch had been mostly smoothed out but still jutted up in places. *One trip and you'd be a goner*, Brooke thought, trying to ignore how badly her legs were wobbling. She didn't dare look down over either side of the branch.

'Oh my days, oh my days,' Dale whimpered behind her.

'Stop being a baby,' Charlie said from behind him.

'What're those glowy thingies?' said Tonya.

Brooke looked up. Little colourful orbs of light were zipping around the leaves just above their heads, winking in and out. She remembered them from the tunnel below The Throat. What were they called again?

'Fire-fairies,' Dale answered for her. He watched one buzz down past him, noticed afresh how high up he was, and dropped to all fours.

'Hurry up,' Willow called back.

Moving in a nervous clump, they continued up the branch and into the leaf canopy. Suddenly, the air was filled with noise and colour as hundreds of fire-fairies swarmed around them, splashing reds and purples and yellows and blues over the mattress-sized leaves of the tree. Tonya swiped at one and Brooke cried, 'Don't touch them!'

'Why?'

'I don't know. Someone told us not to once.'

Then, just up ahead, the quarters of the Empress appeared.

Willow would tell them it was called that later, and Brooke would remember the finer details of how it looked: how intricately the fingers of the branch tip curled back and intertwined to form the dome shape of the building, like an expertly-woven basket; how elaborate, colourful flags and banners had been draped from its windows and balcones, waving gently among the leaves of the tree; how warm, golden light spilled from the front entrance and fire-fairies gathered around the threshold to drink it in. Most of all, she would recall the single bright shaft of moonlight lancing through a gap in the leaf canopy, bathing the whole building in an eerie, silvery luminescence.

But for now, all she saw was the tall, slender Woodswoman with jet-black hair standing in the doorway, and Willow down on one knee before her. Next to her, Rowan-thir had removed the hood of his cloak and was also crouched in a posture of reverent respect.

Brooke, Dale, Charlie and Tonya looked at one another, and then slowly lowered themselves to their knees.

'Is that her?' whispered Tonya. 'Is that the Empress?'

'No,' Charlie replied immediately. 'I don't know who that is.'

The dark-haired Woodswoman, flanked by two guards in green cloaks, motioned to Willow and Rowan-thir. They rose to their feet. Willow looked back and beckoned them.

Brooke suddenly realised her heart was hammering in her chest. Why? What was she scared of? This strange, dark-haired Woodswoman in a silver gown, who Willow had just thrown herself down in front of? Even now, as they came forward, Brooke caught a look on her face she'd never seen before in all the time she'd known the Woodsgirl: anxiousness.

But no, it wasn't that. She wasn't *afraid* of this woman, who studied them through dark, gold-rimmed irises, her green-tinged fingers clasped in exactly the same way as Rowan-thir. It wasn't fear she felt - it was awe. She was *awestruck* by the sheer force of the deep magic emanating from her. It rolled over them in waves.

She knew the others felt it too - Dale looked like he might topple backwards if he didn't kneel soon. Charlie put a hand on his shoulder, pushing him down. The four of them kneeled.

Next to them, Rowan-thir said, 'May I present Maphira, Regent Ruler of Nymm and mother of Orchidema, the Empress of Nymm.'

'Lady Maphira,' said Willow. 'May I present the Other-worlders: Brooke Woods, Dale Reed, Charlie Flint, and Tonya Miller.'

The Woodswoman regarded them thoughtfully, golden flecks dancing in her eyes. No-one spoke or moved; the fire-fairies hummed softly in the leaves around them. Then she smiled, and Brooke felt an invisible weight lift off them all.

'Welcome to Nymm,' said Maphira, spreading long, slender fingers. 'My daughter is expecting you. Won't you come inside?'

Chapter Nineteen: Orchidema

The quarters of the Empress were just as Brooke imagined the home of a Woodsperson to be. She, Dale and Charlie had spent a good deal of time over the summer discussing what Nymm might look like, and while they'd all been fairly wide of the mark so far (apart from there being houses in trees, of course), the inside of Orchidema's home was close to what she'd pictured.

It was all wood, for a start. The floor was essentially a smoother section of the branch, covered here and there with finely-woven rugs, and the walls were simply the intertwined fingers of the branch tip, curled back on themselves to form the dome shape of the building. Again, it was like being on the inside of a giant basket.

Not a luxurious basket either, Brooke thought, looking around as they were led through the main room. There was minimal furnishing and decoration here: flames crackled in a stone fireplace off to the left (*had there been a chimney on the roof?*) and a lantern hanging from the middle of the ceiling bathed the room in warm, golden-orange light; an oak table stacked with very old-looking books rested near the hearth; next to it was a chair shaped like a flower petal, hanging from vines coming down through the roof, and a strange piped instrument in the corner played a soothing melody all by itself. There was a second table by the window covered in a mass of bottles and vials, each filled with a different-coloured liquid, some of which produced puffs of white smoke that floated up to the ceiling. An almost overpoweringly-sweet scent hung in the air - it reminded Brooke of freshly sliced apples and lemons, and she gladly breathed it in.

Another Woodsperson emerged from between curtains at the back of the room, carrying a wooden tray. She started at the sight of them, then ducked her head.

'My lady,' she said. 'The Empress has awakened.'

'Is she well?' asked Maphira.

The servant girl hesitated. 'She was able to drink. She's asked to see Willow-mir.'

'As she wishes,' said Maphira, gesturing towards the curtains.

Willow nodded. Pushing back her hood, she crossed the room and slipped between the curtains. The servant girl left through another curtained doorway near the potion-strewn table. Rowan-thir drifted over to the fireplace.

Maphira turned to them, her eyes glowing gold in the soft lantern light. Brooke felt a dash of that same awestruck fear return and involuntarily shrank back a little.

'You are the Other-worlders,' Maphira said. It wasn't really a question, and none of them dared answer it. The Regent of Nymm smiled. 'My daughter has spoken highly of you, and at great length over these last seasons. If it weren't for you, she may never have left the Ulandai capital alive.'

Brooke tried to speak, discovered her throat was bone-dry, and cleared it. 'It was mostly Willow in the end. And Charlie.' She motioned towards him. He was staring wide-eyed at Maphira.

'Charlie Flint,' the Woodswoman said, looking him up and down. 'The mighty warrior himself. I've heard many tales of your bravery. Orchidema's written extensively about you in her stories. I did, however, imagine you to be taller.'

Brooke wondered if Charlie knew his mouth was hanging open.

'And Dale Reed, the sorcerer. Is it true you destroyed a soulburn talisman?'

Dale nodded slowly.

'Most impressive.' Maphira's eyes travelled to Tonya. 'I'm afraid I don't know of you, my lady. Are you also from the Other-world?'

'Umm… yes?' said Tonya, fidgeting. 'I'm from England, if that's what you mean?'

Maphira chuckled at that - it came out like music.

'I've never heard of such a place. But then again, I haven't left Nymm in a long, long time. But you know that of course, don't you, Lady Woods?'

She met Brooke's gaze and something instantly passed between them. Brooke *did* know it, didn't she? In that moment, she knew more about Maphira than perhaps Willow or Rowan-thir would ever know, and yet somehow, that knowledge was still completely alien to her. It was in her now, buried deep inside, planted.

You'll have the key someday, Maphira's voice whispered softly in her mind. *And when you do, you will see it all.*

'I… yes, I know,' Brooke replied. The others looked at her.

Maphira smiled again, the light in her eyes fading slightly. 'Rowan-thir, has accommodation been arranged for our guests?'

The Woodsman turned from the fire. 'I'm… not sure, my lady. I can check.'

'If you would.'

Rowan-thir nodded, glanced at them once more, and left the room. In the same moment, Willow appeared through the curtains, followed by a much older Woodsman in rich green robes. He held the healing seed reverently in both hands.

'My lady,' he said, a little breathlessly. 'Look what Willow-mir brought us!'

Maphira eyed the glowing purple orb cupped in his wizened old hands. Her eyes flashed and Brooke felt a pulse of electric magic sweep the room.

'Well done, Willow-mir,' she said, her smile widening. 'Well done indeed.'

Willow bowed. 'It's my duty to serve,' she said. 'I only hope it works.'

'It will work,' said the old Woodsman. 'I'm sure of it. I'll start preparing the antidote right away. By your leave, my lady.'

He hurried from the room, still clutching the orb in both hands.

'The Empress wants to see my friends,' Willow said, 'if that's ok with you, Lady Maphira?'

'Of course it is,' said Maphira, beaming. 'Just don't keep her too long, she still needs plenty of rest. But the sight of you will surely lift her spirits.'

Willow turned back to the curtain and they followed. Charlie was right behind her.

***

On the other side of the curtain was a simple bedroom containing nothing but a bed, a chair and a single, flickering candle. Like the chair in the main room, the bed was shaped like a huge flower petal, and Brooke began to wonder if that's what they actually were. It was covered in a smooth, lilac-coloured sheet, and there was a bundle of pillows at one end. And lying under the sheet, her head nestled deep in the pillows, was Orchidema.

'Empress,' Willow said.

Orchidema's eyelids twitched, then slowly drew open. Emerald green irises caught the wavering candlelight as they drifted from the roof to Willow, and then to each of them in turn. A thin smile broke out on the Woodsgirl's pale face.

'Oh, hello,' she said weakly. 'It's been… an awfully long time… hasn't it?'

Brooke had been very young when her grandmother passed away. She'd stood by her bedside in the hospital and held her hand, and marvelled at how frail she'd looked that day. Her grandmother, who not so long ago had been giggling with her in the garden as they chased leaves on a windy autumn afternoon, had smiled and called her 'Brookeworm' - and that was the first time *anyone* had used that nickname, and her mother had called her it ever since - and Brooke had smiled back, and wondered how her warm, jolly granny could possibly look the way she did in that moment.

She saw her grandmother in Orchidema now, and it sent a lump racing into her throat.

'It's been… a while,' Dale agreed.

'Six years,' Brooke croaked, surprising herself.

'But only six months for them,' said Willow.

Orchidema's eyes widened, and seemed to sink further into her face. Brooke thought she looked like a porcelain doll that'd been left in a cardboard box in the attic.

'Six months?' the Empress said in wonder. 'How strange.'

'It's, umm, good to see you… again,' said Charlie. His voice was strange - Brooke looked over and in the dim, intermittent light of Orchidema's bedroom, saw his eyes had turned glassy.

'It certainly is,' Orchidema replied, smiling up at him. Every word from her mouth was just above a whisper. 'I haven't seen anyone new… in so long. Willow's been gone for an age, too.'

'You know why,' Willow said, folding her arms.

'Yes… and you found it.' Orchidema grinned at Willow, and Brooke saw a flash of youthful beauty return to her face. 'Eventually.'

'Hey! You have no idea what I went through to get that seed, Your *Highness*.' Willow's mock indignation was mostly put-on, but Brooke picked up a tinge of sincerity in it. 'I was almost eaten by a full-grown Gnasshmaw in the Stroborian wraithwood, you know. And I got buried in an avalanche in the Golemar foothills, trying to find that seed.'

'You're… so brave,' said Orchidema, and to Brooke's mild amazement, she winked.

Willow snorted. Her eyes bloomed gold in the low light, and Tonya gasped.

'Sorry!' she said, flustered. 'I didn't mean… sorry.'

'No need,' said Orchidema, waving it away. 'I know… how I look.'

Brooke understood why Tonya had reacted like she did. In the brief moment Willow's eyes lit the room, they'd seen the Empress for how she really was - gaunt, sunken, skeletal. Even her hair, normally jet black and lustrous, was thinning to grey.

'Who are you, anyway?' the Woodsgirl said. 'You're… new, aren't you?'

Tonya introduced herself, starting to extend her hand; she drew it back at the sight of Orchidema's shrivelled fingers, which looked like they'd crumble to dust if anyone were to grip them.

'I can't wait… to hear more about your world,' said the Empress, 'once this healing potion… takes effect. Willow, how long - '

'Tomorrow morning,' Willow said.

'And… will it work?'

Willow's expression was a perfect mix of hopefulness and trepidation. 'Yes. It will.'

'Good.'

Orchidema closed her eyes and sighed. For a long moment, no-one spoke. Brooke was about to whisper, 'Is she asleep?' when her eyes opened again.

'It was… all my fault, really,' the Empress said. 'I should've been more careful. They… gave me a drink, while I was on… a diplomatic mission. And it had poison in it. That was all they let me do… during the war. Boring, diplomatic missions. They never let me fight.'

'You don't know how to fight,' Willow said matter-of-factly.

'No-one… ever taught me. At least they… let *you* train.'

'Yeah, and then they sent me away. Because I couldn't do magic right.'

'You know that's not - '

'What d'you mean, "couldn't do magic right"?' said Tonya, and then instantly realised what she'd done. 'Oh, I'm *sorry*! You were talking and I interrupted you… Your Highness.'

Orchidema merely smiled again. 'No-one calls me that. Willow… was joking, before.'

'Still. I'm a butthead.'

'Yeah you are,' said Dale. He gritted his teeth as Tonya's foot connected with his ankle.

'Was it Decymero who poisoned you?'

Brooke and Willow both looked sharply at Charlie, but he didn't seem to notice. His jaw was set, his eyes fixed on Orchidema. Suddenly, Brooke thought he looked five years older than he was.

'Yes,' Orchidema said grimly, meeting his gaze. 'I… know it was him. No-one else in Uland could have done this. He has… agents everywhere.'

'We'll stop him,' said Charlie. 'He'll pay.'

Orchidema smiled, her green eyes sparkling for a second. 'You are brave… Charlie Flint.'

Charlie nodded - Brooke didn't need any more light in the room to tell how flushed his face was. 'It's my, umm… duty, I guess.'

'Your duty?' said Dale.

'Yes.'

'No it isn't,' said Willow, her tone suddenly firm. 'That's not why you're here. It's not anyone's duty to stop him.'

'Maybe that *is* why we're here,' Charlie replied, just as firmly. 'Maybe that's all we were ever supposed to do. We must have these powers for a reason, right? Maybe that's why. We're here... we exist... to stop him.'

'Heavy,' murmured Tonya.

Willow crossed her arms again. 'Well... we can't know for sure, one way or the other.'

'Maybe the Druyads do?' Brooke suggested. 'What about Yulerin? Has he been here?'

Orchidema blinked wearily. 'He could've been. But I haven't seen him... in months.'

Willow turned to her. 'Months?'

'Yes.'

'He *hasn't* been here?' said Willow, turning to her. 'At all?'

Orchidema shook her head. Or rather, she moved it incrementally on the pillows. Willow frowned, pressing her fist to her lip.

'What's wrong?' said Brooke, feeling her heart rate notch upwards without knowing why.

He should've been here.

'He should've been here,' said Willow, 'at some point. He said he was going to the High Druyad temple. He would've stopped here on the way. I'm sure of it.'

'Why?' said Dale.

'He just... would have.'

Orchidema's small hand slid towards Willow.

'Willow-mir,' she said. Her voice was weaker than before. 'How much... have you told - '

The curtain *whished* back behind them. The old Woodsman swept into the room.

'What're you all still doing here?' he snapped testily. 'The Empress needs her rest, the antidote won't be ready for a while. Leave her in peace. Go on!'

He ushered them from the room. Brooke glanced behind her and saw Willow briefly squeeze Orchidema's hand before the curtain fell back into place.

'Seriously,' Tonya said. 'These Woodsmen are *rude*.'

The main space in the Empress's quarters seemed overbright after the gloom in Orchidema's bedroom. Rowan-thir had returned - he was standing by the fireplace with his hands behind his back, gazing into the flames. The Empress Regent was gone.

'Where's Maphira?' said Willow, casting about the room.

'Convening the Council.' Rowan-thir turned to them. 'This is a rather important turn of events, after all. The leadership must be informed immediately.'

'And the Elementals?'

'Supping in the banqueting hall. I've been asked to escort you there now.'

'I know the way.'

'Even so, I've been told to escort *them*.' The Woodsman nodded their way and Brooke felt a bubble of resentment pop in the pit of her stomach. *Or was it hunger at the mention of a banqueting hall?* 'You can make your own way there if you wish, Willow-mir.'

Willow hesitated, looked back at the curtain to Orchidema's room, then turned to the door. 'Fine, I'll go. Come on, then.'

'By your leave, my lady,' Rowan-thir said, with the slightest of smirks.

***

They left the quarters of the Empress, retraced their steps along the branch (slowly, in Dale's case) and started back down the spiralling staircase inside the tree. Willow went a little ahead of them, with Rowan-thir following a few steps behind.

Tonya walked alongside Brooke, bombarding her with questions all the way down.

'So she's, like, in charge of this whole place?

'Yes.'

'Like, a queen or something?'

'An Empress.'

'This doesn't look like much of an empire to me.'

'Well, it is.'

'It looks more like a weird theme park, or something.'

'Ton…'

'Don't get me wrong, it's *cool* n' all. I like the trees and stuff. And that Rowan guy is kinda good-looking, even if he's all rude and whatnot.'

'He's probably, like, a hundred years old.'

'Oh. Bummer.'

They passed more Woodspeople on the way down. All of them stared. Just ahead of them, Willow walked with her hood up and head down.

'And she was in that city, last time you were here? The one you told me about earlier?'

'Who?'

'The Empress. Orchid-eena.'

'Orchide*ma*, yes. She was there. And she was a big deal, like a full-blown celebrity. Also, Charlie loves her.'

'What?' said Charlie from behind them.

'Nothing.'

'I knew it,' Tonya said, grinning. 'D'you think they'll get married, and he'll move here for good? That'd be something.'

'Yeah it would.' Brooke grinned too.

'He'd be a *terrible* Emperor, though. He'd get detention somehow.'

Brooke snorted laughter. Willow glanced back at them.

'What're you two saying?' said Charlie suspiciously.

'Nothing, Charles,' Tonya replied.

Charlie muttered under his breath. Brooke and Tonya giggled all the way back down to the ground floor of the palace.

As soon as they were back outside, Willow stopped.

'You four go on from here. I need to do something.'

'Aren't you hungry?' said Brooke. 'I'm starving.'

'Me too,' said Dale and Charlie in unison.

'I'll be along,' Willow replied, throwing furtive glances at passing Nymmites from beneath her hood. 'Rowan-thir will show you where to go.'

The Woodsman nodded. 'This way.'

He started along the path and the boys followed immediately. Brooke caught Willow's gaze and held it. 'You're ok, right?'

Willow stared back for a moment, the golden hue in her eyes tremoring. Then she dipped her head in more of a bow than a nod.

'I'll be back soon, I promise.'

She turned and headed off down another path, her cloak whipping behind her.

'She still doesn't like me,' Tonya observed.

'Don't take it personally,' Brooke said, following after the boys and Rowan-thir. 'I don't think she liked me either, at first. But she's our friend now.'

They walked along for a moment or two, gazing around at the trees and humming lanterns and Woodspeople; none of the Nymmites seemed to be in a rush - they strolled everywhere, speaking in low, even tones. Brooke saw a group of Woodschildren (*was that the right word for them?*) playing a game of sorts near the path - green sparks burst from their little hands, transforming into daisies as they landed on the grass. The game seemed to be centred on who could make the most flowers appear with each go.

Tonya sighed, her head tilted back. 'This is all so *bizarre*, Brookles.'

'I know, it's like that at the start. Except you've been here for longer than we ever were. You should be used to it by now, Your Highness.'

'Maybe.' Tonya looked down at her hands. 'I *do* like my powers, even if I can't always control them. D'you think we'll have them when we go back?'

When we go back.

'Probably not. But who knows, maybe it'll be different this time.'

'Yeah.'

One of the children squealed as an entire clump of daisies burst from the grass. A passing Woodswoman scolded them and they scurried away.

'Tell me again what happened in the tower,' said Tonya, 'the last time.'

As they walked to the banqueting hall, Brooke told her - in as much detail as she could bear - about the Druyad Tower, and Decymero, and about the soulburn talisman.

***

Willow walked until she was out of sight of the others, and then kept walking. The path wound between tree-buildings and garden groves and fountains of glittering water, going further and further from the tallest trees in the centre of the city, until the paved stones ended and the grass underfoot became wilder, and there were no Woodspeople close by.

Up ahead, the ground gradually steepened to the thick line of white-barked trees ringing the city; beneath the night sky, strange nocturnal creatures roamed through the grass under the light of Uland's stars, keeping a wary eye on the flame-haired Woodsgirl coming their way. Another Enfield, different from the one they'd seen earlier, lifted its head lazily to watch her pass.

She kept going until the sounds of the city had faded behind her, and finally stopped by an old sycamore tree. Its leaves rustled gently above her. She closed her eyes and listened to their music, allowing her breathing to slow back to normal. Then she turned, pushed back her hood and looked up.

Far, far above, the leaf canopy shimmered with colour. Even from the forest floor, she could see fire-fairies dancing between the leaves of the tallest trees.

Woodspeople were in their homes now, dangling from the uppermost branches, oblivious to what was going on elsewhere in Uland. They wouldn't know the Otherworlders were here, not until morning. Then word would spread. They'd want to see.

Word would also spread about the Elementals. They'd blame her for bringing them here, but it no longer bothered her. She was used to being blamed.

How long would it take for them to prepare the potion? Would it be ready by tomorrow, like they'd said? Would Orchidema even have that long?

Willow leaned back against the tree.

The Empress was far worse than she remembered. She'd never seen her look so small and fragile, even when they were young. The poison had taken a deathly toll on her body. If only she'd found the healing seed sooner. It shouldn't have taken this long.

But that didn't matter. Because she'd done it eventually, even if it'd taken so many months. At least now, Orchidema had a chance. She could live, and Nymm could go on.

And when everything was back to normal, she herself could rest. Finally, finally rest.

She'd never been so tired in her life.

Under the night sky on the edge of the city, Willow slowly slid down the tree until she was sitting in the familiar groove between its roots.

Then she cupped her face in her hands, and wept softly.

Chapter Twenty: The Library

Charlie hit the ground hard. Breath puffed from his lungs in a dry wheeze.

'Again.'

The Woodsman stood over him, grinning.

Wincing, Charlie struggled back to his feet, pushing himself up with Quilloran's sword. His body ached from the blows the Nymmite had already landed.

'Ready?'

No.

He took a deep breath and let it out slowly, shifting his feet into position on the grass.

'Ready.'

The Woodman came at him again. The sphere *whummed* through the air on the end of the rope, blurring round and round. Charlie backed up, trying to keep his eyes on the spinning weapon, squeezing the hilt of the sword.

I can do this, he thought. *I* can *do this. I just need one chance. Just… one.*

He saw it, and sprang forward.

The Woodsman had already anticipated the attack. He dodged backwards, let the rope loop around his neck, tossed his head back to unloop it again, and sent the sphere hurtling forwards. The momentum carried it straight into Charlie's chest, knocking the breath out of him all over again. He sprawled to the ground with a gasp of pain.

The Nymmite warrior chuckled, spinning the rope casually in one hand.

'You fight very much like an Ulander,' he said. 'All muscle, no brains.'

Charlie let out a spluttering cough, rubbing his chest. The sphere on the end of the rope wasn't much larger than a tennis ball but it was rock-hard.

'What's that thing made of?' he wheezed.

The Woodsman let the sphere drop into his palm. 'A substance called Duskore. It's only found in the north.'

'Don't they have that where you're from, Other-worlder?'

Rowan-thir had appeared unnoticed on the edge of the training field. He leaned against one of the posts below an unlit lantern, arms folded over his chest.

'No,' Charlie managed, getting back to his feet. 'We don't have that where I'm from.'

He'd woken up early that day in the guest chambers next to the banqueting hall. Dale had still been fast asleep in the bed across the room, snoring like a motorcycle going through a tunnel. The "beds" were really hammocks suspended from the ceiling, and the hammocks themselves were really giant leaves that conformed to their body shape while they slept. Charlie found them more than a little unnerving and was glad to clamber out of his.

After leaving the palace the night before, Rowan-thir had escorted them to the banqueting hall, a big, square tree-building with a single oak table in the centre. A chandelier made from a branch growing down through the ceiling lit the room. Most of the Elemental party was just finishing their meal as they arrived; Luno had apparently gone to the Guildhall to speak to the Council of Nymm and wouldn't be back for a while. The warlocks swept from the room as soon as Rowan-thir entered, and servants quickly cleared the table.

Dinner that night was mostly composed of fruit, berries, nuts and a stew of sorts that may or may not have contained sweet potatoes. Charlie wasn't exactly the biggest fan of healthy food (his stomach had been yearning for pizza all day) but he'd been too famished to care, and had wolfed down a bowl piled high with a bit of everything on offer. They'd all asked for seconds - the Woodspeople had been happy to oblige.

Brooke asked Rowan-thir where Willow had gone. The Woodsman, who'd been sitting in the corner by the banqueting hall fireplace, had simply shrugged and said she frequently disappeared around mealtime. She didn't reappear at all that evening.

As soon as they were done eating, an invisible wave of exhaustion rolled over them and Rowan-thir showed them to their chambers nearby. Brooke and Tonya took the larger room ('I'm a queen, remember?') while Charlie and Dale settled for the smaller one. It was just as minimally-furnished as Orchidema's quarters had been. Charlie had drifted off to sleep thinking of the Empress, and of what he'd do to Decymero if their paths ever crossed.

It hadn't taken him long to find the training field the next morning. The city had been quiet when he left their chambers - the paved roads were mostly empty, the forest floor itself bathed in welcoming dawn light. The grunts and clashes of combat led him directly to the field, a cordoned-off square of grass a little way out from the more built-up centre of the city, where he'd watched the younger Nymmites sparring with their rope-and-sphere weapon (one of them had called it a Moon Hammer) before he was finally invited to duel himself. They'd given him back his sword and he'd soon discovered just how useless it was against their weapons.

'Again?' said the younger Woodsman hopefully. He was a warrior Nymmite, which Charlie gleaned was different from a Woodsperson who used magic in combat, like Willow.

'Yeah,' Charlie replied, 'but let me try that thing.'

The Nymmite glanced towards Rowan-thir for approval. He nodded, amused. The Woodsman handed the Moon Hammer to Charlie, who rolled the sphere in his hand - he was genuinely surprised to find it weighed next to nothing.

'How did *this* knock me down?'

'Duskore gathers energy while it moves,' explained Rowan-thir. Other Nymmites who'd drifted to the edge of the training field to enjoy Charlie's pummelling watched in silence. 'The faster it's spun, the more energy it gathers. Try it.'

Charlie wrapped a portion of the rope around his hand and began to swing it in a close circle. As the sphere moved through the air, it began to *whum* louder and louder with each spin until it was visibly vibrating on the end of the rope, leaving a hazy purplish trail in its wake.

'What now?' Charlie called over the noise.

'Hit the ground,' said Rowan-thir.

'Ok.' Charlie brought the sphere down hard on the grass.

There was a muffled *bang*. Some unseen force slammed into him, tossing him backwards with a yelp of surprise. He landed flat on his back for what must've been the fifth time that morning to gales of laughter from the gathered Woodspeople.

Rowan-thir clapped, guffawing with the others. 'Well done, Other-worlder! I daresay you're wide awake now.'

Cursing under his breath, Charlie hauled himself up again. A shallow crater had appeared in the grass where the sphere connected with the ground. He held it up by the rope and saw it was no longer vibrating, though some of the purple glow remained.

'Perhaps it's time for a rest,' said Rowan-thir, starting to turn away. 'Your friends are in - '

'No,' said Charlie abruptly. 'One more.'

The Nymmites' laughter petered into a general murmur of curiosity. Rowan-thir turned back slowly, cocking an eyebrow beneath his hood.

'One more what?'

'Duel.' Charlie coughed, spitting a glob of blood on the grass. 'I want to duel that guy one more time, with this thing.'

Rowan-thir glanced at the younger Nymmite warrior, who nodded enthusiastically.

'As you wish, Other-worlder.'

A sizable crowd had gathered by the training field now. Charlie guessed many of them had just woken up or had been on their way to work (*did Woodspeople work?*) and had been drawn by the sounds of him getting repeatedly clobbered by this young warrior, who was approaching him now with another Moon Hammer in his hands. And he was grinning.

Let's see what this thing can do.

Charlie began swinging the rope in his right hand, keeping his eyes fixed on how the Nymmite was moving rather than on his spinning weapon. He'd picked up that knowledge at some point during his previous battles, or as the Warrior, maybe he'd always known it.

Watch their feet. Watch their stance. Wait.

They circled one another slowly, edging sideways, their spheres *whumming* in the morning air while the other Woodspeople looked on. Rowan-thir had folded his arms again. He appeared unimpressed so far.

'Come on, then,' said Charlie. 'Hit me, if you can.'

The Nymmite's grin widened.

Suddenly, he spun on the spot, swung the Moon Hammer in a wide arc and, as it came around again, kicked it in mid-air.

The kinetic force gathered in the sphere exploded, sending it hurtling straight for Charlie's face. But this time, he saw it coming and ducked. The sphere shot just over his head, missing his scalp by an inch. In the same movement, he swung his own Moon Hammer low to the ground, going for the Nymmite's feet. The Woodsman just about saw the incoming attack and jumped on his still-standing leg, avoiding Charlie's sphere but losing his balance in the process.

Charlie saw his opponent fall. He jerked his sphere back and let it *whum* past his body in the other direction, allowing the rope to slide smoothly through his hand as far as it would go, angling himself towards the Nymmite. The second the rope went taut, he snapped it back. Without thinking - and not really knowing why - he punched the sphere in mid-flight, straight towards the Woodsman.

His opponent had leapt back to his feet, anticipating another swinging attack. He *didn't* anticipate the abrupt change of direction from Charlie's punch, and couldn't dodge the incoming sphere in time - it hit him square in the chest with a *bang* and sent him tumbling backwards with a cry of pain.

As he hit the ground, a gasp went through the crowd. Charlie snapped his sphere back and caught it neatly in his hand.

'Yes!' he cried, triumphant. Then, a half-second later: 'OW, MY HAND!'

He dropped the Moon Hammer, clutching his right hand in agony. In the heat of the moment, he hadn't felt the impact of the sphere on his knuckles. The pain was sudden and white-hot.

'Geez, I think I broke my hand,' he said, grimacing.

'It's not advisable to… punch… a Moon Hammer, at least without gloves on,' said Rowan-thir, walking across the training field. 'Here.'

He produced a purple Nymm bean. Charlie took it with his good hand and popped it in his mouth. It had a sharp citrus taste and he swallowed it immediately.

'That'll address your pain, but you must have that hand seen to. I believe your beaten opponent can show you where the Halls of Healing are located.'

The younger Nymmite approached them and bowed. 'You fought well,' he said sheepishly, still rubbing his chest where the sphere had struck him.

'Thanks,' said Charlie, eyeing his swelling hand. 'Not well enough, though.'

'Better than any Ulander I've ever seen,' said Rowanthir, with just a hint of admiration. 'And you've never fought with a Moon Hammer before?'

'Nope.' Charlie could feel the bean taking effect already - the pain was subsiding fast. 'But I'm a fast learner when it comes to weapons.'

'So it would seem. We'll have your sword cleaned and returned to you later. Though you may want to continue practising with more of our weapons if you're already so proficient.'

'I'll take you to the Halls of Healing,' said the younger Woodsman.

'Thanks,' said Charlie.

He followed after him and the crowd parted to let them through. As they passed, Charlie heard someone whisper excitedly, 'I *told* you that was him! Charlie Flint, the Warrior!'

He smiled, already forgetting the pain in his hand.

***

Brooke closed her eyes and breathed deep.

The air was heavy with the musty smell of old books. It was an earthy, woody sort of scent, familiar and comforting. She held it for as long as she could before letting the breath out again.

Much like how the training field had drawn Charlie, the library of Nymm had started calling to her as soon as she finished breakfast. Tonya had still been asleep when Brooke woke up and didn't emerge into the banqueting hall until the morning meal was almost done. She'd flopped into the chair opposite her and groggily asked why she was already dressed.

'Ugh, the *library?*' she said, rubbing her eyes. 'We have those back home, Brookeworm.'

'I know,' Brooke replied. She hadn't expected Tonya to come anyway. 'I just want to check something. You stay here, see if Willow comes back.'

'Gladly,' Tonya said, reaching for the fruit bowl. 'D'you think they have hair brushes here?'

Nymm had been wide awake by the time Brooke found the library. The streets between the tree-buildings were bustling with activity: Woodspeople of all ages came and went, gliding smoothly along the paved stone pathways in their earthen clothes; in the canopy far above, more of them drifted along the tree branches, ascending and descending the stairs and ladders with effortless ease. It was balmy that morning, too warm for a cloak, and many golden-hued eyes were drawn to her blonde hair and clear blue eyes as she passed by. She smiled back every time.

A patrolling guard had directed her to the library. It was another domed tree-building near the centre of the city, slightly taller and grander than those around it, with wooden balconies overlooking the grounds on all sides. Brooke had stood alone between the bookshelves for a minute, gratefully breathing in the scent she knew so well. Then a librarian Woodswoman, old and wrinkled with fading brown eyes, came shuffling in; she welcomed her politely and, after hearing her question, led her up a curving set of creaking wooden stairs to the third floor. She was surprisingly spritely for her apparent age.

And if Willow looks our age, Brooke thought, *how old must this lady be?*

'Lindara,' called the librarian at the top of the stairs. 'You have a visitor.'

'Oh?'

A second librarian, somehow just as old and wizened as the first, emerged from behind a bookcase. She held a small lantern in one hand, and raised it higher as she shuffled across the floor towards them. The light from it threw sharp shadows over her face, but her expression was kindly.

'We don't often get visitors this early in the day,' she said.

'I'm, uh, Brooke Woods.'

'Indeed you are,' said Lindara the librarian, smiling. 'The *Seer*, no less. And what brings you here?'

The other librarian disappeared back down the staircase. Lindara started across the third floor towards a wide open balcony, where warm morning light and cool air spilled into the room. The entire floor was one big, circular space, lit only by the light from the open balcony area. Enormous bookcases packed with dusty old tomes spread from the centre of the room in concentric circles, like ripples in a pond.

'I have a question,' Brooke said, 'about a book.'

'Ah, well I believe you're in the right place, then.' Lindara gestured to the bookcases as they passed. 'Are you looking for something in particular? Histories of the continent, perhaps? Tales of war? Magical instruction?'

'Actually, it's about a book I already own. Or, have, I suppose.'

'Well, now. That's intriguing.'

They passed beyond the last bookcase and stepped into the pool of morning sunlight near the balcony. Outside, the gentle din of the city had grown louder.

There were three wooden tables here, each with three wooden chairs positioned around them. Lindara chose the middle table and motioned for Brooke to sit. She set the lantern down, snapped her fingers to put out the flame, and eased herself into the opposite chair with a sigh.

'Curse these old bones of mine,' chuckled the Woodswoman. 'To be as young and eager as you, Otherworlder. How old are you, anyway? Seventy seasons, perhaps? Not a hundred, surely?'

'I'm thirteen,' said Brooke. 'Nearly fourteen.'

The librarian blinked, gold glittering briefly in her grey eyes.

'Thirteen,' she breathed in wonder. 'My, my. I would never have guessed such a thing. Isn't the world a strange place?'

'Umm… yes?'

'Yes indeed.' Lindara inched her chair closer. 'Now, let's see this book.'

Brooke drew Yulerin's book from her internal pocket and placed it on the table. The old Woodswoman peered down at it for a moment.

'Who gave you this?' she asked.

Brooke cleared her throat. 'Yulerin the Druyad.'

Lindara slowly raised her eyes. 'Really?' she said. 'Yulerin?'

Brooke nodded.

'My, my.' Lindara took the little book gently in both hands, staring at the wordless cover. Then she brought it close to her face, closed her eyes and sniffed, long and deep. Her irises sparkled with golden light when she looked up at Brooke again.

'This book is very old,' she said, 'and dripping with magic.'

'I know,' said Brooke. 'It's how we got here.'

'*Really?*' Lindara whispered, astonished now. 'It acted as a *portal*? That really is something, I must say. I've heard of such things, but…'

She placed the book carefully on the table and started to turn the pages.

'You don't mind, do you?' she said.

'Of course not,' Brooke replied. 'It's not mine, anyway. I kinda hoped Yulerin would be here, so he could explain it.'

'He has not been here for quite some time,' said Lindara, her eyes bright with intrigue as she scanned the faded foreign text. 'Nor has his counterpart in the Druyad temple north of here. Those old men used to visit us often, but since the war began we've hardly seen them.'

'There's a Druyad temple near here?'

'Oh yes, quite close. Their temples are everywhere, in every region of the continent. It's how they get around so fast. I've never really understood the appeal of portal-travel myself, but I'm just a librarian after all. I'd rather read about it.'

She stopped turning the pages and frowned.

'What does this depict?'

The book was open at the drawing, the one that'd replaced the map. Brooke noticed the image had grown more distinct since she'd last seen it.

'I'm not exactly sure,' she said. 'I think it might be a tree. And a rock.'

'I see.' Lindara studied it for a moment before turning the page. 'And this part appears… fresh. Did you write it?'

Brooke followed the Woodswoman's wrinkled green finger as it traced over the words scrawled on the ancient paper. They remained unchanged and unintelligible.

'No, I can't write it. But I can read it.'

Lindara looked up, her eyes wide. 'You can *read* this text? How?'

Brooke considered for a moment, but there was no other way to say it. She shrugged. 'I'm the Seer. I guess it's just something I can do.'

Lindara nodded slowly, eyes still wide and swimming with gold. 'Yes, indeed you are.'

Neither of them spoke for a few seconds. Outside, the sounds of the city - fully awake now - drifted up to the balcony. Finally, Lindara said, 'You had a question?'

'Yes,' said Brooke, feeling a little silly now. 'Two questions, actually, though I think you've already answered one.' She tapped the book. 'This is a portal? That's how we got here?'

'It would certainly seem so, yes.'

'Ok.' Brooke stared hard at the book for a moment. 'So my second question is: if it's a portal, why did it only start… portalling… the other day? Yulerin told me it was how we'd get back to Uland, but he never explained how, and I couldn't read the words until recently. Some of the "fresh" writing only just appeared, too. And it's almost as if… I dunno… someone's *adding* to it right now. It even showed me a map when we were in Silversprog, with the Gnomes. It's like it's trying to guide me, or something.'

She sat back, suddenly a little flushed, like she'd blurted out something she shouldn't. But the Woodswoman merely nodded, brushing her fingertips lightly over the pages.

'I'm afraid I can't give you a satisfactory answer to that,' she said, 'because I simply don't know. Perhaps it has something to do with Yulerin himself. Perhaps not. But either way, I suggest you spend some more time reading what's written on these pages. They clearly have something for you, and you alone. And perhaps, if you haven't tried it already, you could try *asking* the book itself for answers.'

Brooke stared at Lindara, then at the book, then at Lindara again.

'Ask… the book?'

'Indeed.' The Woodswoman's eyes sparkled. 'Why not? It may have some guidance for you.'

'I hadn't thought of that.'

'Most wouldn't.'

Lindara snapped her fingers again and the lantern's flame bloomed back to life. She closed the book and slid it across the table.

'I'd also suggest you keep it close,' she said, rising from her chair with a wince. 'I've come across many, many texts in my time, but very few with as much magic inside them as that one. I imagine there are others who would be most eager to get their hands on it. And not all of them would have intentions as pure as yours, my lady.'

'I'll keep it safe,' said Brooke, tucking the book back in her pocket. 'Thank you.'

'A pleasure,' said Lindara, with a little bow. 'By the way, I believe one of your friends is outside right now. You may want to take a look.' She motioned towards the balcony. 'Now, if you'll excuse me, I have a bookshelf to reorganise.'

She shuffled back towards the bookcases. Brooke watched her go for a moment, then walked over to the balcony.

The light here was much brighter. She shielded her eyes from the sun, waiting for them to adjust. An odd mix of sounds reached her ears: leaves rustling, birds trilling, children (*Woods*children, she corrected) laughing and squealing somewhere. And something else. A sound she recognised but couldn't place.

Then, from below, she heard it: 'Well done, Master Reed!'

The glare from the sunlight faded and she blinked her eyes into focus. The third floor balcony looked down on a courtyard of sorts, one she hadn't noticed when she'd arrived at the library earlier. It was a paved square with unlit lanterns in each corner, enclosed on three of its four sides by tree-buildings. A handful of Woodspeople had gathered on the open side, watching something unfold.

Whoosh-bang!

There was the sound she knew, and now she knew why.

Dale was in the square, surrounded on all sides by Elemental warlocks. He was dressed in his full sorcerer garb - deep blue tunic, grey breeches, brown leather boots - and was moving in ways Brooke had never seen before: ducking, dodging, even rolling across the stone slabs, and all the while hurling blasts of bright blue light at the warlocks around him. The Elementals were moving in a similar way, diving to avoid Dale's attacks or blocking them with bursts of light from the heads of their staffs. It was four against one, and Dale wasn't losing.

The Nymmite crowd were enthralled, gasping each time a fireball from one of the warlocks just missed Dale's head or an ice blast ripped across the stone paving, cheering when any of the combatants expertly parried an attack or conjured something new from thin air. Even from the balcony, Brooke could hear Dale and the other men grunt and curse as they fought. She had no idea how they hadn't accidentally set fire to any of the wooden buildings around them.

Then she spotted Luno standing under one of the corner lanterns, resplendent in scarlet robes, leaning on her snow-white staff. Her bright red eyes were fixed on Dale.

Finally, the skirmish deadlock broke. Dale successfully dodged an ice blast from one of the warlocks, who hit another Elemental standing nearby, throwing him back against the nearest building with a yell of pain; Dale used the distraction to blast fire at the first warlock, knocking the staff from his hands as he tried to block the incoming attack. The other two came at Dale in a rage, the stones in their staff heads glowing, preparing to hurl dual bursts of power at him from different angles.

There was no way he could block both attacks at the same time. Brooke's hands clapped to her mouth and she squealed into her palms.

She needn't have worried, though. Dale actually grinned as the warlocks closed in, his eyes flashing blue; they raised their staffs and he dropped to one knee, and his fist connected with the ground.

Whoosh-bang!

A shimmering wave of blue light blasted out from where Dale was crouched - actually *rippled* through the stone slabs of the square - and hit the charging Elementals head on. Both men were sent spinning through the air with cries of surprise. One bounced off a lantern pole, causing the lamp itself to detach and smash to the ground next to him; the other landed hard on the stone slabs and slid into the Woodspeople like a bowling ball.

As the echoes from Dale's shockwave blast subsided, the Nymmites began whooping and cheering. Luno joined in, clapping enthusiastically. Brook took her hands away from her face and whispered, 'When did he learn to do that?'

Dale got to his feet, holding his hands up apologetically. He looked more embarrassed than triumphant, like he hadn't meant to win the fight.

'Bravo, Master Reed!' Luno called, walking towards him. The other Elementals picked themselves up around the square, wincing in pain. 'A most impressive display indeed.'

Dale grinned awkwardly, pushing a hand through his sweaty brown hair. 'I'm sorry, I didn't mean to… do all that.'

'Nonsense,' said Luno, waving a hand dismissively. 'My men underestimated you and paid the price. They'll learn from their mistakes.'

The warlocks gathered together, muttering. One of them was still semi-frozen and had to be thawed out by his compatriots.

Luno put a hand on Dale's shoulder and leaned close, saying something Brooke couldn't pick up from the balcony. An icy finger of unease traced down her spine as she watched Dale's grin widen at whatever the Factionhead was saying.

As the crowd began to disperse, Luno stepped away, patting Dale on the arm. He nodded at something else she said, and in doing so caught Brooke's eye up on the balcony; she offered a brief wave and he returned it, though the smile faded from his face as he did so.

They held each other's gaze for a second longer, then both turned away.

***

Willow finally returned just after dinner. She had news about Orchidema.

'The seed worked,' she said, standing in the doorway of the banqueting hall. 'They made it into an elixir. It took a while, but it worked.'

'Is she all better?' Charlie said, setting his cup of fruit juice down.

'She will be,' Willow replied. She started to turn away again.

'Hey, wait - where're you going?' said Brooke. 'You've been gone all day.'

'You missed a bunch of stuff,' Tonya added. 'I gave one of the servants a makeover. Rowan-thir was *not* happy about it.'

'I had… things to do,' Willow said, a little evasively.

'What things?' said Dale through a mouthful of desert.

'I'll explain later,' said Willow. 'I have to go see the Empress. I'll be back soon.'

'Can we come?' Charlie said, starting to stand.

'No, she needs to rest tonight. You'll see her tomorrow. Everyone will.'

Willow left. The door swung shut behind her.

'She's being weird,' observed Tonya.

'Yeah,' said Brooke pensively. 'She is.'

***

They went back to their rooms after dinner. Charlie said he'd been training most of the day and needed a bath - Tonya agreed, adding something about Orchidema being able to smell him from here. He replied with a casual "whatever" and then practically sprinted to the boys' room.

In the girls' chambers, Brooke told Tonya about her experience in the library, and about how she'd seen Luno speaking to Dale after his duel with the warlocks.

'I don't trust her,' Tonya said, flopping into her hammock. 'I like her hair n' all, but I wouldn't trust her as far as I could throw her.'

'Me neither,' said Brooke, staring at the ceiling above her own bed.

'It's the eyes. The red's creepy. Do they use contacts or something?'

'I think it's magic. They turn their eyes the colour of their chosen element, or something. Red's for fire, blue's for ice, that sort've thing.'

'Weird.'

'Yeah.'

Brooke swung out of her hammock and went over to the mirror in the corner. It looked more like a slice of glass, around which the wall itself was growing. Every structure in Nymm was like that, she realised, marvelling grimly at the dark rings under her eyes. The buildings were grown, not… built. If she wasn't so exhausted and circumstances were different, she could happily have stayed for -

They are coming.

She froze. In the mirror, her blue eyes were wide and unblinking.

Tonya was saying something behind her, but she couldn't hear it. Everything else in the room - the hammock beds, the woven rugs, the softly-glowing lantern in the corner - all blurred away. Her face became the only thing visible in the mirror.

The voice had been so clear, and it'd spoken directly into her mind.

They are coming.

Brooke was dimly aware her mouth had dropped open. She forced herself to close it, leaning closer to the glass. She knew the owner of that voice, didn't she? It was familiar… yet somehow…

They are coming. Soon. You must prepare.

Her eyes ached but she couldn't close them. If anything, they widened further. The cool blue of her irises seemed to swim around her pupils. She could see a tiny version of herself in them. And an even tinier version in the pupils of her reflection. And on, and on, forever. She was falling into those reflections now, falling forward, into the mirror itself while the rest of Nymm melted away behind her in a haze of swirling colour.

It was on fire, wasn't it? The whole city. Trees burning from the roots up. Woodspeople screaming as they fled through billows of black smoke. The tree canopy collapsing from above, crashing to the forest floor far below.

They are coming, Brooke.

She gritted her teeth, reaching back, straining.

Who's coming? Who?

The world spun around her, faster and faster. She was in the mirror now, she knew it. The fires of Nymm roared, melting into the screams of the Woodspeople.

Who? she yelled silently. *WHO?*

The voice came back once more, so loud and crystal clear the owner of it could've been speaking directly into her ear.

Protect the Empress.

The floor fell away. Brooke tumbled forward, plummeting down into the darkness. She heard a distant, high-pitched shriek and realised it was coming from her.

A hand on her shoulder, shaking her. Someone else's voice.

'Brooke! Brooke, wake up!'

She snapped awake and sat bolt upright in her bed. Tonya, who'd been leaning over her and shaking her by the shoulders, jerked back just in time to avoid getting headbutted.

'Brooke!' she gasped. 'What on earth?'

Tonya goggled down at her. She looked like she'd seen a ghost.

'I'm… I'm sorry,' Brooke said, putting a hand to her forehead. She hadn't been anywhere near the mirror. In fact…

'Ton,' she said, 'is there a mirror in this room?'

Tonya's brow furrowed. 'No. There's one in the bathroom. Why?'

Brooke closed her eyes, rubbing her temples. 'No reason.'

'You screamed,' Tonya said in an odd, wavering voice. 'You fell asleep while we were talking, and then you just started screaming. It scared the life out of me.'

'I'm sorry,' Brooke repeated. She swung her legs out of the bed; Tonya retreated back to hers and sat down. 'I had a dream.'

'Seemed more like a nightmare.'

'Maybe.' Brooke shook her head, trying to dispel the screams of the Nymmites and the roar of the fire. 'It might've been more than that.'

'What d'you mean?'

Brooke looked at her. Tonya's face was strained with worry. And something else.

Fright, Brooke thought. *I frightened her.*

'We need to find Willow,' she said.

***

'Who d'you think it was?' said Dale.

Their boots clapped on the stone slabs as they hurried along the road through pools of lantern light. Outside, the evening air was cool and crisp.

'Not sure,' Brooke replied. 'But I think I knew them. Or it sounded like someone I knew, at least. It was hard to tell.'

'Was it like before?' Charlie said. His hair was still damp from his bath. 'Like in the tower?'

'Kinda.'

'And the whole city was on fire?'

'I think so.'

'Oh man,' said Dale.

A tall Woodsman in flowing green robes glanced at them curiously as they passed, his golden eyes blooming in the lower light.

'So what do we do?' Tonya said breathlessly. 'Like, will it definitely come true, or what?'

'Maybe we can stop it this time,' said Dale, 'now that we know. It doesn't have to be like Fort Hammerfall. We'll be ready.'

'For what?' said Tonya.

'Hey!'

The young Woodsman jumped at Charlie's shout, almost dropping the jar in his arms.

'I remember you,' said Charlie as they approached. 'You were at the training field earlier. I was duelling your friend, right?'

'Oh, yes,' said the Nymmite, a little startled by the four panicked Other-worlders gathering around him. 'You fought well.'

'I fought *great*,' Charlie said. 'But that's beside the point. Have you seen Willow?'

The Woodsman frowned.

'Willow-mir,' Brooke corrected.

'Oh, yes actually. I passed her just a few minutes ago. She was on her way to the gardens.'

He nodded towards another road, still clutching the jar in both arms. They thanked him as one and started down the path.

'Isn't this whole place a garden?' said Tonya.

It didn't take them long to find it. The road curved down past a number of smaller tree-buildings - merchant shops and traders, by the looks of things, now closed for the day - to a flat expanse on the forest floor, hemmed in on all sides by a low shrub wall. Spectral white mist rolled across the ground here, curling eerily around their feet as they passed beneath a glowing lantern hanging from a carved wooden archway.

'Where is she?' said Brooke, scanning the area.

Unlike the rest of Nymm, which seemed to have sprung a little chaotically from the ground itself, the gardens were neat and well-kept: paved stone paths bordered by carefully-manicured shrub hedges meandered between flower beds bursting with life and colour; little trees popped up from the midst of the flowers in places, offering shelter for swarms of fire-fairies, which winked in and out amongst their leaves; ornate lanterns dangled from poles around and throughout the garden, bathing the still plants in soft light, colouring the rolling ground mist in places. The only sounds here were the low hum of fire-fairy wings and the whispering rush of gently flowing water.

'There,' said Charlie.

They followed his pointing finger to the centre of the garden, where orange flames flickered in a pyre beneath the navy-purple evening sky. Several figures were gathered around the pyre, silhouetted against its light.

'Come on,' Brooke said, lowering her voice.

The shrub hedges offered some cover as they moved quickly towards the pyre and the people standing around it. None of them really knew why they felt the need to stay low and out of sight, but they all did it anyway. As they drew closer to the heart of the garden, voices began drifting their way.

'... appreciate all you've done, of course…'

'... performed a great service… whole city is in your debt…'

'... have the Empress's eternal gratitude…'

They came within sight of the burning pyre, which rested in the centre of a small square bordered with strange, exotic flowers. There were no lanterns here - the pyre was the only source of light, but it was more than sufficient. They bunched together behind a hedge to listen.

'Once Orchidema is fully recovered, she'll resume her duties,' one of the figures was saying.

They were all robed from head to toe in elegant moss-green gowns. Their faces were shrouded - only their glowing golden eyes were clearly visible beneath their hoods.

'We will, of course, continue to watch over her,' another figure added in a smooth, even voice. 'She will have our constant support and attention.'

'She's still young,' observed another. 'But she is already wise beyond her years.'

'It will be crucial for the rest of the continent to see her again, too.' This voice was female, and somehow familiar. 'When she's able, she should undertake a fresh round of diplomatic journeys. To Ulandai, perhaps. Or even to Elementa.'

'Elementa would be preferable. It would solidify our ties there. We should discuss that with Lady Luno as soon as possible.'

'Shouldn't she stay here for a while? Just to be safe?'

Willow's voice.

Brooke shifted closer to Tonya, trying to peer past the other Woodspeople.

'Ow!' Tonya hissed. 'That's my toe.'

'Sorry,' Brooke whispered back.

Then she saw Willow, standing on the far side of the pyre with her hood up and hands clasped in front of her. She fluttered in and out of view beyond the flames.

'She will have plenty of time to recover,' came the female voice again. 'You needn't worry, Willow-mir. We won't let anything befall her again.'

'There'll be no more need for healing antidotes, I can assure you. That mistake will not be repeated in my lifetime.'

'Here, here.'

There was a pause. Somewhere nearby, water continued trickling through the garden, unseen. Stars glittered through the tree canopy above them.

'And what about me?' Willow said, finally breaking the silence.

Another pause. Then: 'We'll always be grateful for your service, young one.'

'Always.'

'You put yourself in great danger for the sake of your Empress.'

'Nymm will not forget.'

'But,' said the owner of the first voice again, 'the Council concurs on this matter. We believe, now that your duty here is fulfilled, you should return to the service of the Druyads.'

'You were doing a great work there.'

'Most admirable indeed.'

'And we know those ancient old men will be glad to have you back,' finished the original speaker. 'Especially Yulerin. After all, you are still duty-bound to him, yes?'

'Yes,' said Willow.

'Good, then it's settled. You'll leave here tomorrow with the Other-worlders for the Druyad temple in the Evershade Woods. The journey should take no more than a day or two. Once Caelrin has sent your friends back home, you'll be free to return to Yulerin's service.'

'He'll be *most* glad to see you, I'm sure.'

Willow's voice was thick. 'And… when can I come back again? To see Orchidema?'

'That time will come,' replied the Woodswoman gently. 'When it does, we'll summon you directly. Listen for our call, and in the meantime, practise patience.'

'What?' whispered Dale. 'They're just sending her away again?'

'That's bogus,' Charlie whispered back. 'They can't do that.'

'Yes they can,' said Willow.

All four of them jumped. Tonya let out a stifled yelp.

At least seven pairs of golden eyes turned to fix on them. Willow came around the pyre, pushing back her hood. 'Come out,' she said. 'We could hear you a mile off.'

They stood and shuffled sheepishly to the right, where a gap in the hedge let them enter the square. The Woodspeople watched them in silence. Willow folded her arms.

'Spying?' she said.

'No,' said Brooke immediately. 'Just listening.'

'Who told you we were here?'

'No-one,' Charlie lied. 'We heard *you* a mile off.'

Willow made a face. 'You did not.'

'This is a Council meeting, my Other-worldly friends,' said one of the Woodspeople, looming near the burning pyre. 'I'm afraid guests are not permitted.'

'We're sorry,' Brooke said.

'Yeah,' Dale added, 'we didn't mean - '

'How can you just send her away like that?'

They all looked at Tonya. Her hands were on her hips and her head was cocked to one side.

Uh oh, Brooke thought.

'My dear, this is none of your con - '

'*Dear?*' Tonya cut in. 'I'm nobody's "dear", um… sir. I was just asking why, because it seems pretty unfair to me. Willow saved the Empress's life, right? You should build her a statue, not send her packing.'

No-one spoke. Tonya Miller had stunned the Council of Nymm into silence.

Of course she has, Brooke thought, and grinned.

'And what's this about booting *us* out, too? Maybe we're not ready to go home just yet. Did you ever think of - '

'Tonya,' said Willow.

Tonya stopped mid-sentence; she folded her arms.

'It's ok,' Willow said gently, her eyes shimmering in the shadows. 'They're right. I'm duty-bound to the Druyads, and I should go back. It's what I want, too. Honest.'

'Are you sure?' said Dale. 'I mean, one hundred percent sure?'

'Yes,' said Willow. 'That.'

'Why did you come here tonight?' said the Woodswoman.

And for the first time, Brooke realised who she was. She took a half step forward and cleared her throat. 'Lady Maphira, it's because of me. I had… a dream.'

'A premonition,' Tonya corrected, arms still folded.

Maphira studied them both. 'You saw the future?'

'I think so.'

'How?' said one of the Woodsmen.

'This one's the Seer,' explained another. 'She has the Sight.'

'What did you see?' Willow asked, coming closer.

Brooke told them about her bizarre dream experience in their chambers, about Nymm burning and the people screaming. When she recounted the words "protect the Empress", the Council members visibly stiffened.

'Nymm… on fire?' said one.

'And the Empress, in danger…'

'Whose voice did you hear?' Maphira said, her eyes glowing like searchlights.

Brooke felt her face reddening. 'I don't know. But it was… familiar.'

'We should seal off the palace,' said Willow immediately. 'No-one in or out. We can't take any chances.'

'I agree,' said one of the Woodsmen.

'Let's not be too hasty,' said another. 'It's after sunset. If we start fortifying the palace, we'll throw the city into panic.'

'Yes,' agreed another, 'that could do more harm than good. The last thing we need are rumours spreading that - '

'Rumours?' Charlie said incredulously. 'These aren't rumours. She *told* you what's going to happen. You can't just ignore it and pretend everything's ok.'

'She told us what she saw in a dream,' replied one of the Council members calmly. Brooke heard the condescension in his voice and felt heat rise up her neck. 'She told us what *might* happen. We have to consider this with great care.'

'Yes, great care. And time.'

'We will certainly think on this.'

Brooke, Dale, Charlie, Tonya and Willow gawked at the Council members. None of them were able to speak. *It's happening again*, Brooke thought. *It's just like Hammerfall. They're not listening to us because we're young. Because we're not* adults *like them.*

The words broiled up inside her. She opened her mouth to speak, but Maphira got there first.

'We will indeed think on this,' she said. 'And we'll think fast. And in the meantime, I say we seal off the palace, as Willow-mir has suggested. Whether this premonition is true or not, I'm sure we can all agree no chances can be taken with the life of the Empress, especially now that she's recovered. I will take no chances with the life of my daughter.'

The Regent spoke calmly, but her tone invited no debate. In that moment, she seemed to tower over the Woodsmen in the garden. Her eyes burned fully gold.

'Erm, yes, of course,' replied one of the Council members, shrinking back a little. 'Let's return to the palace and give orders for the city to be searched. We'll have the palace fortified, and can continue our consultation there until we have a full grasp on the situation. No harm will befall the Empress tonight.'

'Agreed,' murmured the others, nodding beneath their hoods.

They started towards the gap in the hedge, drifting the way Woodspeople did. Brooke begrudgingly stepped aside to let them through. She saw them eyeing her warily as they passed.

'We'll come too,' said Charlie.

'Yes, we can help,' added Willow, moving to follow the Council.

Maphira turned back. 'No,' she said, 'you mustn't put yourselves in danger. None of you. Stay here for now. We'll send word once we know more.'

'But - '

'There's no discussion to be had, Willow-mir,' said Maphira firmly. 'You must be safe. All of you. We'll send for you soon.'

With that, the Regent swept from the garden after the other Council members, and they were alone. No-one spoke for a moment. Water gurgled and plopped nearby in some unseen fountain.

'They don't believe us, do they?' said Tonya, finally.

'Probably not,' said Dale. 'They never do.'

'It's because we're kids,' Charlie said.

Willow turned away and kicked at a loose stone, muttering under her breath. Brooke watched her, waiting. She hugged her tunic tighter.

This is my fault, she thought. *Me and my stupid dreams.*

'Maybe it's nothing,' she said quietly.

'What?' said Tonya.

'Maybe it was, you know… just a dream.' They all gravitated closer to the pyre as she spoke; there was a chill in the air now. 'It's possible, right?'

'Possible, but not likely,' Dale said.

'You're the Seer, dummy,' said Charlie. 'If you've seen it, it's important. My dreams are about football and video games and dumb stuff I forget straight away. Yours actually matter.'

'Not if we can't do anything about it,' Brooke said, still watching Willow, who was standing with her back to them now. 'They're pretty useless if the adults keep ignoring them.'

'Well, at least that's *one* thing that's the same here,' said Tonya.

'The only ones who ever listen are Jayne and Yulerin,' said Dale. 'And we don't even know where they are right now.'

'Let's just go anyway,' said Charlie, rubbing his hand - it was still swollen from the duel earlier that day. 'We can help. There's no point in standing here while the Empress could be in danger, right? Let's just go to the palace, and if they get mad about it, so what?'

'I have to tell you something.'

They all looked at Willow. She'd turned to face them again. Her arms were crossed and, like Brooke, she hugged her cloak around her.

'Tell us what?' said Dale.

Willow's eyes glowed softly in the wavering light; a breeze went through the garden, nipping at her hair. She cleared her throat.

'It's... something I should have told you already, I think. It's hard to be sure.'

They stood around the pyre, watching her. Flames crackled in the momentary silence.

'It's a secret, you see,' she said. 'I'm not supposed to tell anyone, ever. Almost no-one in Uland knows.'

'What is it?' said Brooke softly.

'Yeah, the suspense is killing us,' said Charlie.

Willow's eyes flashed. 'It's about me. About who I am. And about Orchidema.'

Charlie, who looked like he'd been about to make another wisecrack, closed his mouth.

'We've known each other our whole lives. We grew up together in the palace. I'm a little older than her, but not by much. We've always taken care of each other.'

She dropped her gaze briefly. When she looked up again, Brooke saw the gold in her eyes was swimming.

'Orchidema,' she said, 'is the daughter of the Emperor of Nymm. His name was Aeltherion. He died some time ago. And since then, Orchidema has been the Empress. She never really wanted it, but that's the way things are here. Her mother, Maphira, acts as her advisor. She's been Regent during Orchidema's sickness.'

She paused. They nodded to show they were following.

'Aeltherion was the last in a generations-long royal line. His blood harboured the true ancient power of Nymm. Of all Uland, really. The entire continent was once Nymm - did you know that?'

'No,' said Dale. 'I don't think we did.'

Willow nodded. 'There was a time when our woods stretched the full length of the continent, all the way from Nardren to Suthdren. A Nymmite could travel from one end of Uland to the other without ever touching the ground. That was a long time ago. Now, our empire is only what you see here. We're the oldest Faction in Uland, and aside from the Druyads, we're also the smallest.'

'So… Orchidema has that same blood?' Brooke said. 'The same as her father.'

Willow seemed to hesitate, then nodded again. 'She does. There's power in it. Deep, ancient power. It's always held the magical nexus of our entire world together, but it's been waning for centuries. It doesn't live with any great strength in Orchidema. It barely lived in the Emperor.' She cleared her throat again. 'But it does live in me.'

Brooke's heart caught in her chest. She looked at the others, saw they were all staring at Willow. Dale's face was a picture of dawning realisation.

'You mean…' he said.

'Yes,' said Willow. 'Aeltherion was my father. My mother died just after I was born, so he married Maphira, as is our custom. The Emperor must always have a wife. Orchidema is their daughter. My half-sister.'

'Oh,' said Dale simply.

There was an expression of deep puzzlement on Charlie's face. 'Wait, so you two are *related?*'

'Yes,' said Willow patiently. 'Sisters.'

'But… you're older?'

'Yes.'

'But… that means…'

'*She's* the real Empress of Nymm,' Brooke finished, gazing at Willow. The Woodsgirl met the look, smiling grimly.

'*You're* the Empress?' Tonya exclaimed.

'Yes, but it's a secret,' Willow replied, motioning with one hand for her to hush. 'The only ones who know are Orchidema, Maphira, and the Druyads.'

'Yulerin knows?' said Brooke.

'Yes, he always has. Everin did, too.'

'And Jayne?'

'Jayne knows everything. She's the Seer. But she's never admitted that she does.

'Oh.'

'It was the Druyads' idea to bring me into their service when I got older, to protect me.' Willow folded her arms again, toeing the ground with her boot. 'Just before my mother died, she made my father promise to keep me safe. They saw the power in me - the *Drayocht*, it's called - and knew I'd be in danger if anyone found out. No-one had been born with that same kind of power for a very, very long time. It's rare, almost extinct. It's what's held Uland together since the beginning of time, but not always through so few people. And never through just one.'

'Until you?' Dale said.

'Until me. So my father promised my mother he'd keep me safe. He "adopted" me into his household after I was born - my mother had me somewhere far away and I was brought here after she died. It's not unusual for the Emperor to adopt orphans into the royal household because there are almost no Woodschildren without parents, so no-one questioned it. As far as Nymm knew, I was just someone on whom the Emperor had taken pity. They saw me as Orchidema's adopted sister, and that was all.'

'You said the Druyads took you in?' said Charlie, still puzzled.

'Yes, they did,' Willow said. 'The older I became, the more I struggled to control the Drayocht. There were times when I couldn't contain it. Other Nymmite children grasped basic nature-magic early on but I never could - they thought I was… stupid, or something. But they didn't know *why* I couldn't do simple magic. They didn't know it was because I was doing everything in my power to suppress the Drayocht instead. You saw some of it at Fort Hammerfall.'

'Oh yeah, that was *wild*,' said Dale.

'Kinda scary,' admitted Brooke.

Willow nodded. 'I know. And that was just a sliver. I caused some damage here as a child because of it. They wanted to banish me until the Druyads took me in - many saw that as banishment anyway. But Everin trained me, helped me get my power under control. I'm a lot better now.'

'We think you're awesome,' Brooke said.

Willow smiled, flushing a little in the firelight. 'Most people don't think so.'

'Then most people are dumb-dumbs,' said Tonya.

They all snickered, even Willow. For just a moment, Brooke felt a little stirring of hope, of contentment; for just a moment, they were all kids. Then images from the premonition edged back into her mind, and the contentment quickly receded.

'The… dray-oct,' Dale said, pronouncing it carefully. 'You said you'd be in danger if anyone found out you had it.'

'Yes,' said Willow, brushing a red curl of hair from her face.

'Does… does *he* know?'

'Decymero? Yes, Yulerin thinks so. I'm afraid I… accidentally revealed it at Hammerfall, when I fought Commander Hysst. We think that's why he had the

Empress poisoned, to draw me out. He's been after me for years now.'

'He wants to take the power for himself?' Brooke said. 'Like, make you his apprentice, or something?'

Willow frowned. 'Apprentice? No, nothing like that. If he wants to take the Drayocht, it'll be for one purpose only: to destroy it forever.'

Brooke swallowed. 'And what happens to Uland if he does that?'

Willow met her gaze. 'I don't want to find out. Although, I wouldn't be able to anyway, because I'd be dead.'

She said it so matter-of-factly that all Brooke could do was nod.

'I have a question,' said Tonya, holding up a finger. 'If you can control your power now, why don't you just tell everyone the truth? That you're the real Empress? You could be ruling this place instead of getting… kicked out again.'

'She's not getting kicked out, Ton,' Brooke said. 'She's choosing to go, right?'

Willow nodded. 'Yes, it's my choice. Though I would've liked to stay longer, to make sure the Empress is ok. And I could've shown you round more. You've only seen a small part of the city, really. If we could've stayed longer, it would've been… what's the word you use… cool?'

'Cool,' agreed Dale.

'Fire,' said Tonya.

Willow's brow furrowed. Brooke quickly added: 'We have lots of words for the same things.'

'Oh. So do we, I suppose.' She looked out across the garden. 'I've never wanted to be the Empress anyway. Most of what Orchidema has to do seems… boring. I have a lot of freedom with the Druyads. I would never have met you if I'd been here, as Empress.'

'Good point,' said Charlie.

'And we'd never have known Uland existed,' said Dale. 'That would've sucked.'

'Yes,' Willow said slowly. 'Sucked.'

Suddenly, her head whipped in the direction of the garden entrance.

'Someone's coming.'

They are coming.

Brooke squinted. 'I don't see anyone.'

'Even so,' Willow said. 'Say nothing about what I've told you.'

Then, they heard footsteps. More than one set. They all turned to face the sound, bunching together. Willow drew up her hood, her eyes glowing.

'There you are!'

Rowan-thir appeared out of the gloom, white mist billowed around his feet. Another Woodsman followed just behind him.

'What is it?' said Willow quickly.

'It's the palace,' Rowan-thir said, and for the first time, Brooke heard a Woodsperson sounding breathless. 'Something's happened. You all have to come with me.'

'What's happened?' said Charlie earnestly, taking a step forward.

The Woodsman swallowed; his eyes bloomed gold in the darkness just beyond the firelight.

'It's under attack,' said Rowan-thir. 'We must go. Hurry!'

.

Chapter Twenty-One: The Defence of Nymm

Tonya Miller had never been more confused in her life.

Just when she thought she was getting the hang of this place, the rules changed again. First, Orchidema was the Empress. Now it was Willow.

Who next? Brooke?

The Gnomes had been bad enough, with their over-the-top caution and rigid etiquette (it hadn't taken her long to knock that out of them). But the Woodspeople were on another level entirely. Everything here felt so unreal, like they were floating through a dream haze and would wake up at any moment. The Nymmites themselves were hard to read, too - sometimes they seemed practically human, other times they were like aliens who'd just stepped off the mothership and could barely comprehend basic emotions.

And now Willow - the one she thought she might actually know something about - was, in fact, some all-important leader with ancient, world-altering power flowing through her veins. Did she get that right? It was mega hard to keep up with it all.

More than anything, she just wanted to go home. She'd been there longer than the others and she missed real life comforts: normal food, normal clothes… her *phone*. She'd have missed out on *so* much by now, she'd never be able to catch up.

The whole experience had been scary at first, and then pretty fun for a while (she hadn't minded being the

Glimmerqueen), and then super boring. And now, they were caught up in some battle, and she just wanted to go *home.*

Rowan-thir, the handsome-but-kinda-rude Woodsman, led them at a sprint through the streets of Nymm, weaving between tree-buildings and garden groves beneath the coloured lantern lights, heading deeper into the city. The roads were mostly empty now - Tonya guessed most of the Woodspeople were in the tree canopy high above them - and they encountered almost no-one along the way. Only the patrolling guards remained on the forest floor, and most of them were also running in the direction of the palace.

What're we even *going to do when we get there?* she thought. *Charlie and Dale and Willow can fight, sure, but what'll I do? Shape-shift into a sword or something?*

She liked her power, if she was being honest about it. It'd pretty much saved her life, once she realised she could change into anyone she laid eyes on. She suspected the Gnomes would've locked her in the dungeons straight away if she hadn't transformed into Merriwind. Changing was weird, too - her ears popped like she'd just gotten off a plane every time she did it. And she always felt like she was holding back a sneeze the whole time she was in another form. It was a major relief to shift back into herself.

But I'll still be completely useless if someone comes at me with a weapon, she thought.

'Oh no!'

Brooke was a few paces ahead of them and saw it first. They caught up to her and Tonya gasped.

The base of the palace tree was on fire. Yellow and orange flames swirled around the bottom of the trunk, at least three bus-lengths across. Woodspeople were rushing towards it with buckets of water in their arms. Even from their position some distance away, the air was thick with smoke.

Dale coughed and said, 'Who did this?'

'I don't know,' Rowan-thir replied, his eyes blazing. 'But I can guess.'

'So can I,' said Willow. 'Come on.'

They hurried along the main road leading to the palace. The roar of the flames grew louder as they approached. Nymmites were yelling in panic, dousing the fire with water that seemed to evaporate as soon as it left their buckets. The heat was almost overwhelming.

'We can't get any closer,' Willow said, shielding her face with her arm. The others did the same; Tonya saw Brooke's legs wobbling and grabbed her. 'How do we get through?'

Rowan-thir and the younger Woodsman were peering up at the treetop. Tonya followed their gaze and saw that the fire-fairies were swarming crazily among the leaves. They'd all turned red.

'We can't,' said Rowan-thir, his jaw clenched in fury. 'This isn't just a fire - it's a flame wall. And it's burning all the way around the palace.'

Tonya saw he was right. The fire extended out in both directions and carried on around the tree, blocking off any route into the palace. And, as she stared at the flames, she saw they all burned at an even height with the exact same intensity. There was smoke, and the tree *was* burning, but the fire wasn't moving from its position.

'It's elemental fire,' said Willow, her voice trembling with rage. 'Water won't put it out.'

'It's more than that,' added Rowan-thir. 'Elementals can't conjure magic like this by themselves.'

'Luno,' Dale said. 'It's her.'

Brooke rounded on him. 'What did she say to you earlier?'

'What? When?'

'*Earlier!* After you fought the warlocks. She said something to you. I saw it from the library.'

Tonya looked from Brooke to Dale and back again. She had the impression Charlie and Willow were doing the same.

'She… she just told me I'd done well,' Dale said, frowning. 'She said I'd be a fine warlock someday.'

Willow made a sound that was something between a laugh and a snarl.

'And she patted me on the shoulder,' said Dale, his frown deepening, 'and… now that you mention it… I felt something at the time - '

'Something, like electricity?' said Rowan-thir, looming over him. 'Like it was inside your skin, trying to get out?'

Dale stared up at him. 'Maybe? Yes.'

Willow threw back her head in frustration. 'She took your power!'

'What?'

'Elementals can draw power from others,' said Rowan-thir, glaring into the flames. 'When they can't muster enough themselves, they steal it. Luno stole some of your sorcerer's power when she touched you and used it to make this barrier.'

'Oh,' said Dale. 'I… didn't know.'

'If you hadn't been showing off - ' Brooke started.

'Enough!' Tonya snapped. 'It doesn't matter what happened. They're inside now.'

'There must be a way in,' said Charlie, looking up and down the flame wall. Woodspeople were gathering around them now, shouting and weeping in the harsh light of the fire. 'Can't someone *magic* their way through, or something?'

'I can!' Dale cried, suddenly red-faced and furious. 'I'll teach her to steal my power. Get back, the lot of you!'

They moved away, urging the Nymmites back too. Dale planted his feet on the stone slabs of the road, holding his arms out. Blue light began to glow in his palms, brighter and brighter. Tonya could feel the cold coming off him in waves and thought, not for the first time, *That's Dorky Dale Reed doing that - what the heck is going on here?*

With a grunt of effort, Dale thrust his hands towards the fire. A blast of ice exploded from his palms, swept across the ground and slammed into the fire wall; a hollow *whoosh-boom* sounded as the ice punched through the flames, forming a gap in the wall. Just beyond it, they could see the smouldering remains of the palace doors.

'Hurry up!' Dale cried. His arms were outstretched and trembling, like he was holding open invisible elevator doors. 'Get inside!'

Willow and Charlie sprinted for the gap. Tonya followed, dragging Brooke behind her by the hand. The watching Woodspeople cheered triumphantly and surged towards the opening.

Tonya was almost at the gap in the flames. The heat was so intense she felt like she might collapse before getting through, but she kept her legs moving. Charlie crossed over just ahead of her; she saw Willow looking back, urging them on.

'I can't hold it!' Dale yelled.

'Come on!' Tonya cried.

She ran between the twin walls of fire, yanking Brooke through behind her. The heat was momentarily unbearable; she felt her ears actually sizzle for a split second. And then they were through, barrelling into Charlie on the other side. They all collapsed to the floor.

'Dale!' Willow shouted.

Tonya scrambled to her feet, looking back. Dale was still on the other side of the gap, sweat pouring down his face, his arms trembling.

'I… can't…hold it!'

Then something happened.

The floor on either side of the gap cracked open. Dual lines of thick, soily roots burst from the ground and quickly coiled together to form barriers within the flame wall. The fire instantly began to eat into them.

'Hurry!' Willow cried, her own hands outstretched and glowing with emerald light. 'You'll only have a second.'

Tonya saw Dale eyeing the root barriers, weighing it up. Then, with a yell, he sprinted through the gap, dropping his hands at the last second.

With a roar, the flames rushed at him on either side. Tonya and Brooke screamed.

The roots did just enough. Dale dived headlong through the gap, hit the floor and rolled; the flames surged through the roots, consuming them a split-second after he cleared the opening. The fire wall closed behind him with a *whump* of white-hot heat.

'Dale!' Brooke spluttered, jumping up. Behind her, Willow's arms flopped down by her sides, the green light fading from her hands.

Dale straightened, throwing off his smoking cloak. 'Geez, that was close!' he gasped.

The wall of fire burned hot behind them, just beyond the palace entrance.

'Did no-one else get through?' said Tonya, staring into the flames.

'No,' said Charlie, standing. 'It's just us. We're on our own.'

***

'Well done, Master Sorcerer,' Rowan-thir murmured, gazing into the flames.

Even with his keen eyesight, he couldn't quite make out the Other-worlders and Willow-mir on the other side. The fire wall seemed to have grown in height and intensity the moment it closed back over.

'Did they get through?' said the younger Woodsman next to him. 'I cannot see them.'

'It would appear so,' said Rowan-thir.

'Is there another way in?'

'Possibly.' Rowan-thir tilted his head back, peering up the length of the great tree; embers from the fire floated close to the trunk in the night air. 'Perhaps if we were to climb - '

A horn sounded.

The Woodsman stopped mid-sentence and spun round. The other Nymmites did the same, looking back across the city.

'The call to arms,' said Rowan-thir. His eyes burned gold. 'We are under attack.'

'The city's been breached!'

The cry came from another Nymmite, sprinting up the road in their direction. As he came into the firelight, Rowan-thir saw the terror etched on his face.

'Enemy forces,' he panted, 'coming from the woods to the south.'

A ripple of panic went through the gathered Nymmites. Woodswomen began ushering their young ones away.

'What enemies?'

The Nymmite messenger swallowed, caught his breath, and said, 'Those in black armour.'

'Doomgaard,' said Rowan-thir fiercely. 'We have been betrayed.'

***

Charlie swallowed down the lump in his throat. He tried to look away, and found he couldn't.

'Oh,' was all Tonya managed to say next to him.

Willow stood with the burning palace doorway at her back, her brown eyes slowly sweeping the entrance hall, the green fingers of one hand flexing rhythmically by her side. Her other hand was clamped to her mouth. The firewall swirled and rumbled behind her, tossing her shadow over the bodies strewn across the floor.

'Oh,' Tonya said again.

'What... happened?' Brooke whispered.

Charlie saw Nymmite guards among them. He saw Woodsmen and Woodswomen in flowing robes, all charred and torn. He saw at least one of the Council members from the gardens.

They caught them totally by surprise, he thought.

Willow took her hand away from her mouth. Green sparks began crackling between her fingers. Her whole body was trembling, not in fear.

'They must have known the Council was meeting tonight,' she said in monotone. 'They always meet in the gardens. The palace would've been mostly empty.'

'L-Luno,' Dale stammered, staring at the bodies on the floor. 'Luno did this?'

'She betrayed us,' Brooke said softly. 'She betrayed Nymm.'

'Willow,' Charlie croaked. 'Orchidema.'

Willow blinked, wrenching her eyes from the floor. Golden flecks rushed into her irises.

'We have to help her,' Charlie said.

Willow's gaze burned into him. He could feel her rage from where he stood, pulsing through the smoke-filled air, washing over him in waves.

'I'm going to kill them,' she said plainly. 'All of them. Starting with her.'

'I know.' It was all Charlie could say.

'We're with you,' Dale said, bunching his fists.

'Listen,' said Tonya.

They all listened. Charlie just about heard it: shouts and screams from far above them, barely audible over the roar of the firewall. Something exploded with a dull *boom*. More screams.

'They're going after her,' said Willow. Her eyes flooded with gold. 'Come on.'

She made for the stairs. Tonya and Brooke went after her, stepping gingerly over the lifeless bodies on the entrance hall floor. Dale looked back at the palace entrance, then followed.

Charlie started to go. Then he paused, bent down next to one of the guards, and came up with a long rope attached to a metal sphere.

No sword, he thought, slinging the weapon over his shoulder and wincing at the sharp stab of pain in his still-injured hand. *Moon Hammer it is. Just don't punch it this time.*

He ran for the stairs.

***

'Slow down!' Tonya cried breathlessly.

Willow was almost out of sight on the spiral staircase, her cloak billowing behind her as she raced ahead.

'Willow!' Brooke shouted.

The Woodsgirl stopped, looking back at them with burning golden eyes.

'You're too slow,' she said, not out-of-breath in the slightest. 'I'm going on without you.'

'No you're not,' Dale panted, finally catching up. 'You can't fight them all by yourself. We have to do this together.'

'What he said,' added Tonya, doubled over a couple of steps below them.

Brooke didn't remember the staircase being this long when they were last in the palace, even with Rowan-thir striding ahead of them at top speed. There somehow seemed to be *more* steps than last time.

But of course, that wasn't all. Black scorch marks tore through the staircase in places, ripping into the bark of the walls; occasionally, some of the steps were frozen solid and they had to jump over them. The Elementals had clearly fought their way up through the inside of the tree, blasting anyone in their path.

There were bodies on the stairs, too. More guards, more robed officials. All caught by surprise by their "allies" from Elementa.

'Are you ready?' Willow said impatiently.

'No,' replied Tonya.

'But we're coming anyway,' Brooke finished.

They carried on, climbing higher and higher, their calves burning with exertion. Every once in a while they'd pass a doorway leading onto a floor of the palace. Brooke glimpsed conference halls and war rooms and alchemy chambers along the way, all lit with low-burning lanterns, all empty for the night. She hadn't really noticed any of them the last time.

They must have been halfway up the staircase when Tonya suddenly cried, 'What's happening out there?'

She'd stopped by one of the narrow windows carved into the tree trunk. The others went over to look, grateful for the chance to catch their breath again. Willow reluctantly dropped back to where they were.

'Wait,' Dale said slowly, peering out at the city below. 'Is that… who I think it is?'

Charlie's reply was short and ice cold. 'Doomgaard.'

'From the boats?' said Tonya. 'How are they here?'

'The Elementals must have brought them,' Willow said. 'The depth of their betrayal grows. They'll soon learn, though. Those Doomgaard scum are no match for Nymm.'

'Maybe not,' Brooke replied, inwardly surprised at how calm her voice sounded. 'But there are *more* of them. Look.'

In the distance, flaming torches had begun to appear along the dark perimeter of the city, where the forest floor swept up to the line of white trees. There were hundreds of them, all pouring from one familiar-looking section of the woods.

'The pool,' said Dale. 'The one we came through yesterday. That's how they're getting in.'

Brooke felt her blood run cold in her veins.

'Dale,' Charlie said, giving voice to her fearful realisation, 'how many Elementals came through the gateway with us?'

Brooke saw the other boy thinking it over.

'Six,' he said finally. 'Six, plus Luno.'

'And how many came with us from the ships?'

Dale's face paled. 'Seven.'

Brooke looked up at Willow. 'One stayed behind. He must have brought the Doomgaard.'

The Woodsgirl's eyes widened.

'You mean,' Tonya said slowly, 'the Elementals... and the Doomgaard... are working together?'

Brooke nodded. 'It looks that way.'

'But they rescued us on the lake,' said Dale. 'And they destroyed the Doomgaard galleons, right? They wouldn't have done that if they were *allied*.'

'They would,' said Brooke, 'if they wanted to trick us into leading them directly to Nymm.'

Willow bared her teeth, her golden eyes burning with fury. She joined them at the window.

'Betrayal on top of more betrayal,' she seethed.

'Look - the Woodspeople,' Dale said, pointing out into the darkness. 'They're going out to face them.'

Sure enough, they could just make out scores of Nymmite warriors surging into the open, grassy expanse, heading straight for the gathering Doomgaardians.

'They're putting something together out there,' Charlie said.

Outside in the darkness, Brooke could just make out rows of flaming torches coming down from the trees along Nymm's perimeter. She recognised their movement from Fort Hammerfall, when Commander Hysst's army had lined up on the plains below the city. This time, she also caught sight of huge wooden machines among the black-armoured soldiers, briefly visible in their torchlight.

Catapults.

'I knew this would happen,' Willow said, her voice dripping with anger. 'I *knew* this would happen if we trusted them. If we trusted *her*. How could I have been so foolish? Again?'

'You couldn't have known,' said Brooke, tearing her eyes away from the army massing in the night. 'No-one could have.'

'It's what they do, right?' said Charlie. 'They're liars.'

'But I heard them on the boat,' said Willow, her green fists clenched. 'I overheard something, and I didn't have a chance to tell any of you because then they were *right there*, and they've been with us ever since. I thought I'd maybe… misunderstood, or something… because they helped us get here safely. And Maphira said Luno was gracious in their Council meeting and didn't want anything in return for saving us on the lake, that they were just doing their duty for an ally, but she was *lying* all along. Lying! Just like Hysst, and the Goblins, and Zapharous, and - '

'Willow,' said Dale.

She stopped and looked down. The steps below her feet had broken apart - stinging nettles and black roses sprouted from the cracks, curling around her boots.

'Sorry,' she said, the sun-like glare in her eyes fading. 'It all just… feels like my fault.'

'Save it for Luno,' said Charlie, adjusting the Moon Hammer slung over his shoulder. 'She's the one who's betrayed us.'

'Yeah,' said Tonya, turning away from the window. 'I don't know much about what's happening here, but I know a bad guy - or girl - when I see one. And she's bad news. Let's get her.'

Willow met Tonya's gaze, held it for a second, and started up through the palace again.

Within moments, it seemed, Brooke was out of breath again. Her head was spinning and a painful stitch was already digging deep into her side, but all she could think was:

Willow's the Empress.

Willow!

What does it mean for Nymm? For Uland?

Why didn't she tell us sooner?

And overlaying all of it, the voice from her premonition: *Protect the Empress.*

'When we get to the top,' Dale called from behind her, 'what exactly do we do?' He was just as breathless as Brooke.

'Kill them,' Willow called back.

'Yeah, but how?'

'I'm pretty good with this thing,' said Charlie from up ahead, holding out the Moon Hammer. 'Just give me a fair shot and I'll - '

Whump!

The fireball missed Brooke by no more than a foot, ripping across the staircase and into the outer wall. She screamed and fell back into Dale, who just about managed to stay on his feet as chunks of flaming bark rained down. Ahead, Tonya and Charlie were thrown flat on their faces.

'Meddlers!' snarled the warlock from the doorway on the right. 'You shouldn't be here!' A second fireball was already forming around the head of his staff.

'Get back!' yelled Willow.

Brooke and Dale ducked down as a burst of emerald light struck the threshold of the door; the blast knocked the Elemental back into the room, out of sight.

'Where'd he come from?' Tonya gasped.

'Come on!' Charlie shouted.

Brooke hauled herself up on the wall. She caught a brief glimpse of Charlie before the sizzling trail left by the fireball erupted, blazing flames right up to the ceiling. The sudden blast of heat almost knocked her over again.

'We can't get through!' she yelled.

'Dale, freeze it!' Tonya shouted over the roar.

But Dale was already heading for the damaged doorway, a fireball of his own fizzling to life between his cupped palms.

'Dale!' Brooke cried.

'He'll only come after us!' Dale shouted back, and disappeared into the room.

Brooke looked from the doorway to the flames, back to the doorway. Tonya shouted her name again from the other side of the firewall. The flames were already eating into the wooden walls and steps, threatening to grow out of control.

'Go on without us!' Brooke yelled.

'What? No!' Tonya replied. 'You can't!'

'No choice!' Brooke cried, and darted for the doorway.

She barely made it through before the broken frame came down behind her and the step she'd just been standing on fell away, crashing down through the inside of the tree.

***

'They're gone!' Tonya exclaimed. 'What do we do?'

'We keep going,' said Willow. 'You heard them - they didn't have a choice. And neither do we. The rest of these stairs could come down at any moment.'

She wheeled away and dashed up the staircase.

'But - ' Tonya started.

'They can take care of themselves,' said Charlie, grabbing her arm. 'I think.'

He hauled her after him.

The stairs around the fire wall began to crack and groan.

***

Dale threw himself to the floor just as another fireball fizzed above him - it exploded on the wall, immediately engulfing an ornate tapestry in orange flames. He heard the Elemental cackling on the far side of the room as he scrambled for cover.

'Almost got you that time, Other-worlder,' the warlock called. 'You're not as fast as you looked earlier.'

Gritting his teeth, Dale leapt to his feet again and hurled a blast of ice in the Elemental's direction. He saw his opponent duck behind a table just in time - the iceball skidded across the top of it, instantly freezing a collection of open books and unfurled scrolls, and burst in a snowflake-like pattern on the wall beyond it.

'You're not so fast yourself,' Dale shouted back, dropping back down.

'Dale!'

He looked to his right. Brooke was crouched behind a desk not far from the doorway, which had come down moments earlier and now blocked their escape. He was pretty sure he'd heard the stairs collapse, too.

'What do we do?' Brooke hissed.

'Stay down!' he hissed back.

They were in some sort of conference room. It was huge and perfectly circular, with an enormous round table in the centre. High-backed chairs were still tucked in around the table, and an ancient-looking lantern hung just above it, swinging gently on its chain. Other smaller desks were scattered around the room, and most of the available wall space was covered either in more tapestries or bookcases.

Only the section of wall opposite the single doorway was uncovered. There, a huge, circular window framed with stained glass looked out over the city - moonlight flooded through it, bathing the room in silver.

'Hey,' Brooke said, 'where'd he go?'

Dale peered out around the edge of his desk. He couldn't see past the big central table and chairs. The warlock could be anywhere.

'D'you see the statue thing in the corner?' Brooke said, peeking over the top of her desk. 'I think he might be behind - '

Whoosh!

She yelped and ducked down, just as another fireball ripped across the top of the desk and burst on the wall behind her, showering her in smouldering embers. Dale saw her slapping furiously at her clothes, trying desperately to put the embers out; boiling hot anger surged up inside him and he stood straight up without a second thought.

'There you are, Other-worlder!'

The warlock was indeed by the statue in the corner, half-concealed behind one of its wings. Dale saw the head of his staff already beginning to glow again, saw him bear his teeth in a hideously-malevolent grin. The anger reached his chest and rocketed down his arms, filling his hands with power. The energy ball formed instantly, like a balloon blowing up between his palms, bristling with electricity; he felt it running through his skin, flowing into his muscles and bones and bloodstream, permeating his entire body with sorcerer's magic.

It all happened in half a second.

The warlock pointed his staff in Brooke's direction again. Dale knew the second blast would be twice as powerful - it'd blow the desk to pieces and smash her into the wall. She'd be dead in an instant.

But he wouldn't let him have the chance.

He thrust his cupped palms forwards, shoving the conjured energy as hard as he could. It bulleted across the room in a fizzling blue ball, bright as a bolt of lightning. The warlock saw it at the last second - far too late - and could only tilt his staff towards it.

The energy ball hit the tip of the staff and blew it to smithereens, throwing the warlock's arms wide. His face was a brief picture of total shock. Then the blast lifted him off the floor like he was made of paper and slammed him into the wall, momentarily pinning him against the trunk of the tree; he hung there for just a second, still frozen in shock, before toppling forward. As he hit the floor, his body exploded into a million blue sparks, and he was gone.

Dale's breath came in sharp, ragged gasps. He realised his arms were still outstretched and let them fall limp at his sides. Every ounce of energy had left him. He slumped forward against the desk, knocking an ink pot to the floor.

Then Brooke was at his side.

'Dale!' she cried, grabbing at him. 'Are you ok?'

'Mmm-hmmm,' he replied, his face buried in papers.

Brooke took him by the back collar and pulled him upright again. He slid to his knees, arms spread flat on the desk.

'You did it!' she said. 'You got him.'

'Yeah,' he managed. He turned his head to look at her and his eyes widened. 'Hey, your face! What happened?'

There was a black scorch mark on Brooke's cheek, right next to her eye. She touched it gingerly, wincing.

'One of the embers got me I think,' she said. 'But it would've been a lot worse if it hadn't been for *you*.'

She took him by the arm and heaved him to his feet; his knees almost buckled under him.

'That took… a lot out of me,' he admitted, putting a hand to his spinning head. He realised his other hand was gripping Brooke's shoulder and released her. 'If any more warlocks come, we're in trouble.'

'Don't worry, I think he was the only one. We can't get out of here, anyway.'

They both looked at the doorway, still mostly blocked by the collapsed frame. The gaping hole in the burned staircase was just visible through it. There was no way up or down.

'Now what?' said Dale.

***

The others were almost at the top of the staircase when the next warlock attacked. Tonya saw the blast coming first and shrieked, 'Watch out!'

Willow and Charlie dived in opposite directions. The blast shot right between them, freezing the hem of

Willow's cloak and tearing into the stairs. Ferocious icicles burst from the steps, stabbing up towards the ceiling.

'You'll come no further!' bellowed the warlock, a huge black man in deep blue ropes. 'Go back to where you came from, Other-worlders.'

Charlie steadied himself on the stairs. He started spinning the Moon Hammer, grimacing as the rope cut into his swollen hand.

Just one good shot, mate, he thought, watching the tip of the Elemental's staff glowing blue. *I just need one, and you're toast.*

Willow got there first.

Roots burst from the stairs by the warlock's feet, snaking around his boots. He wobbled on the spot, flailing his arms for balance; before he found it, Willow hit him square in the chest with a blast of emerald light, and he went down.

Her eyes burned gold and she lowered her hands. 'Are you two ok?'

'Just peachy,' replied Tonya, edging around the magicked icicles.

'Never better,' said Charlie. He slowed the Moon Hammer's spin to a stop, catching the sphere in his uninjured hand.

Willow looked past them down the stairs, then started up again.

'When we reach the branch,' she said, 'stay right behind me. They'll try to hit us as soon as we're visible. There are still five left.'

'Including Luno,' said Charlie, following after her.

Willow nodded and said, 'I'll deal with her.'

They came to the end of the staircase. Beyond the opening, the dark green mass of the tree canopy was visible, moving gently in the breeze. The fire-fairies were still there, winking in and out in the gloom.

'Ready?' said Willow.

The other two nodded. Willow held her hands out by her sides, palms down, green sparks flickering between her fingers, and rushed out into the open air.

Charlie barely got out before double blasts exploded just a few yards away from the exit. He half-dived, half-tumbled to one side, landing painfully on his shoulder. Out of the corner of his eye, he glimpsed Tonya going the other way.

He scrambled up. Willow was nearby, furiously hurling bursts of green light at another Elemental, who was parrying them with her white staff, advancing on them menacingly. Each blocked burst of magic exploded with a muffled *bang*, sending an invisible shockwave rippling through the air. Charlie struggled to stay on his feet as wave after wave slammed into him.

'You shouldn't have come here, Willow of Nymm!' the warlock shouted maniacally, drawing closer. Her dyed purple hair flew crazily around her head; her purple eyes glowed in the night. 'You should've stayed far away.'

'You'll pay for this!' Willow yelled back.

With a cry of rage, she threw a bigger, brighter ball of light at the Elemental. The warlock managed to block it, but the shockwave sent her careening backwards across the tree branch.

'Charlie!' Tonya shouted. 'Behind you!'

He turned, saw the other Elemental coming - another woman, dressed in green this time - and started spinning the Moon Hammer. The sphere *thrummed* through the air, beginning to glow as it gathered power.

Hurry up, hurry up!

The warlock stopped, cocking her head. He saw her eyes flash through the blurred spinning rope, her painted green lips curling into an amused grin.

'What toy is this?' she said, raising her staff.

Red for fire, Charlie thought, gritting his teeth as the Moon Hammer rope dug deeper and deeper into his swollen hand. *Blue for ice. What's green stand for?*

The answer came almost instantly.

There was a hollow *boom* as the warlock struck the tree with the base of her staff. Huge chunks of bark, each the size of a basketball, detached from the branch and rose up into the air around her. Charlie guessed there were at least a dozen. The Elemental's grin widened.

Green for earth.

'Uh oh,' Charlie said.

The warlock thrust her staff forward and the chunks of bark shot towards him. He turned the spinning Moon Hammer like a shield, just in time; the heavy wooden projectiles struck it, one after another, and exploded. The air filled with wood chips. Each impact rocked him back but he just managed to stay on his feet, his teeth clenched, his every muscle burning with effort.

The final chunk of bark disintegrated on the Moon Hammer. Through the blur, Charlie saw the Elemental's smile falter. He also noticed the bright blue haze trailing in the sphere's wake. The *thrumming* sound was louder than ever.

'My turn,' he muttered.

He shifted his body, pulled his arm back, and hurled the Moon Hammer at the Elemental. The sphere sung as it bulleted through the air towards her. She'd seen what he was about to do and conjured up a barrier of wood from the tree branch, but it was no good. It may as well have been tissue paper.

The sphere hit the barrier and exploded, obliterating it in an instant. The blast hit the warlock point blank in the chest, sending her flailing through the air. She flew over the side of the branch with a scream and disappeared.

Charlie pulled the sphere back and caught it in his good hand, staring in awe at the little ball of metal. He didn't even feel the pain in his right hand, which was now raw under the Moon Hammer rope.

Tonya appeared at his side. 'When did you learn to do that?'

'Yesterday,' Charlie replied.

'Charlie!'

Willow's panicked cry instantly snapped them back to reality. Charlie turned in her direction and gasped.

She was airborne. The warlock had her in a powerful jet of wind, at least ten feet above the surface of the branch - it rushed from the tip of her glowing staff like a miniature tornado. Roots lashed to Willow's ankles from the branch kept her from simply blowing away, but the wind was too strong for her to get her arms down and fight back. Even as they watched, one of the roots tore free from the branch, leaving her leg flailing in the air.

Purple for wind.

'Help!' she yelled.

Charlie charged, spinning the Moon Hammer again. The sphere began to *thrum.*

But the warlock saw him coming. She turned the twisting tornado towards him - it pulled Willow with it, the one remaining root straining to hold on to her ankle. Charlie felt the wind blast at his face, whipping his hair back, and instinctively threw himself headlong onto the branch.

Tonya wasn't so quick.

The wind caught her and sent her flying back with a scream. She tumbled end over end towards the edge of the branch and the skyscraper-high fall to the forest floor.

Charlie did the only thing he could think of.

With a cry, he sent the Moon Hammer flying in Tonya's direction. The sphere barely reached her in time, hitting her flailing arm. She caught the rope in her hand; Charlie dug his heels into the branch bark to stop himself from being yanked after her. Behind him, he heard the Elemental cackle in triumph.

'Well played, Other-worlder!' she yelled, laughing wildly. Charlie rolled over, saw her purple eyes blazing. 'But you're no match for the might of Elem - '

Roots burst from the branch, snagging her wrists. She saw them and her cackle caught in her throat; before she could react, the roots jerked her hands down, shifting the tornado blast directly below her.

The warlock shrieked as she was catapulted skyward, straight up into the tree canopy above. Charlie saw her vanish into the dark green mass of leaves. The fire-fairies scattered briefly then surged into the leaves after her; she screamed once, long and shrill, then fell silent.

Willow picked herself up, shoving windswept hair away from her face, her hands still glowing faintly green from the spell. She pointed past Charlie and said, 'Help her.'

Charlie turned, saw Tonya lying in a heap nearby, and hurried over to her. She was still clutching the Moon Hammer rope in one hand.

'Ow,' Tonya said, rolling onto her back. 'That… really hurt.'

'Good catch,' Charlie said. He grabbed her hand and pulled her to her feet. 'Are you alright?'

'Yeah, I guess. I don't like these Elemental guys.'

'Me neither.'

Willow came over to them, running the back of her hand over a cut on her lip. Charlie knew she must be just as hurt as Tonya - they'd both dropped from a few feet in the air - but she said nothing about it. Her eyes were already fixed on the branch leading to the quarters of the Empress.

'Two more down,' she said. 'Three to go.'

'They'll have the place sealed up tight,' said Charlie. 'And they'll see us coming a mile away.'

'They'll see *someone* coming,' said Willow.

Charlie followed her gaze to Tonya. The other girl frowned, then sighed.

'Great,' she said. 'Tonya Miller to the rescue. *Again.*'

***

'Oh no,' said Brooke.

'So many,' said Dale.

They were by the big round window, their faces pressed to the glass. Far below, the city had descended into full-blown panic.

Woodspeople had suddenly appeared everywhere, darting up and down streets between tree-buildings, hammering on doors to wake those living on the forest floor. Nymmite warriors were descending from the tree canopy, rushing down the tree trunk staircases while civilians went the other way, heading for the safety of the branches.

But they won't be safe there, Brooke thought, picking out a fleeing Woodsman carrying a Nymmite child in each arm. *Doomgaard will burn the trees down.*

The battle was fully underway now. The Nymmite forces had met the Doomgaard battalion halfway between the edge of the city and the trees lining its outer perimeter, where the buildings gave way to moonlit grassy slopes. Bursts of green and blue lit up the clashing battle lines; even from such a distance, Brooke could see blades flashing in the light and shuddered to think what was going on down there. Further back, the enormous Doomgaard catapults had been completed and were almost ready to begin firing their destructive payloads.

They'll burn everything *down.*

'What do we do?' Brooke said anxiously.

'I'm not sure there's anything we *can* do,' Dale replied, 'except watch, and hope for the best.'

She heard him groan and looked round. He was moving away from the window, hobbling. For the first time, she noticed he was clutching his left arm.

'Are you ok?' she said.

'Yeah,' he said, going to the big table in the centre of the room. 'I think… he maybe got my arm. It hurts.'

She followed him to the table and helped him draw back a chair. They were surprisingly heavy. He winced as he flopped down into it.

'We need one of those Nymm beans,' she said, staring with some concern at his arm. His tunic sleeve was beginning to darken. 'Hang on.'

She did a quick sweep of the room, rifling through papers on top of the desks, pulling open drawers, even checking empty spaces on the bookshelves. Nothing.

'You'd think they'd have *some* lying around,' she said, coming back to the table. 'Willow always seems to have one on her.'

'I'll be ok,' Dale said, forcing a smile. 'It's not that bad.'

'It doesn't look good, though.'

'Don't worry about me.'

'Well, I…'

She trailed off. Dale's gaze dropped to the table. For one long moment, the only sounds were the muffled, chaotic roar of battle in the distance and the intermittent crackle of the lantern above their heads.

Brooke opened her mouth to speak, closed it again.

I hate this I hate this I hate this

Dale shifted his weight in the chair. 'Seriously, I'm fine. Maybe you can figure out what we should do next.'

She swallowed, discovered her throat was dry, and said, 'How should I know?'

'You're the smart one.'

'You're *way* smarter than me and you know it.'

'Not with things like this. I'm good with numbers and stuff. You're the bookish one.'

She sighed, starting towards the window again. Then she stopped.

'Bookish,' she said.

'Huh?'

Brooke hurried back to the table and heaved out one of the chairs. As she sat, she whipped the little leather book from her pocket and heard the words of Lindara the librarian in her mind, clear as day: *Try asking the book itself.*

'What're you doing?' Dale said.

She slapped the book down on the table, undid the twine and flipped to the first available blank page. As she went through them, she caught a brief glimpse of the drawing that'd appeared on the boat: the tree and the rock. It was more defined than before.

'Ok,' she said, pinning the book's next two blank pages open with the flat of her hands. 'Here we go.'

'Here we go with what?' said Dale, frowning.

'Just… stop asking questions for a second.'

She cleared her throat, took a deep breath, let it out slowly, and said, 'We need help.'

Nothing happened. Silence.

'Who… are you talking to?' said Dale slowly.

'Shush.' She leaned closer to the pages. 'We. Need. Help.'

Still nothing.

'I think *you* need help,' Dale said.

Brooke thumped her fist on the table. 'You're not helping here!'

'Helping with what? You're talking to a book!'

'Yeah, so? It worked with the tree at Hammerfall, remember?'

'That was the Wee People's tree. This is a book.'

'And?'

'And have you tried *writing* in it, you dummy?'

Brooke blinked. 'Writing in it.'

'Yeah. Look.' Dale pointed - there was an ink pot on the table next to a rolled-up scroll. And on top of the scroll was a quill. 'Use that.'

Brooke stood, stretched across the table and grabbed the little pot, almost spilling it. The quill, made from a beautifully-patterned tawny feather, weighed next to nothing between her fingers.

'Try writing what you were saying,' said Dale.

'Yeah I know,' Brooke said. 'Give me a sec.'

She positioned the pot next to the book and carefully dipped the quill in the ink; the tip instantly drank some of the black liquid. Taking a breath to steady herself, Brooke put the quill to the blank page and wrote:

We need help.

They both stared at the page as the ink dried. Nothing happened.

Brooke swallowed. 'Maybe... I need to be more specific?'

'Specific how?'

'Like, we need help... getting out of this room? Stopping the Elementals? Rescuing Orchidema? Stopping the Doom - '

'Hey,' Dale said, leaning over the book. 'Look!'

Brooke leaned in too. Words were forming on the page, just below where she'd written. They scrawled into focus, as if some invisible hand was writing them:

They are coming.

A chill ran down Brooke's spine.

'That's... what you heard in your dream... right?' said Dale.

'Yes.'

With a trembling hand, she put the quill to the page and wrote another line:

Who is coming?

They waited. Again, nothing happened for a moment, longer than before. Then:

Turn back and see.

She frowned. 'Turn back and see? What's that mean?'

'No clue,' said Dale. He looked back over his shoulder, shaking his head. 'Nothing here.'

'Who's writing this?' Brooke said. Then she gasped.

'What?' said Dale.

Another line had appeared. Neither of them spoke as they read it:

Turn back and see, Brooke Woods and Dale Reed.

'Ok, so whoever it is knows who we are,' said Dale in a faraway voice. 'Does that mean we know who *they* are? You don't think it's Yulerin?

'Maybe,' Brooke said. 'I suppose that would make…'

She trailed off again. Her heart was thudding hard in her chest now. More words scrawled onto the page in the same hand:

Turn back and see. They are coming. Protect the Empress.

Something clicked in Brooke's head.

'Turn back,' she said, taking the corner of the page, 'and see.'

She turned the page back to the drawing. The tree and rock were more defined than ever. Except now, it didn't quite look like a tree *or* a rock. It was beginning to look like something else entirely.

'Dale,' Brooke whispered. 'What's that?'

He leaned close to the page, squinting at the drawing by Brooke's hand. His hair brushed her cheek but she barely noticed.

'That… looks like the pool,' he said, pointing at the round shape she'd thought was a rock. 'Like the one I almost drowned in.'

'Yeah,' said Brooke. 'I see it too.'

'And that,' said Dale, shifting his finger upwards, 'looks like…'

Not a tree, Brooke thought. *It was never a tree.*

'It's a man,' she breathed. 'And he's… standing over a pool.'

She touched the page. The drawing began to shudder and she felt the familiar warm, tingling sensation beneath her fingertips, just like when she read the words in the book earlier. Then it stopped shuddering and they both drew in a sharp breath. The drawing was now perfectly clear.

'It's not a man,' said Dale. 'It's…'

'It's a Giant,' said Brooke.

Suddenly, the page flipped back over of its own accord. The writing was still there. As they watched, a new, final line scrawled into focus:

They are coming. Turn back and see.

Brooke and Dale looked at each other. Then they pushed back their chairs and ran for the big window behind them.

***

Two warlocks stood guard by the doorway. One wore green, the other red.

Behind them, the quarters of the Empress were sealed up tight. The same warm glow spilled out between the oak window shutters and the fire fairies flitted around the closed entrance, but there was no way inside. The Elementals had seen to that.

They had, of course, heard the fight taking place further down the wide, smooth branch leading to the royal accommodation: the roar of conjured wind, the screams of their fallen comrades. They knew the Woodsgirl and her Other-world friends were here. But they hadn't seen them yet.

Still, they were prepared.

Presently, a figure appeared further down the branch, coming up the slope towards them. She was limping and clutching her arm. Her purple robes were scorched and torn, and one of her bright purple eyes was swollen shut.

One of the guarding warlocks - the one in red - took a step forward, squinting in the dim glow from the lantern above the door. He hated everything about this place, least of all the weak, natural light in which the Nymmites seemed to be perfectly content, with their ugly, golden, nocturnal eyes. He couldn't wait to get back to Elementa.

'Who's there?' he shouted.

'It's me,' the woman called back, waving her good arm. 'It's just me. And I'm… I'm hurt.'

'Hurt how?'

She came closer, moving into the fringes of the lantern light, still limping.

'The Woodsgirl,' she said. 'She… got my arm. Like, really bad.'

'Where is she now?'

'Dead, I think. So are the others. We got them. Can I go inside?'

The warlocks glanced at each other; the one in green shrugged, and turned to unlock the door. The man in red descended the steps.

'You're certain they're dead?'

'Yes. Totally.'

The woman in purple took another step forward then dropped to her knees, wincing in pain. She held her injured arm tight to her body.

'I… I don't know if I can keep going. Can you help me?'

The man in red sighed and started towards her. Behind him, the woman in green unlocked the door. She started to turn.

The vine came from nowhere, wrapping around her ankle. She opened her mouth to scream and another vine lashing itself around her face. A third caught her by the arm, and all three dragged her up into the leaf canopy, coiling around her like snakes. She disappeared in an instant.

The red warlock heard the commotion and turned back, too late.

As he did so, Willow and Charlie came down from the leaf canopy. Willow dropped, catlike, right beside the Elemental; Charlie landed in a heap next to the woman in purple. The warlock spun around, started to raise his staff, and was blown sideways off the branch by a blast of Willow's green light. He disappeared, screaming, into the leaves.

'Ow,' said Charlie, getting to his feet. 'That was a bigger drop than you said it'd be.'

'You misheard me,' said Willow, extending a hand to the woman in purple. 'Well done.'

The warlock accepted the hand up, letting go of her injured arm. She threw her head back and sighed dramatically.

'Seriously, where would you guys be without me?'

'Yeah, you did a lot there,' Charlie said, smirking.

The woman in purple squeezed her eyes shut, and then simply crumpled to the ground. Tonya stood in her place, like she's just shrugged herself out of a costume. She shook out her hair and sighed again, this time with relief.

'I hate playing villains,' she said, stepping away from the Elemental shroud. It dissolved to dust on the surface of the branch.

'Ok,' said Willow, her eyes glowing. 'Stick close to me.'

They approached the quarters of the Empress. The door was still ajar, allowing a shaft of warm light to flood down the steps. As Willow took the handle, the fire fairies around the door frame all began buzzing louder than ever and turned bright scarlet.

'Careful,' whispered Tonya. Charlie took the Moon Hammer rope in his hand, letting the sphere dangle.

Willow pulled open the door and slipped inside. They followed.

Charlie blinked, shielding his eyes from the sudden change in light. Flames crackled in the stone fireplace to the left, and the ceiling lantern swung gently on its chain; the piped instrument in the corner was now silent. The whole room was pleasantly warm and smelled vaguely of peeled summer oranges.

It was also completely empty.

Charlie started towards the curtain at the back of the room, the one leading to Orchidema's chambers. Willow stuck out an arm to stop him.

'No,' she said, 'not there. It's empty, too.'

'How do you know?' he said.

'I just do. And I can hear voices.' Her head swivelled to the right, to the door by the table of vials and potions. 'Through there. Come on.'

They crossed the room soundlessly on the ornamental rugs. Willow paused by the closed door, listening intently.

'I hear… many voices,' she said.

'What's through there?' said Tonya.

'Stairs. Leading to a meeting room,' said Willow. 'They're all down there now.'

'So let's go,' Charlie said, gripping the Moon Hammer rope tighter.

Willow met his gaze, reading him.

'You cannot use weapons in there,' she said. 'There isn't enough space. You may do damage, or hurt someone.'

'I *want* to hurt someone - '

'You may hurt the Empress.'

Charlie swallowed. His grip on the Moon Hammer rope loosened.

'Let me do the talking,' said Willow, looking at both of them. 'If they have Orchidema, they have power over Nymm itself. Luno's the only one left now. She's outnumbered. But she has the Empress.'

Charlie and Tonya nodded. Willow nodded back.

'Alright,' she said. 'Keep your wits about you.'

She twisted the handle and pulled open the door.

***

Dale pressed his face to the glass. 'Do you see anything?'

'No,' said Brooke next to him. 'I mean, I see the Doomgaard, and the Woodspeople. And I see those great big catapults. What're they doing with them?'

'They're getting ready to fire.'

Dale's eyesight wasn't amazing at the best of times, and it was even harder to make out details of the battle through the glass, so high up. But he could see what was happening well enough: the black-armoured soldiers in the rear lines were swarming around the catapults, loading enormous spheres into their throwing arm buckets. And beside every catapult, a soldier stood ready with a flaming torch in his hands.

'They'll burn the city down from there,' Dale said, his voice wavering. 'And there'll be no way to stop them.'

'It didn't work,' Brooke said softly. 'The book, the writing. It didn't work.'

She sniffed, and Dale looked over. Beneath the dangles of blonde hair, her blue eyes were welling up. As he watched, a single tear spilled out and trickled through the dark scorch mark on her cheek.

'It's ok,' he said, without much confidence. 'I mean… it'll *be* ok.'

She saw him looking and quickly swiped the tear from her face, smudging the scorch mark.

'It doesn't feel like it this time,' she said. 'It feels like everything's… I dunno… *stacked* against us, more than before. You know?'

'Yeah. I know.'

Then she was looking at him properly, her bright blue eyes burning into his, and he suddenly felt different. Still afraid, yes, but not because of the Doomgaard. Or their catapults. Or of Luno and the Elementals. Afraid because of her. Afraid that something might *happen* to her… to *both* of them… before he could -

'Wait,' Brooke said, breaking whatever was hanging in the air. 'Do you feel that?'

'Feel… what?'

'That.'

Then he did feel it.

Vibrations under their feet. A rumbling noise.

They both planted themselves against the window again. Brooke jabbed at the glass.

'Look!' she cried. 'There!'

'I don't - ' Dale started, then gasped.

With an audible *boom*, a section of white-barked trees behind the Doomgaard army exploded. Ragged chunks of wood rained down on the black-armoured soldiers. Those in the rear lines started to turn; archers reached for arrows, swordsmen drew their blades.

All too late.

The first Giant erupted from the tree line with a roar that shook the whole of Nymm. He was enormous - bigger even than Murblok, the Factionhead of Golemar - and wielded a club the size of a tree trunk; he swung it in a low arc as he came barrelling down the slope, sending Doomgaard soldiers flying through the night air. Those who managed to dodge the club were mowed down or booted out of the way.

Then another section of the tree line exploded, and a second Giant appeared, even larger than the first. His grey-blue skin, covered all over in tattoos, glistened in the moonlight as the Doomgaard army scattered before him. The ground rumbled and shook beneath their feet.

'It worked!' Brooke cried, clutching her chest. More tears were flowing now. 'Writing in the book worked - you're a genius, Dale!'

'You're the one who did it!' he said, laughing with relief. 'You called for help and it came.'

A third Giant burst through the trees. And a fourth, and a fifth. Soon there were at least ten of them, all different shapes and sizes, all bearing colossal clubs and hammers and axes, ploughing through the panicked Doomgaard ranks. The Woodspeople kept them hemmed in on the other side, blasting the disoriented front line soldiers with bursts of green magic or blue shockwaves from their Moon Hammers.

The first catapult came down with a crash as two Giants slammed into it, sending its spherical payload careening into the nearest Doomgaard soldiers like a massive bowling ball. The second came down even faster. One of the torch-bearers managed to light the sphere in the third one about two seconds before a Giant smashed the arm right off the machine.

Within minutes, it seemed the entire Doomgaard army was in complete disarray. Most of their forces were either running for their lives or surrendering as quickly as they could. Dale saw one of the Giants with a black-armoured soldier in each hand, waving them triumphantly above his head like action figures.

'I can't believe it worked,' Brooke said, wiping her face with both hands. 'They did it. The Giants saved Nymm.'

'They did,' said Dale, stepping back. He suddenly felt light-headed, like a weight had been lifted off him and he was now floating. 'We still need to get out of here, though.'

'Yeah,' Brooke agreed, sniffing again. 'We need to help the others. It's not over.'

Dale started away from the window.

'Wait.' She grabbed his arm and he winced. 'Oh, sorry! I forgot.'

'It's ok.'

He faced her. Beyond the glass and far below, the Giants continued to roar and smash their way through the fleeing Doomgaard forces. The floor still trembled beneath their feet.

Brooke's eyes bore into his and she said, 'Before we go… I mean, *if* we can even get out of here… I want you to tell me.'

Dale's heart leapt in his chest, flooding his cheeks with warmth.

'Tell you… what?' he said.

Her look hardened, just a little. 'You know, Dale,' she said.

'Brooke…'

'Tell me,' she said. And then, it simply burst out of her: 'Tell me why you stopped talking to me when school started again. We spent the whole summer together - you, me and Charlie - and you just acted like it all hadn't happened. Like we weren't friends, like we'd *never* been friends. Like Uland hadn't even happened. Tell me why you stopped replying to my messages. Tell me why you barely looked at me in class. Tell me why you stopped being my *friend*, Dale.'

She paused, took a breath. Her eyes were ringed with red, but she was no longer crying.

'If we don't ever get out of here,' she said, 'I want to at least know *why* first. Before the floor collapses, or the Elementals get us, or whatever. I just want to know. Even if it's because of… what I think it's because of… and that would suck… I still want to know.'

Her voice petered out as the last few words left her mouth. She folded her arms, waiting.

Dale tried to look away and found he couldn't. Part of him wanted to run, to just *run* for the doorway, even though it was blocked off. It was just too much. He couldn't think about it now, when all this was going on. They could talk later, maybe.

What if there never is a later? he thought. *What if this is all either of you have?*

He swallowed. Brooke's eyes were pools of blue and he was falling into them.

Tell her.

'I didn't mean… for it to be like that,' he croaked.

She stiffened, but said nothing. Outside, the Woodspeople were cheering.

'I didn't mean to react like I did, when… when… you know.'

Brooke folded her arms tighter. 'When I said I liked you?'

'Yes,' he replied sheepishly.

'So why did you?'

He shook his head. 'You wouldn't understand. You don't know what's been going on.'

'So tell me!' she cried. Her face was flushed now too. 'I'm your friend, Dale. I'm one of your *best* friends. If I freaked you out or something, I'm sorry. I just… wanted to say it, is all. If you didn't like me back, that's… that's totally fine… but you could've just said so.'

'It's not that.'

'Then what - '

'It's my parents!' he cried suddenly, louder than he'd meant to. She flinched back a little, but he kept going. 'It wasn't because of you. I didn't freak out because you said you liked me. I just… couldn't handle it… in that moment.'

Brooke frowned, hesitated, and said, 'What about your parents?'

Dale turned away. He stared up at the lantern on the ceiling, watching it sway. Finally, he said, 'I think they're getting a divorce.'

There was a long pause.

'Oh.'

He hung his head, realising he'd never said the words out loud before.

'They've been fighting a lot, ever since our school trip. Before then, I suppose. But it just kept getting worse over the summer. I didn't tell you or Charlie because I was… I dunno… embarrassed, or something. And we were all getting on so well. I didn't want to ruin it. And then when we were alone that time and you said you liked me, I just felt so… *guilty*. Like, it wasn't ok for me to be happy when my parents were going through all their stuff together. I know it's dumb, but that's why. That's why I sort of… drifted away from you guys. That's why I couldn't talk to you anymore. I knew you were mad, or sad, or something. And I just felt so bad about it. I felt like such an idiot. But that's why.'

For a long moment, neither of them spoke. He continued staring at the lantern, unblinking, until his eyes ached.

When Brooke spoke again, his entire body froze.

'You're right,' she said. 'You are an idiot.'

He turned back to her, dumbfounded. Her arms were folded again and her jaw was set.

'What?'

'I said, you *are* an idiot, Dale.'

'Brooke - '

'You couldn't talk to *me* about parent issues?' she snapped. 'You thought *I* wouldn't understand?' Then her fists were down by her sides. 'You know my Dad left me and my Mum when I was six, right? You know I haven't seen him in years?'

Dale forced himself not to flinch away from her glare.

'I… sort of knew that,' he said.

Brooke opened her mouth, closed it again, and then whirled away with a cry of frustration. She stomped a few paces across the floor. Dale started to follow and she suddenly whipped back around.

'If *anyone* would've understood, it would've been *me*,' she said. 'I know *exactly* what you're going through, Dale. Maybe I didn't talk about it much either, but… but you never asked.'

He didn't respond. His head felt lighter than ever.

'All this time,' Brooke said with a disbelieving laugh, 'I thought you were avoiding me because I freaked you out. But it was because you were ashamed about something that's not your fault. You big idiot.' She deliberately found his eyeline again. 'You know that, right? You know it's not your fault?'

He stared back. 'Yes.'

'*Do* you?'

He hesitated. 'I… I think so.'

Suddenly, something unexpectedly surged up inside him, something he'd always been quick to force back down. He tried stopping it again, but it was too late. She'd already seen the look on his face.

'Dale.' She came towards him. 'It's *actually* not your fault.'

'I… I know,' he said. That bottled-up feeling was almost at the back of his throat. 'I know it isn't. It's just that… I just wish…'

And then it hit him, and he couldn't stop it. All the anger and pain and despair swept over him, and his eyes filled with hot tears, and a single, aching sob rolled out of his mouth. 'I just wish it wasn't *happening*.'

His head dropped. Brooke was already there.

She threw her arms around him. He buried his face in her shoulder and hugged her back, and tears flowed freely for both of them.

***

Willow knew they were caught before the staff even touched her temple.

'I have you,' said the warlock, his blue eyes glinting malevolently. 'Tell your friends to lay down their arms.'

He moved Willow into the room, keeping his staff aimed at the side of her head. Charlie and Tonya followed, both glaring at the Elemental.

'Guess the seventh one came back,' Tonya muttered.

'Charlie,' said Willow slowly. 'Put it down.'

Reluctantly, Charlie unwound the Moon Hammer from his hand and set it on the floor.

'One wrong move and I'll freeze her head off her shoulders,' said the warlock. 'Now, down the stairs. And keep your hands high.'

Charlie and Tonya descended the curved set of stairs leading from the doorway. The Elemental guided Willow after them, the tip of his staff pointed directly at the back of her head. The staircase ended at another door with runes carved into the wood.

'Inside,' said the warlock.

Tonya opened the door and went through, followed by Charlie. Willow went after them, trying with all her might to keep the magical fury building inside her under control. She couldn't unleash it here, so close to Orchidema.

The moment will arrive, she thought. *Just hold on.*

Then they were in the meeting room. It was a larger space beneath the quarters of the Empress, similarly-lit with a ceiling lantern and stone fireplace in the corner. Several doors around the room led to other parts of the royal accommodation; Willow remembered them all from her childhood, but none were especially useful now.

'Ah, there you are.'

Her heart skipped a beat.

Luno was standing at the far end of the room in a flowing scarlet robe, her ruby eyes glowing in the lantern light. Orchidema sat next to her on a high-backed wooden chair, hands in her lap. She met Willow's gaze with a mixture of fear and relief.

'I wondered when you'd be joining us,' said Luno, smiling.

The Council of Nymm stood in front of them, parted down the middle. Five of the six stood tall, watching them grimly with golden eyes; the sixth, an older Woodsman Willow recognised as Briarwen, was slumped against the wall clutching his right arm, which was badly scorched.

'Please,' said Luno, beckoning them forward.

Willow felt the Elemental's staff prod her in the back. Glowering, she crossed the room towards Luno, passing between the Council members, who averted their gaze as she went by. Charlie and Tonya remained on either side of her; Charlie was muttering words she'd never heard before under his breath.

They stopped a few feet from Luno and the Empress. Orchidema's green eyes swam. Willow could see she was wringing her hands in the folds of her robe, something she always did when she was anxious. Rage bubbled deep inside her, desperate to get out.

Luno cleared her throat and said, 'I assume all my comrades are dead?'

'Every last one,' said Willow, deliberately taking her time with each word.

The Factionhead's smile widened into a sneer and her eyes flashed.

'Sounds like an act of treason to me,' she said. 'I wonder what our allies across the continent will think when they hear of it.'

'You've *literally* taken the Empress hostage,' said Tonya, 'you... you *cow*.'

Luno slowly turned her gaze towards her. Tonya met it without flinching.

'You know,' said the Elemental, 'I'm not sure I have much use for you, Other-worlder. You have no discernible powers, and you're rather childish. I could burn you to a crisp with a snap of my fingers. How would you like that?'

Tonya said nothing. Luno grinned, bearing perfectly-white teeth.

'I thought so.' Her gaze shifted to Charlie. '*You*, however, are most valuable. My master has plans for you, Warrior. You defeated his servant Hysst and he'd like to know how. Who knows, maybe there could even be a place for you among his ranks?'

'Sounds good,' Charlie replied immediately. 'Take me to him. I'll show him what I can do with a sword.'

Willow had been around Charlie long enough to understand sarcasm when she heard it, but the other Nymmites hadn't - a ripple of shock went through them. Someone whispered, 'Surely not?' and Luno chuckled.

'You'll see him soon enough,' she said. 'Once our business is concluded here tonight, he'll be free to visit Nymm whenever he pleases.'

A couple of Council members gasped.

'You'd bring him here, Lady Luno?'

Maphira's tone was cordial, but cold as ice. Willow started to turn her head towards her and felt the staff jab between her shoulder blades.

'Of course,' said Luno, resting a hand on Orchidema's chair. 'I'm sure my lord will be keen to meet his new vassal face-to-face.'

'Vassal?' said Charlie. Willow didn't have to look at him directly to be able to tell he was shaking with rage as he spoke.

'Yes, dim boy,' Luno replied. 'The young ruler of Nymm has agreed to submit herself to Decymero in exchange for the lives of her people. She'll remain Empress under his watchful eye, and Nymm will declare itself a staunch ally of Doomgaard.'

'Doomgaard,' said Willow, now also trembling with anger, 'is currently attacking the city.'

'That's called leverage, my naive little friend. The Empress here would never have even considered bending the knee to my lord if her precious people weren't under threat. I daresay she'd have willingly died at my hand before giving up the city. Am I right, Your Highness?'

'Yes,' Orchidema said, barely above a whisper.

'Indeed. So attacking Nymm became necessary. And thanks to you, dear Willow, bringing the Doomgaard here was no trouble at all. Thank you for that.'

my fault my fault my fault

Luno smiled again, drumming her fingers on the chair. 'So, now that we're all here, let's get this done, shall we? Who has the declaration?'

'I do,' said Maphira. She held up a scroll tied with green twine.

'Excellent, Lady Regent. Do bring it here.'

Maphira drifted towards Luno and Orchidema, her golden eyes blazing. She glanced at Willow as she passed. Next to her Charlie was muttering under his breath again.

'A mother's love,' Luno cooed, gesturing at Maphira as she undid the twine. 'Is there a more potent bargaining tool in all the world?'

The Woodswoman unfurled the scroll with long, elegant fingers. Orchidema looked up at her, twisting her robe in her hands.

'Charlie Flint,' said Luno. 'You're a big, *strong* boy. Make yourself useful and bring that table over here, won't you?'

She motioned to an end table near the fireplace. Muttering, Charlie stomped across to it, lifted it easily, and brought it up to Maphira. As he set it down in front of Orchidema, Willow saw the two of them exchange a look. When Charlie turned back, his face was flushed with more than just anger.

'The mighty warrior,' Luno sneered. Then, gesturing towards the table: 'Lady Maphira, why don't you add your name first?'

Maphira's face remained without expression as she laid the scroll on the table. She produced a quill from nowhere and bent to write her name.

'This is madness!' cried one of the Council members suddenly.

They all looked his way. He was one of the older Woodsmen, probably similar in age to the injured Briarwen, with hair the colour of sea salt. Willow struggled to recall his name for a moment in the midst of her anger, then found it: Sylvara.

Luno rolled her eyes and sighed. 'We've been over this already, old man. And we've established you really don't have much choice in the matter, do you? Now tell me, is it madness to sign a peace-keeping declaration…' - she levelled her staff at him - '... or resist the one holding the keys to your young Sovereign's life, who could reduce all of you to a collective pile of ash faster than you can even utter the word *madness?*'

The last syllable left her lips as a snake-like hiss. Sylvara shrank back and said nothing more.

'I imagined so,' said Luno, holding her staff upright again. 'Now, Lady Maphira - if you please.'

The Regent wrote her name on the scroll and set down the quill. As she straightened up, Luno grinned and said, 'Excellent. Who's next?'

Willow watched with mounting anguish as each Council member approached the little table and scrawled their signatures on the declaration. Orchidema watched too, her deep green eyes gradually filling with tears. Charlie and Tonya were both shaking their heads in disbelief.

Briarwen had to be helped to the table. He grimaced in pain as he bent to add his name to the scroll, but he managed it nonetheless. One of the Council members guided him back to his place by the wall.

Finally, it was Sylvara's turn. The old Woodsman reluctantly approached the table. His face was set and his eyes burned, and Luno's grin grew wider than ever.

'One more name,' she said in a sing-song voice, 'and we're all done.'

Sylvara reached the table and picked up the quill. His hand trembled as he dipped it into the ink and brought the tip down to the scroll. Then he seemed to freeze, hovering over the declaration, gazing at the names already written there. Luno's smile faltered.

'Hurry up, old sir,' she said. 'We don't have all night.'

The Woodsman hesitated a moment longer, still staring down at the scroll. Then he straightened up and dropped the quill onto the table.

'No,' he said. His tone was steady, calm. 'I won't sign this… abomination.'

Willow watched as the scarlet in Luno's irises faded for a split second, then came roaring back. Her blood-red lips curled into a sneer.

'You won't?' she said softly.

Sylvara held his head high. 'I will not.'

Luno lowered her staff, pointing it at the Woodsman once again. The others inched back; Willow braced herself.

'Please,' Orchidema said suddenly, in a tiny voice. 'Spare his life.'

Luno looked down at her, shaking her head grimly.

'I'm sorry, Empress,' she said. 'This man is a coward and doesn't value the lives of your people over his own. There can be no peace without the accord between Nymm and Decymero.' She levelled her staff at Sylvara's face. 'As ruler, you'll need to learn that all actions have consequences. Let me teach you.'

Sylvara closed his eyes. The stone at the head of Luno's staff bloomed red. Someone in the room breathed, 'No…'

Then Luno turned her staff towards Briarwen and said, '*Incadium.*'

With a whooshing roar, a jet of red fire shot from her staff and consumed the injured Woodsman. The whole room lit up with scarlet light. Briarwen screamed once, briefly, and crumpled to the floor. He burned there for a moment. And then he was gone.

Sylvara's mouth fell open in a silent scream of his own and he fell to his knees. The other Council members cried out in despair, staggering back from the smouldering ash pile that had once been Briarwen.

'DO YOU SEE?' Luno shouted over their cries, her staff swaying in the direction of the other Council members. 'Do you see what happens when you defy the will of Decymero? You *burn!*'

Willow felt the tip of the other warlock's staff leave her back. He was distracted.

This was her only chance.

She dropped to her haunches, spun, and thrust out her palms. The Elemental realised his mistake and tried to reposition his staff, but he was too slow. She hit him square in the abdomen with a sizzling blast of emerald light, catapulting him backwards with an 'Oomph!' of surprise. As he flew through the air, his staff - still in his hand - fired a bolt of ice magic towards the ceiling, shattering the lantern. The warlock smashed straight through the door into the stairwell beyond.

For a brief moment, the room was plunged into shadow. Light flared from the fireplace and the eyes of the panicked Woodspeople, who screamed as glass from the destroyed lantern rained down on them. Someone stumbled into Willow, knocking her to the floor.

have to get her have to get her

She struggled back to her feet, swinging back to face Luno.

'*Eydrom.*'

A ball of emerald light burst to life above their heads, flooding the room with green. Maphira stood just below it, her hand raised.

'STOP!'

Willow froze.

Luno was in the same spot at the head of the room. Her eyes blazed red and her face was flushed with rage. She had Orchidema by the scruff of the neck - the tip of her staff was against the Woodsgirl's temple.

Oh no!

'I said stop!' Luno yelled. 'Or I'll kill your Empress.'

One by one, the Council members fell silent, huddling together. Charlie was still standing a few feet from the table and the declaration, fists bunched by his sides.

Luno's fiery gaze settled on Willow. She bore her teeth.

'Silly girl,' she hissed. 'Silly, insignificant *slave* of the Druyads. I might have spared everyone in this room, if not for your stupidity. No longer.'

Willow gritted her teeth. She could feel everyone's eyes on her.

'*You're* the stupid one,' she spat back. 'You sided with *him*. You turned your entire Faction into the enemy.'

Luno grinned again. Her red hair hung crazily about her face now. All her former elegance and beauty had melted away.

'*You* have made yourself the enemy,' she snarled, jerking Orchidema's cloak collar. The Empress's eyes had lost all of their golden lustre. 'Decymero is your new lord, you silly girl. He is the great Vessel of Truth and Power in all of Uland. He is the Harbinger of Destruction, the Prince of the New Age. *See how I serve him now.*'

She threw back her head and shrieked with laughter, pressing the tip of her staff into Orchidema's head. The Woodsgirl winced, squeezing her eyes shut.

She's insane, Willow thought. *He's driven her insane. And she'll kill us all.*

'Lady Luno.'

The Elemental's laughter cut off immediately. She looked across the room, beyond the Council members, and her red eyes bulged.

Orchidema stood by the fireplace, her small, delicate hands clasped in front of her. Her alabaster skin was bright green in the magical light, and her eyes bloomed gold.

Luno's maniacal, triumphant expression dissolved into outright confusion.

'What?' she spluttered. 'How did you… who…'

She looked down. The Orchidema whose collar she was gripping fell away in her hand - Tonya grinned up at her.

She shrugged. 'Umm… surprise?'

With a feline shriek of fury, Luno shoved her away. Both hands went to her staff, angling it in Tonya's direction.

She's insane and she'll kill us all.

Willow ran at her, lifting her hands, summoning her strength.

This time, Charlie got there first.

Before Luno could react, he charged at her and grabbed her staff, just in time; a blast of fire erupted from the end of it, missed Tonya by mere inches and smashed straight through one of the doors leading out of the room. Luno roared something incomprehensible, trying to shake

Charlie off. He held on, doggedly refusing to let go until the Elemental raked her scarlet fingernails across his face; he yelled in pain, releasing his grip.

He'd done enough.

Luno knocked him aside and made to blast him, but before she could, vines burst from the walls and caught her by the wrists. Others snagged the staff, tearing it from her grasp. Roots erupted from the floor and latched onto her ankles. And just as she opened her mouth to scream a spell that could've turned the entire room into a furnace, a concentrated blast of emerald light hit her full in the face. Her head snapped sharply to one side and she slumped into the vines, unconscious.

Willow lowered her hands, breathing hard. She looked across the room and saw Orchidema do the same, the green glow fading from her outstretched palms. The Empress beamed back at her.

'Told you I could do it,' she said.

Chapter Twenty-Two: Homeward

It was almost noon by the time Brooke woke up.

She found her outfit stacked neatly by her bedside, scrubbed and dried to perfection; even her grey leather boots were spotless. She barely remembered dumping her clothes on the floor and crawling into bed the night before, but here they were.

I wonder if Quillorin wants them back, she thought absently, padding to the bathroom.

After washing up, she dressed and hurried down to the banqueting hall, where the others were already having breakfast. Dale and Charlie were shovelling food into their mouths like they hadn't eaten in a week - Tonya watched them with mild disgust. She saw Brooke come in and grinned.

'Brookles, you're up! Quick, eat something before these two scarf it all down. They're like pigs at a trough.'

'Takes one to know one,' Dale replied through a mouthful of food. Charlie snorted, spraying them both with crumbs.

They all ate their fill, and then began picking up their stories from where they'd left off the night before.

Charlie and Tonya described, in vivid detail, how they and Willow had fought their way up the palace staircase, across the tree branch and into the quarters of the Empress. Tonya made it sound as though she'd done just as much fighting as Charlie, who was quick to correct her.

He did, however, concede that she'd ultimately helped win the battle with Luno.

'*Helped?*' Tonya said indignantly. 'If I hadn't switched places with Orchidema when the lantern broke, Luno wouldn't have been distracted long enough for Willow to take her down. I clearly saved the day.'

'It was actually Orchidema who knocked Luno out in the end,' Charlie said. 'But yeah, like I said, you helped.'

Before Tonya could rear up again, Brooke and Dale returned to their story about the warlock and the book and the Giants. They left out the part about their conversation.

'We couldn't believe it worked,' said Brooke.

'Yeah, and not a moment too soon,' added Dale. 'Those catapults were just about to fire.'

'But the Giants smashed them to smithereens…'

'... and the Doomgaard were running scared…'

'... and it was honestly over in no time, right?'

'Right!'

They grinned at one another across the table. Brooke saw Tonya exchange a glance with Charlie and chose to ignore it.

Dale took a swig of fruit juice. 'We were still stuck in the room, though. And it felt like the floor was going to collapse at any minute.'

'Yeah,' Brooke said. 'Thank goodness Rowan-thir came when he did. There was a secret door leading to another passage into the palace. He was able to get us out.'

'We went up instead,' said Charlie, 'into the leaf canopy. And then we came down a different tree. The firewall thing was gone by the time we were on the ground again.'

'What happened to Luno, anyway?' said Dale.

'She's locked up.'

They all jumped. Willow had entered the room without any of them noticing. The Woodsgirl grinned, approaching the table. 'They have her in a holding cell. She won't be going anywhere for a while.'

'Great,' said Charlie. 'Leave her in there.'

Willow touched her own cheek and said to Brooke, 'How's your face?'

'Oh.' Brooke brushed her fingertips over the place where the scorch mark had been - it had almost entirely disappeared overnight, once she'd been seen-to by the healer. 'It's fine, thanks.'

'And your arm?'

'Seems ok,' said Dale, examining it afresh. Willow looked at Tonya and Charlie.

'Bumps and bruises,' said Tonya. 'We'll be fine.'

'Good.'

None of them spoke for a moment. Willow started fidgeting with her hair, a habit Brooke was starting to recognise when she saw it. *She's uncomfortable*, she thought. *Even after everything - even though she's the Empress - she's still just another awkward girl.*

'So what now?' she said aloud.

'Now?' Willow said. 'Well, the battle's over, of course. The Doomgaard didn't stand a chance once the Giants joined the fight. We're still not exactly sure how Yulerin's book was able to summon them, or how they knew which pool to use in Golemar. There are many, and only one leads to Nymm.'

'So *that's* how they got here so quickly,' said Charlie, thumping the table.

Willow nodded. 'It would've taken them days otherwise, even though Golemar is close. Giants can run fast, but not for long. They're always itching for a good fight, though, so they wouldn't have needed much persuasion… however the book managed to persuade them.'

'Are they still here?' said Dale.

'Yes, but not for long. They'll return to their homeland after the feast. Now that Golermar has officially sided with Nymm against Doomgaard, they'll be - '

'Hang on,' said Charlie, holding up his bruised hand. 'Did you say *feast*?'

'You are *literally* eating right now,' Tonya said.

Willow grinned. 'Come outside when you're done and you'll see.'

***

There was an odd air of calm about Nymm that afternoon.

Despite their best efforts, the Doomgaard forces hadn't managed to properly breach the city perimeters, beyond a handful of raiding parties making it as far as the streets. Almost all of Nymm's many tree-buildings were still intact, including (Brooke was glad to see) the library. As they passed by, Lindara waved to them from the balcony, then shuffled back to her books.

While the city itself was mostly untouched, the grassy fields on the northern end of Nymm hadn't been so lucky. Between the rutting wheels of the catapults, the magical blasts hurled by the Woodspeople, and the thundering feet of the Giants, the ground had been torn to shreds, and was now a broken, muddy expanse littered with debris from the battle. Brooke could see Nymmites tossing black helmets and chest plates and gauntlets onto a growing pile in the distance and shuddered, wondering if there were any Doomgaard soldiers left at all.

As it turned out, there were quite a few.

'They'll be kept as prisoners of war, for now,' Willow said, pointing towards a makeshift camp going up on the eastern side of the city as they made their way through the streets. 'It's not our usual custom. But then again, Nymm hasn't been attacked in centuries. So maybe our customs need to change.'

'The Empress could change them,' said Brooke, looking at her, 'couldn't she?'

Willow threw her a half-glance, ignoring the question. 'We'll have to call another War Council, too. The other

Factionheads will meet - somewhere secret this time - and decide what to do next. I don't imagine the Elementals will be invited, though.'

'Are you keeping *her* here, too?' Tonya said.

'No. She'll be sent to the High Druyad temple and kept there for now. It's considered a sacred place to most of Uland. She'll stand trial.'

'I hope they lock her up forever,' said Dale.

'Forever is a long time,' Willow replied. 'But yes, I hope that too.'

As they passed through the streets, Brooke saw some of the Woodspeople bringing tables and chairs outside, setting them up along the edges of the road; others were carrying freshly-picked flowers and jugs of wine and platters of food. The air quickly filled with delicious smells, and to her amazement, Brooke felt her stomach rumble.

'Looks like the feast is almost ready,' Willow said, side-stepping a group of hyper Woodschildren barrelling down the street.

'Is this... normal?' Brooke asked, watching some Woodsmen hoisting a banner over the road ahead.

'Feasts are common across Uland,' Willow replied. 'Here, too. We share in our triumphs, we remember the past, we honour fallen heroes.' She pointed up the road. 'And we celebrate the return of our leaders.'

A ripple of surprise and excitement ran through the gathering street crowds, quickly rising into a reverberating roar of jubilation. Brooke shielded her eyes from the sun, peering ahead towards the palace. Something was happening.

'Come on!' said Willow.

They dashed up the street. Within minutes, it seemed like all of Nymm had joined them - hundreds of Woodspeople surged along the wide, central road towards the great tree, laughing and cheering and singing. Many were waving banners and strips of coloured cloth, even big leafy fronds pulled from the nearest trees. In no time at all, the entire city seemed to have come together, forming a rushing, clamouring river of Woodspeople flowing directly to the palace.

Finally, they came to a lantern-lit square not far from the royal tree, and saw her.

Orchidema was standing just outside the palace entrance, right in the midst of the blackened, scorched earth where the Elemental firewall had burned the night before. The frame of the doorway behind her was mostly gone - in its place were fresh beams lashed together with green vines. Nymmites guards had been posted all around the palace, and at least three dozen were gathered around the Empress herself.

'She looks… so different,' said Brooke.

'I'll say,' said Charlie dreamily.

Orchidema was dressed in a flowing green-and-sapphire-coloured robe. Her hair, black and sleek in the afternoon light, had been tied up in an elaborate chignon, and her head was adorned with a wooden crown patterned with silvery flowers and tangerine-coloured leaves. As always, her skin was alabaster-white, barely tinged with green, and her eyes were emeralds flecked with gold.

She looks older than she did last night, Brooke thought, recalling the brief time they'd spent with the Empress and the Council before retiring to their rooms. *She looks… regal.*

A portion of the crowd had gathered in the square now, waving their banners and branches, singing and cheering at the sight of the Empress. Orchidema waved back, blushing. Maphira was by her side, towering over her, surveying the crowd. The remaining members of the Council hung back, looking somewhat worse for wear.

There were Giants there, too. Four of them stood off to the right, leaning on their tree-trunk-sized weapons. One of them was chewing on a huge shank of charred meat, his bristly grey beard dripping with juice.

Then Orchidema spotted them, and waved both hands enthusiastically. She started to take a step forward -

Maphira touched her arm, said something to her. Brooke saw the Empress look up at her, shake her head, and continue on. Maphira touched her fingers to her mouth, hiding a smirk.

'Come,' Willow said.

They crossed the square, approaching the Nymmite warriors blocking the final stretch of street to the palace entrance. Orchidema came the other way, flanked on both sides by battle-clad guards. A hush of anticipation descended on the crowd.

'Excuse me,' said the Empress politely.

The warriors immediately moved aside and she floated, rather than walked, into the square.

Instantly, every Woodsperson within sight of her dropped to their knees. Willow was the first to bow, her red curls falling over her face. Maphira and the other Council members were next; even the Giants lowered themselves down on one knee, their joints creaking like rusted gate hinges. Brooke, Dale, Charlie and Tonya followed suit.

For a moment, Orchidema looked like a deer caught in headlights, a small figure in the midst of a silent, waiting, bowing crowd. She gazed around with wide, green eyes, the pink in her cheeks deepening. Then she cleared her throat, and in a voice that was louder and more assured than Brooke would have expected, said, 'Everyone, please. Stand up.'

As one, the whole of Nymm rose to their feet. The Giants groaned like old men hauling themselves from their armchairs, pushing themselves up on their weapons.

Orchidema crossed the square soundlessly. Somehow, Brooke thought, she looked simultaneously young and fragile, and also majestic and powerful. There was an unreal quality about her, like they were observing a figure in a painting rather than a living, breathing person. She got the distinct impression the others felt exactly the same way.

Willow ducked her head as the Empress approached. Orchidema did the same, her tentative smile broadening.

'You look well, Willow-mir,' she said.

'As do you, Your Highness. I trust you slept well?'

'Oh, certainly. It was deep and rejuvenating.'

'I'm glad.'

'As am I. So glad.'

They looked at one another for a moment longer. Then their faces crumpled and they both descended into a fit of snorting giggles. Brooke heard gasps and murmurs in the crowd around them; beyond the line of guards, she saw the Council members shaking their heads in disapproval. Maphira was still smirking.

Openly laughing now, Orchidema abandoned all decorum and threw her arms around Willow, who hugged her back fiercely. There were more gasps in the crowd, along with some applause and cheers. Brooke saw Charlie taking a half step towards the hugging Woodsgirls before catching himself.

'Sister!' Orchidema cried, releasing Willow. 'You're my hero once again.'

'I was just doing my duty, sister,' Willow replied. 'And you were the one who - '

'These are your heroes!' Orchidema abruptly proclaimed, sweeping an arm towards them. 'My sister, Willow-mir, loyal servant of the Druyads and Protector of Nymm.'

More applause and cheers from the crowd, growing in volume now. A younger Woodsboy whoop-whooped and a smattering of good-natured laughter rippled around the square.

'Dale the Master Sorcerer! Brooke the All-Knowing Seer!' Orchidema went on, the crowd cheering louder each time. 'Tonya of the Many Faces!'

'That's a new one,' Tonya said, grinning.

'And Charlie, the Mighty Warrior.'

Brooke thought Charlie was going to melt on the spot.

Orchidema beamed at them, joining in with the applause. For a solid minute, the Woodspeople of Nymm clapped and cheered and waved their banners until the sound was almost deafening; the Giants joined in, stomping their massive feet and almost knocking the nearest guards flying. Brooke knew her face was bright red, but for once, she didn't really care.

Finally, Orchidema stopped clapping and the crowd mostly settled down, pressing in around the square. Brooke noticed those who hadn't been able to find space in the street were perched on top of the buildings or in the branches of nearby trees; one teenage-looking Woodsgirl was even hanging nonchalantly from a lantern pole.

'All of you,' said the Empress, turning on the spot. 'All of you fought to defend our city. Our home. You are all heroes. And I am truly, deeply honoured to be here with you again.'

Another cheer began to swell and she held up a hand.

'Today,' she said, 'we celebrate our victory over the enemy who sought to destroy us. Tonight, in the light of the waxing moon, we remember our dead, and the great sacrifice they made to preserve our freedom.'

Murmurs of approval from the crowd.

Spoken like a true leader, Brooke thought.

'Those who betrayed us will pay the price,' said the Empress. 'Nymm will endure. Our enemies will not. We've survived for a thousand generations and we'll thrive for a thousand more.'

Murmurs grew into cheers again. Orchidema's eyes flashed gold as she raised her arms in the air. Green light sparked between her fingers.

'Brothers, sisters,' she said. 'Let's feast!'

The crowd erupted again, and immediately began to disperse along the streets. A song went up and hundreds joined in, laughing and dancing together. All the pain and despair of the previous night was briefly forgotten.

Orchidema dropped her arms and sighed with relief.

'There,' she said. 'My first proper speech. It was a good one, right?'

'You were most eloquent indeed, my liege,' Willow replied, with a mock bow. Orchidema swung for her and she dodged away, laughing.

Sisters, Brooke thought, smiling.

'It *was* a good speech, Empress,' she said.

'Really good,' Dale agreed. 'I think everyone's glad to see you back again.'

'Thank you, Lady Seer, Master Sorcerer,' Orchidema replied, a little breathlessly. 'I haven't felt this well in a very long time. It's quite a relief, really.' Then she turned to Charlie. 'I'm ready for my training now.'

They all stopped and looked at Charlie. His mouth dropped open.

'Oh… right, umm… training… ok.' Red crept up his neck and into his cheeks.

'Had you forgotten you made me that promise?' said Orchidema. 'At Hammerfall, after the battle? You said you'd teach me how to fight. I'm ready.'

'I did? Right, ok… umm…'

'Let's go,' Orchidema said, grabbing Charlie's hand. Brooke was convinced he was about to faint. 'We'll see you all later.'

With that, she dashed off down the street, dragging a flabbergasted Charlie behind her. At least a dozen guards hurried after them.

'Now *that* was funny,' Tonya said.

***

The next few hours passed in no time at all.

A festival atmosphere descended on Nymm; the air filled with music and singing and laughter as the entire city came together for the feast, banqueting in the streets together while sunlight lanced through the tree canopy above them. Brooke, Dale, Tonya and Willow were invited to eat at the Council's table, where the older Woodspeople regaled them with stories about Nymm's ancient past; one of the Giants, who was apparently the leader of their battle clan, also joined them and thumped the table too hard during one of the more amusing stories, cracking it in two.

After eating their fill for the second time that day, Brooke, Dale and Tonya headed back to their chambers, leaving Willow to speak with the Council. It'd become clear during the meal that they now wanted her to remain in Nymm a while longer, but she insisted on escorting "the Other-world heroes" to the Druyad temple in the north first, where they could return home. Maphira and Willow were deep in discussion when Tonya dragged Brooke and Dale away from the table.

'If we're travelling again, I need a catnap first,' she announced. 'And maybe another bath. Have you *tried* the baths here? They're a-*maz*-ing.'

Along the way, Brooke made them stop at the library to see Lindara again, but the old librarian had disappeared and the doors were locked. They also spotted Charlie and Orchidema on the training field, performing a mock duel - the young Empress was casually blasting him with emerald light while he desperately tried to block it with a Moon Hammer. Rowan-thir watched on in the background, arms folded across his chest, grinning.

They returned to their guest chambers. Dale promptly took himself off to bed ('That catnap sounds like a good idea, actually') and the girls went back to their room, where Tonya did indeed go for a bath. Brooke heard her singing tunelessly to herself through the door - Tonya Miller excelled at a great many things, especially in the esteem of their peers at Farmont High, but not when it came to singing. She also clearly didn't care, and was soon belting out pop songs so loudly that Brooke had to leave.

There was a little courtyard between their rooms and the banqueting hall, where jasmine and honeysuckle perfumed the air and fat bumblebees zig-zagged from flower to flower. Brooke sat down on a smooth stone bench and leaned back against the bark wall, closing her eyes for a moment; laughter and singing - decidedly more tuneful than Tonya's - drifted to her from the ongoing feasting in the street nearby. The Woodspeople often seemed far too serious for her liking, but they sure seemed to know how to celebrate when they wanted to.

Warm sunlight flooded the courtyard from above. She turned her face towards it, letting her eyelids go red on the inside. In that redness, she saw the Elemental fire burning around the base of the palace tree; she saw Luno, her insane, scarlet glare turned on them as the Nymmite guards dragged her away; and she saw the softly-glowing lantern on the conference room ceiling, just past Dale's head as she released him from her embrace.

'I like you too,' he'd said, his cheeks still wet with tears. 'I… I think you know that, though.'

'Yeah,' she'd replied, nodding, her own eyes red and puffy. 'You didn't have to say it at the time. And that's why I was so mad at you. You could've just not said it and stayed, but you ran away instead.'

'I know. I get it.' He sniffed. 'I miss being friends with you.'

'Me too.'

She'd waited. She knew something important was going on high above them, but there was nothing they could do about it. There was only this, for now.

'Can we do that again?' Dale had said, meeting her gaze. 'Be friends, I mean. Start again, from there.'

'Yes,' Brooke said, smiling. 'I'd like that. Friends again.'

Dale had smiled back then, and whatever ice had hung between them for so long finally melted away. It'd been a good feeling.

Brooke opened her eyes. Her vision gradually adjusted and the courtyard faded back into focus. She looked down at the little leather book in her lap.

Can you tell me what to do next? she wondered.

But somehow, she knew there was no need.

The book had gotten them back to Uland. It had helped get them to Willow, and she'd brought them to Nymm. And when the time came, the book had helped them defend it.

She didn't know precisely how it worked, or who'd been writing back in response to her questions. She didn't know who'd drawn the picture of the Giant and the pool. She certainly didn't know how or why she was able to read the words when she touched them, or how the Giants in Golemar had been able to find their way to Nymm as a result.

She hoped it was Yulerin. It'd be nice to see the old Druyad again.

For now, she'd leave the twine fastened securely around the book's weathered cover. Maybe she'd give it to Willow before they left. Yes, that'd make sense. She'd know what to do with it. She *was* the Empress after all, even if only they knew it.

Brooke put a hand to her face, where the scorch mark had mostly faded away. It stung a little but she imagined it'd be gone by the time they returned home. The last thing she needed was for her Mum to see it and freak out.

Home.

That was becoming a weird concept again, wasn't it? Each time they were in Uland, home - the *real* world - felt less and less like the place they were supposed to be. Here they had powers, and their actions had impact; back home, they were just kids again. Just kids, to whom the adults never really listened. Nothing special.

She sighed.

How she'd love to stay here longer. How she'd love to see *all* of Uland, even the dangerous places, the parts that were still at war. She and Dale and Charlie and Tonya could travel all over the continent with Willow, visiting strange new cities built on the backs of fallen Giants and exploring dark forests filled with magical creatures and sailing on lakes created by cataclysmic explosions from thousands of years ago. Now *that* would be something worth remembering. *That* would be something worth writing about.

She'd happily do that, instead of *homework*.

One of the tubby bumblebees droned past her face, leaving a golden shimmer in its wake. She moved her hand through it and the shimmer became music, tinkling melodiously in the air.

Brooke sighed again and stood up, slipping the book back in her pocket.

One day, they'd come back here again. Somehow, some way. And they'd stay for weeks and weeks instead of days. Willow wanted to get them home, just in case Tonya's elongated time in Uland had been a fluke ('Maybe because she's the Changer', Dale had suggested) and they all became stone statues. But maybe someday, they'd figure out a way to stay.

Maybe Yulerin would know. Or Jayne.

'Someday,' Brooke said to herself.

She went back inside, leaving the bees to their flowers.

***

And before they knew it, it was time to go.

As afternoon wore on to evening and the sunlight filtering through the tree canopy deepened from gold to mandarin, the feast drew to a close. The singing and dancing stopped and the streets cleared. A sombre mood settled over Nymm, slowly shifting from one of celebration to lamentation. The Woodspeople placed candles by their windows with blue or purple flames - signifying mourning, according to Willow - and the fire fairies flitting among the leaves changed colour to match it. Somewhere in the city, a stringed instrument played a beautiful, haunting melody, and many of the Nymmites took up the song from their doorways on the forest floor and in the trees up above.

Willow and Rowan-thir met them outside their chambers. The Woodsman regarded each of them with the usual scrutiny, but this time also afforded them a half smile and bow of the head. They bowed back, and started after him up the street.

Woodspeople watched silently from their doorways and windows as their small procession made its way through Nymm, heading for the line of white-barked trees bordering the open space around the inner city. Some of them waved, and Brooke waved back every time. But anything beyond that now seemed inappropriate - Nymm had shifted fully into a state of mourning and remembrance. The only citizens still active were those clearing up the battlefield or guarding the Doomgaard prisoners in their camps, who'd been stripped of their black outer armour and were now bunched together on the grass, surrounded by makeshift fences. They may well have been glad of the barriers, too, because an Enfield was prowling in the shadows nearby, watching them hungrily with bright yellow eyes.

After a while, the stone-paved city streets gave way to a rough trail winding through the grass towards the tree line. Brooke noticed they were going back via a different route, moving towards the north-western end of the city perimeter. She could see the trail curling up and into the trees ahead.

'How long will it take to reach the Druyad temple?' said Dale, breaking the silence.

'Not long,' said Willow. 'Once we leave Nymm, it'll only be a matter of hours before we get there on foot. Caelrin can send you back home from there.'

'Ugh, more walking,' muttered Tonya. 'Why did I even *bother* having a bath?'

'You really are royalty, aren't you?' grinned Brooke, throwing an arm around her shoulders. Tonya grinned back, hooking an arm around her waist.

The trail grew steadily steeper as they approached the tree line. Brooke saw Dale pressing at a stitch in his side; next to him, Charlie walked with his head down. He'd looked more than a little forlorn since leaving Orchidema earlier. Brooke wondered if they'd ever see her again - there hadn't been any particular goodbyes exchanged with her or the Council.

Maybe that's just the way Woodspeople are, she thought, remembering how emotionless Willow had often seemed at times when they first met her. *Maybe they don't really say goodbye.*

She was dead wrong about that, however.

They all paused at the tree line for a final look back at Nymm. The city was engulfed in a purple-blue haze from thousands of candles but remained breathtakingly-beautiful in the late afternoon sunlight, glittering with magic from the forest floor to the dark green leaf canopy high above. In the centre of the city, the tree palace stood resplendent, still surrounded on all sides by Nymmite warriors and burning lanterns.

'Come, Other-worlders,' said Rowan-thir.

And then they were in the trees again, and Nymm was gone.

The trail snaked through the dense woodland bordering the city, gradually climbing. They had to walk single-file here, following Rowan-thir and Willow, neither of whom were remotely out of breath. Behind Brooke, Dale was puffing steadily, still pressing at the stitch in his side.

Finally, with the forest growing dimmer around them, they emerged into a grassy, leaf-strewn space among the trees. Stars winked down through the gap in the canopy above. In the centre of the clearing was another pool, much larger than the one they'd come through, bordered with smooth, flat stones. The whole area was lit with silvery light from an ancient-looking lantern hanging above the pool; a handful of fire fairies flitted around it, emitting a low buzz with their tiny wings.

Brooke heard Charlie draw in a sharp breath.

Orchidema was standing by the pool, watching them with green-golden eyes. The hood of her emerald cloak was drawn up and her hands were clasped loosely by her waist. Brooke thought she'd never looked more regal - and, strangely, intimidating - than she had before that moment. And yet, as they approached, she pushed back her hood, smiled toothily and waved, and suddenly she was just another teenage-looking girl. Behind her, a line of guards watched silently from the shadows.

'I wanted to say goodbye,' said the Empress. 'They didn't want me to come up here, but I couldn't resist. And they couldn't say no, really.'

Willow and Rowan-thir both bowed. Brooke, Dale, Charlie and Tonya did likewise. Orchidema dismissed them all with a wave of her hand.

'Empress,' said Rowan-thir solemnly. 'It pleases me to see you've recovered so well.'

'It pleases me too, Rowan.'

'I'm pleased, too,' said Charlie abruptly, taking a weird, staggered step forward. Brooke and Tonya exchanged a quick glance, smirking.

Orchidema smiled at Charlie, her alabaster-green skin dappled with silvery light reflected from the pool. 'I know you are, Charlie Flint. I enjoyed our sparring session earlier.'

'Me too,' said Charlie, suddenly flushing red.

'I'll bet you did,' Dale murmured.

Just then, Brooke noticed Maphira standing among the guards, observing them silently. And next to her, hunched over with her red hair askew and her hands bound securely in metal manacles, was Luno.

Willow seemed to notice in the same instant, and visibly stiffened.

'Lady Maphira,' she said, her eyes flaring in the intermittent light. 'I thought the prisoner was to remain in Nymm for now, until the Council decided on her future?'

Maphira drifted forward. 'The Council spoke this morning and agreed it was best for her to be sent to the High Druyad temple. She'll be detained there until the other Factionheads decide what to do with her. And her presence in Nymm is toxic.'

Luno glowered at Maphira from beneath the tangled strands of her once-pristine hair, furious and crazed now that her powers were stifled by the magical manicals clamped to her wrists. But, Brooke thought, amidst all the rage and bitterness, she also looked… drained. Defeated. She imagined her in a cramped prison cell in the dungeons of Fort Hammerfall, her red eyes glowing weakly from the shadows. Maybe she was looking into the future. She hoped so.

'If that's the Council's decision,' said Willow.

'It is, Willow-mir.'

Willow nodded and turned to them, motioned to the pool. 'It'll be the same as before,' she said. 'Just step in, and you'll find yourself back in the northern forests.'

'I hope it's not *just* like before,' Dale said, shuddering.

'Just try to avoid drowning,' said Willow.

'*Try to avoid* - '

'Wait,' said Rowan-thir, stepping forward. 'The prisoner is to go first, along with her escort.'

He nodded towards the pool and a dozen guards broke from their protective line behind Orchidema, gathering around Luno. As they walked her to the pool, she glared at Willow and spat a gob of blood into the grass by her feet.

'We'll meet again, Woodsgirl,' she said.

'Hopefully not,' Willow replied.

'Enjoy prison,' said Tonya cheerily.

Luno narrowed her eyes at her but said nothing. The guards ushered her into the water (or whatever the substance actually was). It shimmered around them in ripples of colour; they descended into it and disappeared.

Willow went around the pool to where the Empress stood and bowed. Orchidema grabbed her by the hands, straightening her up again.

'Farewell, Your Majesty,' Willow said. 'I'll be back by sundown tomorrow.'

'Farewell, sister,' said Orchidema. 'And you better be.'

They hesitated a second, and then threw their arms around each other. Brooke felt an unexpected lump rise in her throat, even though they weren't saying their goodbyes to Willow just yet. *I wish we could stay longer*, she thought. She glanced at the others and knew they were thinking exactly the same thing. Especially Charlie, whose face was more downcast than ever.

The Woodsgirls broke apart, their eyes swimming. Orchidema cupped Willow's face for a moment, smiling up at her. Then Willow stepped back and pulled up her hood. Maphira observed it all without expression.

Dale went up to Orchidema, bowed, and was immediately enveloped in the same hug. Tonya went next, then Brooke. The Empress was a little shorter than her and still felt fragile after her long illness, but there was a great deal of suppressed strength in her hug. Her hair was scented with jasmine, just like in the courtyard.

As she released Brooke, words spoke clearly in her mind, and she smiled.

I order you to come back soon, Seer.

Finally, it was Charlie's turn. Brooke could tell he was doing his best to appear strong and confident - School Charlie, she supposed - but his legs wobbled as he stepped up to the Empress, and his face was redder than ever.

'Goodbye, Charlie Flint,' said Orchidema, and Brooke was surprised to hear her voice crack slightly. 'You have to come back and train me.'

'I will,' said Charlie.

'I command it.'

'I know.'

She hugged him fiercely, and he hugged her back. It went on decidedly longer than any of the previous embraces. After a solid minute, Maphira cleared her throat.

Charlie reluctantly released her. Orchidema beamed up at him, her eyes brimming with tears, then slipped a hand into her cloak. She pulled some small object out and pushed it into Charlie's still-bruised hand, and said, 'To remember me by.'

He looked down at it, frowned, then met her gaze again. She smiled and brushed a strand of jet-black hair behind her ear, her cheeks growing pink. They both seemed to abruptly become aware there were other people in the clearing, watching them with amusement, and turned away from each other.

'Anyway,' said Willow, a grin tugging at the corner of her mouth, 'who's first?'

'Me,' said Dale, stepping into the pool. 'May as well get this over wi - '

Apparently the pool had no bottom, and Dale dropped completely out of sight before he could finish his sentence. Tonya mounted the stones next, bowed flamboyantly, and jumped into the water. Brooke saw Charlie lingering and grabbed his hand.

'Come on, loverboy,' she said, dragging him to the edge. He went willingly enough, offering a small wave to Orchidema on the way, who waved back. Willow joined them.

'Ready?' she said, her hazel-gold eyes glinting beneath the lantern light.

'Ready,' said Brooke. 'Let's go home.'

They stepped forward and the world fell away.

***

Just like last time, Brooke was plunged into a total nothingness.

The woods were gone, the pool was gone. Charlie and Willow, who'd been on either side of her, were gone. She couldn't close her eyes, even though there was nothing to see.

And like last time, she couldn't breathe.

Hurry up, hurry up, she thought, trying with all her might to ignore the growing pain in her lungs as they screamed for oxygen. Her arms and legs kicked freely in the nothing space. She wasn't moving. *HURRY UP!*

Then she saw light up ahead, glowing in the nothingness. It was either getting brighter or she was hurtling towards it like a rocket, there was no way of knowing. But there it was, growing, growing, growing, and she was falling towards it, into it, through it…

She gasped as her feet touched something solid and cold air rushed into her chest, then cried out in surprise as she fell face-first towards the ground. She just got her hands up in time before smacking bodily into a flat, hard surface.

'Ow!'

Charlie had hit the ground at almost exactly the same moment, but he'd tumbled sideways instead and landed on his elbow. He rolled onto his back, groaning in pain.

Brooke pushed herself up on all fours. Her head was spinning, like she'd just stepped off a merry-go-round moving hundreds of miles an hour, and she promptly collapsed onto her side.

'W-what… what happened?' she managed, flailing weakly at thin air.

Someone grabbed her by the wrist and hauled her to her feet. She saw Tonya's face swim into focus. Six brown eyes stared back at her - she blinked once, twice, and the six became two again.

'Are you ok?' Tonya said.

Her voice was strangely unsteady, and sounded far away. Brooke saw Tonya's breath escape in a white puff when she spoke, and frowned.

'I'm... ok,' Brooke said, trying to keep her head from spinning off her shoulders. 'That was so much worse than last time.'

'You're telling me,' Charlie groaned, getting to his feet.

'Guys...' Brooke heard Dale say.

Her eyes were still adjusting to the sudden change in light. It was much darker here than it'd been in the woods around Nymm? And were they *inside* now?

'Guys,' Dale said again. 'What is this place?'

Brooke saw him now, standing a few feet away, rubbing the back of his head. Willow appeared to her left, her eyes blooming gold in the strange, cold darkness.

'This isn't right,' said the Woodsgirl. 'We're not...'

She trailed off.

Suddenly, Brooke was afraid. She didn't know why - there was nothing to see but darkness, nothing to feel but the chill on her lips and the firm, flat ground beneath her feet.

But... no. Wait. There *was* something else, wasn't there? It was something new, but somehow familiar. Something she'd felt before. Something she couldn't quite put her finger on, but the more she thought about it, the more she leaned into it, the colder her skin seemed to become. Gooseflesh raked up and down her back; the hairs on her arms stood rigid.

Where are we?

'I can't see anything,' said Tonya. Her voice echoed for a split second, then cut off. 'Is it... getting darker, or something.'

'Yes, it is,' said Willow. Brooke saw her move forward, becoming a shadow in the gathering darkness. Then: '*Eydrom.*'

Brooke heard the *snap* of the Woodsgirl's fingers and a ball of swirling emerald light burst into life above their heads. The space they were in was flooded with green. Brooke's neck twisted on her shoulders as she looked up and around, trying to take it in, not really understanding.

'What…?' Dale said.

There were walls, curving up to a curved ceiling; they glinted like glass in Willow's summoned light. There was a floor - black stone, flat and cold - extending to the edges of a huge, round room. And there was nothing else.

Except there was.

There were people, lying on that black, cold floor. People bathed in shimmering green light. People she recognised. And none of them were moving.

'Oh no,' Willow said. 'Oh no, oh please no…'

'*Yes.*'

Brooke felt, rather than heard, the word. She tore her eyes from the bodies strewn over the floor to the shadows opposite them.

He was there, emerging slowly from the darkness.

The wraith from her visions. The intangible figure from her nightmares. The black, wavering shadow from the red portal in the Druyad Temple.

He was there.

'*Finally*,' he said.

Chapter Twenty-Three: Soulburn Talismans

None of them moved.

Brooke felt as though her feet were cemented to the floor. Maybe they were. She couldn't tell, because she couldn't look down - her eyes were locked on the man on the other side of the room.

The man. He's not *a man.*

She could hear someone's breath coming in short, sharp bursts. Was it *her*?

No, it was Charlie, to her right. She could see him in the farthest corner of her eye, arms by his sides, chest heaving under his red leather doublet. His fingers flexed near his hip, where his sword should be.

They forgot to give back the sword, she thought, her mind working desperately to stay focused. *The Gnome's sword. Quillorin. Charlie isn't armed.*

That's right, Brooke Woods.'

The voice again, floating across the room on a chill, turning her spine to ice.

He can hear me.

'Right again,' he said. 'I can hear every word going through that dainty little head of yours. Charlie is indeed unarmed. These, however, were.'

They all saw the gnarled, bony hand extend from the shadows and sweep the room, gesturing to the lifeless Nymmites scattered over the floor. The hand disappeared again, and a deep, inhuman chuckle wafted their way. Brooke realised she was shivering all over.

'Just like the Woodspeople,' said the thing in the darkness. 'So trusting. So very *naive.*'

Willow screamed and thrust her hands forward. A blast of bright green light rocketed across the room, straight for the source of the voice.

In the same instant, a spinning ball of flame shot from the shadows in the corner and struck Willow's magic in mid-air; they all recoiled as a blast of green and red light exploded, briefly illuminating the whole room. For a split second, Brooke saw everything: the floor, the walls, the ancient stone doors directly opposite them just beyond the black figure, who seemed unaffected by the light.

And she saw Luno, creeping from the darkness with fire blazing in her eyes. Her wrists were no longer bound and there was a staff in her hands once again.

The Elemental tossed back her head and cackled, gleefully insane and bristling with magical power. Willow's palms remained up and ready, sparks dancing back and forth between her fingers. Brooke saw Dale slowly raising his hands, too.

'Ah Willow,' Luno laughed, her hair tumbling about her ghostly-white face. 'You silly, foolish girl. Do you see what you've done? Do you see where you *are?*'

Brooke tried to swallow but her throat had gone bone dry. She'd seen it. When Willow and Luno's blasts connected, she'd seen the room in full. The walls glinted black, tinged with red, glassy in the magical light. There were hundreds of them, maybe thousands, all embedded into the stone of the walls and ceiling. No, more than that - they were *made* from them.

Soulburn talismans.

They were in a room made from soulburn talismans.

Luno cackled again, wiping a pale hand over her mouth. Above their heads, the green glow from Willow's summoned light was fading.

'Do you see, little Woodsgirl?' Luno sneered.

'She sees.'

At the sound of the voice, Luno spun on her heel and dropped to her knees, bowing her head almost to the floor. If Willow had wanted to blast her again, she could have. But she didn't. And neither did Dale. Her light was almost out.

Snap.

The dying emerald ball turned scarlet, flooding the room red. The soulburn talismans in the walls responded as though they were alive, glowing evilly in the retreating dark. For the first time, Dale and Charlie seemed to realise what they were, and all the fight left them.

The hand slipped back into the folds of a black cloak. Brooke stared at its owner. She saw him now, saw him in full for the first time.

And her eyes burned.

Decymero came forward into the blood-red light, his footfalls echoing around the room, making the space seem simultaneously larger and more claustrophobic than it actually was. The talismans glowed brighter in response, pulsing now, expectant. Brooke felt the air grow thick and cold, turning her lungs to ice, and no matter how hard she tried, she couldn't take her eyes off him.

Here he was, the dark figure from the other side of the portal, walking slowly towards them.

He was real. Far, far too real.

He wore a black cloak that disguised most of his body, though Brooke could easily tell he was very thin beneath it, almost skeletal. And yet his boots thudded heavily on the stone floor, as if a troll was approaching them rather than a man; his footsteps echoed up to the ceiling, sending responsive red light rippling through the talismans. He walked with a kind of subtle elegance - grace, even - yet his gait was strangely uneven, as if one of his legs was crippled or shorter than the other.

A hood was drawn up over his head, making him seem taller than he'd first appeared in the shadows. He wasn't *especially* tall, though, in Brooke's uneasy estimation. Had she expected him to be tall? What *had* she expected?

He drew closer, moving beneath the hovering ball of red light. His hands were behind his back, like a displeased school teacher bearing down on unruly students. What Brooke wouldn't have given to be back in school now, far away from here. Far away from *him*.

He stopped then, standing perfectly still in the centre of the room, observing them. No-one spoke, no-one moved. They *couldn't* move, could they, even if they wanted to? Just like in the Druyad Tower, their feet were pinned to the floor. Some unseeable force was holding them in place, gripping their limbs, sliding over their skin like an ice-cold hand.

Fear. It had all of them. *He* had all of them.

Luno shuffled to his side, head dipped, eyes downturned. Brooke found herself inwardly marvelling at her, this proud, fearsome woman, now reduced to a snivelling waif in Decymero's presence.

'My lord,' she said. 'Would you like me to kill them, too?'

Too? Brooke's eyes went to the bodies of the Nymmites scattered on the floor by Decymero's feet. *Luno killed them?*

'No,' he replied. Every word he spoke seemed to pour directly into Brooke's ear, like he was whispering to her alone. 'You will not harm them, though I know you'd very much like to.'

'Yes, my lord,' Luno said, her eyes gleaming hungrily. 'I would. Very much.'

He turned his head towards her, and they saw his face properly for the first time, unshrouded by the shadow of his hood. Tonya gasped.

His skin was corpse-white, pulled taut over razor-sharp features, as though there was no flesh beneath. They may as well have been looking side-on at a skull. He had a hooked nose, a pointed chin and a high, unlined forehead that transitioned into a widow's peak just below the rim of his hood. The corners of his mouth were drawn up in a wide, fixed grin, as though there were invisible hooks tugging at the ends of his colourless lips. His teeth were all pointed and glinted red in the light.

At the sound of Tonya's gasp, his eyes shifted back to them, and his hideous grin somehow drew wider. The eye on the left was emerald green, the right one glacial blue. Both looked as though they'd been placed into the sockets of his skull, like they weren't supposed to be there. They were rimmed in black.

'Don't be afraid,' he said softly, his bony jaw working beneath paper-thin skin. 'This is a safe place.'

He walked towards them. Every atom of Brooke's body screamed at her to run, to fling herself back into the portal.

But it's closed now, she thought. She didn't have to see it. *We can't go back. It's stone.*

Decymero nodded at her, as if she'd spoken out loud. 'You cannot go back,' he agreed. 'And why should you want to? You are where you were always meant to be. With *me*.'

He approached Charlie, hands still clasped behind his back. As he bent to scrutinise him, Brooke saw dangles of unkempt black hair slither from beneath his hood.

'The Warrior,' said Decymero, looking Charlie up and down. 'Yes, I see it. So much rage, so much *power*. What'll you do with it, though? Hmm?'

Charlie was shaking from head to toe, desperately struggling against his invisible bonds. His teeth were clenched together and saliva trickled from the corner of his mouth.

'You'd kill me, wouldn't you?' Decymero said softly. His face was inches from Charlie's now, studying him like a specimen in a jar. 'You'd do it with your bare hands. I believe you could, too. You aren't especially good at most things, Charlie Flint, but you have the heart of a true killer.' Decymero drew a hand from behind his back, unfurled a long, skeletal finger and poked Charlie in the chest. 'I like that. I could *use* that.'

Please, Brooke thought, fists bunched by her sides, tears welling in her eyes. *Please don't hurt him.*

'I told you already, Brooke Woods,' Decymero said, without looking at her. 'You're safe here. I won't hurt you.'

Luno glowered at them over his shoulder, grinding her teeth. Decymero straightened up and turned to Tonya, who shrank from him.

'Well, well,' he said, strolling up to her. 'You're new, aren't you? A surprise guest. I didn't intend for you to be here, yet here you are.'

The pale hand came out again. One long, gnarled finger tilted Tonya's chin up towards him; Brooke noticed, with mounting revulsion, that the fingers were tipped with cracked, claw-like nails.

Decymero held her gaze, reading her. Brooke could see Tonya struggling to look away, straining to turn her head. A bead of sweat trickled down from her temple, curving along her cheek.

'Tonya,' whispered the dark creature, his green and blue eyes locked on hers. 'Tonya… Miller. And… ah yes… you have some power too, don't you? Fascinating.'

'She's a shifty little changer,' Luno practically spat. 'A lying, deceptive rodent.'

'Yes, she certainly fooled you, didn't she?' He straightened again, and Brooke was sure she saw him wince. 'The great Luno of Elementa, outsmarted by a child of the Other-world.'

Luno's eyes flashed. She went back to grinding her teeth.

'I'll come to you in a moment,' Decymero said to Willow, whose back was to Brooke; her shoulders were slumped and her head was down. 'First, I have a question for the Seer.'

'Don't you touch her!' Dale yelled abruptly, startling everyone.

Decymero grinned malevolently and snapped his fingers.

Dale's hands suddenly jerked up, his palms twisting towards his face. They held there, trembling, glistening with sweat. A single, tiny flame sparked between his fingers.

'Now, now, Master Sorcerer,' said Decymero, his eyes still fixed on Brooke. 'I could burn your head right off your shoulders with your own fire, if I wanted to. Or…' He snapped his fingers again and Dale's right hand swung, puppet-like, towards Brooke. '... I could have you turn her to ash, right here and now. How about that?'

Dale seethed for a second, then closed his eyes. The flicker of flame between his fingers fizzled out.

'Good,' said Decymero.

He snapped his fingers once more and Dale's arms returned to his sides.

'And now, for you,' he said, looming over Brooke. 'I'm particularly pleased to make your acquaintance, Lady Seer.'

She could smell him now, a dank, pungent odour, like an exhumed corpse. Her stomach turned inside her and she had to hold her breath as his face came within inches of hers. His green-blue eyes searched hers, his jaw working from side to side.

'Here's my question,' he said finally, holding up one pale, skeletal finger. 'Are you ready?'

Some invisible string tugged twice at her hair, forcing her head to nod.

Decymero grinned and said, 'Who did you think was writing to you in your little book?'

Brooke's eyes widened. He saw it and chuckled, dousing her with a burst of sickeningly-stale breath. Behind him, Luno had begun to pace the room.

'You didn't know, did you?' he said. Her blood temperature seemed to drop a degree at every word from his mouth. 'All along, you had no idea who was holding the pen. The wise, all-seeing Brooke Woods of the Otherworld didn't even *consider* it.'

That single bony finger travelled up to her forehead; the jagged nail on the end of it pressed into her brow.

'If you're going to be the Seer, you'll have to use your brain,' said Decymero. 'It's too good a thing to waste. And if I start to suspect you *are* wasting it, well, I might just have to pop open that little blonde head of yours and scoop it right out.' The finger came away from her brow, leaving an indent in her skin. 'Let me show you who you've been writing to all this time.'

He abruptly wheeled away and strode across the room. The string holding the back of Brooke's head released and she gasped, sucking in a lungful of air. She'd forgotten she was holding her breath.

Decymero motioned and said, 'Come.'

Brooke's feet started moving, walking her involuntarily across the stone floor. The others were doing the same. She could see Charlie struggling against it, but it was no use. Luno giggled and skipped after Decymero.

'I… I can't stop,' said Tonya, her arms swinging by her sides.

'Neither can I,' Dale said. 'Willow, do something!'

But Willow's head was still down, and her shoulders were still slumped. The invisible magical strings moved her with ease.

She's given up, Brooke thought with ever-increasing alarm. *She's given up!*

There was a loud *clunk* and the double doors at the far end of the room swung inward, spilling a harsh red glow into it. The swirling scarlet ball winked out and the soulburn talismans went black again. Decymero strode through the doors, hands behind his back once again, the hem of his cloak brushing the floor in his wake. Luno bowed mockingly to them as they followed after him.

Brooke blinked as her eyes readjusted to the changed light. They were in another circular room, larger than the first, with walls and floor of grey, cracked stone. There were no talismans here. The doors clunked shut behind them and Luno swept up to their side, the base of her staff *thunking* rhythmically next to her.

'What… where are we?' whispered Tonya.

The room was mostly empty. The only features Brooke could see were a handful of candelabras positioned around the walls, all burning with red flames, and a large black wooden table directly opposite the doors they'd come through, covered in bottles and vials and open books. A lantern hung lopsidedly on a hook over the table, flooding the area in red light.

Everything was in shadow. Everything, apart from the windows.

Two enormous round holes had been cut into the wall on one side of the room, spaced evenly apart. Through them, Brooke could see the night sky glittering with stars, with the moon just visible on the right. There was a strange, reddish glow along the bottom of each window.

Decymero crossed to the table, motioning absently towards the windows as he went. 'Take a look,' he said. 'The view is quite impressive.'

Suddenly, Brooke felt the magical grip on her limbs release. They'd been keeping her on her feet more than she realised, and she almost slumped to the floor. The others did the same, staggering like toddlers. Willow dropped to her knees.

Luno looked anxiously from them to Decymero, but he seemed to have momentarily forgotten them. He was over by the table, his back to the rest of the room.

'Willow,' Brooke said, dropping down next to her. She put an arm around the Woodsgirl's shoulders and found they were shaking. 'Come on. You have to get up.'

Willow sniffed, her face hidden beneath her hair. 'Why?' she said, barely above a whisper. 'What's the point? He has us now. He's won.'

'No he has not,' Brooke replied, surprised at the stubbornness in her voice. 'He… he doesn't get to win. Not like this. Get up.'

Willow reluctantly allowed Brooke to help her back up. She kept one arm around her, gripping one of her slender green hands in her own.

'Oh my days,' said Dale dully.

The others were over by the window on the left. Brooke and Willow crossed the room unsteadily, joining them. Decymero continued working at the table, paying them no attention.

Brooke looked out and her heart began pounding harder than ever.

They seemed to be at the top of an enormous castle made from black stone, overlooking a city. At first glance, it looked somewhat like Fort Hammerfall, with hundreds of individual buildings, towers, paved streets and squares lit with red light. And there were people down there, going about their business as the dying embers of dusk gave way to full nighttime. The whole city sprawled beneath the castle, hemmed in on all sides by a dense, dark forest.

But among the civilians, Brooke saw soldiers patrolling the streets, dressed in black armour. And she saw black flags fluttering in the breeze from the tops of the towers. And, to her horror, she saw grotesque, hairy beasts with glowing red eyes prowling the edges of the forest, drawing thin lines of white mist in their wake.

Ghouls.

'We're in Doomgaard,' she whispered.

'Indeed you are,' said Decymero. Brooke pried her eyes away from the dark city and saw him standing by the table, facing them now. 'You're in Obsidian Fell, no less. The oldest keep in all of Uland. This room, in fact, was formed from the skull of a Giant called Vandruk - you're looking through one of his eyes right now. That's quite an honour, you know.'

'An honour they don't deserve,' muttered Luno.

'Nevertheless.' Decymero trailed a hand along the edge of the table; Brooke noticed, in the midst of her dizzying fear and confusion, that each of his hands were significantly different in appearance. 'And now, let's answer some of those questions I hear swirling around inside your heads.'

His trailing hand plucked a small vial of red-orange liquid from the table and he turned to the centre of the room.

'This is Uland,' he said.

He snapped the fingers of his skeletal hand, and a huge map materialised on the floor. Its lines glowed red against the grey stone, depicting the entire continent. Brooke spotted Canyon Lake in the middle of it, but much of the rest was unknown to her.

'We are here,' said Decymero, tipping a drop from the vial over a portion of the map. When the liquid touched the floor, it immediately sprang up into a tiny, solid castle, with the rest of the city puddling out around it. 'Doomgaard, the last bastion of true power in the world. Resting place of the fallen Vandruk, most bloodthirsty of all the ancient Giants. And this…' He tipped another drop onto the map, just above the thick red line of a river. '... is Hammerfall.'

A much larger city appeared on the map, resting on the side of a mountain. Brooke recognised it, and now understood that the thick river line south of it was the Thunderflow, where Dale had been wounded by the ghoul. And south of that, appearing as a dull wedge across a narrow stretch of land, was The Throat, and goblin-infested Crookedstone.

'I'm sure you remember this city well,' said Decymero, looming wraith-like over the glowing mountain. 'It was, after all, the place where you helped defeat my army. The place where Sol - that insipid fop - tried in vain to rule until that wasting disease finally took him two years ago. The place where my servant Hysst died so mysteriously in that dungeon after his capture.' He glanced pointedly at Luno, who averted her gaze. 'And it was the place where you, dear Willow, revealed your *true* self.'

Brooke felt Willow stiffen beneath her arm, which was still draped around the Woodsgirl's slender shoulders.

'That power of yours,' Decymero went on, his eyes gleaming, 'is *delicious*. That of a true Empress, indeed. I wasn't sure if I'd ever taste it again in my lifetime.'

'What do you mean?' said Luno sharply.

Of course, Brooke thought, struggling to maintain a firm grip on her mind. *She doesn't know.*

Decymero gestured nonchalantly towards Willow. 'I mean, Lady Luno, that you and I are now standing in the presence of royalty. This slave of the Druyads is the *real* Empress of Nymm, not the weak, naive youngster you attempted to capture last night.'

Brooke felt Willow's body begin to tremble at the word "weak", and she knew it had nothing to do with fear. She could feel the rage building in her.

'*She* is the Empress?' Luno exclaimed, genuinely shocked. '*Her?*'

'Yes.'

'Then why, my lord, did you have us aid them on the lake, when your Doomgaard vessels wrongly attacked their ship? Why the ruse? Why have us infiltrate their hidden city and win their trust, and take their imposter Empress hostage, when *she* was the one you wanted all along? Why -'

Decymero turned to her and she stopped mid-sentence. The vial of red-orange liquid glowed in his thinner, gnarled hand.

'I appreciate your passion, Lady Luno,' he said. 'It's why I chose you in the first place, when I could have chosen so many others. And it's how I brought these young Other-worlders and their Woodsgirl companion here tonight. When you passed through that portal pool for the second time, leaving the hidden city, I could *see* you, and I could see *them.* You were the connection I needed. And with the newly-acquired power at my disposal, I was able to open the gateway that brought all of you to Doomgaard instead of the forests in the north. It was no mean feat.'

Luno's face had grown paler in the gloom.

'You… knew I'd be defeated, then?'

'I knew no such thing,' said Decymero. The words came out of him in a sigh. 'You could have been successful. The forces you helped gain entry to the city could have been victorious. Or you could have been killed. All were distinct possibilities. But either way, they wouldn't have kept your body in Nymm a moment longer than they needed to, whether you were alive or dead. Your compatriot on their little Council helped see to that. And as long as they passed through the pool while the waters were still disturbed from your departure, I could determine their destination.'

He turned to them again, spreading his hands.

'I'm sure that answers some of your questions, at least.' He raised a finger. 'And here's another: *I* did not send the Giants. They were an unexpected twist in last night's story, but their interference ultimately failed to alter *your* fate. I lost a great many men, which is always a shame. But I gained the Empress of Nymm and the ancient power locked deep in her heart, which beats so ferociously as we speak.'

Grinning at the shocked expressions frozen on their faces, he went back to the map, walking across the lake to its eastern side.

'Here is the Glimmerglen,' he said, tipping another drop. It puddled into an area around the shore, with Silversprog appearing at the northernmost point. 'This is where my hired bounty hunters laid the trap for you, dear

Willow, after my messengers planted word in your ear some weeks ago about the healing seed. I knew that's precisely where you'd go, after all my failed attempts to capture you before. I knew your love for your half-sister, your *desperation* to see her restored, would drive you to complacency. And if things had gone more smoothly, I may never have needed to involve Nymm in the entire process at all. But even I can't foresee everything - I can only trust that fate remains on my side, on the side of *justice*.'

'You're insane!'

They all looked at Dale. The words had erupted from him, and he was now shaking with fury where he stood. Decymero didn't take his eyes off the map.

'On the contrary, Master Sorcerer,' he said, drifting towards the northern end of the lake. 'I'm very much in my right mind. How else could I have devised all this? An insane being would have been tripped up long ago, but I carry on.' He tipped a drop onto the map and a glowing tree sprang up where Nymm must be.

'Why us?' said Brooke, fighting the waver in her voice. 'Why're we here again? Why did you bring us back, just to die here?'

Decymero paused then, hovering over Nymm. Brooke could feel him probing gently at the recesses of her mind and pushed back; he retreated, but she was fully aware he hadn't really been trying. They were in his domain now and he could look inside each of their minds whenever he liked.

'I did not bring you here to die,' he said slowly, still gazing down at the map. 'I brought you here as a test. And, crucially, I did not bring you here through my power alone.'

Brooke swallowed. A terrible feeling was building inside her. It was more than just a human feeling, too. She could *see* something coming.

'Whose power?' Charlie said hoarsely.

Decymero started back across the map towards the table.

'First,' he said, 'the test. There's something I must know, before we go any further.' He replaced the vial in its holder on the table, and the glowing depictions on the floor map dissolved. 'I'm certain at this point, in my heart, that young Willow here is, in fact, the true Empress - '

'You don't have a heart,' Tonya said, matter-of-factly.

'But the heart,' Decymero continued, ignoring her, 'often misleads. I must be sure *here*.' He pointed to his head, the horrid smile on his ghostly-white face widening. 'The test will determine, for sure, whether or not Willow is who I believe she is. Who *she* believes she is. So let's begin.'

He snapped his fingers. With a strangled gasp, Tonya dropped to the floor.

'Ton!' Brooke cried, going to her.

Tonya writhed on the spot, clutching her throat. Her eyes bulged.

'No?' Decymero said. 'Not that one?'

Snap.

Charlie crumpled, palms pressed flat to his eyes.

'Argh!' he cried, rolling on the stone, 'I can't see. It *hurts!* ARGH!'

Brooke looked desperately from Tonya to Charlie, then to Willow. The Woodsgirl's golden eyes were growing steadily brighter, her hands squeezing into fists. In the shadows, Luno cackled gleefully and clapped her hands.

'Stop it!' Brooke yelled. 'Please! Don't do this!'

'I'm sorry, Lady Seer,' said Decymero regretfully. 'It's all part of the test. As is this.'

Snap.

Dale slumped to the floor, grabbing at his chest. His eyes bulged wider than Tonya's. Red began seeping through his tunic, exactly where his Ghoul scar had once been.

'STOP IT!' Brooke screamed. 'STOP!'

'I can't,' Decymero said, shaking his head. 'Not until *she* stops me.'

Willow's eyes were blazing now. Emerald light pulsed from her hands, flooding the place where she stood. Her skin turned fully green and began to glow.

'Stop,' she said. Her voice sounded far away, like it was no longer her own. Brooke felt the floor beginning to tremble under her. 'Stop this.'

'*You* stop this,' Decymero replied, baring his pointed white teeth.

Tonya was convulsing in Brooke's arms now. Charlie was screaming, clutching his eyes.

'Willow!' Brooke yelled.

'Stop this,' Willow said. 'STOP THIS.'

Dale was no longer moving. His tunic was soaked in red.

'WILLOW!' Brooke shrieked.

With a roar, Willow thrust her hands forward.

A shockwave of emerald light exploded from her with a *boom*, knocking Brooke over. Luno was sent flying into the far wall with a cry of surprise. The table was overturned - vials and bottles crashed to the floor, bursting with coloured flame, and books scattered everywhere. Decymero was knocked back a step but remained on his feet, his green-blue eyes burning triumphantly.

'Good!' he cried, laughing heartily. 'Thank you, Empress.'

Brooke saw him snap his fingers. Tonya rolled onto her front, sucking in air, then exploded into a fit of coughing. Charlie lay still on his back - he took his hands away from his face, blinking up at the ceiling with bloodshot eyes. Dale sat up, clutching his soaked shirt, grimacing.

Next to them, Willow folded to her knees, breathing hard. The blazing sunlight had left her eyes, but her hands and face still glowed emerald. Green shoots broke through the stone between her fingers, unfurling into dandelions.

'I'm sorry, my dear,' Decymero wheezed, bringing his laughter under control. 'I'm sorry it had to be this way. But I had to know for sure. And now I do.'

'Are you ok?' Brooke whispered to Tonya, still gripping her tightly.

'Yeah,' Tonya replied, rubbing her throat. 'I'll be ok. I think.'

'Here sits the true Empress of Nymm,' announced Decymero, spreading his arms. The top of his undershirt had fallen open, revealing more of the same ugly, grey skin stretched over a skeletal collarbone beneath. 'You passed the test, young Willow. My theory is confirmed.'

'What theory?' Brooke said coldly, glaring at him.

'That Willow here only reveals her true power in *your* presence.' He pointed at Dale and Charlie. 'All three of you. Four, now. She did it at Hammerfall, and she's done it again. I had to be sure, before we went any further. Too much time would be wasted otherwise.'

'That's why you brought us back,' groaned Dale, holding his chest. 'To *test* her?'

'Indeed, Master Sorcerer. And it worked beautifully, in spite of the timing and location of your arrival. I wasn't even aware such a thing was possible until Lady Woods opened her little book again. And by then, I knew what had to happen next.'

He is *insane*, Brooke thought, listening to him gleefully explain everything. *He's taking pleasure in our pain.*

'Not so,' said Decymero, answering her thoughts aloud. 'I take pleasure in the fates aligning, as they've done here tonight. I take pleasure in seeing a carefully-constructed plan finally come to fruition after *years* of waiting while this continent warred pointlessly beyond my walls. And I take pleasure, Lady Woods, in revealing the final piece in this puzzle. Two pieces, in fact.'

He came forward now, arms still spread like he was welcoming them, the false grin fixed on his face. All they could do was watch helplessly from the floor.

'I told you I didn't bring you here in my power alone,' said Decymero. 'I couldn't. Even the power of two could barely get you Other-worlders through that portal, and even then I couldn't determine *where* you would end up. But the power of three…' He laughed again, long and slow this time, savouring it. 'The power of three was enough. It brought you right here, into my very castle, fallen now at my feet. And I have your friends to thank for it.'

He snapped his fingers and the candelabras around the walls suddenly blazed bright, flooding the whole room with scarlet light. Decymero tilted his head back. They all followed his gaze to the ceiling, where the shadows had been driven back.

Brooke looked, and felt the life drain out of her.

There, hanging above them at the highest point of the room, were two people. They were both spreadeagle against the ceiling, pinned to the inside of the Giant skull with faintly-glowing strips of metal (*magic-suppressing manacles*, were the words Brooke heard). Both their heads hung limp, their faces partly covered with their hair, but they all knew exactly who they were looking at.

'Oh no,' Brooke whispered.

One of them was a man, old and wrinkled, with a long, tangled white beard swinging from his chin; the beard had once been tied in two plaits which looked as though they'd been forcibly pulled apart. He wore a simple grey cloak, and his feet were bare.

The woman next to him wore a fine, sky-blue dress and brown leather bodice, and a blue sash around her waist. Chestnut brown curls hung over her face, which was bathed in red from the burning candelabras. Her eyelids fluttered in the changed light and she groaned.

It was Jayne. And next to her was Yulerin.

'What have you done to them?' Willow said in a very small voice.

'This and that,' replied Decymero airily. He gazed up at them - head cocked to one side, hands behind his back -

like he was observing a painting in a gallery. 'The Druyad's been here for a while. The Seer arrived just two days ago. My men captured her trying to flee the Gnomish city.'

Jayne groaned again, and now Yulerin was stirring. Brooke felt as though her knees were about to give way.

'Let's bring them down, shall we?' said Decymero.

He snapped his fingers - the magical manacles vanished instantly. Yulerin and Jayne dropped straight towards the floor, falling like two lifeless rags.

'NO!' Dale and Brooke cried in unison, leaping to their feet.

At the last second, Decymero snapped his fingers again. The Druyad and the Seer abruptly froze in mid-air, just a foot above the hard grey floor. Jayne's long hair brushed the stone. Decymero motioned with his gnarled hand and the two rose up into standing positions, their feet floating an inch above the floor. Their heads rolled on their shoulders.

'Heavens,' said Decymero, 'they look somewhat worse for wear, don't they? I suppose that's what hanging upside-down on a ceiling for days on end without food or drink will do to a person.'

Charlie snarled in anger and charged, crossing the floor with lightning speed. He almost reached Decymero, his fist drawn back and ready to swing, before the dark lord intercepted him with a casual flick of his hand. Charlie stopped dead, frozen mid-punch, eyes bulging. Brooke stared, horror-struck, her limbs suddenly locked in place again, and thought, *Charlie, no!*

Decymero grinned. 'Not yet, Charlie Flint.' He turned his palm inward and motioned with his long, horrible fingers, and Charlie slid closer, dragged forward on an invisible string. Decymero studied him again. 'You have a strong, noble face, my boy. Perhaps it'll be my next one - the one I'm wearing now is getting rather tired.'

With a flick of his fingers, he sent Charlie tumbling sideways into Dale, who let out an '*oomph!*' as the other boy crashed into him. The two collapsed to the floor in a heap.

'No more of that, please,' said Decymero. 'We're short on time. The ghouls will have heard this commotion by now and will be on their way up here. I'm not sure I have the energy to dissuade them from eating all of you, either.'

'What've you done to them?' Willow said again, staring glassy-eyed at Jayne and Yulerin. They both appeared to be awake now, blinking in the harsh red light.

'I used their power,' Decymero replied, circling them like a lion assessing its prey. 'The old man was most useful, for a time. His ancient magic, combined with my own, allowed me to communicate with Lady Woods in the Other-world. I planted some seeds, nurtured them carefully, and waited. Sure enough, your friends found their way here once again. That little book really is an *extraordinary* portal, you know. And then, when Lady Butterfield graced me with her presence, I had everything I needed to bring you all here.'

Yulerin moaned something.

'What's that?' Decymero sidled up to him, taking one side of the old man's face in his gnarled hand. 'Something to say, Master Druyad? Speak up, sir!'

Yulerin's cracked lips parted. 'Re… release them. They are… only children.'

Decymero green-blue eyes flashed; the grin on his false face drew wider.

'*Children*,' he hissed. 'Children, who thwarted me once before. Children, harbouring the power of the Uland Seven, in whose presence the last, great Empress of Nymm reveals her true nature. These are not mere *children*, you foolish old man. These are destiny incarnate, harbingers of the Reckoning. I've been waiting for them for *centuries*.'

Yulerin moaned again. Decymero let go of his face and his head dropped to his chest.

'They're not going anywhere,' the dark lord rasped. 'This is their new home, where they'll remain. If I am to extract Lady Willow's magic, I need them with her, for as long as it takes.'

'You… cannot take… what doesn't belong to you,' Yulerin wheezed, his head still hanging limp. 'It must… be given - '

' - willingly,' Decymero finished, nodding. 'Yes, I know. I too was there when the rules were written, old man, or have you forgotten me all over again? A magical life force cannot be taken - it must be surrendered, at the will of its owner.' He turned to Willow. 'And the Empress here *will* surrender hers to me.'

Willow, who was still on her knees, slowly lifted her head.

'Never.'

Decymero didn't flinch. 'No, not immediately. But you *will* give your power to me, Woodsgirl. Eventually.'

'I'll die first.'

'I won't let that happen. Your death would do me no good, especially if your soul ends up in one of those talismans in the next room, trapped for all eternity. No, I will keep you alive for as long as is required for your mind to change, whether that's a month, a year, or a century. I can wait, I have all the time in the world. Your friends, however, do not. I wonder how long your resistance will endure when I begin torturing them? Like I said, I take no pleasure in the pain of others. But I will do what's necessary to take what's rightfully mine. I hope you can understand that, my dear.'

Willow stared up at him, shivering. There was no more gold in her eyes.

Then Brooke heard it: *Don't let her do it.*

'If… if you'll let them go,' Willow stammered, 'maybe I… I could - '

'No!' Brooke cried. 'Don't you dare!'

Decymero glared at her. For the first time, his fixed grin turned downwards into a sneer.

'Begging won't save you, little Seer,' he growled.

'I'm not begging,' Brooke shot back, fighting to keep her knees from buckling. 'I'm telling her *no*. She can't do it. I won't let her.'

'Me neither,' said Tonya defiantly. Charlie and Dale agreed, clambering to their feet.

Willow looked at each of them in turn. Decymero's sneer became a scowl.

'I'll feed you all to the ghouls,' he said. 'They'll make short work of you.'

'No, you won't,' Brooke said. 'You can't.'

'She's right,' said Dale. 'You just said you need us alive.'

'And we can withstand torture,' added Charlie. 'We have to go to school *every day*.'

Willow rose slowly to her feet. Her hair, bright red in the candelabra light, fell about her face.

'I won't give it to you,' she said. 'You can keep me here for a thousand years and I'll never, ever let you have it. You're fading. You think I can't see it, but I can. I'll let you fade away to nothing before I give you a drop of my magic.'

For a split second, Decymero appeared taken aback. His jaw worked soundlessly, his skeletal fingers flexing. And then, the evil grin carved its way into his face again.

'So be it,' he said softly. 'Keep it for yourself. It'll only prolong your life while you rot in my dungeons and I burn this world to ash. I'll send all of you there right now. You'll never see another sunrise.'

He stepped forward. Willow's hands went to her sides, sparking green.

'Wait.'

They all stopped and turned.

With some effort, Jayne raised her head, blinking dazedly at them. Her deep, brown eyes were bloodshot and wearied.

'Don't… harm them,' she managed.

Decymero slowly turned to her. 'And why not, Seer?'

No, Brooke thought suddenly, seeing it coming. *No, don't!*

'An exchange… instead,' said Jayne. 'My power… for their freedom.'

'NO!' Dale yelled suddenly. 'You can't!'

'No, I won't let you,' Willow said, shaking her head furiously. 'I *won't*.'

Decymero stroked his chin.

You can't, Brooke echoed in her mind. *Jayne, you can't.*

I must, came the gentle reply.

'An intriguing proposal indeed,' said Decymero. 'The power of the Seer - that would certainly be a difficult gift to turn down.'

'And you'll… let them go?'

A long pause. Then: 'Yes.'

No!

Jayne met his gaze. 'Then do it.'

Decymero shrugged. 'As you wish.

He lifted both his hands - the long, skeletal one and the smaller, withered one - and Jayne was suddenly propelled backwards, the toes of her boots hovering an inch above the floor. Yulerin toppled sideways, crumpling in a heap. Willow rushed to him.

The double doors they'd entered through creaked open and Jayne floated towards them, her long chestnut hair dangling over her face. Decymero walked after her, hands still outstretched, grinning madly.

Brooke found herself on her knees next to Willow, who was holding Yulerin's head. The old Druyad was white as snow, but his eyes were open.

'Yulerin,' Willow whispered. Her eyes brimmed with tears. 'Master.'

He looked up at her, and then at Brooke.

'I… I… am sorry,' he croaked. 'Forgive me.'

'Don't be silly,' said Brooke, and immediately felt silly for using the word. But her heart was heavy and her mind was a dizzying blur. 'You don't need to say that.'

'No, you don't,' added Willow, cupping his head tenderly.

Yulerin's cracked lips worked for a second before the next words came. 'Help… Jayne.'

Brooke looked up. The Seer was now in the centre of the next room, floating higher off the floor, the hem of her sky blue dress waving around her feet. Decymero stood in front of her, hands out, palms up, a black shadow in the soulburn room.

'How?' Willow said, shaking her head. 'She's already given herself willingly. There's nothing we *can* do.'

Yulerin closed his eyes for a moment, then sighed. 'Bring me… to her.'

With some effort, they started helping Yulerin up. Out of the corner of her eye, Brooke saw Luno stirring in the far corner of the room, groaning. Then Dale was there, and Charlie, and Tonya. Together, they all hauled Yulerin to his feet. The Druyad looped an arm over Charlie's shoulders - Dale and Tonya ducked under the other one, and Tonya took his hand.

Yulerin met Willow's watery gaze and nodded. 'Go.'

'Come on,' said Brooke.

They hurried into the next room, their boots clapping on the stone floor. As soon as Brooke crossed the threshold, she felt the temperature drop and the air thicken. All around them, the soulburn talismans flashed their evil red light, responding to their presence; for the first time, Brooke also noticed the archway they'd entered through - it was now a wall of smooth, grey stone.

No way out, she thought. *Trapped.*

Decymero laughed then. She wasn't sure if he'd read her mind again or if Jayne had said something to him, but the sound made her skin crawl.

'It's good of you to join us,' he said. His voice was raspier than ever. 'Lady Butterfield was just telling me how very *special* each of you are. I knew it, naturally. But the Seer's words have extra weight.' He glanced over his shoulder. 'As will yours someday, Brooke Woods.'

Brooke glowered at him, following Willow as she circled around him. Jayne's head was tilted back towards the ceiling now, her arms hanging limp by her sides. The rings on her fingers flashed in the intermittent light cast by the talismans.

'What are you going to do to her?' Brooke said.

Decymero smiled. 'I'm going to do as she asked. I'll take her power, which is given willingly. And then she'll be no more.'

Golden flecks were beginning to gather in Willow's irises again. 'If you're so great,' she said, 'then why take her power? You don't need it.'

Decymero sighed. 'I'm afraid that's where you're wrong. I *do* need it, if I'm to carry out my intentions. Bringing you all here was quite draining, you see. As *great* as I am, it would still take me some time to recover my full strength. So I do need Lady Butterfield's power, which she surrenders most willingly. It is a gift. And I do not despise *gifts*, my dear.'

The others had managed to help Yulerin into the room now, circling around to the other side of Jayne and the dark lord. The talismans shimmered as the Druyad passed in front of them.

'So, once again,' Decymero said to Jayne, 'you offer yourself in place of the Woodsgirl?'

Jayne's head rolled on her shoulders.

'Yes.'

'You willingly surrender your power to me? Every last drop?'

'Yes. All of it.' Her voice was weakening with each passing word.

'Good.'

I can't believe this is happening, Brooke thought desperately.

Jayne's head tilted forward and her brown eyes met his gaze, held it. Around them, the soulburn talismans pulsed hungrily in anticipation.

'And… you swear to let them go… after?'

Decymero nodded. 'I swear. Most solemnly.'

Brooke turned to look at Willow. Her eyes blazed gold, but her mouth hung open in disbelief. She looked across the room at the others, who appeared just as stunned. Dale caught her eye and a deep wave of sadness cut into her heart.

This is *happening.*

She looked up at Jayne again. The Seer continued to hold Decymero's gaze, refusing to break it. The dark lord stared back, grinning, waiting. For one long, painful moment, nothing happened. Jayne hung there, unwavering, while the soulburn talismans glimmered around the room. Brooke saw Decymero's hands beginning to tremble, and for a split second, a flicker of hope sparked inside her.

But Jayne's words snuffed it out.

'Take it,' she said.

'Gladly,' Decymero replied, twisting his palms towards her.

With a rumbling *whoosh*, silver light exploded from Jayne's chest. Her head was thrown back and her limbs went rigid. Brooke caught a brief glimpse of the Seer's face, her mouth wide open in a silent scream, before the light enveloped her. Decymero's head was also thrown back in a gale of insane laughter as Jayne's ancient magic flowed into his hands, up his arms and into his chest; his feet lifted off the floor as the light swirled into his body, rolling off him in waves, thundering into the walls, turning the talismans bright silver. The noise became too much - Brooke clapped her hands to her ears and sunk to her knees, vaguely aware she was screaming while Jayne's voice reverberated over and over and over in her head

HE IS LYING HE WILL BETRAY YOU GET BEHIND ME

and the entire room became silver light, and everyone disappeared.

And then, silence.

She opened her eyes. The light gradually faded, revealing her friends across the room, and Willow by her side. Decymero remained where he was, head down now, breathing hard.

Jayne was gone.

get behind me

The words still echoed. Brooke got to her feet, not really knowing why, and took Willow by the arm. The Woodsgirl blinked at her through a haze of gold.

'Come,' Brooke said.

She ushered Willow towards the back of the room, to the blank stone archway. The others saw them go and started after them. They all gave the place where Jayne had been a wide berth. Around the walls, the soulburn talismans had gone black and glassy again.

get behind me

Decymero uttered a long, cathartic sigh and slowly lifted his head. His palms and irises glowed with silver light. His mad grin was gone, replaced with one of deepest pleasure.

'How long… have I waited,' he breathed, 'to feel this power again.'

Brooke got Willow to the archway, directly behind where Jayne had been. The others gathered next to them, still supporting Yulerin. The Druyad appeared numb with shock.

'Thank you, Lady Seer,' said Decymero, tipping his head back, spreading his arms. 'I accept your gift, given so willingly. Thank you.'

Brooke looked at the others, who were all staring at him. Only Dale looked back at her.

Decymero's head rolled forward again. His smile widened.

'Of course you know I can't let you leave,' he said.

he will betray you

'You're here to stay, my friends. Guests of Doomgaard, for the remainder of your days.' He bared his white teeth, his eyes burning silver. 'How lovely to have you.'

'Liar.' Willow choked out the words. 'Betrayer.'

'My dear Empress, what *exactly* did you expect?' He laughed again, deep and menacing. 'You're here now, and I will have *your* power as well. No matter how long it takes to get it.'

'Monster,' Tonya whispered.

'A monster with the power of the Seer,' Decymero said, looking down at the silvery glow in his hideous hands. 'And it is indeed *exquisite*.'

'You said you'd let us go,' Charlie said, his voice trembling with indignation. 'You *swore*.'

'The promise of a liar, my boy,' Decymero said, shrugging, grinning. 'Besides, even if I wanted to open that portal and send you home, I wouldn't know how - '

Suddenly, his hands jerked up. The silver light in his palms bloomed.

With a roar, the blank stone wall beneath the archway vanished and electric blue light spilled into the room. Brooke felt a rush of air erupt past them, and then immediately tug them backwards. Decymero's eyes bulged, his fingers hooking into claws, his grin curling into a grimace of abject horror.

'NOOOOO!'

They all fell backwards into the portal. As they went, Brooke heard Jayne's words in her mind, one last time.

Make it count, Brooke Woods. Make it count.

Decymero and the soulburn talismans and Doomgaard blurred into the distance and disappeared, lost in the portal's shimmer.

And then they were falling, falling, falling upwards into swirling blue-white light, the familiar roar building, Uland pulling away as their world rushed towards them once again.

***

The Year 9 corridor was quiet and empty. Elsewhere in the school, the Halloween party was in full swing.

Brooke's locker was still ajar. No-one had noticed the metal door hanging open.

No-one, that is, apart from Alex Johnson, who'd glanced at it curiously on his way to the bathroom. He'd thought about shutting it, but quickly decided against it. Brooke might be nearby, or might've left it open for a reason. Besides, he had more pressing matters to attend to - he'd drank far more punch than even his large frame could handle and needed to get to the loo, fast.

It was a close call in the end, but he made it.

On his way back, he heard a metallic *bang* from the Year 9 corridor up ahead. He paused at the corner of the hallway, listening. If Zac and Noah were round there, stuffing Dale Reed into a locker, he'd rather wait until they were done. They'd never get him into one, of course, but it might not stop them from trying.

He saw a flicker of weird, blue light reflect on the glass of a trophy cabinet to his right, and heard a succession of muffled thumps. Someone said "Ow, you landed on me!" and someone else - a girl, Alex thought - apologised. There was a scuffling of shoes on tiles and murmuring voices, low and urgent. *Was someone crying?*

Alex waited as long as he could, then screwed up his courage and walked around the corner.

Four people turned quickly to face him.

'Alex!' said Dale Reed. 'Hey.'

'Hey,' Alex replied, raising one of his big hands. He looked at each of them and frowned. 'When did you guys change costumes?'

He saw them exchange glances. Brooke Woods turned away, wiping her eyes.

Tonya Miller put her hands on her hips, smiled and said, 'Oh, just now. We, umm… wanted to win the costume contest, you know?'

'Yeah,' agreed Dale. 'The contest. Great prize this year.'

'Isn't it, like, a coupon for an ice-cream shop?' said Alex dubiously.

Brooke Woods tossed something in her locker and slammed the door. Her eyes were red.

'Everybody loves ice-cream,' said Charlie Flint. Then, with some effort, added: 'Especially you, right Johnson?'

Alex felt his face redden.

'Fat joke,' he muttered. 'Original.'

Charlie shrugged, but his face had gone red too.

For a moment, no-one said anything. Alex stared at them, and they stared back. He sensed they wanted him to leave.

'Well, see you back at the party,' he said.

'Yup,' said Tonya.

As he passed, he nodded at Dale. 'Nice blood. Looks real.'

Dale looked down at his chest. 'Oh yeah. Thanks.'

Alex carried on down the corridor, heading for the gymnasium. He glanced back once before turning the corner, and saw something he never thought he'd see in Farmont High.

Brooke, Dale, Charlie and Tonya were huddled together by the lockers, their arms around one another's shoulders.

Epilogue

The half-term break came and went. Brooke spent most of it in her room, staring at her ceiling or attempting to do homework. She knew her mother was worried about her ('Did something happen at the party?') but she didn't have the energy to even lie about it. She simply avoided the subject, and waited until the holidays were over.

She didn't see the others again until school resumed. They all looked just as haggard and depressed as she felt. But at least they were able to talk again. None of them had been able to face trying since Halloween.

'What d'you think happened to them?' Dale murmured over lunch.

'I saw them in… the portal,' Tonya replied, trying to ignore the staring eyes of their classmates, who'd never seen the four of them eat together. 'They sort of… flew away ahead of us and disappeared.'

'Maybe they went back to Uland?' Brooke suggested. She looked at her ham and cheese sandwich, thought of Jayne, and dropped it into her lunchbox. 'Maybe they're in Nymm again.'

'Or they're with *him*,' Charlie muttered darkly.

'Hopefully not,' said Dale.

They all picked at their food in silence for a minute.

'So… what now?' said Tonya.

***

Weeks went by.

The never-ending dreariness of November finally gave way to December. Scattered, crunchy autumnal leaves turned to mush in the streets; the air became crisp and chilly, and winter quickly set in. In no time at all, every window in town glowed with festive light, and the familiar old tingle of Christmas excitement began to build.

Brooke didn't feel it, of course - their last memories of Uland still hung over her like a shadow, draining the usual joy from the holiday season. But for the sake of her mother, who loved Christmas and always made a big deal about it, she kept a smile on her face and tried to avoid spending too much time in her room, where the little leather-bound book was hidden away beneath a sheaf of papers in her desk drawer.

She'd taken it out every night since their return, just in case. But the pages were more brittle than ever, and no new words had appeared. In fact, all of the existing text and drawings were already fading away. She knew they'd be gone soon. And with them, their hope of ever getting back to Uland.

Maybe it was just as well, she reasoned one night, half-watching an old Christmas movie with her mother by the fire. Maybe Willow and Yulerin really *were* back safely in Nymm, and Jayne's sacrifice had done enough to stop Decymero, and there was peace there now. Maybe Uland was better off without them.

But something told her that wasn't the case.

She knew, somehow, that it was far from over.

***

Then, just a few days before the Christmas holidays, it happened.

She snatched up her phone and rang Tonya first, then Dale.

'What d'you mean?' he replied groggily. It was nine-thirty on a Thursday night, and he'd been getting ready for bed.

'There's writing again!' Brooke exclaimed, trying to keep her voice down. 'New words!'

'What do they say?'

She told him, and his voice changed instantly.

'Let's go, then!' he said.

'Tell Charlie!' Brooke replied, and hung up.

She dressed in a hurry, pulling on a warm coat over her wool jumper and jeans. Tucking the book in her pocket, she slipped from her room, and then decided there was no point in trying to be coy. Her mother would be more suspicious if she snuck out.

'I'm meeting my friends, Mum!' she called nonchalantly, thudding down the stairs.

'You're what?' her mother called back from the living room.

'I have my phone and everything, don't worry.' She snatched her bobble hat and scarf from the coat hooks by the door. 'I'll be back soon, I promise!'

'Wait, who're you… take your scarf!'

Brooke lived fairly close to the centre of town. She knew it'd take less than ten minutes to walk there, and guessed it'd be about the same for the others. Even so, she was shivering by the time the giant Christmas tree in the square came into sight.

There weren't many people there so late on a weeknight. A handful of window-shoppers strolled by the brightly-lit store fronts around the square, peering through the glass at the festive offers inside; a weary-looking barista was gathering in chairs from outside a still-open cafe on the corner; Christmas music drifted from the doorway.

Brooke hugged her coat around her and walked over to the tree, gazing up at its star. For a brief moment, she saw the palace in Nymm again, and her heart thumped just a little harder in her chest.

I hope Orchidema's ok, she thought sadly. *She won't know what's happened. Unless…*

'Hey.'

She turned. Dale was crossing the square, bundled up in an enormous, padded coat.

'Hey,' Brooke said. 'You look cosy.'

'My parents made me wear it,' he grumbled.

She grinned and play-punched his padded arm. 'You look like a Christmas tree bauble.'

'There you are!' Tonya came around the tree, wearing a jacket that looked far too expensive for a thirteen-year-old. She shivered dramatically. 'It's *freezing* here!'

'It's not *that* cold,' said Dale, turning awkwardly in his huge coat.

'Maybe not for you,' Tonya replied, and punched his arm.

'Ow! Why does everyone keep doing that?'

'Let's see it then,' said Tonya.

Brooke saw Charlie approaching, hands jammed in his pockets, and dug the book out.

'It just appeared tonight,' she said, flipping through the pages. 'Completely out of nowhere. It's the first time it's happened since we left.'

Charlie arrived at her shoulder and squinted at the book. 'What's it say, again?'

Brooke tugged one of her gloves from her hand and gently ran a finger over the foreign letters on the page. They shimmered, grew warm beneath her skin, and formed new words:

Meet us at the big tree of lights.

'The big tree of lights?' Charlie read. 'That's a bit weird.'

'You're sure they meant here?' Dale said.

'Who's "they"?' Tonya said.

Brooke took her hand away from the page. The words remained.

'I don't know who wrote it,' she said. 'But I know they meant here. Now.'

They all looked around. The window-shoppers had moved on, heading back to their cars; at the cafe, the final customers of the night were beginning to gather their things. A chill breeze curled through the square, rustling the branches of the enormous tree.

'You don't think… it was *him?*' said Tonya nervously. 'Like, luring us here, or something?'

'Geez, I hope not,' said Dale, his coat creaking with every movement. 'My powers are long gone.'

'I can still fight, if I have to,' muttered Charlie, balling his hands into fists.

'Maybe it's something good,' Brooke said. 'Maybe we can go back.'

'Not yet.'

They all jumped. The voice had come from right behind them, deep and hoarse. They spun around, and stared.

An elderly man stood there, dressed in a heavy winter coat and hat. A tartan scarf was wrapped tight around his neck. He was leaning on a wooden walking stick with a bare, wrinkled hand, gazing at them through thick, horn-rimmed spectacles. When he spoke again, the words came from behind a wispy white moustache.

'We're glad you came.'

Brooke swallowed and said, 'We?'

A teenage girl stepped out from behind the old man, dressed in a baggy grey hoodie, flared jeans and scuffed boots. She hesitated, then pushed back her hood, revealing smooth, pale skin, deep hazel eyes and an untidy crop of red hair. Smiling awkwardly, she raised one slender hand in a wave.

They all stood there for a moment, dappled in coloured light from the Christmas tree, staring at each other. Then the old man cleared his throat, and smiled.

'Hello again, my friends,' he said. 'I believe we have much to discuss.'

The end.

ACKNOWLEDGMENTS

This second instalment in the Book of Uland series flowed out of me in a matter of weeks. Returning to these characters was a joy, and I loved walking them through their next steps. Brooke, Dale, Charlie and Willow are a pleasure to write.

Once again, certain people in my real life made this continued journey smooth and easy: Christine, my Ideal Reader, whose endless patience I'll never deserve; my diligent beta readers (Becca, Megan, Erin, Trudi and Margaret) who offered such helpful, constructive feedback; my publisher, Richard, for all his support and guidance; and JV Arts, who were extremely patient with me during multiple iterations of the cover design process.

Finally, thank you, Dear Reader, for joining me in Uland once again.

Here's to many more adventures in the Unseen Realm.

ABOUT THE AUTHOR

David writes from his home in Northern Ireland, where he lives with his beautiful wife Christine and their two dogs, Lupin and Ghost. He loves books, movies, football (he's better at watching than playing), and getting his hiking boots dirty.

Subscribe to David McIlroy Fiction here:

SCAN ME

More books by Burton Mayers Books

When an enchanted garden is threatened with ecological disaster, an unlikely gang of fairy-tale friends must work together to save their home.

www.ingramcontent.com/pod-product-compliance
Lightning Source LLC
Chambersburg PA
CBHW060221030726
47499CB00004B/1134
* 9 7 8 1 9 1 7 2 2 4 1 7 8 *